Frances M. Trollope

Gertrude, or, Family Pride

Frances M. Trollope

Gertrude, or, Family Pride

ISBN/EAN: 9783337103033

Printed in Europe, USA, Canada, Australia, Japan

Cover: Foto ©Andreas Hilbeck / pixelio.de

More available books at **www.hansebooks.com**

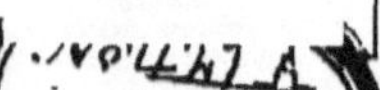

A. LELLAN.

GERTRUDE;

or,

FAMILY PRIDE.

GERTRUDE;

OR,

FAMILY PRIDE.

BY

MRS. TROLLOPE,

AUTHOR OF

"THE LIFE AND ADVENTURES OF A CLEVER WOMAN," "MRS. MATHEWS,"
"WIDOW BARNABY," ETC., ETC.

LONDON:
CHAPMAN AND HALL, 193, PICCADILLY.
1864.

GERTRUDE.

CHAPTER I.

In sitting oneself down to the somewhat idle occupation of "Old tales telling of loves long ago," it is much safer, for many reasons, to give fictitious names to the various scenes in which the circumstances occurred, than to challenge the criticism which might discover either to much, or too little of truth in the details, were the real names to be given.

Most of the circumstances upon which the following story is founded, occurred in Germany, and it is therefore to Germany that I will beg my reader to follow me.

It was upon a very fine morning in the month of June, that two individuals, who are the first of my dramatis personæ to be presented to him, might have been seen climbing steadily and perseveringly, but at no very rapid pace, the steep hill which overhangs the pretty little town to which I shall give the name of Hindsdorf.

These two travellers were neither mounted knights "pricking o'er the plain," or the hill either; nor had they, in truth, the appearance of belonging to any station to which the act of walking was not likely to be the ordinary mode of conveyance along any highways, or bye-ways, by which it might be necessary for them to travel.

But, nevertheless, few could have looked at them steadily for one moment without feeling inclined to bestow a second, for the purpose of looking at them again; for both were very decidedly well-looking, and being male and female, it would have been difficult not to believe that the earnestness with which they were conversing, and the deep attention with which each looked at, and listened to, the other, proceeded from that tender passion which is universally considered as being particularly interesting.

Both were in the earliest bright perfection of adult comeliness, but the girl looked somewhat the elder of the two. This was not the case, however, for the young man was three years her senior; but being, as Rosalind says of herself, "more than common tall," and having, moreover, a remarkably firm step, and upright carriage, the girl looked considerably older than she was. The dress of both was scrupulously neat, but shewed no pretension beyond the Sunday garb of decent, well-conditioned peasants.

If examined by a critical eye, however, the young man might have been suspected to be of a higher class than his companion, for his linen was of a finer fabric than the most gala attire is thought to render necessary among persons of the rank to which it seemed evident that he belonged.

Any one within reach of hearing, as well as seeing them, as they pursued their way, would have discovered that there was a difference of opinion between them, or some very interesting point which they were discussing, notwithstanding the air of love and devotion which each seemed to feel for the other.

"Fear nothing, my dear friend!" said the beautiful, tall, upright girl, as she stepped firmly and actively on beside her companion; "fear neither harshness, nor difficulty of any kind, from the venerable man we are about to visit. All will go smoothly with us, depend upon it."

And then, after the silence of a moment, she added, the words however, being tempered by a most lovely smile, "Nay! I will turn round, and run away! I will indeed, if you permit yourself to be thus overpowered by terror. Why, your arm positively trembles!"

"And can you wonder it should tremble?" he replied, looking at her almost reproachfully. "Oh! do *you* not tremble too!"

"Nay, take my hand, and hold it steadily," she replied, laughingly. "Do you find any symptom of trembling, my good man?"

"Surely, surely, you cannot love me as I love you, or you could not be thus brave at contemplating the possibility of our being parted for ever!" he answered, in a voice of deep emotion, as he pressed the hand she placed in his.

"But I contemplate no such possibility," she replied; adding, in a firm but gentle voice, well calculated to soothe the feelings which she affected to chide, "I contemplate nothing but the returning with you along this self-same path within an hour or so, as your wedded wife; and I see nothing in that at all likely to make me tremble."

The young man only answered these cheering words by a passionate caress, and then they pursued their way in silence for a minute or two.

But this silence was again soon broken by him, for, in a tone which sounded a little as if he were relapsing into the fears for which he had been chidden, he ventured to whisper, "But if this priest *should* declare that he would not marry us? If he *should* say that it was his duty to be assured of the consent of our parents and friends?"

"Why, in that case, my good man," returned his still smiling companion, "in that case, we must take our leave of him very respectfully, and betake ourselves and our wedding-fee to another."

",But do you not rest too much hope and faith upon that large wedding-fee, dearest?" said the youth, shaking his head.

"It is possible I may," she replied; "but till experience teaches me the contrary, I am strong, very strong, in the faith and hope which the amount of it inspires. They say, that is, the worldly-wise, of course; but the worldly-wise do say that the priesthood (of the present day) have a great respect for money. Perhaps they think that the possession of it may enable them to do much good. And they are right there, my friend. Money is certainly a powerful agent, either for good or evil, as the case may be. If he be a reasoning, right-thinking man, he cannot fail to perceive, from the amount of the sum we are about to offer him, that the attachment between us is a very true one. It must be a rare thing for people of our station to offer so large a sum for the purpose of being permitted to enter the pale of holy matrimony. And though it is likely enough that he will guess, from the secret manner in which we present ourselves, that our respective parents are probably at feud, and, therefore, would oppose the marriage, he must, at the same time, be aware that there would a great and useless cruelty in attempting to keep asunder a pair who love each other well enough to part with a sum which, of course, must be so important to them! Moreover, a very little common sense will suffice to convince him that, if he will not marry us, some other priest will."

This conversation, earnest as it was, had not impeded their pace, and they had now reached the summit of the hill they had long been ascending. The level they had thus obtained, however, did not continue above a quarter of a mile, before they arrived at a somewhat steep declivity on the other side, which terminated in the little town which they trusted would prove the termination of their excursion; for there dwelt the priest whom they hoped would consent to unite them in the bonds of holy wedlock.

The young girl had never visited this little town before, but it was sufficiently well known to her companion, to enable him, as they descended the hill, to point out to her the dwelling of the priest whom they came to seek; which humble dwelling seemed to make part and parcel of the little church within whose walls they hoped to receive the benediction which was to insure their mutual happiness for life. Something like a tremor seemed to pass over her, however, as he pointed out the spot, and said, "There is the church, dearest; and there, under the same roof, as it should seem, is the dwelling of the priest.

He felt that she trembled as he pronounced these words, and suddenly stopping, he dropped the arm which rested on his, and placing himself directly before her, he fixed his earnestly enquiring eyes upon her face, and said, "Do you REPENT? It is not yet too late to say say. Speak!"

The young girl did not immediately obey him. She did not speak, but she fixed her eloquent eyes upon his face, and let them speak for her; and truly it may be doubted, if a more perfect model of human beauty, than she then gazed upon, ever met the eye of a mortal, since the original of the Apollo stood before the statuary who has given him an earthly immortality.

She looked at him very fixedly for a moment; and then she sighed. But it was the sigh of tenderness, and of passion. Regret had nothing to do with it; and in the next moment she smiled again, and smilingly recovered possession of his arm, and drawing him back to his place at her side, only replied to his question by a gentle pressure, and an accelerated pace.

His reply to this silent decision was also given in silence. A look, and again a gentle pressure of the arm, said quite as much as any words could have done, A few moments brought them to the arched gateway of the little town of Hindsdorf, and a few more to the door of the priest's house.

"Was the priest at home?" was the question asked with trembling eagerness by the young man. The answer was in the affirmative, and about two steps more brought them from the humble door of the house to another equally humble, which opened upon a small snug room, near the open window of which sat the holy man, whose services they came to purchase; he held a book in his hand, but his eyes were fixed upon the blooming little flower-garden, on which the window opened.

It would not have been very easy for even more experienced eyes to have formed any very decided opinion upon the temper and character of the man whose face was turned towards them, as soon as she became aware that the door of the room was opened. His age appeared to be about sixty, or something beyond it, but though rather a spare man, he had still a look of health and activity, and his eye had lost nothing of the keen expression for which it must ever have been remarkable.

The old woman who had admitted our lovers, lingered for a moment in the doorway, as if wishing to hear them declare their errand; but her master checked her indiscretion by saying, in an accent which was, however, only remarkable from its peculiar distinctness, "Shut the door."

This command was as promptly obeyed as it was given; and then the old man turned to his two young visitors, and said, "What is your business?"

"We are come to Hindsdorf to be married," replied the young man, without adding another syllable.

The old priest looked at them both rather earnestly for a moment, and then raised his eye-brows, and shook his head. Any description of the scene which followed would be quite superfluous; it is enough to say, that the young girl had not rested a vain hope upon the influence of the wedding fee which they had contrived to bring with them. The names of both were equally, and utterly unknown to the old man, whereas the value of their gold was a matter of no mystery whatever.

Nor did he think it necessary to make any great difficulty about the matter. He very hospitably regaled them with the best refreshment which his house afforded, and exerted himself very actively while they were engaged in taking it, in order to get everything in order for the ceremony which was to follow.

The priest of Hindsdorf was greatly respected in his parish, and he found no difficulty in obtaining proper and sufficient witnesses for the ceremony he was about to perform.

In a word, the purpose of the unfriended young couple was achieved with no bustle, and with as little delay as possible; and the most remarkable circumstance which I have at present to relate respecting it is, that though they walked so lovingly together to the town of Hindsdorf, they left it by two different routes, which appeared to lead them as far asunder as it was possible they could go.

CHAPTER II.

WE have all read stately stories of proud old barons in more lands than one; and if our researches into the annals of the race have led us far back, we may have read too of predatory barons, nay, of murdering barons also; each one furnishing a theme fruitful in incident, and precious to all the numerous class of readers who love excitement better than example.

I, too, have a story to tell about a baron, and, moreover, about a German baron, which is, I believe, considered as the most romantic species of the class; but unfortunately the date of my story is not so favourable as I could wish it to be, for it is too recent to furnish authority for any of those highly-wrought descriptions of awful acts, and startling facts, which are so readily welcomed by the imagination, when the period at which they occurred is sufficiently remote to render the application of the test of probability, only a mark of ignorance as to the prodigious difference between the present and the past. Such as my story is, however, I will tell it without further preface, only begging for a little more of the indulgence which has so often been granted to me.

The Baron von Schwanberg was already an old man when my narrative begins, but still young enough, nevertheless, to be as self-willed and headstrong a gentleman as could easily be found at any age. He was, moreover, one of the very proudest men that ever existed; but there was such an honest and undoubting sincerity of belief in his own greatness, that few of those who approached him could refuse to sympathise with his feelings sufficiently to prevent their betraying any very decided doubt of his greatness; for it was easy to perceive that no such doubt could be betrayed to him, without producing a more violent effect than any reasonable person would wish to witness.

Had he lived more in the world, this half-insane state of mind must of necessity have been cured; but every circumstance of his life had unfortunately tended to increase it.

He was early placed, with all the distinction usually shewn to rank and fortune, in one of the most favoured regiments of the Emperor of Austria; and if he had remained there, he

would have been sure to learn, notwithstanding this grace
and favour, that he was but a man, though a very noble one.
But unfortunately his father died within a year after the young
officer had attained the age of twenty-one years, and, as the
country was then most profoundly at peace, no objection of any
kind was made to his withdrawing himself to his estates in
Hungary, which were indeed large and important enough to
render the personal superintendence of their possessor extremely
necessary.

Setting aside the sort of monomaniacal pride above mentioned,
the Baron von Schwanberg was far from being a bad man; and
if he believed that the duties which devolved upon him at the
death of his father, were only second in importance to those
which fell upon the Emperor himself, when his imperial parent
was removed from the earth, he believed also that great and
grave duties devolved upon him likewise, and very earnestly did
the youthful baron determine to perform them faithfully.

Having, by very careful and judicious inquiry, ascertained
both the character and the position of the many families in
his immediate neighbourhood, who were either the tenants,
or the labourers on his property, he made various regulations,
all tending to encourage and reward their industry; and it
would have been difficult to find in any land an estate, upon
which the toiling labourers, who converted its soil into gold,
had less reason to complain of their lot.

That these labourers were considered by the baron as no more
of the same order of beings as himself, than were the docile oxen
which they led to plough, or the milky herds which enriched
their dairies, is most certain; but the Baron von Schwanberg
was as unconscious of committing any fault or folly, by so thinking, as he was when selecting a rose from his flower-garden, and
testifying his approval of it, by permitting it to bloom for his
especial pleasure on his drawing-room table.

But, nevertheless, though his gigantic estimate of his own
greatness did not weigh upon his conscience, it was in many
ways troublesome to him. It cannot be doubted, that such a
young man as the baron, almost as far removed from frivolity
of all sorts as from right thinking upon most subjects,—it
cannot be doubted that such a man had not long found himself at the head of his illustrious house, before he began to
turn his thoughts towards the necessary and all-important business of forming such a matrimonial alliance as, while it provided
for the continuance of his race, should add no symbol to the

bearings on his shield which could be consid red as unworthy of
a place there.

But the task he thus set himself wa , in truth, no easy one.
Not for a moment during the many years through which this
difficult search lasted, did he ever permit his eye to wander
in pursuit of beauty, however attractive, or his heart to soften
under the influence of the sweetest smiles that woman could
bestow. Some adverse fate seemed to be at work against him ;
for, although, in addition to his noble descent, and his large
and unincumbered estates, he was decidedly a very handsome
man, his hand had been more than once rejected. It is probable
that he was too much in earnest in the real object which he had
in view, to disguise his comparative indifference on other points ;
for it would be really difficult to account for his many disap-
pointments on any other ground. At length, however, his
persevering researches were rewarded by what he considered
as the most brilliant success ; for during his annual visit to
Vienna he had the happiness of meeting, wooing, and winning a
young countess, who really seemed to possess every qualification
to make the marriage state happy, save and except the paltry
article of wealth ; but as he really would have considered a large
fortune in his wife a very useless superfluity, the want of it was
by no means considered as an obstacle to the union ; and at
length, therefore, a few months before his fiftieth birthday,
the Baron von Schwanberg was united to the young, beautiful,
and high-born Countess Gertrude von Wolkendorf.

When a marriage so every way desirable has been achieved by
a lover, he is apt to think that he has reached the happiest moment of his existence ; but this was not exactly the case with
the Baron von Schwanberg. He was certainly greatly delighted
to find himself, at length, married to precisely such a noble
young lady as it had been his wish to find ; but not even from
her would he have attempted to conceal the fact, that the happiness of possessing her was a blessing of conderably less importance
than that of the heir which he anticipated as its result.

Fortunately, the prospect of this crowning blessing soon became
evident, and the delight of the Baron von Schwanberg thereupon
was almost too great to be restrained within any reasonable
bounds. His young wife was often at a loss to know how
she ought to receive these vehement demonstrations of his
happiness. Like most other women, she gladly welcomed the
trial that awaited her, for the sake of the treasure which her
womanly hope told her would reward her for it ; but as to sym-

pathising with the almost convulsive raptures daily and hourly expressed by her husband, it was beyond her power. She was by nature thoughtful, gentle, and rather undemonstrative, than the reverse; and moreover, she was as true as she was reasonable; and the sort of affectation which it would have required to enable her to appear in a state of ecstacy equal to his own, would have required a sacrifice of sincerity which it was not in her nature to make.

As it never entered the head of the Baron von Schwanberg, to suppose it possible that any lady who shared with him in all the honours and glories of his position, as his wife, should be insensible to the happiness of transmitting them to an heir, he very soon began to torment himself with the terrible idea, that the preternatural composure and indifference, as he called it, of his wife's manner, arose from ill-health; and from the time this idea first suggested itself to him, he never for a moment lost sight of the possibility, nay, probability, that all his hopes might at last prove abortive.

Grievously did he torment his unfortunate lady, who, to say the truth, was in very excellent health, by his unceasing anxiety about her condition; till at length, finding that the most tender and persevering enquiries could obtain from her nothing but reiterated assurances that she was "quite well," he suddenly took the resolution of adding a domestic *accoucheur* to his establishment; and as he did not deem it either necessary or judicious to explain to his lady all the parental terrors which had induced him to take this step, Madame von Schwanberg was a good deal surprised by the lengthened visit of the grave and not very amusing individual whom her husband now introduced to her as one of his particular friends.

This introduction, however, was, of course, enough to insure her treating him with all the consideration due to an honoured guest; nor, to say the truth, was she at all insensible to the relief she might experience by her magnificent husband having the society of a friend, whose presence might occasionally excuse the necessity of her own, and leave her thereby at liberty to listen, in the retirement of her own apartments, to "those silent friends that ever please;" an indulgence which, if not absolutely denied to her, had been very greatly restricted since the Baron von Schwanberg had made her the partner of his greatness.

But, by degress, it seemed as if this particular friend of her husband's was inclined to assume the right of being her particular friend also. Again and again, it chanced that when the Baron brought him to pay a daily visit of compliment to his lady, in her own particular sitting-room, he lingered behind, when the lord of the mansion retired ; and, by degress, this very superfluous degree of attention was rendered still more remarkable, and still more disagreeable, by his removing from the place he had occupied during the presence of the lady's husband, and taking a seat next to her, often, indeed, on the very sofa she occupied.

And then followed, before she could quite make up her mind as to the best mode of escaping this annoyance, the inconceivable audacity of his taking her hand, and holding it for several minutes in his, despite her very decided efforts to withdraw it.

The Baroness von Schwanberg was one of the last women in the world to suspect a gentleman of falling in love with her; but it appeared to her impossible to suggest any other solution capable of explaining the extraordinary conduct of the Herr Walters.

For several days, however, after his idea first occurred, she very earnestly endeavoured to persuade herself that it was impossible; and nothing but the persevering repetition of the offence could have induced her, at length, to confess to her husband that she did not like the manners of his friend, the Herr Walters; that he was a vast deal too familiar in his mode of addressing her, to suit her notions of propriety; and that she greatly wished that a time for his departure might be fixed as soon as possible.

It would be difficult to conceive anything more ludicrous than the manner in which the Baron von Schwanberg listened to this remonstrance. He had cautiously avoided mentioning to his lady the profession of his guest, from the fear of endangering her health by creating a feeling of alarm; and it was, therefore, with no appearance of surprise, but with an aspect of the most serene satisfaction, that he now listened to her observations respecting the offensive familiarity of his manner.

The Baron von Schwanberg had much too profound respect for the noble lineage of his lady, to make it easy for him to allow, even to himself, that she had any of the faults or defects to which inferior people are liable; but, nevertheless, there was one trait in her character to which, with all his efforts, he could not be wholly blind, and which, assuredly, often occasioned him something very nearly approaching to vexation. And no wonder, for this defect in lady's character was the apparent absence of that noble feeling which the vulgar call pride, but which all higher classes of the human race more properly designate as a high-minded appreciation of their own position. It was, therefore,

with a greater degree of satisfaction than can be easily imagined
by persons differently situated, that the Baron von Schwanberg
now listened to his lady's indignant observations on the too great
familiarity of the Herr Walters' manners towards her.

The baron was not of a caressing disposition, or he would
probably have testified his feelings by giving his lady a warm
embrace. But, although he did not do this, he testified his
feelings in a manner equally eloquent, for he immediately stood
up, and placing his right hand on his breast while he saluted
her, by touching the left with his lips, he made her a very profound bow, and said, with an approving smile, as he recovered
his perpendicular position :

"Your feelings, my dear lady, are exactly what I would wish
them to be. That you should resent anything, and everything,
that could suggest the idea of impertinent familiarity, is not only
what I should expect from the lady whom I have so carefully
selected as my wife, but it is precisely what I should most honour
and most admire in the lady of my choice. And now, having
done this justice to you, and to myself, let me also do justice to
the very respectable individual whom you have been led to consider as defective in that perfect respect and deference which
your father's daughter, and my wife, have such undoubted right
to expect. And now permit me to explain to you the real cause
of the conduct which has appeared to you as objectionable in the
worthy Herr Walters."

And having said this, the Baron von Schwanberg sat himself
down on the sofa beside his lady, and proceeded to explain to
to her the nature of the attention which their new inmate had
bestowed upon her.

There would be no use in attempting to describe the transition
from one species of displeasure to another, which was the result
of this confidential disclosure to the persecuted baroness, for it
may be very easily imagined.

The prevailing quality of her temper was gentleness, or, more
correctly speaking, tranquility. No lady living ever troubled
herself less concerning the affairs of other people, nor was she at
all disposed to suspect that other people took the liberty of
troubling themselves about hers; and the now finding herself
the object, and the avowed object, of the unceasing observation
of her very particularly tiresome husband, and his professional
assistant, was a sore trial to her usually dignified composure of
manner.

If the medical gentleman had touched her pulse at that moment,

he would assuredly have felt himself called upon to declare that
it made no very "healthful music;" but, fortunately for her
patience, she escaped this trial; and when her observant spouse
perceived that his statement respecting the Herr Walters' position
in his family caused a very considerable augmentation of colour
on the delicate cheek of his lady, he permitted himself to look at
her with a sort of patronizing smile, as he promised to indulge
the timidity of her youthful shyness, as far as it was possible to
do so without withdrawing the attention necessary to her
precious health!

"The timidity of her youthful shyness!" The feeling which
her unsuspicious husband thus described, might have been called
a movement of almost ungovernable rage, with much more
justice.

The baroness half rose from her chair, and her project was,
probably, to leave the room; but she conquered herself sufficiently
to resume her seat, and another moment enabled her to avoid the
folly of expressing anger that would be equally unintelligible,
and disregarded. For a second thought sufficed to suggest a
wiser course. If their strange visitor was retained in the house
for the express purpose of examining the state of her health, he
might (she thought), if he had been as great a fool as his
employer, have made himself still more troublesome than he had
been already; and although his doing so might have saved her
from the ridiculous blunder into which she had fallen, it would
have left less hope of her being able to prevent his annoying her
for the future.

The destiny of the unfortunate baroness had, unhappily, precluded the possibility of her acting on any occasion wherein her
husband was concerned, with the frankness and sincerity which
was originally a part of her nature; and after meditating very
seriously for the first few weeks after her marriage upon the
comparative evils, and the comparative sins, attending a systematic course of falsehood, and a systematic course of truth, in
her intercourse with him, she deliberately decided upon the
former.

It took but little time to prove to her, beyond the hope of
mistake, that her husband was a pompous fool, incapable of acting from rational motives; incapable of forming a rational
opinion; and pretty nearly incapable of uttering a rational word.
Should she be doing right if she so conducted herself as to make
it evident to himself, and to others, that such was the opinion
she had thus formed of him? She thought not. And having

come to this conclusion, she acted upon it with a steady, quiet perseverance, which not only prevented his happiness from being troubled by any doubts concerning either his own wisdom or hers, but which puzzled many an intelligent looker-on as to the strange phenomenon of such a woman as the Baroness von Schwanberg thinking it right and proper (as she so evidently did), to listen with attention to the Baron von Schwanberg whenever he thought proper to speak; let his language be ever so frequent, or ever so long.

At length, however, a very remarkably clever man, when discussing this puzzling subject with a friend, observed, that he saw but one way of accounting for it; which was, by supposing that the high-born baroness was at heart quite as proud as the high-born baron, although she did not betray the feeling so openly as her husband; "and in that case," added his philosophical observer, "you may depend upon it, she really does think every word he utters is worth listening to."

But we must return to the *tête-à-tête* which these remarks have interrupted; no so sooner had the idea occurred to Madame von Schwanberg, that the physician might not be the fool which he was probably fee'd to appear; than she determined to give him a hint or two which might prevent the thraldom in which she was placed, from being utterly intolerable. Fortunately for all the parties concerned, born and unborn, she found him apt; and from that time, till his final dismissal after the birth of her child, he proved himself a very useful friend, cleverly contriving to become the recipient of the baron's parental meditations, whether hopeful or fearful, and procuring thereby something like comparative peace to the unfortunate object of his anxiety.

CHAPTER III.

But, at last, the great, the important day arrived, which was to repay the Baron von Schwanberg for all the anxieties he had endured, by blessing his longing eyes with the sight of the illustrious little baron, whose distinguished destiny it was, to perperpetuate the honours of the Schwanberg race.

tunate father; for, however powerful the description might be, it could only convey an idea of his real condition to those capable of conceiving it, and fortunately the great majority of human beings would, judging from their own feelings, conceive such a description to be unnatural.   Yet such things are.

The judicious Herr Walters took care to prevent his perfectly contented patient from being disturbed during the first days of her convalescence by the presence of her husband, lest the real state of his mind might become apparent to her; and by so doing he certainly contributed very essentially to her comfort; nevertheless, the lady would probably have progressed with equal certainty towards recovery, if these precautions had been omitted; for the temper, the spirits, and even the feelings of Madam von Schwanberg, had become pretty near callous to all the superb absurdities of her husband; and most assuredly it would have been greatly beyond his power to have expressed or manifested any feeling concerning the arrival of her new-born treasure, which could in the least degree have lessened her happiness in possessing it.

Meanwhile the little Gertrude grew, and prospered; and as it was the will of Heaven that she should be an only child, not even the inferiority of her sex could prevent her becoming a person of considerable consequence, even in the estimation of her father.

To her devoted mother she certainly appeared to be as near perfection as it was possible for any mortal mixture of earth's mould to be; and even her disappointed father soon began to think that, although unfortunately she was not a son, she was such a daughter as only the house of Schwanberg could produce.

Allowance must me made, however, for the natural partiality both of father and mother. Gertrude von Schwanberg was a splendidly handsome child, and showed early symptoms both of intelligence and good temper; but nevertheless, the young baroness was very far from being the perfect being her progenitors supposed her to be; for in truth she inherited, in a very considerable degree, the faults of both. But she wore these faults with a difference; or rather, the fact of their being blended, produced a result by no means very exactly resembling the character either of the one or the other.

From her father she certainly inherited a kind temper and a generous hand. Like him, she could never witness want or suffering, without feeling a very earnest wish to relieve it. But she inherited from him also no inconsiderable portion of pride.

This last-named quality, however, was more changed by trans-
mission, than these before mentioned; for Gertrude inherited
from her mother, not only a bright intelligence, but also the
clearness of head, which, if it has fair play, leads to that most
precious of all faculties, common sense ; and where this is found
in action, pride, though it may exist, must cast off its fooleries.

The mental superiority of her mother, however, could not,
either by inheritance or precept, obliterate the self-willed pertinacity of character which was so remarkable in her father; but
her mind being of larger scope, her self-will could never have
been as perfectly satisfied as his, by the preservation of an unblemished coat of arms.

And excellent as her mother was, she too had her faults.

If the baron had too much pride in one direction, she had too
much pride in another ; and their child was as likely to suffer
from this sort of inheritance on the mother's side, as on the
father's.

The Baroness von Schwanberg's adoration of talent, and contempt for the want of it, might very truly be said to know no
bounds ; and to communicate these feelings to her child, speedily
became the great object of her life.

Had the father of this child been a little less absurd in his
estimate of human affairs in general, and of his own position in
particular, the feelings of his wife towards him would have been
very different, for, in that case, her estimate of her respective
duties as a wife and a mother, might have been more justly
balanced ; but, as it was, she felt as if she had done her child
great wrong by permitting herself to be persuaded to form the
alliance which had given her so unintellectual a father; and in
order to atone for this, she put but little restraint upon herself
when discussing the inanity of his pursuits, or the absurdity of
his notions.

But, fortunately for both parties, nature seemed to take the
feelings both of the father and the daughter into her own hands,
and that, too, without changing the intellectual condition of
either. The baron, perhaps, never quite ceased to lament in his
inmost soul that his daughter was not his son ; but, nevertheless,
a very few years sufficed to teach him that a daughter was a
thing that might be very dearly loved; and he did love his
beautiful Gertrude very dearly.

The young girl, on the other hand, guided by the same kind
of unerring impulse, soon discovered that though papa did not
know so many things as mamma, it was still very nice to have a

father so fond of one; and perhaps the worst effect of this divided duty was, that it taught her to feel how much more important she was to both, than either of them was to the other—a discovery which was likely enough to lead to the dangerous conclusion, that she was able to manage them both.

And that this was, in a great degree, the case, is very certain; and had the young heiress been a little-minded girl, she would have been ruined by it; but fortunately, she was not. She had a multitude of faults, both heriditary and acquired, but littleness of mind was not among them.

She would have no more condescended artfully to use her influence on either, for the purpose of obtaining any childish indulgence, than she would have cut off her own little finger; but she certainly did not scruple to profit by the indulgence of both, in the way most agreeable to each. It was with her father, therefore, that she enjoyed the great delight of cantering on her beautiful little pony, not only over every part of his wide domain, but considerably beyond its confines, when the doing so could afford her an opportunity of looking on upon the chase, in which her father delighted, and in which he very frequently indulged, considering it as the only amusement which could be strictly considered as truly and exclusively NOBLE.

In this much-loved recreation her mother could take no part, for she had never been a horse-woman; but having all confidence in the care taken of the little girl by her father in these excursions, her good sense and right feeling taught her to rejoice instead of lament, that there was some portion of her daugther's days which might be passed in the society of her father, without either positive loss of time or positive privation of pleasure. And this portion, and her presence at his daily meals, appeared to satisfy the good baron completely.

Her mother, on the other hand, was equally well contented by the portion of this precious daughter's hours which was allotted to her.

The only stipulation on which she insisted was, that she should have no governess but herself. Her own education had been well attended to. She was an excellent musician, drew with taste and correctness, and was quite as good a linguist as she wished her daughter to be; all this, she was quite aware, might be also acquired by her Gertrude, by the aid of an accomplished woman, who might easily be hired for the purpose of teaching her; nor was she at all unconscious of the fact that she should herself be spared many hours of fatigue by this arrangement.

But the steadfast-minded mother had what she conceived to be much higher objects in view than could be obtained in the ordinary routine of education by the assistance of a governess. She had long ceased to lament, with anything like bitterness, the fate which had given her one of the dullest men that ever lived as a husband and companion; for she had enough of practical wisdom to be aware that her happiness would have been much more effectually destroyed by a man who, with less of dullness, had a greater propensity to interfere with the opinions of his wife, and who might have interfered more fatally still with the occupation of her time.

But although she felt that there might be qualities in a husband worse than dullness, the terrible vision, which was long the *bête noir* of her existence, arose from the fear that the intellect of her child might resemble that of its father.

Her chief reason for deciding that she would herself be the instructress of the little Gertrude, arose from the conviction that so only could she be able to form a just estimate of her faculties and disposition. "Should I," thought she, "find my spirits or my strength unequal to the task, I can resign it; but this shall not be done till I have enabled myself to form something like a correct judgment of what she is."

The experiment was made, and the result was most propitious in every way.

It required no maternal partiality to convince her that, although the little girl might inherit the Schwanberg estates, it was quite impossible that she should ever give evidence of her lawful right to them by any resemblance to their present possessor.

The fate of Madame von Schwanberg had certainly not hitherto been a happy one. She had known what it was to love, and be disappointed. She had known, too, the weariness, not to say misery, of becoming the wife of a man utterly incapable of being a companion, and yet, perhaps, not quite deserving the feeling he inspired.

But, be this as it may, she soon discovered that her only resource against something very like despair must be sought in herself; and, fortunately, she was not long in discovering that she should not seek it in vain. The quiet baron had not the slightest objection to her exercising her own taste in the arrangement of her apartments; and if her constant additions to his fine old library had cost him thousands instead of hundreds, he would have made no sort of objection to it, for it would have caused him no inconvenience; nay, even if it had, and that his forests, or his flocks either, had been thinned to furnish what she needed, he would greatly have preferred making the sacrifice to enduring the idea that his wife, the Baroness von Schwanberg, should want anything which the most powerful of German nobles could obtain. Of course, this sort of indulgence, together with the perfectly well-founded conviction that the baron did not expect his baroness to bestow much of her company upon him, in a great degree reconciled her to her lot.

And then, heaven graciously sent her the little Gertrude!

Her satisfaction at the arrival of this precious treasure would have been more perfect still, had not the fears before-mentioned blended her hopes with doubts.

The scheme she had hit upon, of being herself her little daughter's governess, was extremely well imagined, and perfectly successful; for, before the little baroness had completed her tenth year, her mother had become very comfortably convinced that there was as little intellectual resemblance between the father and daughter as she could possibly desire; and having ascertained this important fact very completely to her satisfaction, she prayed God to forgive her for having been so very anxious about it; and also for the extreme gratification which she derived from the result of her watchful study of infant character.

This important question being thus settled to her satisfaction, the baroness, like a good woman as she was, took care not to impede, but, on the contrary, to foster, by every rational means in her power, the growing attachment between the father and daughter.

The little girl had her mother's beautiful eyes, hair, and teeth, but she also, in many respects, resembled her father. Her growth, and finely-formed limbs, seemed to promise that, in a feminine degree, she would prove a worthy scion of the stately house of Schwanberg; and it was, happily, very evident also that, in the vigorous healthfulness of her constitution, she much more nearly resembled her father than her mother.

Of this resemblance the baron was fully as conscious as his lady could be of the child's intellectual features; and it would be difficult to say which parent was best pleased by the resemblance which each traced.

The good baron, however, reasoned about it much less than his philosophical-minded lady. It is very possible that, sincerely as she wished that a strong mutual attachment should exist between the father and his child, she might have been less willing to see them so well pleased in each other's society, had the resemblance between them been of an intellectual instead of a physical kind. Could she have believed that, during the many hours in which they were riding or walking together, the spirit of the child would have kindled into the same sort of eager animation, that it was the delight of her heart to witness, when she was herself the bright young creature's only companion, a feeling of no very pleasant kind would have been the result. In short, had the father and daughter been more intellectually alike, the mother might have been less willing to see them share so many hours of exercise and amusement together.

〜〜〜〜〜〜〜〜〜

CHAPTER IV.

But Madame de Sewanberg was not quite right in supposing that those very hours could be thus passed *tête-à-tête* with her father, without producing some effect upon the child's mind, and manner of thinking. In forming this opinion, she had forgotten that the mind of the baron had its particular *hobby*, as well as her own, and that her feelings of love and reverence for genius and knowledge, were neither more active nor more ardent, than his for high descent and aristocratic station. Nor did the ample stores of her library furnish more fitting materials for making her child intellectual, than the ample extent of his domain offered for rendering his heiress proud.

And, in fact, she rode by his side, and listened to the long stories he recounted of the succession of noble ancestors who had possessed, and ruled over, these fields and forests, and indulged their subject tenants, and their favoured friends, by permitting them to join in the glorious chase, to which their magnificent extent offered such rare facilities, till the little girl certainly did begin to think that her papa was a very great man indeed.

Nor did he permit her to remain long in ignorance of the agreeable fact, that she was destined by providence to become, in the course of time, a very great woman herself. At first, she only laughed at this, and thought he was joking; and then, when she perceived he was in earnest, she blushed, and felt half shocked, and half frightened, at the idea of becoming the ruler and the queen over so many grown-up people.

Upon the whole, however, the idea was by no means disagreeable; and by degrees she began to wonder that her dear mamma (who must, of course, know all about her future greatness as well as her papa) had never said one single word to her on the subject. By degrees, too, this reserve became painful to her; and when she was about twelve years old, she suddenly took the resolution of asking her mother why, among all the things she taught her about what was right, and what was wrong, she never said anything as to the sort of way in which she ought to behave when she came into possession of her father's great estates.

"I could give you many reasons, Gertrude, for never spending any of our precious time upon such a subject," replied her mother.

"Pray do tell me some of them, mamma!" returned the child; "for I want very much to know all about it."

"One reason for my silence might perhaps be, that I know very little about it myself," said the baroness; "and another certainly is, that I consider it very unlikely that you should ever find yourself in a situation to require the information you ask for."

"How can that be, mamma?" said Gertrude, slightly knitting her beautiful brow; "is it not certain that I shall be my papa's heiress?"

"No, not quite certain," returned her mother, carelessly; "for I may die before your father, and he might marry again, and have a son. But, even if this does not happen, there is very little danger, my dear, that you should ever be troubled about the management of the estate. Of course, you will marry, as other girls do, and there will be no more occasion for you to trouble yourself about the estate, than there is for me to do so."

There are no auditors in the world more amenable to the influence of common sense than children. There is neither fallacy nor puzzle in it, and there is always a sort of self-evident truth about it, which is to the mind what light is to the eye; and the statement that we believe what we see, is as correct respecting the one, as respecting the other.

Gertrude troubled herself no more respecting the difficulties attending the management of her future dominions; but it was not very long before the idea suggested itself to her, that although she might never have much to do with the management of her estate herself, it would be proper for her to be very careful not to marry any one who was not well qualified to manage it for her.

This task of selection, however, did not trouble her much; but, nevertheless, a tolerably firm resolution took root, almost unconsciously perhaps, in her young mind, that the said selection should be made by HERSELF.

Her life, meanwhile, was one of almost unmixed enjoyment, for the wearisome dullness of her father was unfelt when she was galloping at his side, up hill and down dale, upon the very prettiest pony that ever carried a young heiress; and every hour passed with her mother was so enjoyable, that she only wondered how she could ever bear to leave her, even for a gallop; for when they were not talking together, or singing together, or drawing together, they were both reading, at no great distance apart, in the snug retreat afforded by the fine old library, where no chance visitors were ever permitted to enter, and from the threshold of which the magnificent master of the castle instinctively retreated, as if conscious that there was some quality in its atmosphere decidedly hostile to his constitution.

Different people would have doubtless passed different judgments on the conduct of the baroness, respecting this reading portion of Gertrude's education, had her system been made known. What was coarse and gross, was so repugnant to her own feelings, that she would no more have permitted anything of this nature to come in her daughter's way, than she would have suffered poison to be mixed with her food; but she rather wished to encourage, than restrain the perusal of whatever argumentative works excited her interest, being deeply persuaded that TRUTH will make its way to the mind, wherever free discussion is permitted between herself and the blundering falsehoods by which she is perpetually assailed.

Madame de Schwanberg's idea on the subject was, that with a fair field, and no favour, there was no more danger that truth should be conquered in the strife, than that a six-foot grenadier should be overthrown by Tom Thumb.

She had herself read much more widely and deeply than the majority of her sex, and her opinions upon many points still contested by mankind, were as firmly held as they were carefully formed; but she recognised no law which, in her opinion, could justify her insisting upon her daughter's adopting her opinions; and Gertrude was in a fair way of profiting as largely by the baron's polite liberality in the constant purchase of books, as her mother had been before her.

But this is forestalling; for there are events of her childhood to be recorded, which occurred before the liberality of her parents, either in money or mind, enabled her to cater for herself in this particular.

It would be doing great injustice to the parternal feelings of the Baron von Schwanberg to deny, that however constant he might be in theory, to his preference for a male heir, he had become, in practice, to be most fervently attached to his little daughter; and there was no page in the history of his country, that he now dwelt upon with so much pleasure, as that which recorded the greatness of MARIA TERESA. In short, if he had not changed his mind upon the superiority of a son to a daughter, he had, in a great degree, forgot to think about it; and in contemplating the beauty, the vivacity, and the high spirit of his heiress, he could find no room in his heart for any feelings but love and admiration.

But, of all her accomplishments, he was decidedly most vain of her horsemanship. He was never weary of pointing out to all who would listen to him, the undaunted courage displayed by the little girl, when she accompanied him in the chase; and he believed, as firmly as that the earth was created by God, that the noble daring she displayed was derived from the untainted blood of her long descended line of ancestors.

Such being his feelings on the subject, it may easily be supposed that he lost no opportunity of exhibiting her beauty, and her fearlessness on horseback, whenever he indulged his more aristocratic neighbours, by inviting them to hunt upon his land; and as the baroness had the most perfect confidence in the knowledge and discretion of her husband in all matters appertaining to the chase (the more perfect, perhaps, because unmixed with any suspicion of his superiority on any other subject); no objection was ever raised, on her part, to her daughter's sharing in a pastime which she enjoyed with quite as much fervour as the baron himself.

It happened soon after she had passed her twelfth birthday, that a grand hunt was proposed, in a direction not very frequently taken by the baron and his sporting friends, on account of the intervention of a stream that was not always easily fordable. But the young baroness having previously, with her father at her bridle-rein, tried her pony very successfully at the spot where they intended to cross, the party was arranged, and a gayer field had never been assembled at Schloss Schwanberg than that which left it upon this occasion. The weather was delicious. Every thing seemed to smile upon them; but, alas! "malignant Fate sat by, and smiled" too.

It certainly was a very pretty sight; and the gay, blooming, fearless little Gertrude, making her spirited little pony pace daintily along, close to her father's horse, was not the least attractive part of the spectacle.

After about an hour's riding, they reached the spot where they were to cross; and it was arranged between the baron and his friends, that they, and the servants, should all precede him and his precious charge, to prevent the possibility of frightening the pony by the unwonted sound of splashing hoofs behind him. They all made the passage without the slightest difficulty, the steep descent down the high bank beneath which the little river ran, being by far the greatest impediment to their progress. But Gertrude was far too good a horse-woman to mind this; and gathering up her reins in as scientific a manner as it was possible for the little hand to achieve, she reached the border of the stream as safely, and as gracefully too, as if she had been riding across her father's lawn.

"Now then, Gertrude," said the baron, "put him to it. Let him step in."

Gertrude paused but a moment to gather up her long riding-dress, and obeyed. For the first few paces the little animal seemed to find no difficulty, and made none, but stepped as steadily forward as if conscious of the important duty he had to perform, and the necessity of being more than usually careful.

The sheltering projection of the steep bank which they had just descended, so effectually impeded the current at the point where the road entered it, that its waters ran almost without a ripple; but having passed this shelter, Gertrude's little steed stopped short, and neighed to his brethren who had preceded him, as if to consult them concerning his progress.

It is true that he had crossed at the same ford before, and had made no difficulty about it; but whether the largeness of the party of which he now made one had shaken his nerves, or that the stream ran deeper in consequence of more recent, or more abundant rain; in short, whatever the cause, he not only stood still, but shewed very evident symptoms of being frightened.

Not so his high-spirited young reader. But if ignorance is bliss, it is not safety. It was evident that the pony was more aware of the real state of the case than Gertrude, or she would have patted him gently, and waited for her father, who followed her at the distance of a few feet; but instead of this, she gave her little favourite the sharpest touch of her whip that she had ever bestowed upon him, and in order to obey it, he made so great an effort that he was immediately taken off his feet, and the terrified baron had the misery of seeing his heiress floating down the stream, very evidently against her will. That it was against the pony's will also, was equally evident; for though the action of his head and neck very plainly showed that he was endeavouring to obey the rein which Gertrude still held steadily in her hand, he was unable to do it. Her father's first impulse was to follow her; but the powerful animal on which he was mounted had no intention of swimming, and strode resolutely onward to the bank, which the rest of the party had reached, without heeding either the heel or the hand of his rider.

Meanwhile, more than one of the sportsmen who had crossed, turned their horses' heads down the stream, in the hope of finding some point at which they might dash into the river, and by heading the pony and seizing his rein, be enabled to rescue the precious burden he was so evidently carrying to destruction. But this plan was more easily formed than executed. The bank on the side which the advanced party had reached rose rapidly, and the swimming pony had already passed the last point at which those who wished to rescue the young girl could possibly have reached the stream.

At this terrible moment, when the thought had occurred to more than one of the party, that it was not the classic Tiber only which was destined to roll its waves over youth and beauty; it was it this terrible moment that the slight figure of a young lad was seen on the side of the river which they had just quitted, running with the swiftness of an antelope to some point which evidently he was desperately purposed to reach; and he had already outstripped the swimming pony, when he was seen to turn suddenly to a projecting ledge which overhung the river, and then hastily unclasping his belt, and divesting himself of the loose garment which would have impeded his purpose, he took a vigorous forward spring, which brought him within a few feet of the advancing pony and his helpless burden.

After this plunge, the bold boy was for a moment lost to sight, and more than one of the gasping spectators of this frightful scene exclaimed, " He is gone ! "

He was not gone far, however, for, though he had sunk to a perilous depth beneath the surface of the water, he speedily rose again, and vigorously seizing the falling girl with his left arm, he swam with her, by the help of the right, to a little pebbly cove on the same side of the stream which he had just quitted, and the next moment she was lying, not dry, certainly, but high enough above the water to insure her for the present from any danger of being drowned.

The scene which followed may be easily imagined. Not only the half-dead and half-bewildered father immediately set himself to discover the readiest mode of joining the dripping pair, who appeared lying side by side, and equally motionless, on the beach, but every individual of the party—masters and men—were evidently intent on the same object.

It took not long to decide what was to be done.

In the next moment the whole group were galloping back to the ferry, which they recrossed as rapidly as was consistent with their recently-acquired knowledge of its danger; and in a few minutes afterwards they reached a point of the cliff, down which they scrambled with no great difficulty, having dismounted, and consigned their steeds to the care of their servants; and then they very speedily reached the object of their anxiety.

Poor Gertrude was perfectly insensible, and for a few terrible moments her miserable father believed she was dead. But more than one of his truly-sympathizing companions, though not a little flurried by the scene they had witnessed, were, nevertheless, sufficiently in possession of their senses to perceive that the adventure, perilous as it unquestionably had been, was not likely to end in so tragical a manner.

As there was no one present likely to quote Shakspeare, and exclaim, "Too much of water hast thou"—a very sensible individual of the party ventured to try the experiment of applying a little more; and as he did this very judiciously, by dashing from a drinking-horn, which he carried in his pocket, a pretty copious libation of the fluid in her face, it proved to be, like many other things, both bane and antidote, according to the mode of its application, for the beautiful eyes of the young Gertrude immediately opened at its startling touch.

She first breathed a somewhat sobbing sigh, and then looked about her, very much as if she wanted to find out where she was, and not at all as if she intended to die before she had satisfied herself on this point.

There were several stout-hearted gentlemen present upon that occasion, who were heard to declare more than once, in the course of their subsequent lines, that they never should forget the countenance of the Baron von Schwanberg at the moment he first perceived that his daughter was alive.

Of all the party present, he had perhaps been the only one who had even for a moment hopelessly and completely believed that she was dead; and his agony under this conviction had been terrible to witness. His heavy, haughty, but very handsome face, had assumed a sort of livid paleness, which it was frightful to look at; and the features had such an expression of misery, so fixed and immovable, that he looked as if turned to stone. The transition from this condition to the full conviction that he still possessed the precious heiress bestowed on him by Heaven (expressly for the purpose of proving the absurdity of the Salique law), produced an effect which, for an instant, seemed to overpower him, and he caught hold of the branch of a neighbouring tree, to prevent himself from falling; but, in the next, he was sufficiently recovered to be on his knees beside his treasure; and it certainly must have have been a hard heart which could have witnessed the embrace which followed, without emotion.

I have not, perhaps, on the whole described the Baron von Schwanberg in very agreeable colours; but, dull as he might have been on some points, he was not dull enough to be insensible to the immensity of the obligation which he owed to the poor boy who had saved his daughter's life, and who was still lying on the bank beside her, very nearly as pale as herself; for he had dislocated his ankle while dragging the young lady to land, among the unsteady pebbles and stones of which the river, sometimes a very powerful stream, had thrown up a tolerably steep ridge.

With one arm still clasped round his daughter, he employed the other in trying to raise the pale lad, who certainly did not at first give any very certain indications that his own life might not be the sacrifice he was doomed to pay for having preserved that of another; but, though in great pain from his ankle, he was neither dead nor insensible, and was soon sufficiently recovered to reply to the questions kindly, and even anxiously, put to him by the baron, as to the distance to his home, and the best way of conveying him thither.

The brave boy's reply to the first question was agreeable to the noble questioner in more ways than one, for it conveyed the information that he was the nephew of a priest well known in the neighbourhood, and that a short cut across the country would speedily bring him to the good man's home, which, for the present, was his own also, as well as that of his mother, who was sister to the worthy and much-respected ecclesiastic.

"I am glad to hear it, with all my heart!" exclaimed the baron, with great energy. "Your uncle shall become my confessor in the place of old Father Ambrose, who has grown too infirm

to come to the castle, and too deaf to hear me confess.   He shall
be pensioned, and your uncle shall be promoted; and so shall
you, too, my young hero, you may take the Baron von Schwanberg's word for that."

And then followed a consultation among the numerous group
which was now assembled round them, as to the best method of
conveying the lamed boy to his home; and as it became perfectly
evident, upon his attempting to stand, that he was totally incapable of walking, it was speedily decided that the carriage,
which was already sent for to convey the uninjured but dripping
Gertrude, should convey her preserver to the castle likewise;
while another domestic was dispatched to the Unterthal dwelling
of the priest, to inform both him and his sister that the young
Rupert was safe, and that both of them would be welcome at the
Schloss Schwanberg, if they would come thither to visit him.

There might be traced in the well-pleased tone in which the
baron said this, a self-approving consciousness that the invitation
thus given must necessarily be so highly gratifying to the persons
to whom it was addressed, as to be almost of itself a fitting
reward for the service it was intended to acknowledge.

But the Baron von Schwanberg was no niggard either in his
gratitude or in the manner in which it was his intention to show
it; and having paused for a moment after pronouncing these
flattering words, he added, in a tone that had a good deal of
solemnity in its earnestness, "Nor will their welcome to the
castle of Schwanberg be the only proof given by its lord of his
gratitude for, and his admiration of, the high courage and the
noble impulse by which the life of his heiress has been preserved."

The pale-faced hero of the adventure, for pale he still was, and
still suffering considerable pain, contrived nevertheless, to smile
as he replied, with a disclaiming shake of the head, "There is
nobody in the world, I believe, my Lord Baron, who would
not have done just the same thing, if he had happened to have
been by."

"It is well and highly becoming that you should say so, my
good boy," returned the baron, with a gracious nod; "but it
would be quite the reverse of this, if I could either think or say
so."

The boldest rider and the best mounted of his train, had
already been sent back to the castle by its master, to order the
countess's coach to be instantly prepared, and brought with all
possible speed to the spot where the accident had happened.

"And, for God's love! bring back a bottle of brandy or wine

with you," screamed a ready-witted individual of the party, who having turned his eyes towards the young hero of the adventure, when he replied to the baron in the manner above-mentioned, perceived that he was either fainting or dying, and very considerately uttered this injunction as the surest way of rescuing the sufferer from both.

CHAPTER V.

It certainly was not the intention of the baron, when he thus hurriedly dismissed his messenger, that his lady should be made to suffer still greater, or, at the least, more lasting, misery than he had endured himself from the accident; but such was the result of the unmitigated clamour which rang throughout the castle, within a few moments after the summons for the carriage arrived at it.

Either the evident urgency of the case, or their habitual promptitude in obeying the commands of the baron, produced such instant obedience to his message, that the carriage was fortunately already on its way to the spot where it was so eagerly waited for, before the alarming report of the adventure had reached the unconscious mother in the quiet, and somewhat remote retreat of her library.

But her respite lasted no longer, for scarcely had the equipage rattled off over the moated entrance, when her own personal attendant, followed by the steward of the household, and the portly housekeeper, all rushed into her presence together, exclaiming in very discordant chorus: "For mercy's sake, don't alarm yourself, madam!"

"It will all end in nothing, you may depend upon it!"

"These things are always made the very most, and worst of, my lady!"

"For Heaven's sake, tell me what you are all talking about," cried the bewildered lady; "is the castle on fire?"

"No, my lady, no! God forbid! Such a noble castle as this! The whole body of saints and martyrs that lie in the chapel cloisters yonder would rise to put it out, my lady, if it was so," said the old steward, who was renowned for his exemplary piety, and who now, taking courage from the dignity of his office, and his long service, approached the lady's reading-desk, and bent himself down with a sort of protecting air over the back of her chair.

She turned suddenly round to him, but ere she could pronounce the inquiry which was upon her lips, her waiting-woman had dropped on her knees before her and began chafing her hands as if she had been in a fit, while the old housekeeper stood by, in an attitude very eloquently expressive of woe, with the corner of her handkerchief in her eye.

It was certainly scarcely possible that all this could go on without suggesting, as it was intended to do, the idea of something very terrible, which is the usual mode, I believe, of preparing people for the disclosure of some great calamity; the reasoning in such cases being, that it is better that people should suspect something worse than the worst, at first, in order that when they know the real truth, it may bring with it a feeling of relief.

Whether such suffering can ever be really beneficial, may be doubted; but in the case of poor Madame de Schwanberg, it was very decidedly the reverse, for her daughter being now always the first object of her thoughts, the idea immediately suggested by the moaning around her was, that she had been thrown from her horse, and was killed!

"My daughter is dead!" she exclaimed, and having distinctly uttered these fearful words, she uttered a piercing shriek, and fell back in her chair as pale and as motionless as a corpse.

It was in vain that the three raven messengers now screamed in chorus: "No! No! No! not dead, my lady!" She heard them not; and although she had moved her limbs, and once or twice partially opened her eyes, she was still nearly insensible, when the carriage conveying the hero and heroine of the adventure retured to the castle.

On entering the hall, Gertrude, who, excepting the injury done to her pretty riding-dress, was not in the least degree the worse for it, stood for a moment irresolute as to whether she should run first to embrace her dear mamma, and wish her joy of still having a troublesome daughter; or fly to the housekeeper's room, to order that a bed should immediately be prepared for the young hero who had saved her.

It was much to her honour that she decided upon the latter, for strong was her longing to embrace that dear mamma, and witness her happiness at having her safe at home again. But the selfish thought was speedily dismissed; one glance at the pale face of her preserver, as the servants assisted him from the carriage, being quite sufficient both to decide and accelerate her movements.

But her active gratitude was of no avail, for it was in vain she sought the important functionary at her usual post; and not finding her, she at once decided that "mamma" was the properest person to say what was immediately to be done in order to obtain for the poor sufferer the relief of lying down, with as little delay as possible.

Though the distance from the housekeeper's domain to the library, was much more considerable than the inhabitants of our degenerate mansions are accustomed to tread, in passing from one part of a house to another, the space was rapidly traversed by Gertrude; but the feeling of thankful happiness with which she was about to throw herself into her mother's arms was changed to terror, when, on entering the room, she beheld her mother stretched upon a sofa as pale as a corpse, with her eyes closed, and giving no sign of life save deep-drawn sighs, every one of which seemed to be a gasping effort to recover breath.

The servants, who still stood trembling around her, hardly knew whether she was conscious of their presence or not, for she had not spoken since the first heart-broken exclamation which she had uttered upon being told that she was "not to alarm herself."

Deadly pale as were her cheeks and lips, however, she was not insensible, for no sooner had the voice of her child pronounced the words "Mamma! dear, darling mamma!" than the closed eyes opened, and the seemingly helpless arms raised to receive her.

"Is it about me, mamma?" cried the frightened girl, kneeling down beside her. "Did the people tell you I was hurt, mamma? It was very, very wrong of them if they did, for I am not hurt, not the least bit in the world; but HE is hurt! The dear, brave boy that saved my life, without thinking for a moment about his own!" And then the eager girl, addressing the group of servants who still hung round her mother, as if they were performing thereby a most important duty, she added: "I tried to find one, or all of you, even before I came here, that you might get a bed ready, if only for him to die in! Oh! I wish you had seen him, mamma!" she continued, while tears of gratitude started to her eyes. "He seemed to think no more of his own danger, when he sprang into the water to save me, than if he had been already as immortal as an angel."

"Go, go, good Agatha!" cried the baroness, who seemed restored to life as if by miracle; "and you too, Hans, go both of you, and see that everything is provided for this boy—this benefactor. And tell him—tell him that I would come to him myself, but that my dear dripping girl must be attended to."

The two servants she addressed obeyed her command with all possible celerity; for, in truth, they were as curious, as obedient, and as eager to wait upon this wonderful young hero, and to hear all that was to be known about him, as their mistress could be that he should be taken care of.

But no sooner was this duty of dismissing them on their errand performed, than transferring a portion of the attention she had been bestowing upon her daughter's bright face, to her dripping garments, she almost relapsed into terror for her life, when she became aware of their condition.

She rose from the sofa, from which, a few minutes before, her attendants had doubted if she would ever rise again, and offering her arm to her radiant daughter as if her steps wanted support, prepared to lead her from the room, exclaiming, in the very extremity of eager haste, "Oh, Gertrude! Gertrude! why did you not tell me that you were in this condition? It may be the death of her still, Teresa!"

"It will be the death of you first, my lady," cried the terrified abigail; "you that have been lying here senseless for an hour or more, to be starting up in this way! Let me alone for taking care of the young baroness. Come along, my dear!"

Teresa was an old servant, and a privileged person upon most occasions, and might now have said whatever she chose without the least danger of being chid; but as to preventing the resuscitated baroness from attending Gertrude to her room, she might as well have attempted to make Gertrude herself turn pale.

The trio, therefore, sought the young lady's dressing-room together, and nothing certainly could be less like sickness or sorrow, than the aspect of both mother and daughter, when they were startled by a knock at the door.

Teresa immediately opened it, in obedience to a sign from her mistress; and to the astonishment of them all, they beheld the stately master of the castle standing before it.

Now the castle of Schwanberg was a very large castle, and the apartments allotted to the different members of the family were not only perfectly distinct, but at a considerable distance from each other.

It might be for this reason, perhaps, that the baron, who was not only a very ceremonious, but (except on horseback) a very unlocomotive person, had rarely, or never been seen before on the spot where he now presented himself.

If Gertrude had been a little more inconvenienced by her accident, or if her lady-mother had been a little less thoroughly recovered from her false alarm, the effect of this very unexpected visit would have been less remarkable.

But the poor baron had, with his own eyes, beheld his darling daughter and heiress in such real, and very near danger of death, that he had himself by no means recovered from the shock, and the sight of the mother and daughter sportively engaged in contemplating the condition of the drenched garments, nay, positively laughing heartily at some of Teresa's tragic exclamations as she gazed upon them, so astonished, and in truth, so shocked him, that he dropped into the nearest chair with a look of absolute dismay.

The baroness saw how matters stood in a moment; and knowing that it would be impossible to make him gay, she might awaken him to a feeling of happiness, she turned from her laughing girl, and laying her hand kindly on her husband's arm, said to him, with a very sweet smile, " Gertrude is wild with joy at her own escape, and the sight of my happiness."

" I would rather see her grateful than wild for her escape," replied the baron, very solemnly; "and though, of course, I cannot but rejoice at finding her so perfectly recovered, I should have been better pleased if she appeared to think more seriously of the danger she has escaped."

" Do not suspect her of ingratitude for this great mercy; and do not suspect me of it, either," replied the baroness, while very pious tears rushed to her eyes, as she raised them in gratitude to Heaven.

" Of course, wife, of course!" returned the baron, crossing himself. "God forbid that I should suspect either of you of impiety! A proper service will be performed with as little delay as possible in the chapel of the castle to return thanks for the special interference of Providence in my favour, nor can I for a moment doubt, that you will both of you join in this service with feelings of devotion becoming the occasion. But the gratitude to which I allude is of a different kind. The young lad who so bravely endangered his own life for the purpose of saving that of

4

my daughter, is now suffering, under the shelter of my roof, from the effects of the perilous effort which he made to ensure her safety; and having already had my mind set at ease by the report of my daughter's safety, I have taken the liberty, wife, of seeking you here, for the purpose of stating to you my opinion, that the condition of this suffering boy well deserves and (considering the cause of it) demands some sort of hospitable attention on your part."

It must be confessed that it was a very rare thing for the baron's harangues to produce so great an effect upon those who listened to him, as on the present occasion. Both the mother and daughter were sincerely shocked and repentant, at thinking that one to whom they owed so much, should have been for a moment forgotten; and the baroness hesitated not to leave her daughter to the care of Teresa, and the consequential individual who had formerly officiated as nurse to the young lady, and who had now joined the party in Gertrude's bed-room.

It was impossible for the baron to feel otherwise than satisfied on perceiving the effect he had produced; and it was, therefore, very nearly in his most gracious and condescending manner that he now presented his arm to his lady, in order to conduct her, as in duty bound, to the chamber of their suffering guest.

Nothing could have been more fortunate for the young hero of the adventure, than this fancied superiority of noble feeling and amiable conduct on the part of the baron; for it at once caused him to identify the lad with himself as one party, while his thoughtless young daughter, and her seeming ungrateful mother, formed another. This was of itself quite enough for a man so intensely vain as the Baron von Schwanberg, in order to make everything concerning the boy, a matter of interest to him.

It is quite certain, that his marriage with the high-minded woman who had been given to him by her family for his wife, had been as little a source of happiness to him, as to her. To comprehend, or understand her character and qualities, was beyond the scope of his ability; but some faculty, apparently approaching to instinct, produced a very disagreeable sort of vague conviction on his mind that she was, in some way or other, above him. This feeling would have been more painful still, if his vanity had not taken refuge in the constant recollection of his lady's high birth, which being, undeniably, still more illustrious than his own, accounted very naturally, and almost satisfactorily, for the sort of involuntary deference which he paid her.

But now it was quite evident that in nobleness of character he was her superior; for had he not himself stood for several minutes by the young stranger's bed, in order to be sure that he was placed safely in it, while the heedless mother of the heiress whose life had been saved by the young stranger's valour, was childishly at play with her daughter in the most distant part of the castle!

Nevertheless, he was generous enough to abstain from uttering a word more of reproach on the subject; contenting himself by observing, in a very solemn tone, as, with a very solemn step, he led her to the chamber of the sufferer, that "he trusted the humble station of the individual they were about to visit would be forgotten, or excused, in consideration of the immense blessing which Providence had ordained that he should bestow on the house of Schwanberg."

It is impossible to deny, that the lady to whom this harangue was addressed, had taught herself to hear the pompous platitudes of her lord without permitting them to interfere greatly with the course of her, probably, very distant thoughts; and she was now so occupied by the important question which had just arisen in her mind, as to the possibility of Gertrude's having taken cold, that when his speech was ended, which happened just as they arrived at the door of the boy's room, she replied, "Oh, certainly," in so very careless a tone, that the baron breathed a silent vow, as he turned the lock, that this unnatural indifference on the the part of his wife, should be atoned for on his, in a way that should do his grateful feelings justice in the eyes both of God and man.

Notwithstanding her momentary oblivion, however, of the errand she was upon, there was nothing like ingratitude in the heart of the baroness; and even if there had been, it would have given place to a very contrary feeling, the moment she beheld the suffering boy who had saved the life of her child.

The paleness which had been the first visible effect of the pain he had suffered from the injury he had received, had now given place to the bright hectic of fever. The least experienced eye could hardly fail to perceive, at the first glance, that the fervent glow of his cheek, and the preternatural brightness of his eye, were the result of suffering, and not of health; yet, nevertheless, the first feeling of Madame de Schwanberg, as she looked at him, was that of unmixed admiration. She thought she had never beheld such perfect beauty before; and perhaps she was right; for lovely as her own daughter certainly was, the face which she now saw before her, was lovelier still. The forehead was large

' 4—2

and beautifully formed, and the dark eyebrows were of the form
which best helps expression, without being themselves a too con-
spicuous feature. The nose, mouth, and chin might have furnished a precious model to a statuary who wished to emulate the
type of Greece, without the sort of exaggerated regularity which,
except in a few rare instances, destroys the expression of great
intelligence. The rich natural curls of his dark hair were in
what could not fail, from their beauty, to be " *admired* disorder;"
but, nevertheless, they had been so wildly handled by the feverish
hand which supported his head, that the effect was painful, for
his whole aspect suggested the idea of incipient delirium.

The first effect that his appearance produced on the lady of
the castle was, as before stated, admiration; but a moment's
contemplation of it produced alarm, and her first words were expressive neither of gratitude nor welcome; for she only said,
with hasty abruptness, "I hope, baron, that you have sent some
one for Dr. Nieper!"

The baron was positively both shocked and angry. "What a
reception to give the youthful hero who had saved her child!"
were the words he muttered, as he turned his head away from
the offending lady.

"Do you fear infection, madam?" was the reply he made to
her; and it was spoken in a tone of so much contempt, that she
really hoped for a moment that her fears were absurd; and she
answered, with something like a smile, "Oh, no!" but then
added, "I really scarcely know what I fear; but I am of opinion,
baron, that medical advice will be necessary."

This certainly was said without any smile; but so strongly
persuaded was the baron that no one but himself had sufficient
feeling and discernment united, to be aware of the boy's real
condition, that he still thought she was speaking ironically; and
it was really with a very awful frown that he replied, "I believe,
madam, that the best thing you can do, is to return to your
daughter; concerning her condition I have no anxiety, having
accompanied her home in the carriage, enjoying thereby the great
happiness of perceiving that she was never in better health and
spirits in her life. I shall, as I have already said, take care that
a proper service, at which you will, of course, assist, shall be
performed in the chapel, as an acknowledgment to the Virgin for
her special care of our child. As for this youth, I will at present
trouble you no more concerning him. He would, doubtless, be
more interesting if he were of higher birth, but, nevertheless, I
feel myself, as the head of a noble house, bound to testify, by

every means in my power, my thankfulness for the service he has rendered it. Give yourself no trouble whatever about him. I will take care that he shall neither want medical aid, nor anything else that can be of use to him."

The experienced baroness plainly perceived, by the stately manner in which this speech was delivered, that her noble husband was in one of his magnificent paroxysms, though what it meant on the present occasion she was at a loss to conjecture; but at that moment she was too much occupied to care about it, and gently replying, that she quite agreed with him as to the necessity of immediately sending to the neighbouring town for their medical attendant, she has hastened from the room, eager to consult her old housekeeper, who was the most experienced person in the family, as to the real state of the poor boy, and the best manner of treating him before the doctor arrived.

The baron, meanwhile, was exceedingly relieved by her absence. Like all slow-minded people, he adhered very pertinaciously to an idea, when once he had got hold of it; and he was now brimful of the comfortable persuasion, that his noble nature had enabled him to conquer, as if by miracle, all the ordinary feelings of the high rank to which he belonged, in order to prove his devoted love to his child, and his feeling of gratitude to the humble being who had saved her.

Had he taken it into his head that his lady had displayed these feelings instead of himself, his conduct towards his young benefactor would have had assumed a very different colour.

As far as the boy was concerned, nothing could be more fortunate than this delusion; for, being as obstinate as he was shortsighted, the baron never for a moment lost sight of the idea that the family pride of his wife had caused her to treat him with great ingratitude; and the amiable contrast to this, which his own conduct exhibited, was not only a source of the most satisfactory self-applause to the last hour of his existence, but insured the continuance of his favour to the boy, with the most steadfast and unwearying constancy.

CHAPTER VI.

The baroness, notwithstanding her sincere anxiety for Rupert Odenthal, saw no reason why it should detain her any longer from the greatly-longed-for presence of her daughter; and it was to her room, therefore, that she summoned the venerable Agatha, in order to consult with her as to what it would be best to do for the suffering boy before the doctor arrived.

On re-entering Gertrude's apartment, she found the young lady still on the bed, in obedience to orders, but looking as well and as gay as if she had never sat upon a swimming horse in her life.

"How is he, mamma?" were her first words, as her mother approached her.

"I really know not how to answer you, my dear child," replied the baroness, "for you father seems to think that it is his own special duty to take care of him. This is very kind and grateful on his part, and I should be sorry to check it by any interference of mine; but, nevertheless, I feel very anxious about the boy, who seems to have a great deal of fever."

"Then, send for the doctor, mamma, at once," replied Gertrude, promptly.

"Your father has promised to do so," returned her mother; "and, in the meantime, I have sent for old Agatha to come here, that I may hold a consultation with her as to what we had better do for him, before Dr. Nieper arrives."

This important Agatha soon made her appearance, and, in reply to her lady's question as to what she thought of the boy? she replied, without a moment's hesitation:

"I think he is very ill, indeed, my lady."

Gertrude burst into tears.

"Do you mean to say that you think he will die, Agatha?" she exclaimed in great agitation. "I would rather die myself, mamma; I do really think I would. As long as I live, I shall always feel that I have killed him!"

"Don't take on in that way, my dear young lady," said the housekeeper. "I did not say—did I?—that I thought he must die. I do certainly think, however, that he has a great deal of fever."

"But we have many drugs that check fever, Agatha," replied the lady. "You are a very good doctor yourself, and I am sure you can give him something cooling before Dr. Nieper arrives."

"But I can't set the broken bone—if it be broken—my lady; and the fever won't stop till that has been done," returned Agatha.

"Is the baron still in the boy's room?" said Madame de Schwanberg.

"I can't say for certain; but I have very little doubt of it,"

replied the old woman, with a queer sort of smile. "Master
always likes to be Number One in every way, and about everything, when he chooses to meddle at all. And every word he
says about the boy shows that he thinks it a part of his greatness,
like, to take the whole management of him upon himself. But
I'll go and see if I can be useful, my lady. It won't be like
your ladyship's going."

Perhaps Gertrude did not quite understand the old woman's
meaning, but the baroness did. She made no commentary upon
it, however, but dismissed the sagacious housekeeper with a silent
nod, being very much in earnest in her determination that no
interference of hers should check her noble husband's intention
of proving himself the most generous of men.

It was for some hours, however, a very doubtful question
whether all these magnificent projects of showing to the whole
world how great a man's gratitude could be, would not be defeated
by the speedy death of the individual who was to be the object
of it.

The distance to the doctor's dwelling was considerable, and
the doctor's pony not fleet; but at length, however, they both
arrived at the castle, and it was the baron himself who ushered
the astonished Dr. Nieper into the patient's room.

The baron, too, very clearly perceived the impression produced by this extraordinary condescension on his part, and, on
reaching the chamber of the invalid, paused for a moment before
he opened the door, and said:

"I can easily believe, my good friend, that my accompanying
you to the sick-bed of an individual of the rank to which your
patient belongs must surprise you. But, in my estimation, Dr.
Nieper, gratitude in noble minds should never be in just proportion to the obligation received; and the father of the heiress
of Schwanberg will prove to the whole world that, in his estimation, the humble youth who saved her life is worthy even of
such attention as I am paying him now. Of course, my good
sir, a fitting service will be performed in the chapel of the castle,
that, in like manner, my gratitude to heaven also may be made
manifest to the eyes of all men."

Having at length concluded this speech (which the baron's
slow enunciation rendered rather long), he opened the door, and
placing himself at the bottom of the bed (at each side of which a
female domestic was seated), made a sign to the doctor to
approach. A very short examination sufficed to enlighten the
the practitioner upon the state of his patient; the ankle was dis-

located, and the drive which had followed had placed the injured limb in so fatiguing a position as greatly to increase the inflammation.

Fortunately, Dr. Nieper was no bungler, and the painful operation necessary upon such an accident was performed without loss of time, and with very considerable skill; but, nevertheless, the boy fainted under it, and when restored to animation, he was perfectly delirious, and manifested every symptom of fever.

As the baron (who, with all his pride, was far from being a hard-hearted man) had left the room during the operation, and only returned to it upon being informed that it had been very successfully performed, he was both shocked and surprised at finding the boy talking incoherently, so much so, indeed, as to make him break off in the speech, which he had began to utter as he entered, concerning his purpose of having a special service performed in the chapel of the castle, etcetera.

He was, in fact, exceedingly alarmed, and began to fear that the first duty which would devolve upon the boy's uncle, upon his promotion to the post of confessor at Schloss Schwanberg, would be to administer the last sacraments to his unfortunate nephew.

The noble gentleman, in fact, looked so completely dismayed, that Dr. Nieper was induced to give him assurances, somewhat more undoubting, perhaps, than his own opinion, that his patient was likely to do well.

"It may, nevertheless, be right, my Lord Baron," he added, "that the boy's relatives, if he has any, should be informed of his condition; for, in cases of this kind, where fever supervenes so violently as it seems inclined to do here, no practitioner in the world can be sure of the result. Does your lordship happen to know anything of his family?"

"Providentially, I do!" replied the baron, solemnly. "His uncle is a priest, and lives with this boy's mother, who is his sister, at the distance, I believe, of a mile or two."

"Then let them be informed of the accident immediately," returned the doctor; "it is certainly very proper that they should be sent for."

"Your suggestion, doctor, is the echo of my own thoughts. They shall be summoned immediately. Alas! it had been my intention to summon the priest without delay, in order that he might commence the duties of the place to which I meant to promote him, by performing in the chapel of the castle the special service which it was my intention."

"And if I were you, my Lord Baron, I should include his mother in my invitation," said the doctor, rather abruptly interrupting him; "for although these young women look very gentle and kind, it would be much better, when his reason returns, that he should not find himself surrounded by strange servants."

"Alas! alas!" replied the baron, very piteously; "I grieve that it should be so! But there are some minds, my good sir, upon which the effect of conscious high rank is not exactly what we might wish it to be. The Baroness von Schwanberg, born Baroness von Wolkendorf, is a lady of *very* high rank; and I have certainly never seen her so deeply and strongly influenced by the remembrance of this, as since your suffering patient was brought to the castle. I will not dwell upon the circumstances which have occurred, and which have all tended to prove her averseness to take any personal interest in the fate of one so much beneath her in station. I will not, I say, dwell upon this, farther than to remark, that I trust my own conduct gives sufficient evidence of the much deeper impression which this poor boy's courageous conduct, and subsequent suffering, has produced on my own mind. Nevertheless, I flatter myself, doctor, that I have never shown myself unconscious of, or indifferent to, the dignity of the position in which, by the will of Providence, I am placed. I will, indeed, venture to say, that the baroness herself cannot be more deeply impressed by the consciousness of her own dignified station than I am, or of that in which I and my high-born daughter stand likewise. Nevertheless, I am of opinion, that on such an occasion as the present, an occasion which, I conceive, calls for the performance of an especial service in the——."

"Nothing can be more clear and satisfactory, my Lord Baron, than your view of the case, which I comprehend perfectly, without your condescending to explain it farther," said the doctor; who, with his eye fixed upon his patient, had perceived sundry twitches indicative of pain and restlessness, and not feeling quite certain that the sonorous voice of the baron had much to recommend it, by way of a soothing lullaby, he ventured to apply a little of his professional courage to stop it.

The lord of the castle looked more startled and astonished, than angry; and thereupon the clever doctor, laying his head upon his own hand, shut up his eyes, and slightly snored, whereupon every trace of suspicion, or surprise either, vanished from the magnate's countenance; and making sundry pantomimic signs of intelligence, he walked out of the room with as little noise as a very stately baron, who did not tread very lightly, could contrive to do.

The poor boy, however, was neither sleeping, nor likely to sleep, as the worthy doctor well knew, for he was evidently still in pain, and very feverish; and although these symptoms were too inevitable, after what had happened, either to surprise or alarm him, he felt anxious to preserve him from such weighty annoyance as the presence of his host was sure to bring with it.

The two attending damsels who had been stationed beside the bed by the baron's orders, and who had left the room on his entering it, now returned, and stood before Dr. Nieper, waiting with great docility for his commands. The first he gave was to the younger of the two, signifying his wish that she should seek her mistress, and inform her that he desired to see her before he left the castle; adding, that, with her permission, he would immediately wait upon her. He then gave instructions to the other, to prepare some cooling beverage, which she was to keep ready at hand, and administer freely to the patient.

In order to obey this command, it was necessary that the person who received it should apply to the house-keeper; and while the woman went in search of her, the doctor took her place by the bed-side, awaiting the summons which he hoped to receive from the baroness.

As this intelligent mediciner had long been the professional attendant in ordinary of the Von Schwanberg family, he had placed but little faith on the baron's statement respecting the feelings of his lady towards the suffering boy; but nevertheless he was rather surprised to see her accompany the messenger he had sent to her, into the room of his patient, and that so promptly, as to prove that she had lost not a moment in seeking him.

She gave a hasty glance round the room on entering; and having ascertained that the baron was no longer there, she stepped gently to the bed-side, and after gazing earnestly for a moment on the fevered face of the patient, she turned a sorrowing, anxious look to the physician, who then stood beside her, and whispered the words, " Does he sleep?"

Dr. Nieper shook his head, and taking the hand which she had extended to him in friendly salutation, he led her to a distant part of the room, and forestalled her question by saying, " I flatter myself, madam, that he is not in danger. Worse accidents are, at his age, often met with sufficient strength to render recovery from them an easy matter. The dislocation of the ancle, however, is the least part of the mischief. His sufferings, probably from being in a constrained attitude in the carriage during his return, have brought on a very considerable degree of fever; but if he is properly attended to, and kept perfectly quiet, I dare say we shall conquer it. I should be sorry to lose such a patient as that," he added, turning towards the bed; "I think, madam, that, excepting your own, and your daughter's, it is the most beautiful countenance I ever saw."

"I could readily forgive you, doctor," replied the lady, "even if you had omitted the polite exception; for most assuredly I never saw, either in the glass, or out of it, any face which, in my estimation, can compare with it in beauty. God grant that he may do well! You must take care to be very clear and very explicit in the orders you leave about him, for the baron does not seem to approve my attending upon him myself, which I do assure you I should wish to do; and we all know, that however much we may rely on the fidelity of servants, we can trust nothing to their judgment."

"The baron seems to think, madam—" began Dr. Nieper in reply. But, for some reason or other, he deemed it best not to finish the speech he had begun; for he abruptly added—"Do you know, madam, if the boy has any mother within reach?"

"Yes, indeed! my housekeeper told me that his mother is living at Francberg with her brother, a very worthy priest, known by the name of Father Alaric."

"Francberg?" repeated the doctor, in an accent of considerable satisfaction; "Francberg is at no great distance; a man and horse might get there in an hour, if they kept to the bridle path. The carriage road is considerably longer. Let me recommend you, dear lady, to send to the house of Father Alaric immediately; and order your messenger to tell both the mother and uncle of this poor boy, that it would be desirable that they should, one or both, come to him immediately. Nothing should be more carefully avoided than letting our patient find himself, upon fully recovering his senses, in the midst of strangers. It might produce a very alarming return of delirium."

"I am quite aware of it," replied the baroness, earnestly. "But I should greatly wish that you should state your opinion on this subject to the baron himself."

"I will do so instantly," he replied; "and in my judgment, it will be better that you, madam, should not remain in this room. The servant now sitting by him may administer all the

assistance he wants, till his own mother arrives to wait on him—
and it may, perhaps, accord better, on the whole, with the baron's
wishes."

It is probable that there is no class of men, seek for them in
what country you will, who form, individually, such correct
judgments respecting their fellow-creatures (mentally as well as
physically) as those who attend them in a medical capacity.

The power of the priesthood in this respect is nothing in comparison to it.

For even if we take a penitent at the last gasp, terror may
almost involuntarily give a false colouring to his disclosures. But
in a sick room, there is always, to an acute observer, a great
facility given to the discovery of truth, not only as to the state
of the invalid, but likewise as to the mental condition of those
around him.

Dr. Nieper had been the medical attendant in ordinary at
Schloss Schwanberg for more years than its present lady had
been known there; he knew its master well; and the pompous
harangues in which he indulged, were as familiar to him as
was the sound of the sonorous monster bell which announced
the arrival of all comers.

His lady, on the other hand, was not only blessed with that
excellent gift in woman—a gentle voice, but she was habitually,
especially on matters of business, a succinct, rather than a ver-
bose, speaker; and the value accorded respectively to their words
by the doctor, might be fairly compared to that given to a huge
copper penny-piece, and a tiny golden half-sovereign.

In reply to this gentle hint respecting the "baron's wishes,"
she said nothing, but she made a slight movement with her head;
and thereupon it was as well understood between them, that the
baron was to make as much fuss as he liked, without let or
hindrance of any kind, and that everything required for the comfort of the boy, should be furnished without any fuss at all—as
if they had discussed the subject for an hour.

The positive commands of the baron, aided by the persuasive
urgency of his lady, caused the messenger dispatched for Father
Alaric to perform his errand both fleetly and featly; but it was
not till about half-an-hour after he had set off, that the slow-
paced baron was made to recollect, that although the messenger
he had sent was well mounted, those he had been sent to
summon, were not likely to be mounted at all, and might therefore be some hours before they could reach the castle.

How strictly the baroness thought it best to adhere to her

resolution of not interfering in any way, was proved by her
making no observation on the subject of their conveyance; and
she only learnt the fact of its having been omitted, by Gertrude
asking, "What carriage had been sent?"

Fortunately, however, the baron had thought fit to repeat his
visit to his daughter's room soon after the messenger had been
dispatched; and almost the first words she uttered after he
entered, were, "You are a dear, good papa, for sending for the
poor boy's parents! What carriage have you sent for them? Not
the great coach, I hope, it will be so long coming!"

"Carriage! my dear child! Mercy on me! I never thought
about a carriage. His uncle is only a village priest, my love, and
his mother is of the same modest class. I don't suppose they ever
rode in a coach in their lives, Gertrude!"

"But what difference does that make, papa? They can't fly
like the birds, you know, though they do not keep a coach. And
if you do not send some carriage for them, it is quite clear that
they won't be here to-night. And do just think, papa, what a
dreadful thing it would be for me, if I were ill, instead of this
dear, good boy, and had to wait hours, and hours, and hours,
before I could see mamma!"

"My noble-hearted Gertrude!" exclaimed the baron, with
great energy; "how exactly your generous feelings answer to
my own! I was to blame in not coming to you before I dispatched my messenger. But in my haste to serve these poor
people, I positively forgot what it was most essential to remember! Excuse my leaving you so abruptly, my dear girl; but you,
at least, are aware, if nobody else is, that it is, and ought to be,
my first object at this moment to obtain every assistance and
comfort for the young hero who hazarded his own life to preserve
that of *my* daughter."

There was just enough emphasis in the pronunciation of the
word *my*, as might suggest the idea, that if the person saved had
been any other man's daughter, the saving part of the adventure
might not have taken place; and a sort of half glance from the
saucy bright eyes of Gertrude towards her mother, might have
been received by a less discreet person, as a commentary upon it.
But upon this occasion, as upon many similar ones, the baroness
appeared to be rather short, or, perhaps, dim-sighted, for no
glance whatever was vouchsafed in return.

It is not improbable, that the baron might have lingered some
time longer at the bed-side of this important daughter, (for he
certainly felt inclined to dilate a little upon various points of his

own conduct, all tending to prove that he was the most generous, as well as the most noble of men,) had not Gertrude sent him off by clapping her hands, and exclaiming, "Go! go! go! my dear, darling, noble baron of a papa, or these poor, dear belongings of your hero will be struggling about the road in the dark, before the carriage can reach them."

The baron obeyed in a moment, as, to say the truth, he was very apt to do, when the will of his daughter was made known to him by her own irresistible lips. He only lingered at the door for one moment, to say, "If anything could add to my happiness in witnessing your present safety, my beloved child, it would be, the perceiving that your high-born spirit is in exact accordance with my own, in the feelings of gratitude due to your preserver!"

For about a minute after the door closed upon him, there was silence between the mother and daughter; and this, also, was apt to occur when the grandiose lord of the castle disappeared from before them, after having pronounced one of those high-sounding harangues which it was his delight to utter, and which it might have been somewhat amusing to them to hear, had not a sense of propriety, or, perhaps, even a feeling of duty, checked the mirth of both.

It generally happened, however, after one of these decorous pauses, that the next words exchanged between them were of a purport, and in a tone, which might justify a laugh; and so it was now; for Gertrude broke the silence by exclaiming, as she half sat, and half lay upon her bed:

"What a joke it is, mamma, to see me lying here, as if I too had dislocated a limb! Will you please to give me leave to get up? And will you please to give my respects to Madam Agatha, and tell her, when she makes her next visit, that I only got up, because I could not lie any longer in bed?"

And without waiting for an answer, the wilful young lady was upon her feet in a moment, and, investing the said little feet in the silken slippers which stood in waiting for them, began frolicking about the room in a style that gave very satisfactory proof that she, at least, was not at all the worse for the morning's adventure.

CHAPTER VII.

THE day was by this time drawing to its close, but there was still an hour of good driving light left, and the mother and daughter began to speculate upon the probability that the carriage might return before the hour at which the baroness usually retired to rest.

"I shall not like to go to bed, Gertrude, till I see the mother of this dear boy sitting beside him," said she.

"And I shall not like to go to bed to-night till you do, mamma," replied the young lady, with somewhat of the accent of spoilt-child pertinacity.

But Gertrude was only partially spoilt, not thoroughly; the spoiling stopped short of the heart, though the head sometimes showed symptoms of giddiness from it; and when, upon the present occasion, she saw her mother looking pale and harassed, upon her reiterating her wish to remain watching, she instantly changed her tone, and said, "Don't look so grave, dearest mamma! I am ready to go to bed again this moment, if you wish it."

It was therefore alone that the very anxious baroness awaited the return of the carriage. The baron's noble feelings kept him in very unusual activity till his usual hour of retiring to rest; but having eaten his supper, and inhaled the last breath of his beloved pipe, he announced to his lady that it was his intention to retire to his own apartment.

"Of course, my dear, you will retire to yours," he added. "I have given orders that several servants shall remain up all night, or, at least, till the carriage returns with the relatives of the heroic boy who has insured my gratitude for life; and the gratitude of Von Schwanberg can neither slumber nor sleep, whatever his eyes may do. But I mean not for a moment to insinuate that I wish for any watchfulness on your part. On the contrary, I rather wish to make it evident that the gratitude of the Baron von Schwanberg is sufficient, without the aid of any other human being, to repay whatever obligations may have been, or can be, bestowed upon him. Good night, my dear lady! Good night!"

The obedient baroness returned the salutation, and retired.

Gertrude had already been fast asleep for an hour or two; and

when at length Teresa, in obedience to her instructions, gave her
mistress notice that the baron's personal attendant had left him
snoring; she quickly took her way to the sick boy's bed-side, and
having dismissed the watchers, who by the baron's orders were
hanging about him—retaining only her faithful Agatha as her
companion—she prepared to pass the hours which might yet in-
tervene before the arrival of his mother, in watching his feverish
slumbers, and administering the medicines which had been prepared by Dr. Nieper for his use.

Notwithstanding the promptitude with which the suggestion of
Gertrude had been obeyed, night had ceased to be at odds with
morning before the carriage returned. For the roads of the
short cut, which had been ventured upon by the coachman, had
never been intended, in their best days, for the accommodation of
so dignified a visitor as a four-wheeled carriage; and they were
now so much the worse for the wear, that the frightened pair, in
whose honour it was sent, had to trust to their feet more than
once in the course of their *trájet*, in order to save their bones from
the danger of an overturn.

It was not much past three in the morning, however, when
the equipage and its anxious passengers arrived at Schloss
Schwanberg.

Notwithstanding the sleepy propensities which generally prevail at that hour, there were enough watchers ready to conduct
the expected guests to the chamber where they were so impatient
to be.

The baroness, who had been much too anxious for their arrival,
to have enjoyed any repose deserving the names of sleep, heard
the approach of the carriage, and was standing outside the door
of the sick boy's room, as the priest and his sister reached it.

The baroness, being wrapped in a very simple white dressing-
gown, with her usual night-gear on her head, suggested no idea
to her visitors, as she extended a welcoming hand to each, but
that of a sweetly kind-looking attendant, who was attentively
awaiting their arrival, with friendly anxiety, but without weariness or impatience. Their address to her, therefore, was perfectly
unrestrained and unceremonious. "How is he?" said the priest,
fixing his mild, anxious eyes upon her face.

And, "Is he alive?" said the pale mother, with an almost
convulsive pressure of the hand that welcomed her.

"More quiet. Much more quiet," replied the baroness, at once
perceiving, and rejoicing at their mistake; for the wearisome
parade of her proud husband, had for years made her rank a

burthen to her, and it was a positive relief to be thus addressed as a *woman*, and not as a sovereign "*Lady Baroness*." And those whispered words, accompanied by a kindly return of the pressure her own hand had received, were followed by her saying, "Now you are come to bless his eyes whenever he opens them, I feel confident, quite confident, that all will go well."

The trio then entered the room together, and the effect of the first glance exchanged between the mother and the son was very painful, for it was quite evident that he did not know her.

As the fact that the poor boy had become delirious was already known by every one who had approached him for many hours past, there was nothing in this which could justify the increased alarm which seemed to seize upon the baroness and her servants; but the agony of the mother, at finding herself stared at by him as a stranger, was so great, that it was impossible to witness it without sympathy; and not only the gentle Madame de Schwanberg herself, but her handmaids also, were soon weeping for company.

As for the good priest, though he had certainly visited more sick beds than his companions, and might therefore be expected to witness even this most painful symptom of fever with more philosophy, he seemed as much overpowered as the rest; and when he kneeled down, and took from his bosom the well-worn book from whence he was wont to draw the doctrines of resignation and hope, his tears flowed so abundantly, that he could scarcely articulate.

Till now, the hopeful opinion which Dr. Nieper had given of the boy's case, had so effectually sustained the spirits of those who were left in attendance on him, that the notion of his dying had scarcely occurred to any of them after he had uttered it; for his judgment was held in high estimation at Schloss Schwanberg; but now all favourable predictions were forgotten, and there was no one present, who did not begin to think that they were watching at the bed of death. The feelings of the baroness were not only those of a woman, but of a mother; and the true sympathy with which she beheld the intense misery of the unhappy Madame Odenthal, produced so violent an effect upon her, that Teresa, who was beside her, and who had been terrified by the condition to which their alarm for Gertrude had reduced her in the morning, very properly used a little gentle violence to make her leave the room. It may be doubted, however, whether the remonstrances of her waiting-woman would have proved so effective, if the experienced old housekeeper had not whispered in her ear,

"My master will be so vexed if he finds that you are here! He will be sure to know all about it, if you stay longer."

The only reply of the baroness was a very slight nod, but she remained no longer in the room than was necessary for the arranging that every comfort and accommodation possible, under the circumstances, should be provided for her sorrowing guests; and when this was accomplished, she again took the hands of Madame Odenthal in her own, and having repeated the assurance she had before given, that the doctor would be with them by the break of·day, she pressed the poor woman's forehead with her lips, and left her.

"Who is that sweet, kind-looking woman?" said Madame Odenthal, to one of the servants, as soon as the baroness had left the room.

"Woman!" repeated the housemaid, with a look of dismay; "that is the Baroness von Schwanberg, the lady of the castle."

"The baroness? The lady of the castle?" repeated the good woman, with a look of dismay. "Oh dear! oh dear! what dreadful falsehoods people do tell! All the country round says, that though they are good and charitable, they are too proud to be spoken to. Why, if she was as poor as I am, she could not be more kind and gentle; and yet it is the saying of the whole country, that they are the very proudest."

"Pooh! pooh! old lady, you are talking nonsense," said the sagacious Agatha. "There can only be one at a time, you know, that is the very proudest—and my lady is not that one, you may take my word for it."

As the Frau Odenthal was by no means a stupid woman, it is very possible that she might guess who the individual was, who had a right, in this matter, to be honoured with the·superlative degree. She was much too discreet, however, to ask any further questions, but quietly sat herself down beside the bed on which her son lay, but with a curtain between them; for she thought, and, perhaps, with reason, that though it was evident he did not know her, yet there was a sort of restless, painful, puzzled look in his eye, when it met hers, which seemed to indicate that though not recognised as his mother, she was not wholly forgotten, and that her presence, if he were conscious of it, might disturb, though it could not soothe him.

The priest, meanwhile, as is usual, I believe, with all the professional individuals of his communion, selected as convenient a corner as might be for the purpose of kneeling down; but in no outward respect does the reformed church differ more essentially from the unreformed than in such moments as these. It is difficult while watching a Roman priest under such circumstances, to believe that his thoughts even accompany, still less that they inspire, the words he mutters; and, if it be otherwise, who is there that will venture to deny that such service is a dangerous mockery? Nevertheless, Father Alaric was a very worthy man; and, if he "prayed the gods amiss," it was the fault of his teaching and not of his character.

The hours which followed till the day broke, and the doctor arrived, were as miserable for all the parties concerned as such hours always must be. Anxiety and weariness possessed them wholly, though not exactly in equal proportions throughout the group.

The baron was habitually an early riser, but, upon this occasion, he quitted his room a full hour before his usual time; for having learned that the mother and uncle of the boy had arrived during the night, and also that Dr. Nieper was expected at daybreak, he was steadfastly determined, as it was well possible for a gentleman to be, that his noble sense of the service which had been rendered him should be made manifest to everybody in the most striking manner possible.

And, assuredly, the doctor was a good deal surprised upon entering the sick boy's room, to find that he had been preceded by this high and mighty personage.

But his emotion upon this unexpected occurrence was as nothing when compared to that experienced by Father Alaric and his sister.

The great object of the Baron von Schwanberg's life had been to impress the whole country round with an idea of his greatness; nor had these unceasing efforts been in vain, for he was not only considered the greatest man in the neighbourhood, but as being probably one of the greatest in the empire—the Kaiser and his race excepted. When, therefore, his tall person, his brocaded dressing-gown, his embroidered cap, and his velvet slippers entered the room where the sick boy lay, the effect he produced was everything he could desire.

The sleepy priest, who had been sitting humbly on a low straw chair, with his head resting on the back of another, started to his feet with a degree of agility which persons of his profession are seldom seen to exhibit; and, crossing his hands reverently upon his breast, bowed low his head, with a look that had more of veneration in it, than of mere respect from one man to another; but he did not venture to utter a syllable.

5—2

The unwearying mother, who was still bending over her child, and soothing herself with the idea that he breathed more tranquilly, raised her eyes as the door opened, and beheld the overpowering spectacle with a degree of emotion that caused her pale cheek to become crimson.

The two female servants who had been commanded by the baron to remain in the room, started from their respective attitudes of repose, and looked very considerably startled by this unexpected apparition. But the almost awful emotions caused by it were speedily relieved by the entrance of Dr. Nieper, who followed him into the room; for the baron had timed his visit well, assisted by the obedient watchfulness of his valet, and mounted the stairs as the doctor dismounted from his horse.

Nothing could be more satisfactory than the scene which followed, for, in addition to the fervent expressions of gratitude uttered by the priest and his sister, who seemed to have recovered their senses in some degree upon the entrance of the physician, the doctor himself joined the chorus of praise and admiration, saying :

"Upon my word, my Lord Baron, your conduct has been as noble as your name, and that is saying a good deal for it. But, truly, your contriving to get these good people here, notwithstanding the distance and the darkness, has been most kind and most considerate. And now, my Lord Baron," he added, "I believe that I may venture to pronounce the words which your kindness will make the most welcome to you. This brave boy here is now very healthily asleep, and, I venture to predict, that, when he wakes, his delirium will have left him, and that he will be in a state to join his friends in returning thanks to you for the great kindness which has been shown to him."

The baron, upon this, bent his head forward, very nearly an inch from the perpendicular, and, with a charming mixture of condecension and dignity, replied :

"I should be unworthy the name I bear, my good doctor, had I done less: nor shall I be satisfied till I have done much more. I should be grieved if it could be supposed by any one throughout the whole district in which I live, that my gratitude for the preservation of my daughter and heiress should not prove such as to influence the destiny of this brave youth through life. I have decided, in my own mind, that reference shall be distinctly made to him in the service which I shall order to be performed in the chapel of the castle, and,"——

"Hush!—please hush!" whispered the mother of this

highly-favoured individual; "I think, doctor, he is going to wake!"

"Well, good woman, and if he does, there is no harm in that," replied the doctor, cheerily. "I want him to wake. I want to see if he knows you."

"He did not know me when I spoke to him only a very few minutes before he went to sleep," she replied, in a whisper; "and I thought it only disturbed him when he looked at me."

"That is very likely: but I have got his pulse under my thumb, you see; and if he fairly wakes up, I will bet a florin he knows you now."

A very few minutes proved the doctor to be right. Rupert Odenthal did fairly wake up, and immediately gave the most decisive proof that he recognized his mother; for he placed his hand in hers, and, in a minute or two, relapsed into quiet sleep again.

<hr>

CHAPTER VIII.

The recovery of the boy from the effects of the accident was both rapid and complete ; and if the Baron von Schwanberg had been of an inconsistent character, which he really was not, he would have scarcely found time to change all the generous projects he had formed in his favour, before the boy was in a condition to profit by them.

Having, however, exhibited his magnanimous condescension in the remarkable manner recounted in the last chapter, he did not appear to deem it necessary that the future favours he meant to bestow should be accompanied by any similar excess of personal familiarity.

His pledged word was most faithfully redeemed by the special introduction of his name into the service, etc. etc. etc.—which was performed as an act of thanksgiving in the chapel ; moreover, the whole adventure was at full length recorded on a marble tablet erected in the vestibule of the said chapel. Neither did he forget his promise of providing a comfortable retreat for his venerable confessor, Father Ambrose, and of appointing Father Alaric to the office in his stead.

The judicious professional attendant of the lady had succeeded in persuading him, that the most serious and deplorable consequences might ensue, if the latter part of the time, which preceded the anticipated event, were not passed by her in the unbroken repose of her own dressing-room ; and it is highly probable, that this friendly precaution, on the part of the rational and kind-hearted individual, who, from an involuntary persecutor, had become a pitying friend, saved her from such a fever on the spirits, as might have endangered her own life, if not that of her child ; for if the ceaseless worry and impatience, in which the father expectant passed this interval, had been shared, or even witnessed by his unfortunate wife, it is scarcely possible that it could have failed of producing very painful effects.

As it was, however, the Baroness von Schwanberg brought forth in safety. But, alas! her offspring· was a daughter! I. will not attempt to describe the state of mind into which the announcement of this fact threw the baron. This was an occurrence which, from a strange sort of infatuation had never occurred to him as possible. In fact, his mind, which was not a very expansive one, had been, not only since his marriage, but long before it, so fully and wholly occupied by the idea of having a son, that the possibility of his having a daughter had never occurred to him.

The Herr Walters was not only a kind-hearted, but really a sensible man, which was proved by the manner in which he had contrived to prevent his very unnecessary presence in the family from being an annoyance to its unfortunate mistress. But it should seem that he was not a brave man ; for his courage failed him altogether, when he remembered that the baron had made promise to come to him in person, as soon as the child was born, that he might at once learn his opinion exactly as to its state of health, and so forth.

But the good doctor really dared not face the baron under such circumstances. The task of telling him that all his noble anticipations of seeing before him the glorious prospect of an endless race of barons were vain, and that, instead of this, he must content himself with being the father of a little girl, was more than he had courage to perform. The direful tidings were therefore conveyed to the unfortunate nobleman by one of the attendants, with an intimation that Herr Walters was in attendance upon the baroness, and could not leave her just at present.

It would be equally vain and needless to attempt describing the condition into which this announcement threw the unfor-

But when all this was done, his daughter, Gertrude, said to him one day, in her pretty spoilt-child manner, " You are a dear, good papa, for caring so much, and doing so much, all about me. But you have not yet told us what you mean to do for poor Rupert himself. I am not going to complain about what you have done for his dear, darling of a mother, for I really do think that she is the most "——

" The most what? My dearest love ! " said her father, gazing at her according to custom, as if he were in presence of an oracle.

" Why, really I don't know what to call it," replied Gertrude, laughing; " the most hugable, and kissable dear soul in the world; that is what I mean, I believe. And as to your new confessor, Father Alaric, if you were to make him an archbishop, or a cardinal, I should think it very right and proper; but you know, papa, after all, the real truth is, that it was Rupert who jumped into the river to pick me up ; and therefore I do think you should give him something beside physic, and that is all he has had, as yet, to reward him."

To say the truth, it would have been a difficult matter for Gertrude to say anything which her father did not think the very cleverest thing that ever was said under the circumstances ; and it is no wonder, therefore, that the speech above quoted, appeared to him so admirable, that he almost thought it was uttered from a species of inspiration.

" It is a very remarkable thing," he said to his lady, the next time he found himself *téte-à-téte* with her; " a very remarkable thing, that so young a girl as Gertrude, should never give her opinion on any subject, without displaying a degree of judgment which might, and must, make most full-grown people feel themselves her inferiors. I mean, of course, her inferiors in ability ; her inferiors in station, most persons must, unavoidably, be. She has just been speaking to me of her obligations to the poor boy, Rupert Odenthal, and HER obligations are, of course, MY obligations, also. ' And yet, excepting that I commanded his name to be mentioned in the special service which I caused to be performed in the chapel of the castle, she is perfectly right in stating, that as yet, the whole of our efforts towards remuneration have been confined, as far as the boy himself is concerned, to obtaining the necessary medical assistance for him. How has it happened, baroness, that this has escaped your observation ? There was an acuteness wonderfully beyond her years in the remark, that the only reward which he has hitherto received for the immense obligation he has laid upon us, has been in the shape of physic ! "

The well-disciplined baroness did not laugh; she did not even smile; in truth, she had pretty effectually drilled herself into a systematic and constant avoidance of any such equivocal demonstration of the effects of the baron's eloquence; but she replied, "that she doubted not but that, sooner or later, some arrangement would be made, which would properly remunerate the boy for the service he had done them."

The baron kept his large dull eyes fixed upon her as she spoke, and when she ceased, he uttered a deep groan.

After this, he paused for a moment, as if to collect his thoughts; and then he said, "You must forgive me if I express myself both shocked, and surprised, at the cold indifference which you display, madam, on a subject which is, in my estimation, the most important that can by possibility be presented for our consideration. For it does not concern the demonstration of my gratitude, the gratitude of the Baron von Schwanberg, for the preservation of his only child and heiress? I implore you, baroness, not to mistake me, and not to imagine for a moment that I mean to reproach you. I can never forget, that you are of the noble house of Wolkendorf, or cease to remember, with proper deference and respect, that you are also Baroness von Schwanberg. But the difference in our characters and manner of thinking, is too remarkable, not to produce often an emotion approaching to wonder and astonishment. Happily, however, this marked difference of character between us is not likely in the least degree to lead to any mischievous result. Your principles as a virtuous wife, and honourable lady, will, of course, ever prevent you from interfering in any way that would trouble or annoy me; and it really seems like an especial blessing of Providence, that our daughter, who is to be my successor here, should, in all things, inherit the character, qualities, and opinions of her father. On the subject of the noble-spirited youth who has made us so deeply their debtors, I think it will be desirable that we should have no farther discussion. It is evident, that your feelings towards him are by no means in unison with those of my daughter and myself; but your daughter knows her duty too well to utter to *you* anything that should be mistaken for a remonstrance on the subject; and you, on your side, will, I am sure, consent to promise me, that you will not interfere in any way with my intentions respecting him."

The baroness readily gave the promise required, and the more readily, from her conviction, that Gertrude was not the least likely to mistake her non-interference, for either indifference or ingratitude towards the individual to whom she certainly owed her life.

How matters might have gone on, however, if it had not chanced, before the occurrence of the conversation above recited, that Gertrude had overheard her mother and old Agatha discussing together their hopes, that the baron would make some permanent provision for the boy, it is impossible to say; for, till the young lady had made the pertinent remark above cited, respecting her hopes, that Rupert would have something beside physic as his reward; it is certain, that his being permitted to remain with his mother in the house (probably, because he was still too lame to walk out of it), had appeared to the lord of the castle, to be the very perfection of the most generous and condescending hospitality.

But no sooner had the half-jocose remonstrance of his daughter been uttered, than he determined, however playfully her reproach had been spoken, that HE would consider the matter seriously, and that he would go as far beyond his daughter's grateful wishes, as he had appeared hitherto to fall short of them. But, as I have before stated, the baron was a slow man, as his only reply to Gertrude's remonstrance, was in these words:

"You are as right on this subject, my dear child, as I hope and expect my daughter ever will be on every subject, upon which she may condescend to bestow her attention. I will inform you, my dear Gertrude," he added, "what my purpose is respecting this very meritorious lad, as soon as I have had leisure to consider all the circumstances of his position."

How much, or how little, this meant, Gertrude did not very clearly understand; and she therefore, as in all cases of doubt, applied to her mother.

"Papa has been talking most royally about what he intends doing for Rupert; only he says, he must have more time to think about it. I think he ought to tell Father Alaric at once, what he means to do about him. What do you think, mamma?"

"Why, to tell you the truth, Gertrude," replied the baroness, "I perfectly agree with your father, as to the necessity of taking time to deliberate, before any particular destination for him is proposed. He is only now just beginning to let me talk to him as if he were not afraid to answer; and till we can get him to speak freely of himself, and his former pursuits, and future hopes, I think it would be injudicious to propose any particular career to him."

Gertrude looked in her mother's face, and laughed.

"What is there in what I have said," said the baroness, smiling, "which appears to you so superlatively ridiculous?"

"Ridiculous!" repeated Gertrude; "my laugh was the laugh of triumph, mamma, and not of ridicule."

"Explain," returned her mother; "and then, perhaps, I may enjoy a laugh, too."

"And so you ought," said Gertrude; "and it should be a very thankful, happy laugh. I was thinking, what a very clever pair we must be! Papa says, that everything *I* say is right; and I think everything *you* say is right. What lucky people we are! But when shall you begin to bestow some of your most particular cleverness upon Rupert, in order to find out whether he is most fit to be a priest like his uncle, or a soldier like his father? His father, you know, mamma, was killed in battle."

"No, Gertrude, I did not know it. But there are more professions and occupations than two. Perhaps I had better begin by talking a little with his mother."

"Right again, mamma! You ought to be called the wise woman of Schwanberg Schloss. May I be present at the talk? Do you know, mamma, that if I see her often, I shall love that sweet mother of his better than anybody in the whole world, except yourself? There is not one of all the baronesses, and countesses, or princesses either, that I have ever seen, that I like one half quarter so well."

"There is something peculiarly pleasing in Madame Odenthal," replied the baroness, thoughtfully; "I, too, feel that I should get very much attached to her, if she were to be much with me. I am greatly inclined to believe that her education was befitting a higher station than what she now holds. Not that she ever talks to me of the pursuits of her youth, or having been at all different from what they are at present; but nevertheless, there is something in her language, as well as in her manner of thinking, which leads me to suspect that she has been better educated than her present station seems to account for."

"Then, of course, I *am* a marvellously clever person, mamma; for I must have made the same discovery without being conscious that I had made it," said Gertrude. "You laugh, mamma," she continued, very gravely; "but I am quite in earnest. I have thought again and again, quite to myself, as you know,—for if I did not talk about it to you, I certainly should not talk about it to anybody else,—but I have thought over and over again, when I have been listening to the Frau Odenthal, that she did not talk like the other people, who appear to be of the same rank, as far as outward appearances go. Papa and I, you know, ride about in all directions; and though he does not seem to think it proper to speak much to any people who live in cottages, that are not upon the Schwanberg estate, he is constantly stopping to talk at the doors of those who are. And very long talkings they are, sometimes, for though his manner to them is very stiff, and stately, he seems very much interested about them all; but I never, in all these visitings, met with anybody at all like Madame Odenthal."

"I quite agree with you, Gertrude," replied her mother; "and I am glad to hear you make the observation, though I don't think it shews any *marvellous* cleverness, dearest, because the fact is so obvious; but, at least, it shews something like the power of discrimination, which is always desirable. But is your cleverness enough to make you aware, that our discovery adds greatly to our difficulties respecting the son of this mysterious Frau Odenthal?"

"No, mamma, I don't see that, at all," was the reply. "Why should it be more difficult for papa to benefit the boy, because his mother has been well educated?"

"If you were really very clever, I think you might guess, Gertrude. You ride about, as you truly say, a great deal with your papa, and I am quite sure that you must have been present on many occasions when he has shewn himself able, as well as willing, to assist his deserving tenants in the difficult matter of disposing of their sons advantageously. No year passes in which he does not benefit some of them in this way. But can you not perceive, that he would find it much more difficult to do this, in a case where the boy whom he wished to serve, had been brought up by a mother whose education had enabled her to instruct her son in a manner very likely to unfit him for any of the humbler stations of life?"

"Yes, mamma, I do see it," was now her more grave reply.

"His uncle's profession is the only one, that I know of, in which a good, or, at least, a somewhat learned education, is found in so humble a state of life as that of Father Alaric," resumed the baroness; "and I certainly am of opinion," she continued, "that the obligation we are under to this boy, ought to be rewarded by our placing him in a more comfortable station of life, than any which Father Alaric is likely to attain. Your father might easily obtain for him a place as clerk, in some government office; but if he resembles his mother, such an appointment would not satisfy my ideas of what we ought to do for him."

The conversation between the mother and daughter was interrupted here by the arrival of a noble neighbour, who had driven in state some half-dozen miles or more, in order to learn all particulars respecting the young baroness's perilous adventure, and to offer congratulations for her providential escape, etc., etc., etc.

CHAPTER IX.

WITHIN a day or two after the conversation had occurred between the Baroness von Schwanberg and her daughter, which has been recorded in the last chapter, it happened that the noble lady, and the humble guests whose manners had formed the subject of it, met accidentally in one of the alleys of the castle garden.

Gertrude was enjoying, with her thrice-happy father, the first gallop to which he had invited her since her accident; for he had deemed it necessary, or, at least, proper, that the pony should be daily exercised for a fortnight after it had occurred, before the young lady was again permitted to mount him, in order to ascertain that he had not been taught to start by his misadventure.

Poor Rupert, meanwhile, though quite recovered as to his general health, was still too lame to walk beyond the limits of his room, or, at least, of the floor on which he was lodged, for the getting up and down stairs was still forbidden by Dr. Nieper; and it was therefore in solitude that his mother availed herself of the baroness's permission, or rather invitation, to walk in the beautiful pleasure grounds for which Schloss Schwanberg was justly celebrated.

The salutation with which the baroness treated the Frau Odenthal, was as usual, full of kindness; and it was no feigned interest, as to the state of Rupert's health, which gave so soothing a tone to every question she asked concerning him. But these enquiries being all satisfactorily answered, the grateful mother of the boy stood aside, to make way for the onward course of the lady of the castle; but instead of passing Madame Odenthal, the baroness turned, and putting her arm under that of her modest vistior, she said, " Let us walk together, my good friend. I am pretty sure that our thoughts have often, at least, one subject in common. Let us discuss it together. You will easily guess that I allude to Rupert, and I will almost venture to say, that you are not more occupied about his future plans than I am. You must be aware, from what the baron has already said, both to you and to him, that it is his purpose to remunerate him (as far as such a service can be remunerated), for having saved the life of our child, to say nothing of what he has suffered since, himself, in consequence of his perilous enterprise."

"Indeed, madame," replied the Frau Odenthal, with great sincerity, "I believe Rupert considers himself as very amply rewarded already. Your condescending kindness to him, and the delight he has had from the freedom with which you have permitted me to furnish him with books, has made 'this period of lameness,' as he says, 'the happiest portion of his life.'"

"Has he indeed said so?" returned the baroness with animation. "Such a statement from him has a two-fold value. In the first place, it is a great comfort to hear that he has not suffered so heavily from the restraint of his confinement, as I feared that he must have done. And secondly, it is of far greater value still, as furnishing a hint as to the choice of an occupation for his future life. A boy of his age, Madame Odenthal, who can feel that pain and confinement may be atoned for by reading, must not be placed in any situation, where time and opportunity for reading would be denied him."

"Alas! my dear lady," replied Madame Odenthal, "that thought is no stranger to my mind. But it is, I am afraid, a dangerous one for those to cherish, who must employ their hours in such a manner as to obtain for themselves the necessaries of life. I fear, that intellectual pleasures are among those which must be set apart among the recreations of the rich."

"That is a question which will, I think, be more fully and practically discussed in days to come, than it has been in days past," said the baroness; "I have a great inclination to believe, that if man was taught to make the best, and the most of his faculties, ways and means might be discovered, by which the action and development of his mind might assist, and not impede his means for providing for the wants of his body. But this is too wide a discussion for us to enter upon now."

In saying this, the baroness turned her eyes towards the face of her companion, and could scarcely suppress a smile, as she marked the expression of it.

The complexion of Madame Odenthal was, like that of her

son, rather pale, than ruddy, but now the face was flushed; her lips were parted, as is generally the case when under the influence of surprise; and the dark eyes which met hers, said, as plainly as eyes could speak, "how came you to guess that I could comprehend you, if you did discuss it?"

But the four very intelligent eyes which encountered thus, withdrew themselves as by common consent from further questioning; and after the pause of a moment, the baroness resumed, "I am sure you will agree with me, Madame Odenthal, that it will be impossible for us at the castle to make a judicious choice of a profession for your son Rupert, unless we know more about his character and past pursuits, than it is possible for us to acquire by our own observation. How old is your son?"

"He wants two months of fifteen," was the reply.

"How has he been educated? Has he ever been at school?" demanded Madame de Schwanberg.

"No, madam, never," said Madame Odenthal. "All the instruction he has received," she added, "has been from myself, and his uncle."

There was again a short pause in the conversation, and then the baroness said, "Has it ever occurred to you, that you should wish him to adopt his uncle's profession?"

As the baroness said this, she again turned her eyes towards her companion; and the dark eyes of her companion again encountered hers. It was but for a moment, however, and then Madame Odenthal quietly replied, "No, madame."

After another short silence, the baroness again resumed the conversation, by saying, "The avocations of a priest must, I should suppose, leave abundant time for reading."

"I do not know," replied the mother of Rupert; "women," she added, "however nearly related by blood to the ministers of the Roman Catholic religion, know but little respecting their private studies."

"I was not aware of that," said the baroness; "none of my ancestors have belonged to the profession, excepting one cardinal, I believe, a century or two ago. But there certainly must be many more hours in the life a priest which might be devoted to study, than could be afforded in any other profession."

The arm upon which the baroness leant had a slight, a *very* slight movement in it; but the Frau Odenthal said nothing.

"Is your brother disposed to be a reading man?" said the baroness.

"Father Alaric is only my half-brother," replied Madame

Odenthal; "he is many years older than I am, and I know but little about his private studies now, and still less respecting his education."

"He seems to be a very good, kind person," said the baroness.

"He is, indeed, very good and kind," replied the sister, eagerly, and as if relieved from embarrassment by being able to speak so cordially, and so completely, without restraint. "I am quite aware," she resumed, "that our being with him must be a heavy burthen upon him, for his professional income is very small, and he has nothing else. But when my husband died— my husband was a military man—an officer, and a brave one; but when he died, my boy and I were, literally, almost starving, my little pension being scarcely more than sufficient to lodge and clothe us; and though, by being a very good needlewoman, I contrived to live, the kindness of my brother in offering us an asylum in his little home, was, as you may believe, madam, most gratefully accepted. Since that time, I have been my boy's only instructor, for Father Alaric's parish is large, though but a poor one; and moreover, to say the truth, I believe it was less troublesome to him to feed my boy, than it would have been to instruct him. My brother Alaric is a good man; good, because he endeavours conscientiously to do what he believes to be right; and to avoid doing what he believes to be wrong."

"If all men did so," replied the baroness, "the world would go more smoothly for us all."

"I suppose so," returned Madame Odenthal, meekly; "but in order to make so conscientious a system of important utility," she added, "the judgment must be put into wholesome training. If a man blunders between right and wrong, his conscience may lead him to commit, instead of avoid, sin."

The baroness very nearly stood still, while, for a moment, she again fixed her eyes on the face of her companion; but she gained nothing by doing so, for the eyes which she wished to look into, were fixed upon the ground.

"But the priesthood takes this responsibility upon itself, I believe," returned Madame de Schwanberg, after a short silence.

"Not in all lands," said Madame Odenthal; adding almost in a whisper, "my mother was an Englishwoman."

It would not be easy to describe the effect which these few words produced on the lady of the castle. The history of her own mind, of her long years of solitary reading, and solitary thinking, must be given, in order to make such a disclosure intelligible. A very gentle pressure of the arm on which she leaned, was the only reply made at that time to this avowal of her new acquaintance; but the new acquaintance seemed, by some sort of freemasonry, to understand its meaning, and to feel sufficiently encouraged by it to add:—

"This will make you understand, madam, why it is that I have never wished my son to adopt the profession of his uncle."

"Yes," replied the baroness, "I understand it perfectly; and I am glad that you have had sufficient reliance on my discretion to state this fact. Fear not that your confidence should be abused. It is important, while considering the future prospects of your son, that I should know what you have just confided to me, but the knowledge of it need go no further. Is Father Alaric aware that your son——. Is he aware what your opinions are?"

"I hardly know, madame," replied her companion; "my brother Alaric was a very sickly boy when his father married his second wife; and I have often heard from himself, as well as from my father, that she was as kind to him as if he had been a child of her own. Alaric, himself, is very kind-hearted, and this behaviour in his step-mother naturally softens his heart when speaking of her, and I never heard him make any unkind reflections upon her creed. And then, it must be confessed, that my brother Alaric is, both mentally and bodily, very indolent; and I really doubt, if he has, during the whole course of my life, ever given one whole hour's thought as to what my opinions really were. The father of Rupert was a soldier; and it always seemed to me, that as long as the rank and file of a regiment went as regularly to mass as to parade, their officers were less troubled by the priests, than most other people. I lost my dear kind husband at a very early age; and few people, brought up as I have been in a Roman Catholic country, have been so little interfered with by the priests as myself. One reason for this was, no doubt, my having a priest for my brother; and when I and my little boy took up our residence in his house, it was, of course, supposed, by anybody who took the trouble of thinking about us at all, that we wanted no other religious aid than what he could give us."

The Baroness von Schwanberg listened to this statement, not only in silence, but with great attention. Her answer, however, was very brief.

"I feel flattered," she said, "by the confidence in my good faith and discretion, which you have proved to me by the openness of your statement. Like you, Madame Odenthal, I have been a licensed reader through life, and wherever this has been the case, the result will, in all probability, be, on some points, very similar. We will not discuss any forbidden subjects together, because it is far more likely that danger and mischief might be the result, than advantage to either of us. You will easily believe, without my dilating upon the subject, that what you have now said to me must have increased my individual and personal interest for your son. It is certainly possible, that this feeling may have some influence on the future destiny of the boy; but it is by no means certain that it should do so. From the moment I learned that I owed my daughter's life to him, I have felt very deeply that he had a claim both on my heart and my justice, and what has now passed between us has certainly not tended to diminish either. And now, for the present, farewell. I hope I have not detained you from him too long."

It might be difficult to say, which of the two women who then shook hands, and parted, was most surprised, and gratified, by the unexpected confidence which had sprung up between them.

CHAPTER X.

There was a good deal in the conversation above recited, which was likely to awaken a lively interest in Madame de Schwanberg, both for the mother of the boy whom she wished to serve, as well as for himself.

The baron had frequently alluded, in his grandiose style, to his purpose of providing for Rupert Odenthal; but all he had said on the subject was so vague, that, excepting, as Gertrude had truly observed, in the articles of physic, no very certain conviction had reached Madame de Schwanberg's mind that any positive advantage would be the result.

But, as she knew also that if it actually happened that the boy and his mother were permitted to walk off, with no benefit more positive than the reiterated assurance of his generous intentions, it would only be because nothing feasible had occurred to him on the subject. She had long determined to tax her own inventive powers for the purpose of hitting upon some expedient by which the patronage of the great man of the castle might be practically useful.

Had the boy been half-a-dozen years older, it might have been easy enough to place him in a farm upon the estate, on such terms as might ensure its being beneficial to him, without having recourse to the somewhat degrading alternative of offering him a sum of money, as payment for having hazarded his life. But the conversation which had now passed between the boy's mother and the lady of the castle, had thrown a perfectly new light upon the subject, and led to the suggestion of a proposal which seemed likely to remove all difficulty at the present moment, and to afford time, and perhaps opportunity also, for due consideration of what might be done for him at a more advanced age.

The plan which she now thought of for him, was one which might immediately be adopted, without any risk that the employment it would give should be too fatiguing to him, although the injured limb had not yet fully recovered its strength.

The baroness, who had gone on increasing the already very large library from the first year of her marriage to the present day, had long felt the want of a librarian capable of classing and arranging it, in such a way, as might save her the trouble and fatigue of endeavouring to keep it in order, an undertaking which it was, in fact, quite beyond her power to accomplish.

The strong appetite for reading which the invalid had evinced during the tedious lameness which had resulted from his accident, had suggested to her the idea that, young as he was, he might very probably find himself sufficiently at home among books, to be useful to her as a librarian; and the neat handwriting displayed, in consequence of her having told him to write down the title of any books he particularly wished to read, convinced her that he might be profitably set to work upon an undertaking which she had long wished to achieve, but had never yet found courage to attempt. As far as her researches had reached, she had been unable to find any trace of a catalogue, and the extent of the collection was such as to render the want of it a constant inconvenience. But this very obvious method of placing the boy in a most desirable situation, without any trouble to the slow-moving baron, was rejected almost as soon as conceived, from the idea that the nephew and *élève* of a Romish priest, might be as much shocked, as astonished, if his reading habits should lead him to examine all the books which she was in the habit of adding to the venerable collection. But although the converstion which has been just rehearsed as having taken place between the baroness and the boy's mother, was much too vague to convey to either any very decisive information respecting the religious

6

opinions of the other enough had passed to persuade the baroness (who, like the rest of her sex, perhaps, was apt to jump to a conclusion), that she should run no risk of being troubled by the Inquisition, by permitting the young Rupert to set down in his catalogue of the castle library, all the very fullest titles of the books which she was constantly placing on its shelves.

What followed may be told in a very few words.

Gertrude was a very quick, intelligent child, and required wonderfully little prompting on the present occasion. Nothing could have less the appearance of a plot, than the manner in which she said to her father, as she sat knitting beside him, while he smoked his pipe, "I will tell you what you shall do for Rupert, papa, besides giving him physic. You shall have him here always in the house, to keep the library in proper order. I am almost as fond of galloping over the books, as over the grass; but my dear pony does not make half so much confusion among the flowers, as I do among the volumes. I don't think I am so naughty about any thing, as I am about the books; for when I have got all I want out of one of them, I never can find out the right place to put it in, and so, of course, the confusion goes on getting worse and worse every day. And it is a great shame! I know that too, papa, for mamma says that quantities and quantities of them have belonged to our grandee ancestors, since the days of Noah, I believe. Now if you will tell Rupert that he is not to go away at all, but to stay here, and keep your books in order, everything will be right."

The baron looked at her with admiration and astonishment, and for a moment or two appeared to be in deep meditation, for he said nothing; but he spoke at last, and then, as was very usual with him, it was to express his admiration of her extraordinary abilities.

"Gertrude!" he said, very solemnly; "Gertrude, my dear, you certainly are a very superior young lady. I ought not, however, either to express, or to feel any astonishment at this. You ought, from the name you bear, to be a very superior person. I do not suppose that there ever has been a descendant of the Von Schwanberg race, who has not been superior; but yet, nevertheless, my dear daughter, I will not deny that I never remark in you any of the superior qualities for which our name is celebrated, without feeling a very strong sensation of pride and pleasure. It is impossible, my dear, not to perceive, in the words which you have just spoken, a very striking proof of the superiority to which I allude. It consists—" And here the baron paused for a moment, to take breath. Whenever this happened, Gertrude never failed to take advantage of it; for, to say the truth, these long harangues about her own superiority, had long become exceedingly fatiguing to her. She was much too sharp-witted not to perceive that there was so little mixture of truth in the view he took of her, and her qualities, that any one who heard *him*, and knew *her*, would be inclined to doubt which made the most ridiculous figure of the two.

A pause, therefore, was always joyfully welcomed, and turned to excellent account. Sometimes, by her hiding her laughing face with her hands, and running off, as if too modest to hear any more, and sometimes, as in the present instance, by her throwing her arms round his neck, and stopping his lips by a kiss.

In neither case did the adoring father betray any displeasure; and if she seized the next moment to make, or reiterate a request, she might be tolerably sure that it would not be refused.

On her now gaily clapping her hands, and exclaiming, "Well, then, dearest papa! you will let this good boy, who nearly killed himself to prevent my falling into the water—you will let him stay at the castle, and take care of the Von Schwanberg library, and he must be called *the librarian*, you know. I believe that he is rather young for a librarian, but that does not signify, for he deserves to be treated like a grown-up person, because he behaved like one."

"Quite true! Perfectly true, Gertrude," said the greatly pleased baron; who, by some lucky chance, happened to know that the Emperor had a library, and a librarian. "Of course, as you grow up, my dear, it will become necessary for me to make several additions to my establishment. As soon as ever you are old enough to be presented at the different courts, where I mean to introduce you, I shall have a groom of the chambers, Gertrude, for the purpose of announcing to you in a proper manner, all persons who may have the honour, wherever we may be, of being permitted to wait upon you and your mamma."

During this last important speech, the baron had held the hand of his daughter in his own; but as this restraint was becoming particularly troublesome to her, she emancipated herself by a sudden movement, and then danced out of the room, kissing the rescued hand to him as she went. The certainty that everything she said, and did, would be considered as right, and well done, was rather a dangerous sort of experience to be acquired by a very lively young lady of twelve years old.

Such, however, was the fate of my heroine; and her gentle

6—2

mother often sighed, as she thought how very little it was in her power to do, to counteract the dangerous effect of it.

On the present occasion, however, there seemed to be no room for regret of any kind. A real difficulty had been got over, and a real convenience obtained; and slow as the movements of the Baron von Schwanberg generally were, but few hours were permitted to elapse after Gertrude left him, before he dispatched a man and horse to the residence of Father Alaric, requesting his immediate attendance at the castle.

The newly appointed confessor lost no time in obeying the summons; and in the course of the interview which followed between him and his noble penitent, he had, while doing honour very justly due to the acquirements of his young nephew, the good fortune to dwell upon one of his acquirements, which added in a very important degree to the satisfaction with which the baron contemplated the idea of adding the youth to his establishment.

"We can never be grateful enough," said the humble-minded confessor, "for the noble generosity with which it is your excellency's pleasure to recompense my nephew for the service which the special Providence of the Holy Virgin enabled him to perform to the precious heiress of Schwanberg; but my happiness, from this flattering arrangement, is very greatly increased, by my thinking, that the education which my nephew has received by the help of his mother, may be of service in more ways than one to your excellence."

"By keeping the valuable library, bequeathed to me by my ancestors, in good order," said the baron, with dignity.

"Not only that, your excellence, but it is a comfort to me to think that, by the careful instructions of his mother, who is an excellent scholar, he writes so beautifully well as to be quite capable of performing the duties of a secretary to your excellence."

Now, in truth, the noble Baron von Schwanberg had no more want of a secretary, than of a milliner; but he was perfectly well aware, that very great men did employ a secretary; and though the idea of adding such an appendage to his establishment had never occurred to him, he no sooner heard it mentioned by Father Alaric, than he felt suddenly convinced that he should find such a functionary extremely useful; but that he had been very neglectful of his own ease and convenience by neglecting to provide himself with this very necessary attendant before.

But though taken a good deal by surprise when listening to this novel proposition, he did not so much forget his habitual dignity as to betray any feeling of the kind. His wife, excellent woman as she was, would often have given gold, could she have escaped thereby from the painful, yet smile-provoking consciousness, that there was something marvellously resembling the comic solemnity of the owl in the physiognomy of her noble husband, whenever he happened to take it into his head that he was called upon to look particularly dignified and sagacious; but happily for Father Alaric's well-being as confessor to the Baron von Schwanberg, he had no such stuff in his thoughts; and during the interval which followed between his proposal of permitting his nephew to add the duties of secretary to those of librarian, he remained seated, exactly in front of his new penitent, but with his own eyes humbly fixed upon the ground.

After the interval of some few minutes, however, the baron slowly unclosed his lips, and began to speak.

"What you have just said, Father Alaric, has a great deal of very sound sense and good judgment in it. That a secretary would be very useful to me, is most certain; but it can be scarcely necessary for me, I should think, when speaking to a man of your inspired profession and excellent understanding,—it cannot be necessary for me, I say, to point out to such a one the extreme importance of not appointing any one to the situation, of whose merits and capacity I can have any doubt."

The confessor raised his meek eyes, and looked very much as if he was going to speak.

"I must beg you, Father Alaric, to wait till I have concluded what I was about to say," said the baron, with much dignity.

The confessor coloured slightly, crossed his hands over his breast, and again fixed his eyes upon the ground.

"Of course, Father Alaric," resumed the lord of the castle, "I must frequently have been inconvenienced by feeling the want of a secretary. To a man of my extensive connections, and very large property, it cannot be otherwise than troublesome and fatiguing to be without one. But the fear of bringing into contact with myself any individual whose appearance and manners might be objectionable, or in any way distasteful to me, has constantly prevented my offering the appointment to any one. Your present proposal, however, has much in it to make me hope that I might now safely venture to make this very proper addition to my establishment; and I fully authorize you, my good Father Alaric, to impart to your nephew, the doubtless welcome news of his appointment to the joint offices of librarian and private secretary to the Baron von Schwanberg."

And then he added, after returning, with great dignity, the humble and grateful obeisance of the ecclesiastic; "And I flatter myself, Father Alaric, that this appointment, with such a salary as I shall deem it fit and proper to annex to it, together with my having caused his name to be specially mentioned in the solemn service of thanksgiving which I commanded in the chapel of the castle, will be considered by the friends of the young boy, as well as by the world in general, as a sufficient proof that I am not ungrateful for the service which your nephew was fortunate enough to confer on me and my race."

Perhaps there is no attitude better suited for the reception of a long speech than that of crossing the hands with a sort of submissive passiveness upon the breast, and fixing the eyes upon the ground. It is an attitude familiar to the Romish priesthood, when listening to their superiors; and it was that to which Father Aalaric had recourse on the present occasion. But when the baron ceased, he raised his eyes, and having gently murmured a thankful acknowledgment for the favours bestowed on his nephew, made a low bow, and departed.

<center>~~~~~~~~~~~~~~~~</center>

CHAPTER XI.

THE style in which this same appointment was communicated to the baroness, differed considerably from that in which it was made known to the father confessor; for it was with a dancing step, and a joyous clapping of hands, that Gertrude entered her mother's dressing-room, and announced the news.

But it was in vain that the elder lady assumed an aspect of the most perfect propriety, as she listened to the intelligence; for Gertrude, with her bright eyes sparkling through her clustering curls, and her laughing lips vainly attempting to screw themselves into a suitable expression of solemnity, related the harangue of her father (including at full length all his compliments to herself) in so very a heroic style, that for a moment the baroness's gravity forsook her, and it was in vain that the very useful veil so often furnished by the ever-ready cambric, was called to her assistance; for, despite her utmost efforts, her mischievous daughter perceived that she had succeeded in making her laugh. It was but for a moment, however; for fondly as she loved the fearless playfulness of her petted child, she was most truly desirous of veiling from her as much as possible the deficiencies of her noble father.

But this task was every day becoming more difficult; and when it happened, as in the present instance, that her own gravity gave way, she generally cut short the conversation by saying, "Gertrude! you are giving me pain."

But now she felt that a still stronger rebuke was deserved, and her own inclination to laugh speedily gave way before her wish to correct a propensity in her child, which seemed likely to conquer much more valuable feelings.

"You have made me laugh, Gertrude," she said; "but it is a poor triumph, my child! The ludicrous movements of a monkey might have the same effect. Our muscles are not always under the command of our judgment. On this occasion, particularly, I should have thought that the kindness of your father, in so immediately complying with our wishes, would have created a feeling very far removed from ridicule."

The manner in which this was said, as well as the gravity of the words themselves, was well calculated to produce the effect desired; and it did produce it. Gertrude never again mimicked the manner of her father, when repeating to her mother anything which he had said to her; and much was gained thereby on many subsequent occasions; for the more Gertrude increased in years and stature, the more did she find it necessary to confine to her own bosom the judgment which she was led to form of her father's intellectual capacity.

But though relieved from the saucy commentaries of her daughter, Madame de Schwanberg found it no very easy task to place the highly-intelligent boy, whom they had almost made one of their own family, in his right place. She had not passed by far the greatest portion of the last twelve years in miscellaneous, and sometimes in deep reading, without acquiring that sort of insight into the rarities and peculiarities of human intellect, which enables an acute observer to form a tolerably just estimate of the faculties of those with whom they are intimately associated. The boy Rupert was not, either in intellect or character, by any means a common boy.

Observant persons, who direct their attention to the fact, may often find that a mixture of race produces many striking rarities, both of intellect and character. The mother of Rupert was English by her mother's side, and Prussian on that of her father; and her husband, the father of Rupert, was a native of Innspruck.

How this variety of lineage affected either the *morale* or the *physique* of the boy, I will not attempt to trace, or even to guess, but content myself by stating the fact, that he was, in more ways than one, a remarkable boy.

In most things, however, he resembled his mother more than he did his father, especially as to the character of his intellect. In that peculiar beauty of countenance, which had struck Madame de Schwanberg when she first saw him in his sick chamber, he decidedly resembled both his parents; but the tall stature which he had already attained, was evidently inherited from his father.

It took the baroness but little time after the young librarian had been fully established in his office, to convince her, that if her gratitude for the service he had rendered her child, had placed before him all the employments and occupations which the world could offer, it would have been impossible for him to have fixed on any which would have suited him so well.

His passion for reading appeared insatiable; and no sooner had she perceived this, than she was induced by various causes to indulge him in it. In the first place, there was her gratitude, which prompted her very earnestly to promote his well-being and happiness, by every means in her power; and in no way, according to her own estimate of the comparative value of the various sources of enjoyment granted to us in this life, could she so effectually administer to it, as by indulging his inclination for reading.

Moreover, it appeared to her, that this occupation, "never ending, still beginning," was the best, if not the only way of supplying him with constant employment, for she did not expect that much business would come upon him as secretary to the lord of the castle; and although she certainly anticipated a good deal of active work for him in the library, she anticipated also that many an idle hour would be left upon his hands, if he had no other employment than keeping his books in order.

During the first week or two after this arrangement had been decided upon, and that his mother had returned to the dwelling of Father Alaric, the baron seemed desperately determined to prove to all whom it might concern, that the appointment of this favoured youth to the place of private secretary to the illustrious lord of Schloss Schwanberg was no sinecure, whatever other advantages it might offer.

To do him justice, he took good care that it should be well salaried, that the room appointed for so distinguished a functionary should be extremely comfortable, and that the domestics, from one end of the establishment to the other, should be very distinctly given to understand, that his private secretary, the Herr Odenthal, should be treated and attended upon in all respects like a gentleman.

The arranging all this was not only easy, but agreeable to him; for he was liberal by nature, and so truly grateful for the service the boy had rendered him, that every opportunity of treating him with generosity and kindness, was a real pleasure to him.

So far, all was well; it was only when the unfortunate baron had to find employment for his secretary, that his troubles began.

The first idea which occurred to him in this dilemma, was, that he should dispatch notes to one or two of his neighbours, inviting them to dine at the castle. He really ought to have had his picture taken while dictating these notes; for never, perhaps, had he looked more superbly dignified during any moment of his existence. Rupert, too, at the moment he was summoned to attend him, had been most deeply and delightfully occupied in the perusal of a volume of newly-arrived English poetry, which the baroness had good-naturedly put into his hands, proved the honest earnestness with which he desired to perform the duties assigned to him by the promptitude with which he closed the precious volume, and followed the servant who had been sent to summon him. His eye was still bright, and his cheek was still flushed by the excitement caused by the "Lay of the Last Minstrel;" but the feelings of the baron were of too grave and solemn a kind, to permit his noticing the animated appearance of the official he was about to employ.

A table, with all that was necessary for writing and sealing very carefully placed upon it, awaited the arrival of the young secretary; a chair also was very attentively placed for him, exactly where it ought to be, and the baron himself was seated in a very large and pompous-looking *bergère*, at no great distance.

When the youth was near enough to make his salutation to his dignified employer, the baron acknowledged it by graciously bending his head, and waving his hand towards the vacant chair, as an intimation that the secretary was to seat himself in it.

The youth obeyed, and in like obedience to another wave of the hand, accompanied by the words, " I wish you to write for me;" after placing himself in the vacant chair, drew towards him the implements for writing, which were placed before it.

"I wish you," still more solemnly resumed the baron, " I wish you, Mr. Rupert, to write several letters for me."

Rupert, upon hearing this, took the pen in his fingers, and with a look of awakened diligence, dutifully determined to forget Branksome Tower, and everything belonging to it.

"He—hem!" quoth the baron.

The pen of Rupert already touched the paper. A pause followed; and then the baron, again clearing his voice, said, very distinctly: "My dear sir"—but there he stopped.

Having waited for what appeared to the unpractised secretary a very long time, the youth began to suspect that he had made a blunder in supposing the dictation to have been already begun, and that he was himself the "dear sir" addressed; whereupon he said, very respectfully: "Did you speak to me, my Lord Baron?"

"No! my good lad, no!" was the immediate reply. "I am addressing myself to one of my noble neighbours, by letter. My dear sir," he again began; but these words being already written, Rupert could only refresh the dot over the *i*, which he did.

Another interval of silence followed, and then the baron said: "I am not quite certain, Mr. Rupert, whether the use of the third person is not the more correct and dignified mode of expression upon these occasions. Put aside that sheet of paper, if you please, and begin again."

Rupert obeyed, as far as the sheet of paper was concerned; but having very carefully laid another before him, he had to wait several minutes before he received any instructions concerning the use to which it was to be put.

At length, the baron spoke again, and, in a still more impressive tone than before, pronounced the words, "The Baron von Schwanberg presents"—but having proceeded thus far, he again paused, and Rupert, having inscribed the words in fair characters upon the paper, paused too.

But, this time, the pause was longer, and there was evidently doubt and difficulty in the mind of Rupert's master, as to what was to follow; nor was it till the noble author had repeatedly pressed his forehead with his hand, that he again spoke. But, at length, he said: "You have been over-hasty, my good boy. Nothing should ever be written in a hurry. I have still doubts as to which mode of address is, upon the whole, most unobjectionable."

Rupert, thus reproved, changed the attitude of his hand, and, instead of placing himself in an act to write, took the attitude of the most respectful listener. This state of things, also, lasted for some time, and then the baron said: "On the whole, perhaps, the first person may be preferable. Take fresh paper, if you please, and write carefully, according to my dictation."

Rupert dutifully listened, and faithfully obeyed, inscribing on the fresh paper, in fair characters, the following epistle:—

" My DEAR SIR,—It will give both the Baroness von Schwanberg and myself the sincerest pleasure, if you, my dear Count, with the amiable Countess your lady, and the charming young Countess your daughter, will afford to the Baroness von Schwanberg and myself, as well as to our young daughter the Baroness Gertrude, the honour and pleasure of your company at dinner, on Thursday next, the 19th of the present month, at the hour of four.

" I remain, my dear————."

Rupert had already written " SIR," when the baron stopped him, by saying, somewhat sharply, " What is that you have written, young man ? I must desire you to observe, that my secretary must not write faster than I dictate : I had no intention whatever of repeating the phrase, ' dear sir.' Nothing is worse in composition than repetition. My purpose was to conclude with the words, ' dear Count.' "

" I beg your pardon, my Lord Baron," said the boy, colouring; " I will write it over again in a moment, if you will permit me."

" Yes, Mr. Rupert. I not only permit, but must insist upon it. It must not, however, be done in my presence. You cannot suppose, young man, that I can bestow any portion of my valuable time, in sitting by while my secretary corrects his own blunders. Take these papers with you to the library. If I mistake not, the baroness permits your proceeding with the necessary business of making a catalogue of the books in my library, without your making a point of leaving the room when she enters it; and, fortunately, the noble size of the apartment permits her doing so without any inconvenience to herself. Take these papers with you, my good lad, and on no account permit yourself to be in a hurry. Rather than that you should be so, I would permit you to have a holiday from your work in the library for the remainder of the day. Your enjoying the joint offices of private secretary and librarian, will, of course, render it occasionally necessary that the great work of forming a catalogue should be suspended. Now leave me, Mr. Rupert. My time is very valuable. You are too young and inexperienced, as yet, to be aware of the many calls upon the time of a nobleman of my position; and therefore, for the present, I can only impress upon you the necessity of never breaking in upon me without having received especial permission to do so."

Rupert bowed low, and was leaving the room in respectful silence, when the baron recalled him, to say: "Of course, you are aware, young man, that you are not to presume to sign my name to this document. I will not believe, as it is evident that you have received a very decent education—I will not believe, I say, that you would be likely to commit such an offence. It is, however, my duty, having received you as an inmate into my family, that I should not trust your being aware of so important a law, to chance. It is not impossible, indeed, or wholly improbable, that when you have listened to such a prohibition as that which I am now enforcing, you may have heard it accompanied by the formula, '*with intent to defraud.*' But this qualification, though enough, if attended to, to exonerate you from danger in the eye of the law, is by no means sufficient, in the case of a secretary to a nobleman holding my position in society. The law contemplates only the pecuniary injury which may be done; but the feelings of a nobleman, on such subjects, are far more refined than it is within the reach of mere lawyers to understand. Do you hear me, Mr. Rupert? And do you comprehend what I mean?"

"I quite well comprehend," replied Rupert, fixing his eyes upon the ground, "that in no way, and for no reason, my Lord Baron, would you hold me excusable were I to write your name."

"You have expressed yourself very properly, my good lad," replied the baron, evidently pleased by the clear and distinct manner in which his young dependent had worded the important law he had laid down; "and now," he added, "you may leave me, my good Rupert; I have business of importance to transact, in which I shall not require your assistance."

If the boy had looked in upon his noble master ten minutes later, and seen him, as he would have then found him, fast asleep in his arm-chair, it is possible that he might have suspected this august master to have been uttering a jest when he thus dismissed him; but, in that case, the boy would have blundered, for nothing in the least degree resembling a joke occupied the mind of the solemn baron. Perhaps he thought that he really was going to perform important business; perhaps he had some dreamy sort of notion that he would ring the bell, and tell the footman to tell the butler to tell the cook that it was probable there would be a company dinner given at the castle on the following Thursday.

But if any such active project really occurred to him, the fatigue he had undergone in transacting business with his secretary, had incapacitated him for that, or for any farther exertion; for, in truth, although he placed a hand on each arm of his chair, as if he intended to rise from it, he was too much overpowered by drowsiness to achieve the doing so; and having gently sunk back into a leaning position, had fallen into a sound sleep, which lasted till the first dinner-bell had sent its rousing peal through the castle.

CHAPTER XII.

When Rupert returned with his papers to the library, he found the baroness and Gertrude rather lazily occupied; for, to say the truth, neither the mother, who had sat down with an intention to read—nor the daughter, who had sat down with an intention to draw, could fix their attention sufficiently upon what they were about, to prevent their thinking a good deal, and talking a little upon the subject of Rupert's *début*, in his capacity of secretary to the baron.

They had both been for some days aware that he had been appointed to this important office, but this was the first time he had been called upon to perform the duties attached to it.

Unfortunately—*very* unfortunately—as the excellent baroness often told herself, the young Gertrude von Schwanberg had a peculiarly acute sense of the ridiculous; and there was, perhaps, no point of her education which had given her mother so much trouble as she had found in keeping this unfortunate propensity in subjection. The excellent motives which had made this sort of discipline appear so peculiarly important to Madame de Schwanberg, may be easily guessed at.

Her consciousness of her own deficiencies in the respect and love with which it is the duty of a wife to regard her husband, was a subject of never-ceasing regret to her; nay, there were times when the far bitterer feeling of self-reproach was mixed with this regret; for she was ever perfectly ready to acknowledge, even to her own heart, that her noble husband was possessed of many excellent qualities, and that his obliging and observant conduct to herself had been such as ought to have atoned to her, more than they had done, for his slow and weak intellect, as well as for the many traits of character which often excited both smiles and frowns on her part, when, as she was quite ready to allow, they ought not to have excited either. But it was much easier to plead guilty to her faults in these her secret self-examinations, than to correct them in her intercourse with her husband; all that she could do, therefore, for the ease of her conscience, was to guard as much as possible from betraying any species of disrespect to him, in the presence of her daughter.

This cautious circumspection on her part, at least, produced one good effect, and that a very important one, for it prevented their ever indulging together in a smile at any of the numerous absurdities of the worthy baron. How far, in the case of Gertrude, this restraint proceeded from her own convictions of what was right and proper, and how far from compliance with the example so stedfastly exhibited by her mother, it might be difficult to say, nor did her mother seek to know.

When Rupert entered the library, with his hand full of papers, and his eyes full of fun, while the flush upon his handsome face showed plainly enough, that he had passed through some scene which had more than usually excited him, both the baroness and her daughter behaved admirably well; and that it was their purpose to do so, was proved by their not even exchanging a glance together.

The library at Schloss Schwanberg was a very noble and spacious apartment. That part of it which was farthest removed from the door of entrance had three large windows, which commanded a view of the porch. It was here that the baroness and her young daughter spent by far the greatest part of their days.

Each of them had their own place there; a separate table large enough to contain materials for various employments, and a chair ready to be occupied by the person employed. Each of these tables was so placed as to command the view afforded by the two windows most distant from each other; while between the two, and in front of the third, was a somewhat longer table, with a sofa, well calculated for the accommodation of two lounging ladies, the table in front of it being tolerably well laden with books.

But this portion of the apartment occupied only one-third of its entire size; the lofty ceiling being in three divisions, each one marked by a very noble arch, and supported by columns of very noble proportions, which, though not advancing above three feet from the wall, gave a sort of enjoyable snugness to the three divisions of the room, which, without them, might have looked too large for comfort.

Each of the lower compartments had its separate window, and the middle one seemed dedicated to music, for there stood the grand pianoforte, which both mother and daughter touched so ably, and there also stood a harp, and music desk.

How the lower end of the room had been arranged before the Schloss Schwanberg establishment had been augmented by a librarian and secretary, it boots not to say; but at the time of which I am now speaking, a very substantial writing-table, with all appurtenances and means to boot, was placed at a convenient distance from the lowest window; and on this table was placed not only all implements necessary for writing, but a goodly show of very ample volumes, ready to receive from the hand of Rupert the titles of the many thousand volumes which were ranged on the massive book-shelves which surrounded the room.

It should seem, from the aspect of this very noble apartment, that the climate was a cold one, for each division had its separate stove.

On the entrance of Rupert in the manner above described, the two ladies raised their eyes from their respective employments, and then, having looked at him for a moment, resumed them.

Rupert, too, for one short moment looked at them; but as they did not address him, or give any other indication of wishing him to approach, he quietly seated himself at his especial writing-table, and in a minute or two afterwards, appeared to be busily occupied with his pen.

But the sharp eyes of Gertrude speedily perceived that he was not at work upon his catalogue; and after watching him for a little while, without affecting to conceal that she was so doing, she suddenly started up, exclaiming, " Mamma! I must see what it is that papa has given him to do, before I can fix my attention upon anything I wish to do myself;" and without waiting for any reply, she bounded down the room with a very active and resolute step, and placed herself behind the chair of the young secretary.

Rupert behaved admirably well, for he did not, even for an instant, turn round his head to speak, or even to look at her. It might be, perhaps, that he dared not meet her eyes, from fearing that he might laugh. But, whatever was his motive, his demeanour was exactly what it ought to be; a fact, of which the baroness, who had followed her daughter's movements with her eyes, was perfectly aware.

She certainly gave the lad credit for his discretion, in so steadily pursuing the occupation which had been given him, without permitting the frolicsome approach of the young lady to withdraw his attention from it; but she was not aware of half his merit; for there lay all the various sheets of papers before him, on which he had made his first abortive attempts at performing the duties of a secretary, by writing from dictation; and considering their mutual acquaintance with the peculiarities of the other party concerned, which would have required nothing more than a simple exposure of the various folios, in order to make the ludicrous scene which had passed, as obvious to Gertrude as it had been to himself; Rupert indulged not himself by making any such display; but, on the contrary, contrived to mix the paper with which he had returned so skilfully, with what he found on his table, that he thought that not even the sharp eyes of Gertrude could make any very important discovery concerning the business which had been transacted between the Baron von Schwanberg and his newly-appointed secretary.

The words, as well as the movement of Gertrude had made her mother aware both of her object, and of the unscrupulous mode she had taken to obtain it; and as the baroness happened to be so placed, as to be able to follow her wilful daughter with her eyes, without changing her own position; she had an opportunity of observing the behaviour of Rupert, as well as that of Gertrude; and she gave him great credit for the manner in which he contrived to defeat her unscrupulous curiosity, without even appearing to notice it.

She felt that the boy deserved to be trusted, and the feeling this, was really and reasonably a great satisfaction to her; for had the case been otherwise, the familiarity of intercourse, which was the almost inevitable consequence of his employment in the apartment they chiefly occupied, would have been very objectionable.

But although the baroness gave him honour due for the quiet, yet effective manner in which he had avoided the indiscretion, as well as the familiarity, of making the young lady acquainted with the business which he was transacting with her father; she was very far from being aware, either of the amount of this forbearance on his part, or of the importance of it on that of her daughter.

Well prepared as she was to give the baron credit for very great absurdity, she by no means supposed that any scene so ridiculous as the one which has just passed between him and his secretary, could have taken place; and she therefore attributed no merit to Rupert, beyond that of well-behaved discretion.

Rupert might, indeed, very easily have repaid himself for the heavy moments which he had passed in the performance of his difficult duty to his master; for the mere exposure of the various abortive dispatches to eyes and intelligence as quick as those of Gertrude, would have been quite sufficient to have explained the whole matter to her; and there was merriment enough in one smile of hers, to have atoned for more than all the heavy dullness from which he had just escaped.

But Rupert Odenthal had other good qualities, besides the courage which had urged him to spring into the water, for the purpose of saving Gertrude's life. Rupert Odenthal "had a conscience." The difference of age between himself and the young baroness, was only three years; but when the senior is only fifteen and a-half, such difference is apt to appear greater than it really is. Moreover, Rupert was a very manly boy of his age, and much older in proportion, as far as judgment went, than the over-indulged heiress of the Baron von Schwanberg.

There was a bounding gaiety of step in the manner in which Gertrude now approached him, which made him shrewdly suspect, that the young lady might be so indiscreet as to quiz her papa, if he afforded such an opportunity for it, as the variations in his correspondence with his noble neighbour might give; and he accordingly placed the sheets which he had brought back with him (by a hasty movement), between the pages of his blotting-book, bringing forward, almost at the same instant, a fresh sheet of paper, which he placed before him, while he commenced the dilatory operation of mending a pen.

But Gertrude had been too quick for him. Ere she had reached his chair, her eye had caught sight of the characters upon the various sheets which had been taken, and rejected; and the real state of the case was revealed to her, as distinctly as if she had been present at the scene.

Her prompt suspicion of what had passed, was, of course, materially assisted by her foregone knowledge of the dull baron's extraordinary slowness and uncertainty upon all occasions of the kind; and for one short moment she anticipated considerable merriment, from the account which Rupert, who was by no means a dull narrator, was likely to give of the affair; but a

7

second thought brought a repentant blush to her cheek, and she
walked back again to her own little table, without saying a
word. Madame de Schwanberg saw all this, and understood it
too, and gave both parties the credit they deserved. Rupert was
permitted to proceed with his important task as secretary without farther interruption; and when, after the judicious delay of
about half-an-hour, he carried the fair-written document to the
baron for his signature, that illustrious individual felt such an
agreeable accession of dignity from this royal mode of giving it
value and effect, that from that time forth, he never made any
other use of his pen than what was necessary to sign his name;
and it would, perhaps, be difficult to trace as much ingenuity
and invention in any other circumstance throughout his life, as
he displayed at finding occasions for performing this important
ceremony.

CHAPTER XIII.

THE instance given in the last chapter of Rupert Odenthal's
discreet conduct, and more than discreet feeling, went farther,
and did more, towards giving Madame de Schwanberg a respect
for his character and confidence in his principles, than might
have been produced by a multitude of excellent traits, all perhaps exhibiting great ability, and even good feeling also.

But the poor baroness was so deeply conscious of the profound
feeling of contempt with which her noble husband's intellectual
deficiencies had inspired her, that she dreaded nothing so much
as seeing her beloved Gertrude fall into the same sin. So blame-
less had been her own life, and so truly benevolent and indulgent
were the feelings of her heart towards every human being with
whom she had come in contact, with the sole exception of her
wearisome husband, that the consciousness of this exception lay
very heavily on her spirit, and the idea of her child's being by
any means betrayed into the same sin, was really terrible to her.
The strong persuasion, therefore, that, instead of being led to
this, she would be guarded from it, by the good sense and high
principle of the boy, whom accident had thrown into such intimate contact with them, was most welcome, and consolatory.

Had Madame de Schwanberg's practical knowledge of the world been equal, or in any fair proportion, to the information she had acquired from books, this dread, lest her daughter should sympathise too completely with her in her feelings towards the baron, would not have taken such painful possession of her; for with more experience of the world and its ways, she would have learnt that Nature never blunders as hopelessly as we sometimes blunder ourselves.

Save in some few rare and perfectly exceptional cases, we never see any *dis*like between parents and children, that can compare, in bitterness and intensity, to what may frequently be seen to exist between husband and wife.

The community of their worldly interests, and still more, perhaps, the community of their parental feelings, go far towards checking this; so far, indeed, that in a multitude of instances, domestic peace is not disturbed openly, by the want of personal attachment between the parties; but where parents have authoritatively interfered to bring those together whom inclination, on either side, would keep asunder, they have to answer for the heavy sin of charging the unhappy victim with a weight too heavy to be borne patiently, and a duty too difficult to be sincerely performed.

It was such an authority as this, which had made the high-minded, intellectual Baroness von Schwanberg the companion for life of the prejudiced and heavy-minded baron.

It has been already stated, that this unfortunate lady's greatest cause of anxiety, during the infancy of her daughter, arose from her dread, lest her child should inherit the weak and slow capacity of its father; and the happiest period of her married life was decidedly that, during which the bright faculties and clear intellect of her child were displaying themselves under her own able and ardent tuition, in a manner very effectually to convince her, that all such fears were vain.

It is was only since the domestication of the young Rupert in the family, that this new cause of natural uneasiness had suggested itself to her. Hitherto, the reading of Gertrude, though extremely agreeable both to the teacher and the taught, had for the most part been selected more with a view to solid instruction than present amusement; and though the enchantment created by poetry was beginning to be felt by the young student, it had as yet only reached her in the form of, or,·at least, blended with instruction.

Before her accident, too, so large a portion of her favourite exercise, and her favourite pleasure, was enjoyed with her father, and derived solely from his care and attention to her wishes, that her mother's tender conscience was perfectly at ease respecting the mutual feelings of both father and daughter. But the terrific accident which had led to Rupert Odenthal's becoming a member of the family, had, for some time, greatly checked and curtailed this enjoyment; for the baron, himself, had been too seriously terrified to be very eager for a speedy renewal of the exercise; and the mother's agony at the idea of it was such, that Gertrude, from very love and pity to her, was long before she ventured to propose the renewal of her favourite exercise.

But, somehow or other, it seemed as if the taking the catalogue of the library supplied a source of occupation and amusement, sufficient to make them forget the want of any other. The baron, of course, continued his usual habit of spending some hours of every day on horseback; and many weeks elapsed before he even wished to enjoy the much-loved delight of seeing Gertrude riding by his side, so fresh was still the recollection of what he had suffered from seeing her life in danger.

During this interval, the baroness, and her aidful daughter also, had not only found the examination and arrangement of the library to be an occupation full of interest and amusement; but they found also, that, in order to bring it into the condition in which it ought to be, it would be absolutely necessary that Rupert should have all the assistance they could give him.

They had neither of them, as yet, been very careful librarians; but, nevertheless, they knew their way among the shelves well enough to render his task very much easier than it would have been without them. For the first few days that they thus worked together, the efforts of the trio, though they had all the same object in view, namely, the orderly arrangement of the volumes which were, as yet, for the most part, placed side by side, without any regular arrangement at all; for the first few days of their labour there was little or no attempt among them to pursue any fixed plan of operations, though one and the same ultimate object was always in view; on the contrary, indeed, a looker-on might have been tempted to declare, that the object of each was perfectly different and distinct from that of the others. The baroness might have been observed to bring the German, French, and English books, which furnished the fund from which she drew her own resources, into the part of the room where she usually sat; while it was quite evident, that Gertrude's selection of permanent lodgings for the favourites to whom she looked for future companionship, in a great measure depended upon altitude of position, as she carefully avoided placing any volume which it was her purpose to read, above the easy reach of her own hand.

Rupert's manœuvres seemed to be regulated on a principle quite different from either; for he very sedulously divided the volumes according to the different languages in which they had been written, but placing them with very little regard to anything else.

The tremendous business of dusting, it must be observed, had been previously performed under the eye of the house-steward, who, by the help of some half-dozen assistants, had, in the course of a few days, taken down every volume, and replaced it again, so as to leave both shelves and books in a condition to be approached and handled, without any risk to the bold invader of being smothered.

So far, therefore, all seemed to go on smoothly; till one day, when Rupert had been, if possible, more than usually active, he suddenly suspended his operations, and approaching the baroness with somewhat of a melancholy aspect, and accosting her with a very ominous shake of the head, he said, "My lady baroness! we are all wrong! This will never do! How can a catalogue be made out in any regular order, where there is no order in the books themselves?"

The baroness immediately suspended her own operations, and looked and listened with great attention.

"Explain yourself, dear Rupert," she said. "What is it that you would propose?"

"I scarcely know, myself, dear lady," he replied; "but I am quite sure, that if the books are left as we are placing them now, no catalogue that I can make, will ever assist any one in finding the particular volume that may be wished for."

The lady of the castle raised her hand to her forehead, and remained for some moments in meditation. At length she replied, with rather a deep sigh, "I am very much afraid that you are right, Rupert."

"And I am afraid so too," replied the anxious-looking boy. "But if we are to begin all over again," he added, "you must please to promise me, that neither you, nor the young baroness, will do any more with your own hands. You look tired now, dear lady! Will you promise not to take any more trouble?"

"But what terrible labour is it you are going to propose? I assure you, I like the work, Rupert; and if I give you the promise you ask for, I should really be promising to give up a very great pleasure. Remember what your mother's darling poet says. 'The labour we delight in, physics pain.'"

"Yes, dear lady! I understand that, and I feel it, too. But when labour has been performed, the having to undo it, and begin over again, is likely to produce a more disagreeable consciousness of fatigue. Do you not think so, madam?"

"Why, perhaps I do, Rupert," replied the baroness, laughing; "but do you really think that we are in that unhappy condition?"

It was with some reluctance, and a great deal of modesty, that Rupert was at length fully brought to explain himself, and to show, which he certainly did very clearly, that a catalogue continued upon so very miscellaneous a scheme as that which he had began, accompanied by such an unsystematic arrangement of the volumes on the shelves, was not likely to insure either the information or the inconvenience which had been contemplated.

Rupert Odenthal and his fair assistants were by no means the first, and will probably not be the last, who have been sorely troubled in finding out the easiest way of getting at the one book we want, among many thousands that we do not want; and whether the tri-partite ingenuity which was upon this occasion brought to bear upon the question, produced the best result which has been as yet hit upon, I will not pretend to say; their labours had at least, one effect, which was certainly very agreeable to all the parties concerned, for it would have been very difficult to hit upon any device which would so quickly have led to an equal degree of friendly intimacy and practical equality among the trio thus employed; and the modest bearing and boyish age of Rupert, as well as the childishness of Gertrude, so effectively prevented all objection to the sort of domestic familiarity which ensued, from even suggesting itself, that Rupert might have been heard issuing orders to "Gertrude," and Gertrude might have been seen very meekly obeying them, without any thought ever occurring to the busy baroness, that it might be as necessary to keep noble girls and plebeian boys exactly in their respective places, as folios and duodecimos in theirs.

And yet, it is scarcely fair to employ such a phrase, on such an occasion; for, if all the boys and girls in Christendom had been brought together for judgment, it would have been impossible any pair so brought, at the respective ages of fifteen and twelve, could have been found, who would have given less reason to their mothers and fathers, their pastors and masters, for any anxiety respecting their conduct, separately or conjointly, than did Rupert Odenthal and Gertrude von Schwanberg.

Nevertheless, wherever it is thought desirable that an immense distance should exist through life between individuals, the wisdom of placing them in very close juxta-position, at first setting off, may fairly be questioned.

There was also another point on which the judgment of Madame von Schwanberg showed itself defective.

She carried her dislike, or rather her dread of ignorant dullness, to such an extent, that during the first ten years or so of Gertrude's life, it had positively become the *bête noir* of her existence; and, assuredly, she must, in what she would have considered her most reasonable moments, have been ready to declare, that there would have been less of lasting misery to her in seeing her child die, than in seeing any positive symptoms in her of intellectual deficiency.

It is certain that her anxieties on this subject were effectually and for ever removed at a somewhat earlier period of her daughter's life than she could have reasonably expected; for Gertrude was not only a sharp-witted child, but, her animal senses being as acute as her intellect, she manifested, at a very early age, a more than ordinary degree of intelligence.

No sooner did this great question appear to be settled in her favour, than Madame von Schwanberg became perfectly reconciled to her own destiny.

"It would have, doubtless, been very agreeable," thought she, "to have found a companion in my husband; but if, at this hour, the choice were offered me, I would rather, ten thousand times, find that blessing in my child!"

Such being the result of her most secret meditations, and such the genuine feeling of her heart, it was natural enough that, in educating her daughter, she should take the most especial care to keep her bright young mind free from the only peculiarity which appeared with sufficient strength and vigour to be fairly considered as a marked feature in that of her father. Nor must this strong feeling, on her part, be considered as any proof of personal hostile feeling towards her husband. That pride of race was the master-feeling of his mind, no one who approached him could long be permitted to doubt; but her conviction of this fact rather led her to form a higher notion of his intellect than it deserved; for she considered this overgrown and ill-regulated feeling as a species of mental fungus, which had spread over and diseased his faculties, so as to produce very nearly the effect of monomania; whereas the real state of the case was, that, if the noble baron had not happily got hold of this idea, he would probably have passed through life without enjoying the high human prerogative of being conscious of having any positive idea at all.

That, under these circumstances, the cultivation of Gertrude's mind became the first object of her mother's life, may easily be understood; and it took her but little time to discover that, if Rupert's courage and dexterity had saved the young girl's life, his bright and varied intelligence might be of almost equal utility in assisting the powers of her young mind to develop and strengthen themselves by the help both of example and emulation.

The good baroness either was, or fancied herself to be, peculiarly unfortunate in the intellectual peculiarities of most of her neighbours. At any rate, she made no blunder when she became, at length, fully, though reluctantly, convinced that there was not a single *reading* human being within twenty miles of Schloss Schwanberg. This she felt to be a grievous misfortune to herself on her own account, as well as a serious disadvantage to Gertrude; "for how," thought she, "shall I ever be able to make her comprehend that, if she ever lives to mix with the world, she will not find all its inhabitants quite as ignorant or as dull as the noble neighbours of Schloss Schwanberg?"

It is extremely probable that she was right in this; but highly as most assuredly she ought to rank, even amongst the most intellectual and the most highly-instructed of her sex, there was one point upon which the Baroness von Schwanberg very decidedly deluded herself.

She would have been very indignant, and have considered herself as very cruelly misjudged, had any one told her that she might be fairly charged with displaying a more decided proof of deep-seated aristocratical feeling, than ever her husband had done.

"I?" methinks I can hear her exclaim—"I?—who, from my very soul, abhor all such paltry and childish distinctions? Where is the human being who estimates more highly whatever superiority nature has bestowed, or more lowly the trumpery distinctions conferred by man?"

It may be difficult to answer this challenge; but will our philosophical baroness tell us what is the feeling, and whence it arises, which causes her to look upon it as an event *absolutely impossible*, that her daughter Gertrude should join in the pursuits and studies of Rupert Odenthal so thoroughly, and with such sincere participation and sympathy of heart and soul, that she should at last arrive at the conclusion, that—" She of living men could love but him alone?"

What is the feeling which makes such a conclusion appear impossible to the baroness, and whence does it arise? The feeling can correctly receive no other name than PRIDE—for it can only arise from the deep conviction that the space dividing the noble and the plebeian is too vast, too profound, too incalculably great, for any person in their senses to contemplate the passing it as a thing possible.

That such was, in truth, the persuasion of Madame von Schwanberg, cannot be doubted; and upon no other theory can her conduct be explained or excused. Notwithstanding her painfully-low estimate of her husband's intellect, his station as a high-born nobleman, important to his country, both from his wealth and his alliances, was recognised as fully by her as by himself; and though she might have allowed that the overthrowing the dynasty of the Emperor would be a crime more awful in its consequences, she would have scarcely considered it as more decidedly the reverse of *right* than any act by which the pure nobility of such an escutcheon could be compromised.

Those who would declare that such a state of mind, in such a woman, would be unnatural, blunder as much as a born-and-bred citizen does in doubting the fact, that a thorough-bred sporting-dog would fast, almost, if not quite, to death, rather than feed on game. It is idle to call it unnatural.

If it be an art, it is " an art that Nature makes," as she does *that* by which the culture of the gardener can metamorphose a flower.

The most satisfactory source of comfort in contemplating the existence of such a fantastic vision, in such a mind as that of the Baroness von Schwanberg, arises from remembering that Nature gives us as ample powers for the inoculation of good as of evil varieties; and that, even at this present NOW, with half the nations of the earth trying to make mince-meat of each other, without any one of them very clearly knowing why, " there's a sweet little cherub sits perched up aloft," who is busily employed in making many of us go in the right direction, though without showing us exactly where it may lead us.

CHAPTER XIV.

As it was by no means a difficult matter to excite in the mind of the Baron von Schwanberg a feeling of admiration concerning every thing that he could call his own, the orderly arrangement of the Schwanberg library, and the daily growing catalogue of the volumes it contained, soon became a new, and favourite theme for his eloquence; and as it was evident that Gertrude listened to him with more than usual interest, when he was expressing his wonder and admiration at all that had been done in that department, he went on admiring Rupert's extraordinary industry and cleverness in the business, so warmly, that the baroness, on one occasion, took an opportunity for saying, that she was almost afraid the young man worked too hard, and that he scarcely allowed himself sufficient time for air and exercise.

"Do you really think so, my dear lady?" exclaimed the baron, with a most unusual degree of animation. "I should be very sorry to let any of my people injure their health by over-fatigue in my service; and with respect to this excellent lad in particular, I would rather permit the great work he is upon to be suspended altogether, than that his health should suffer from his devotion to it. We must never, under any circumstances, my dear lady, permit ourselves to forget the enormous benefit he has conferred upon us. In fact, there would be a very great impropriety in my permitting an individual, whose name I caused to be specially alluded to, nay, positively mentioned, in the service which my influence with the church enabled me to command, in the chapel of the castle; there would decidedly be a very great impropriety in my permitting a youth residing in my family under such circumstances, to run the risk of injuring his health in the performance of a task which I have assigned him, and which was done in the hope of providing him with an honourable and profitable employment, instead of doing him a serious injury."

The baroness, as was her wont, remained in the attitude of a listener, till her noble husband had ceased to speak; and then she replied, that she agreed with him perfectly, and that it would give her much pleasure to see so well-disposed and every way deserving a lad, permitted, and indeed encouraged, to take a little more exercise and amusement.

It so chanced, that within an hour after this conversation had taken place, the baron and his daughter accidentally met in the hall of the castle; upon which, Gertrude stopped him, and said, with great glee, "I am so very glad, dear papa! for mamma tells me that you are going to be so kind as to order dear, good Rupert to walk about and amuse himself, now and then, instead of staying in the house all day, as he does now, about the catalogue. I never guessed that you had such a quantity of books, papa! I really can hardly believe that the Emperor himself can have a much larger library than you have. I think you will be astonished to see the catalogue when it is finished. And the library is looking so different! It is grown quite magnificent."

"I am very glad to hear you say so, my dear love," he replied, with a look of very great satisfaction. "Magnificent is exactly the word which I should like to have applied to every part of my property; for the remembrance that you are to inherit it, my dear child, gives everything a greater value and importance in my eyes now than it ever had before. Come into the library with me now, Gertrude. I should like to see what has been done there."

The effect produced upon the noble master of the castle on entering this fine room, arranged and decorated with equal taste and industry as it now was, by the trio who for many weeks past had devoted all their time and talents to its embellishment, was much greater than they had either of them hoped to produce, and his approbation was signified in a manner intended to be very gratifying to them all.

To his lady he made a speech of considerable length, signifying his entire approval of everything she had done, and hinting, in a whisper, not intended to reach the ears of Rupert, that however well she might have been assisted by the lad whom he had so fortunately fixed upon as his librarian, it was quite evident that nothing but the taste and judgment of a person as nobly born as herself, could have suggested the different alterations which had given so noble an air to the apartment.

He turned to Gertrude, who was on the other side of him as he said this, and added, "I now perfectly understand, my dear child, what you meant when you said the room was magnificent. It *is* magnificent, Gertrude, and your mother, as well as yourself, have shown, on this occasion, as I am quite sure you will on all others, the invariable result of being descendants from a noble race."

This harangue was listened to with a smile, pretty equally

made up of satisfaction and fun. She was exceedingly well pleased at finding "dear papa" so perfectly contented with all the bold innovations by which they had so greatly altered the aspect of the room, and infinitely amused at the idea that these alterations had been achieved by the *vis inertiæ* of a noble pedigree.

But Gertrude had something more in her head at that moment, than the powers of a noble pedigree or the beauty of a fine room; and having set her heart upon obtaining a very particular favour from her dear papa, she permitted neither fun, nor anything else, to turn her from her purpose; and having respectfully waited till he had completed his speech, by the solemn repetition of his conviction, that he should consider himself as guilty of great impiety could he doubt that it had been the especial purpose of Heaven in bestowing strength and courage upon Rupert Odenthal, to save the life of the heiress of Schwanberg, she quietly replied, "Yes, papa, he must indeed have been very strong, and very courageous, or he never could have done it; and I have been thinking, papa, that it would only be acting like your dear, kind self, if you were to buy a nice little horse for poor Rupert, that he might have a holiday sometimes, and ride out with us."

"You are a noble-minded, generous young lady, my dear Gertrude," replied the baron, looking at her very approvingly; "and if every high-born nobleman did his duty towards the race from which he sprung, as scrupulously as I did mine, Gertrude, when I took your mother for my wife, we should probably see many more instances than we do of young ladies as high-minded and generous as yourself. Your very proper suggestion shall be immediately attended to, Gertrude; and it would doubtless have occurred to me before, as a proper thing to be done, had not the multitude of affairs, which every man in my exalted position is obliged to attend to, occupied me too completely to leave me as much leisure as I would wish to attend to minor concerns."

So the nice little horse was bought for poor Rupert, who thenceforward became not only as well mounted a cavalier as could easily be found in the land wherein he dwelt, but a fearless and graceful one into the bargain.

But if the gratitude of the baron thus led him, in the strength and fearlessness of his greatness, to bestow favours upon the low-born boy with no more caution than he would have thought necessary in petting a poodle; the baroness, on her side, displayed a still more perilous want of forethought; for whereas the baron only mounted him upon a well-bitted little horse, the paces of which might be displayed without danger to anybody, his lady had the rashness not only to encourage by every means in her power the cultivation of his fine and powerful intellect, but to lead him, solely as it seemed for her own gratification, to display in familiar, daily intercourse with herself and her young daughter, the very brilliant faculties with which Nature had endowed him.

And this went on from month to month, and from year to year, without any thought of possible mischief from it, ever entering her head for a moment!

But Gertrude was not, by any means, *so thoughtless a child* as her mother imagined her to be. So much, indeed, did she think, and so justly did she reason, that it is highly probable the danger which now threatened would, to her, have brought no peril at all, had her own judgment been her only guide; but it was not so.

Had her father made it less evident that he considered his young secretary as no more belonging to the same class of beings as himself, than was the horse on which he had mounted him, neither the heart nor the intellect of Gertrude would have rebelled, as they now did, against the impious absurdity of so classing him; while on the other hand, she never would have ventured to place him, upon the authority of her own judgment alone, so greatly above the generality of his fellow-mortals, as she was now disposed to do.

In short, every individual of the four who now formed the domestic circle at Schloss Schwanberg, was in a false position, excepting only the young librarian himself.

He was permitted to eat at their table, because, as the baron told him, his being nephew to the holy man who had been appointed confessor to the castle, made it extremely fitting and proper that he should pronounce grace at its owner's table; and having once been told that he was to dine there, and for the especial reason so stated, he thought no more about it, but took it for granted, that it was perfectly right and proper that he should do so; and his common sense, to which he alone applied for counsel on the occasion, made him feel that being thrown into the domestic society of his patron's family, it was desirable that he should, as much as possible, both in dress and demeanour, assimilate himself to them.

As to the many very busy, and also very delightful hours, which he passed in the great room on the other side of the castle, he certainly found nothing at all likely to puzzle him in any of them. The vocation for which he was expressly hired, seemed to make him part and parcel of the library; and as we are told, that men are sometimes so placed, that " their talk is of bullocks," so with him, it was quite as inevitable that his talk should be of books.   And so it certainly was—and being so, it speedily became more amusing and more interesting to the ill-matched baroness than any she had listened to for years.

Never once did it occur to her as possible, that there could be anything wrong or mischievous, in listening to the eager, ardent criticisms of the intelligent lad, as he dashed on from one gifted page to another.   Never once did it enter her head as a thing *possible*, that what she listened to with pleased amusement, might steal into the heart and soul of her young daughter with an effect as lasting as it was delightful.

In short, a more false, or, at least, a more mistaken, position than that of Madame de Schwanberg, when presiding over the occupations of her quiet library, cannot easily be imagined.

As to the poor baron, his little greatness, and his great little-ness, have already been dwelt upon too fully, to require any further description here.   But amidst all this blundering, it was the unfortunate Gertrude who was the most likely to stumble outright, for she was really led to believe that she was not only displaying, but feeling, the very noblest sentiments, while cherishing precisely the thoughts and feelings which *both* her parents would have the most deeply deplored, could they have been made aware of them.

And on—and on—and on—went weeks and months, and the noble inmates of Schloss Schwanberg took little heed of them. Gertrude grew tall, and taller, and very tall; but the eye which first seemed to take note of this, as well as of the bright dawn of the beauty which every day seemed bringing to perfection; the eye which first seemed to think this dawning beauty worthy of especial note, was not within the castle walls, but seven miles beyond them.

The young Count Adolphe von Steinfeld was the son and heir of one of the noblest and richest of the neighbouring proprietors, and was almost considered, even by the baron himself, as having a right to associate with him on terms of equality.

This young Count Adolphe it was, whose eyes and heart first did homage to the beauty of Gertrude von Schwanberg.

The two families had been upon friendly visiting terms before Gertrude was born; but it was not in the nature of the Baron von Schwanberg to be intimate with any one, and nothing less active and less daring in its nature than the " sweet passion of love," could even have led to an intercourse so nearly approaching intimacy, as that which had lately grown up between the castles of Schwanberg and Steinfeld.

Love is not only active and daring, but wonderfully ingenious; not all the good qualities of the young Count Adolphe, and he had very many such, would even have availed in obtaining for him the easy access he now enjoyed to the library at Schwanberg, if he had not continued to run up a very familiar and intimate friendship with its young librarian.

I should, however, be doing both the young men injustice, if I left it to be supposed that the feeling on both sides, which brought them so frequently together, was not originally that of mutual and very cordial liking; but it may be fairly doubted, if this alone would so very frequently have caused Count Adolphe's steed to be stabled at Schwanberg, as was now the case.

This young son and heir of the wealthy and right noble Count von Steinfeld was, in many respects, a good deal out of the ordinary routine of character commonly found among the young aristocracy of Southern Germany. Accident had made him a scholar; for it was to accident he owed the having been almost wholly educated by an English tutor; and his natural temperament had led him to be a *reader;* a peculiarity less common in his class and country, than in any other upon earth, who have made equal advances, in other respects, towards civilization.

It was during a long riding excursion that these two young men first fell into a conversation together, sufficiently long, and sufficiently unrestrained, to make them both feel that they had got hold of something out of the common way, and that they should like to have a little more of it.

One must have been resident in such lands, and familiar with their inhabitants, before any such freemasonry as this can be comprehended.

In Southern Europe it is possible (and a good deal more than possible) to live for years in habits of constant friendly association with a great variety of well-born persons, moving in the very highest society, without having your intelligence once called upon, or in the least degree awakened, to the consciousness of being in the society of persons *au courant* of the age in which we live.

To those (whether foreign or native) whom accident has jostled out of this routine, every collision with persons who have been equally lucky, is exceedingly agreeable; and thus it was with the highly-born Adolphe and the lowly-born Rupert.

More than once in the course of that same ride, the stately horse of the young Count might have been seen pacing with enforced condescension beside the clever little steed of Rupert; and if the young plebeian was less startled, and less excited, by the tone and pith of the young nobleman's remarks than his well-pleased companion was by those he himself uttered, it was only because the relish with which one listens to truth, was less new to him.

The consequence of this was, that the young Count, upon coming to Schloss Schwanberg, and inquiring for Herr Rupert Odenthal, was shown into the library.

All that followed was so pretty nearly inevitable, that it scarcely needs recounting.

With all the tact of her charming manners, and all the kindness of her womanly heart, the baroness immediately contrived to put the two young men at their ease together, under circumstances which, had the baron been present in her stead, would have been exceedingly embarrassing; but, while giving Adolphe a very cordial reception as a family friend, she took care to make it evident that she understood his visit to be intended for Rupert; a fact which had been made evident to her by the servant, who had proclaimed, when he announced him, that he inquired for the Herr Rupert.

As to Gertrude, though this unwonted occurrence did not suggest to her the necessity of "looking beautiful with all her might," she very civilly laid her book aside, and so far joined in the conversation as to listen to it, and even "to speak when she was spoken to."

This was quite enough, and no great wonder, either, to convince Count Adolphe that she was not only the most beautiful, but the most intelligent girl he had ever seen; and what with the aspect of the room, which set him longing for something like it at his home, and what with the friendly kindness of the baroness, and the unaffected ease and spirit with which Rupert sustained the conversation (for, not having a particle of vanity, the feeling of shyness was, of course, unknown to him),—what with all this together, the Count Adolphe thought of little else, as he rode home, than of the finding some good excuse for speedily repeating his visit, which most assuredly was, for some cause or other, by far the most agreeable he had ever made in his life.

CHAPTER XV.

Count Adolphe von Steinfeld was a warm-hearted, ardent-tempered young man, with fewer faults than might have been expected from one who had undergone so much of the spoiling process, as handsome young sons, heirs, who have no younger brothers to rival them, are usually exposed to.

It was decidedly a very strong proof of the goodness of his nature, that, before he gave himself up wholly and entirely to the "soft passion of love" for the beautiful Gertrude, he determined to find out whether the extremely probable circumstance of his new friend Rupert's having fallen in love with her also, might not already have taken place. This was the more generous, because he was quite aware that he would himself be considered as a match in every way desirable and proper, even for the heiress of Schwanberg, whereas he could not doubt that it would be quite sufficient for Rupert to be caught looking at her with the eyes of affection, in order to ensure his being turned out of his present paradise without an hour's delay.

But his perfect conviction that in thus thinking he made no mistake, had a precisely contrary effect upon him, from what it probably would have had upon most other people.

If he had believed himself as superior in talent, or even as superior in the less important advantage of good looks, as he truly believed himself to be the reverse, he would have been vastly more inclined to take advantage of it, even at the cost of sacrificing his newly-formed friendship to his newly-felt love; but the idea that, if both fairly weighed together, Rupert could only be found wanting in weight of metal, was repugnant to him, even though that metal was gold.

It required no great time to enable him to decide irrevocably against running the risk which might endanger the happiness of all, from any such rivalry; but it took him rather longer, before he could make up his mind as to what would be the best method

8

of proceeding, in order to ascertain whether, in truth, Rupert were as much in love as himself.

That he should have lived in the same house with Gertrude, and escaped being so, certainly seemed to him to be pretty nearly impossible; but, nevertheless, he determined to have better authority than this, before he decided upon what his own conduct should be.

The result of all his meditations on the subject, was his writing and sending the following letter :—

"MY DEAR ODENTHAL,

"Though we have so well managed our pleasant rides as to get more talk amidst our gallopings than, I believe, most people could have done, and though the friendship thus began between us took a very vigorous step onward during my unconscionably long visit in the Schwanberg library yesterday, I still feel that I want to know you better yet; and I am inclined to think that a good long *tête-à-tête* walk together, would be one of the most agreeable modes of attaining my object. What say you? I know that you are not such an idle, useless fellow as myself ...... I don't believe I should have liked you so well if you had been ...... It must be for you, therefore, to fix the day and hour that will best suit your convenience for our ramble ; I shall hold myself in readiness to meet you when and where you please.

     " Believe me,
       "Dear Odenthal,
         " Very sincerely yours,
           "ADOLPHE STEINFELD."

The receipt of this note surprised Rupert Odenthal a good deal, but it pleased him considerably more. He had been, for the last year or two of his life, much too busy a personage to have had any time to spare for day-dreams ; but, had he indulged in such, the offered friendship of such a man as the young Count von Steinfeld, would decidedly have been of the number.

But though his service was a very easy one, he felt at that moment more decidedly, perhaps, than he had ever before done, that he was not quite so free a man as he might wish to be. But ere he had positively breathed a sigh as he remembered this, he threw down his pen, with a smile, as he remembered, also, that it was to the lady of the castle, and not to its lord, that it was necessary to apply for permission to accept the very agreeable proposal which the note contained.

It was with a flushed cheek, and a brightly sparkling eye, that he approached his ever-kind patroness, and placed the note in her hand.

He had no sooner done so, than Gertrude, with her accustomed unchecked impetuosity, sprung from her own table to that at which her mother was sitting.

"It is not a secret, I suppose, mamma, is it?" said she, bending over her mother's shoulder, with the very evident intention of reading the note she held.

"Fie upon you! naughty Eve, as you are!" said her mother, laughing. "You may perceive it is addressed to Mr. Odenthal," she added, holding up the note so as to exhibit the address; and, therefore, it is Mr. Odenthal's permission, and not mine, which is necessary."

"Indeed, mamma!" said the young lady, bounding back to her accustomed place still more vehemently than she had left it; "I have not the very slightest wish to force myself into Mr. Rupert's confidence. Will it be more discreet for me to leave the room? Or will it do, if I go down to the very farther end of it?"

"Let me read it aloud, Rupert—shall I?" said the greatly-pleased Madame de Schwanberg. "Silly child as she is, I think it will give her almost as much pleasure as it does me; and I am quite sure it would, if she as well knew its probable importance to you."

She then read the note aloud, and addressing her daughter as she gave it back to Rupert, she said, "You see, Gertrude, that we are not the only people in the world who find Rupert an agreeable companion. But the messenger is waiting, my dear boy. Sit down and write your answer."

"But you have not yet told me, dear madam, what that answer is to be. What will you give me leave to say to him?"

"Oh, Rupert! if I were mamma, what a rage I should be in with you!" exclaimed Gertrude, with cheeks as red as scarlet. "Do you really think that mamma wants to make a slave of you? Don't you feel that you hate him, mamma? If I were in your place, I am quite sure that I should!"

"Not unless you misunderstood his application to me as completely after you had got into my place as you evidently do now, Gertrude," replied the baroness; "our friend Rupert might as reasonably be accused of being a slave because he opened a door for me, or offered me his arm in a walk, as because he consulted me as to the best time of appointing Count Adolphe to meet him."

8—2

"Oh! if that is all, mamma, it is all very right and proper; and, of course, I was a fool for supposing that Rupert could mean anything else."

"Suppose you name mid-day, to-morrow, Rupert," said the baroness, after meditating upon the subject for a moment; "and you had better say in your note," she added, kindly, "that we should be very glad to see him here to dinner afterwards, at four o'clock."

Thus authorized to return precisely such an answer as he wished to send, Rupert was not long in despatching his reply; and this being done, he quietly sat himself down to continue the employ-ment upon which he had been occupied when this agreeable interruption stopped him.

But Gertrude seemed determined to atone for her cross fit, by becoming so gaily frolicsome, as to render it impossible for any one within reach of the sound of her voice to employ themselves seriously.

"What is come to you, Gertrude?" said her mother, laughing with her, because it was impossible to resist her gaiety. "Upon my word, you give us reason to suppose that you are beyond measure delighted at the idea of seeing our agreeable young neighbour at dinner, to-morrow; and I cannot chide you for it, if you are, for there are very few people that I like so well myself, as this Count Adolphe."

"And I can go farther than that, mamma!" replied the young lady, with great energy; "for I can truly say, that I never in my whole life liked any one so much."

Her mother looked at her earnestly for a moment, and during that moment she certainly became more conscious than she had ever been before, that Gertrude was no longer a child.

But neither by look or word did she betray the discovery she had made, to either of her companions. She quietly resumed her own employment, and Rupert proceeded with his; but Gertrude had less command of herself, and might have been seen, if her companions had been at leisure to watch her, more occupied in plucking the feathers from her grey goose quill, than in writing with it.

Nothing intervened to interfere in any way with the projects which had been formed for the following day; and with exemplary punctuality to the hour named, the two young men met at the spot indicated by Rupert, in reply to Count Adolphe's note.

The meeting was joyously cordial on both sides, and they set forward on their projected ramble with as much satisfaction as if the pedigree of the one was precisely on an equality with the pedigree of the other.

For the first hour or so of their walk, it was Rupert who seemed to lead the conversation; and many interesting themes were touched, not one of which but might have furnished a wider scope for interesting discussion than many a morning's ramble could have allowed time for.

But at length, just as Rupert was waiting a reply to a somewhat bold speculation, Count Adolphe suddenly stood still, and darting off from the subject they were upon, he exclaimed, "What a lucky fellow you are, Rupert Odenthal! I envy you that library! I envy you the companions with whom you seem to live there! I really know no man living, whose existence seems to pass so exactly as I would wish my own to do. There is but one anxiety which could, I think, interfere to torment me in such a situation."

"And what is that, Count?" said Rupert, with a smile, as he thought of his right noble patron, the Baron von Schwanberg.

"Nay," returned his companion, colouring. "I assure you that the danger to which I am alluding has no mixture of jest in it. I do really and truly think, friend Rupert, that if I spent as many hours as you do in the society of the Baroness Gertrude, I should be in great danger of falling in love with her."

The sparkling eyes of Rupert again kindled into a smile.

"Were such an adventure to befal me," he replied, "I should most certainly consider it as a very terrible mishap; but I don't see why it should be so in your case."

"On account of the contiguous estates, you mean, and all that sort of stuff. Fie! fie! Rupert! I did not expect to hear such trash as that from you. Do you really think that I should consider my happiness ensured by being married to Gertrude, at the command of her father and mine?"

"No, indeed, Count Adolphe!" returned his companion; "I think no such thing. But neither do I think, on the other hand, that the well-pleased consent of both ought to be any drawback on your happiness."

"I did not exactly mean that, either," returned Adolphe, colouring more perceptibly than before. "All I should want or wish, would be, that they would let us alone. But what I want most particularly to know at this moment is . . . . . . whether you are in love with her yourself, Rupert?"

Rupert, in replying to this very important question, really and truly did all he could, both to look and speak seriously, as he answered, "No, my Lord Count. I am not!"

"Thank God!" exclaimed the young nobleman very fervently; "I am sure you would not deceive me, dear Rupert!" he added, "and, therefore, I welcome this very delightful assurance, with the most perfect conviction of its truth. But how you have escaped, is to me a perfect mystery! Tell me, Rupert, did you ever see any one whom you thought more beautiful?"

"I am almost afraid to answer you, dear Count!" said Rupert, casting down his eyes, and assuming an aspect of great solemnity; "but, at any rate, I will not take refuge in an untruth, in order to propitiate your favour. Yes!" he added, "yes! I have seen two people who, according to my judgment, are both handsomer than the Baroness Gertrude von Schwanberg." And here he stopped.

Count Adolphe raised his arms in an action of astonishment, but this was accompanied by a smile, which plainly proclaimed that his offence was forgiven.

"Go on!" said the Count.

Upon which Rupert meekly bent his head, and pronounced, in a deprecatory tone, "I think the baroness, her mother, is handsomer."

"And the other?" said Adolphe, with rather a contemptuous shake of the head.

"The other is a little girl, whom you have probably never seen, my Lord Count; for she is the daughter of a poor woman, who lives in the village of which my uncle Alaric is the priest."

"And you are not speaking in jest, Rupert?" said the young nobleman, gravely.

"No, indeed, I am not!" returned Rupert, with all the simplicity of truth. "As to our baroness at the castle, I scarcely ever look at her without thinking that she is the exact model of what a poet might fancy as the lovely sovereign of some enchanted land. Some of Spenser's descriptions remind me of her. I do not think her daughter will ever be so exquisitely graceful as she is...... And as to my little nymph of the fountain—for it is when fetching water from the fountain that I have generally seen her—she is more like a picture, or a dream, than anything made of flesh and blood. The eyes of your young baroness are very much like the eyes of her mother, and they are, therefore, exceedingly handsome; but you must see my nymph of the fountain before you can understand, *how* beautiful eyes may be."

"Yes!" returned Adolphe, rather solemnly; "eyes may assuredly be very beautiful; but what a providential arrangement it is, friend Rupert, that the judgment of the eyes of those who look, varies as much as the beauty of the eyes looked at. It is long since I felt as light-hearted as I do at this moment, for to tell you the honest truth, I was desperately afraid that you too might be in love with this peerless young Gertrude. And yet, my good friend, a moment's consideration ought to be enough to suggest the heavy fact, that although she may not be in love with you, nor you with her, yet nevertheless it does not follow as a necessary consequence, that she will therefore some day be in love with me! Nay, how do I know that I may not at this present moment, be the object of her peculiar dislike? Gracious Heaven! What a dreadful thought! And yet my common sense tells me that it is quite as likely that it should be so, as not...." And having uttered these terrible words, in a tone of unmistakeable sincerity, the agitated young man suddenly quitted the arm of his companion, and throwing himself on the turf beside the path, buried his face in his hands.

"It certainly is a strange choice, Count Adolphe, that has put it in my power to give you hope on such a subject as this," said Rupert, gaily throwing himself on his knees beside him; "but so it is, and that too, without any breach of confidence on my part. But when your letter to me was brought into the library yesterday morning, my ever kind friend and patroness, the baroness, expressed her pleasure at such an unequivocal proof of your amiable readiness to forget the distance which station places between us, and spoke of you generally, my good friend, in the terms which you so well deserve. Whereupon, the young baroness, Gertrude, blushing like a new-blown rose, exclaimed, with an earnest energy, of which I would fain give you an idea if I could, 'I can go farther than that, mamma; for I can truly say, that I never in my whole life, liked any one so much.' Does that satisfy you, Count?"

"Satisfy me!" exclaimed the delighted young man, springing up. "Did she really say this, Rupert? But I know she did, for you are incapable of deceiving me."

"Indeed I am, dear Count," replied Rupert, gravely. "If I know myself, I am incapable of deceiving you in any way; and trust me, in a case where your happiness is so deeply concerned, I would not only be true, but cautious also. But my memory has not failed me, dear Adolphe! She spoke the words with even greater energy than I have repeated them; and her mother was evidently conscious of this, for she positively started, and blushed too, almost as brightly as her daughter."

I will not attempt to describe the state of happiness produced on the young Count by this observation. He seemed to walk on air; nor was his reception, on returning to Schwanberg, at all calculated to check the hopes which it had created.

The baron was as courteous as a baron so very solemn could be; the baroness was all genuine kindness, and the blooming Gertrude went as far as it was possible for a well-behaved young lady to go, in making it evident to the guest that she liked very much to see him there.

CHAPTER XVI.

Once fairly convinced that he had no rival to fear in Rupert, and that the fair object of his passion was by no means disposed to frown upon him, the course to be pursued became equally hopeful and easy to the young lover. In the first place, as in duty bound, he requested a private interview with his father.

The Count von Steinfeld was in many respects an amiable and estimable gentleman; and if his attachment to his son (his only son) had something approaching to fanaticism in it, the fine qualities, and excellent conduct of the young man, offered a great excuse for it. The revenues of Count Steinfeld were very nearly, if not fully, equal to those of his neighbour, the Baron von Schwanberg; and his nobility as unblemished, though not, perhaps, of so high antiquity. The hopes of the young Adolphe, therefore, had nothing deserving the imputation of presumption in them; but there is so much of true timidity for ever mixed with true love, that it was not without trepidation that the young man presented himself before his father, to beseech his consent to his offering his hand to Gertrude.

Now the only feature in the business in the least likely to check the satisfaction of Count Steinfeld on hearing this proposition, was the recollection that he was himself but just above forty years old, and that his son was not yet twenty. His high rank

and ample fortune had produced in him an effect diametrically
different to what similar causes had produced on the Baron von
Schwanberg; for whereas the baron had found it so difficult to
discover a lady in all respects deserving the honour of being his
wife, that he had nearly reached the age of fifty before he accomplished it, the Count had fallen desperately in love when he was
about the same age as his enamoured son was now; and though
he could not plead his own example as a warning, for he had
been very particularly happy both as a husband and a father, yet
still he felt that there were some rational objections against such
very early marriages.

The first effect of Adolphe's solemn proposal was to make his
father laugh; whereupon the young man blushed still deeper than
before.

"Is there anything ridiculous, sir, in my selection?" said he,
with very considerable dignity.

"No, indeed, Adolphe!" returned his gay father, still laughing.
"If you have really made up your mind that you are in want of
a wife, I really do not think that you could have chosen better."

Somewhat mollified and consoled by this assurance, Adolphe
replied, almost with a smile; "Then may I ask why you laugh
at me?"

"Not at you, my dear boy...... My dear man, I mean. Not
at you, Adolphe! Your choice is an admirable one, in all ways.
I only laughed at thinking what a lot of dowagers there will be
in a few years, if your progeny follow our example."

"You were very fortunate, my dear sir, in meeting my mother
at an age, which was likely to ensure you a long life of happiness.
But at any rate, my dear father, my choice can involve no consequences which should lead you to object to it as imprudent in a
pecuniary point of view. The Baroness Gertrude is an only child,
and her father is already an old man."

"True! quite true, Adolphe," replied his father; adding, in a
tone which had nothing of jesting in it, "Woo her, and win her,
my dear son! Depend upon it your happiness shall find no impediments from me. If it be settled, as I think it should be, that
you should have an establishment of your own, I shall be ready
to double whatever income the baron may think proper to settle
on his daughter."

It may be easily predicted by what I have stated, that no time
was lost by Adolphe in ascertaining whether his friend Rupert
was right in believing that he had made a favourable impression
on the heart of the young Gertrude.

The dinner which had succeeded to their morning walk, showed her ever ready to listen when he spoke, and to show, moreover, by her replies, that she had listened with pleasure; and he deserved very great credit for the self-command which enabled him to say farewell when he left her, without uttering a word that might lead her to guess, that before he saw her again he would probably have asked, and obtained permission, from both their fathers, to kneel before her, and ask for her hand in marriage.

The interview with his own father, which has been already described, took place early on the following morning; and within half-an-hour afterwards, he was galloping over the three or four miles which divided the two mansions. He had the good luck of meeting his friend Rupert at the distance of a five minutes' walk from Schloss Schwanberg; whereupon he sprang from his horse, and throwing the reins over the saddle, he suffered the docile animal to follow him, while he profited by the meeting, by making Rupert understand that he came to offer his hand to Gertrude with the full consent of his father.

"Bravo!" cried Rupert, joyously; "I wish you joy with all my heart, for I am neither so blind nor so dull as not to think our young baroness very charming, though not quite so beautiful as her mother. But we must manage a *tête-à-tête* for you at once, Sir Count, somehow or other, for the beauty of the mother will not atone for the inconvenience of her presence at such a moment."

"Good heaven! No!" cried the lover, in a tone which betrayed great perturbation. "Manage this for me, Rupert, and I will cause your name to be specially mentioned in the castle chapel the first day I am the master of it."

"Nay, traitor!" replied Rupert, laughing, "if you turn my own jokes against me, I will so manage as to bring the mighty baron himself to be present at the very moment you are making your proposal!"

A little coaxing, however, so effectually softened the heart of Rupert, that he not only undertook to promise that the baron should not appear, but also that he would invent some means or other of causing the baroness to leave the room immediately. It is not necessary to describe the gratitude of the lover on receiving this promise; suffice it to say, that it was kept, and that Adolphe Steinfeld and Gertrude Schwanberg very speedily found themselves *tête-à-tête* in the Schwanberg library.

The reception which Gertrude had given to the young Count upon his entrance, was by no means calculated to discourage him;

for it was with a smile, not only bright and beautiful, but too eloquently expressive of real pleasure to be mistaken.

The young man lost no time, but had explained the object of his visit, with equal eagerness and grace, within a few moments after the successful manœuvring of his friend had placed him *tête-à-tête* with the young baroness.

Getrude, too, on her part, displayed more self-possession and propriety of demeanour during these agitating moments, than might have been reasonably expected from so young a girl. That they WERE agitating moments, was proved by the deep blush which suffused her beautiful face, and by a tremor in her voice, which reduced it almost to a whisper.

"Your attachment, Count Adolphe," she said, "would do honour to a much worthier object than such a childish creature as I am; but my esteem for you is too sincere to permit my pleading my youth as an objection to your addresses; and I will say to you now, what I am quite sure I should say, under similar circumstances, were I many years older. I was but seventeen my last birthday, Count Adolphe; but, if I were of full age, I should tell you that I refer you wholly to my father for your answer. It is not, believe me, because I have any doubts of your merit, or, on that point at least, any great doubt of my own judgment; but people of our station of life have duties to fulfil, which may not be neglected with impunity. My own case, as you must be aware, is a peculiar one. I have learnt, even from my dear mother herself, that my father's disappointment at not having a male heir has been bitterly felt by him; and I think that I can never be grateful enough for the tender affection which seems almost to have reconciled him to his disappointment. The only adequate return I can make for this affection, is referring myself implicitly to him on such an occasion as the present."

"May I see him now?" said the impatient young man, more inclined to bless his noble birth and broad acres at that moment than he had ever been before.

Gertrude answered him with a blushing smile, which made him forgive the delay she proposed.

"No!—not to-day, Count Adolphe! Depend upon it, I know best. Let it be to-morrow, at this same hour, if you will: and even *so*, he may think you, perhaps, over-hasty. Oh! what a little time ago it seems since we were both children!"

"And do you really insist upon my waiting till to-morrow?" said the young man.

"Yes," she replied, holding out her hand, in token of farewell.

He saw that she was in earnest; and he not only took the hand, but ventured to kiss it, as he said, "Farewell, then, dearest Gertrude!—farewell till to-morrow!"

She turned her head only as she repeated this farewell. . . . But, on the whole, he was far from being dissatisfied by the interview; and never in his life before, had he contemplated with so much satisfaction the stately aspect of his father's noble residence as he did upon returning to it now, with the comfortable belief that the Baron von Schwanberg could not be insensible to its splendour, or ignorant of the ample revenues by which it was sustained.

No sooner had the door of the library closed behind him, than Gertrude reseated herself, with the look and manner of one who had been sufficiently agitated to make solitude and repose very welcome. She did not, however, permit herself to enjoy either very long, but, hastily rising, began seeking amidst the miscellaneous objects which covered her own particular table, and selecting from them a very tiny volume, put it into her pocket, and left the room.

CHAPTER XVII.

It was to the apartment in which her father generally dozed away the interval between his heavy breakfast and his before-dinner ride, that Gertrude now betook herself; and, although he certainly looked more than half asleep, she approached him with a sort of resolute step, that plainly showed that it was her purpose to arouse him.

"Are you at leisure for me to talk to you a little, papa?" said she; "for I have something I want very much to say to you."

"I am not quite sure that I could find leisure at this moment to converse with any one else, my dear Gertrude; but you well know that I always contrive to find it for you."

"I well know, my dear father, that you are always kind and indulgent to me, even when I come to you like an idle child, to talk to you for my own amusement. But the case is different now. I am come to tell you, even before I mention it to my mother, that the young Count Adolphe von Steinfeld has made me an offer of marriage."

"You have behaved, as you always do, with the greatest possible propriety in bringing this intelligence to your father, to the head of your own noble house, Gertrude, before you communicated it to any one else. I am sorry," he added, after a pause—"I am sorry, Gertrude, that the young man has not shown an equal sense of what was due to me on such an occasion. However, I presume he must be forgiven on the score of LOVE. I am quite ready to believe, Gertrude, that he is too much enamoured to have entirely the command of his own judgment."

"You are very kind, papa, to judge him so leniently. I am quite aware that he ought not to have spoken to me on the subject till he had obtained your leave to do so."

"Right again, my dear, as you always are," said the baron, taking her hand. "I am proud of my daughter, and I have reason to be so. However, Gertrude, we must not be too hard on the young man, either. You are certainly a very fair excuse, my dear, for a little blundering at such a moment. Moreover, it is impossible that I can deny the value of the compliment he has paid you. The only son of my distinguished neighbour, the Count von Steinfeld, is a very great match for any lady. The estate is a very noble one, and perfectly unencumbered; and, moreover, it is contiguous to mine. The two estates, when united, would certainly make one of the finest properties in the country, my dear Gertrude; and I confess to you, that I think it would be difficult to find a more eligible connection for you."

Gertrude, who had seated herself, and was placed immediately opposite to her father, with her eyes fixed on the carpet, remained silent for a short interval after he had ceased speaking, and then, almost in a whisper, repeated the word, "*connection?*"

"Ah, Gertrude!" said her father, relaxing so far from his usual stately demeanour as to smile; "ah, Gertrude! I suppose your young heart is too much interested for the young man himself, to permit your giving a single thought to his position in life. Is it not so?"

"No! my dear father! no! It is not so," replied Gertrude, with a degree of earnestness that had something almost solemn in it. "Can you believe that *your* daughter can be so lamentably the slave of any passion, as to make her unmindful of the race from which she sprung? Can you forget the hours we have passed together, in which you have explained to me the pure nobility of your blood, and of the higher station still which the family of my mother holds? If *you* forget this, dear father, I do not; and so deeply have your words and your feelings been impressed upon my heart, that I believe myself utterly incapable of feeling for any man such an attachment as a wife ought to feel for her husband, unless he were one whom my pride might select as well as my love."

And then she stopped, again turning her eyes upon the ground, which, while speaking, had been earnestly fixed upon her father's face.

"When I listen to such words from your lips, my noble-minded Gertrude, it is like listening to the sound of my own thoughts!" replied the baron in a sort of ecstacy that positively made his lips tremble; "and deeply indeed should I despise myself, could I in the choice of a matrimonial connection for you, suffer any consideration of any kind to interfere with what we owe to noble blood and high alliances. But this young man, my sweet Gertrude, is a nobleman of high birth, nor do I remember to have heard that his race has ever been degraded by an ignoble marriage!"

"But has it ever been embellished, my dear father, by such alliances as I have traced in our own pedigree?" returned Gertrude solemnly. "Have I not myself heard you say," she continued in the same tone, "that instead of marrying early, as most men of your rank and fortune are apt to do, have I not heard you say that you waited till what is generally considered as an advanced age for matrimony, solely for the purpose of giving yourself an opportunity of improving your magnificent escutcheon? And how deeply do I feel indebted to you for this! There are bearings on the Wolkendorf shield, of which sovereign princes may boast with pride."

"You speak nothing but the truth, my daughter, in saying so," replied the baron, with the quiet but dignified demeanour of one conscious of merit of no common class.

"And while you acknowledge this, my dearest father," resumed the beautiful heiress; "can you not sympathise with the feeling which leads me to plead for *time*, before I engage myself to any man? When you remember how young I still am, I think you must allow that I have enough time before me to justify my pleading for some few years' delay, before I resign the dignified position I hold as your daughter and heiress, in order to become the wife of any man whose pedigree is less illustrious than your own."

"Admirable! admirable young creature!" exclaimed the baron, "most safely may you be trusted in this matter, and I do, and will trust to you implicitly. Fear not, Gertrude, that I should ever urge you to marry any one whose escutcheon you could not explain to your children with as good effect as I have explained mine to you. But are you quite sure, my dear love, that this might not be the case if you accepted the hand of Count Adolphe von Steinfeld? I really do not remember to have heard of any degrading alliance contracted by that family."

"Perhaps not, papa," replied Gertrude. "*Degrading* is a very strong epithet, and I confess to you that the mere fact of their not having degraded themselves by their alliances, would not be enough to satisfy me. I have sometimes thought, papa," she resumed, after a short pause, "I have sometimes thought, that I knew a way by which I could very easily decide whether any one who proposed to me, had any right to hope for an alliance by marriage with your family or with that of my mother."

"And what way is that, my noble child?" eagerly demanded the baron.

"Why, by just going carefully through the pages of the Almanack de Gotha. There is one member of your family mentioned in it about seventy or eighty years ago, I think, on the occasion of one of the daughters forming a matrimonial alliance with a relative of a reigning duke; and there are no less than three of mamma's remote ancestors, whose names are to be found there in the same way. Now it seems to me, that as I am thus honoured on both sides of my house, my name also ought to find its way, by means of marriage, into the same august memorial."

"I would, indeed, wish that so it should be," said the baron, solemnly; his whole form seeming to dilate as his daughter thus fed him with the food he loved. "I willingly agree to accept of this as a criterion. But are you quite sure, Gertrude, that our neighbour, Count Steinfeld, has never been happy enough to find his way to the pages of this ennobling record? His estate is a very fine one, and perfectly unemcumbered, which is a circumstance which, I believe, very often leads to advantageous marriages."

Gertrude did not immediately reply, but she put her hand into her pocket, and drew thence the tiny volume, which she had taken from one of the library tables.

"I have examined this book, papa, very carefully, from the first page to the last," she said; "and I pledge you my word, that the Count Steinfeld is not fortunate enough to have found a place there."

"Enough, my dearest love," replied the baron; "I have

pledged *my* word to you, Gertrude, that I will trust to your own discretion in this matter. You are as yet, as you well observe, extremely young; and with your birth and fortune, to say nothing of your rather striking personal attractions, I certainly feel that I need be in no hurry to part with my daughter."

"You have made me very happy, my dear father, by trusting me to my own discretion in the important business of marriage," she replied; "I shall not be in a hurry, dear papa! There is no reason whatever to render it desirable that I should be. *Your* daughter really ought not, child as she is in age, to be married to the first boy who may happen to fancy that he likes her; or to one who may happen to think that he should like to obtain possession of the Baron von Scwhanberg's castles and domains. We are very happy as we are, dearest papa! and if we are wise, we shall make up our minds to remain so for many happy years yet, unless, indeed, some one were to propose, who might place my name in this dear little book!"

"You deserve to be *my* daughter, my high-minded Gertrude; and I flatter myself that I am not altogether unworthy of being your father!" returned the baron, fervently.

"But you must not leave me yet, my beloved child!" he added, seeing that she had risen as if to quit the room; you really must tell me, and tell me precisely, my dearest Gertrude, in what way you would wish me to dismiss this young man. I should be very sorry to offend either him or his family. What you say about the Almanack is unanswerable; and God knows I am the last man in the world, my love, to disregard such an observation, made, too, in so truly noble a spirit! But it would be difficult to explain all this to him. What do you think I had better say, my dear Gertrude?"

"I am not very well versed in such affairs as yet, papa," replied the young baroness, gravely; "but the only child of the Baron Schwanberg is not likely to escape proposals of this sort; and, therefore, dear father, I would recommend you to decide at once, upon the manner in which you will think it best that your answers should be given."

"Certainly, my dear! certainly! Nothing can be more right and sensible than what you say. But it won't do, you know, my dear, for me to learn by heart a form of words about it, because it cannot always be the same, my dear Gertrude. For if you were the daughter and heiress of a king, you must be married at some time or other, you know; and then, my love, as your own good sense must tell you, the answer must be different."

"Yes, papa, I am aware of that," she replied, in the quiet accent which implies assumed conviction. "But we are agreed, you know, in thinking that there is no occasion for us to be in a hurry about it. A young lady in my position ought to be allowed time to see a little of the world, before she exchanges the immense advantages of such a position for any other . . . . . . less than regal."

"Quite true! Most perfectly true! And it is a sentiment worthy of yourself, my darling Gertrude! But still, you know, dearest, I should not exactly like to say *that* to Count Adolphe. Think about it, my love, and let me know the result of your thoughts. I know that I have very considerable command of language myself, but, nevertheless, I think you might be able to assist me."

"On such occasions, my dear father," replied Gertrude, looking a little alarmed; "I should think the most concise method would be the best, and I am quite sure it would be the kindest. It will be quite enough to say that you cannot accept his proposal, and that you hope he will very soon forget having made it; for that you should be extremely sorry to lose him as an acquaintance and friend, and so would your family also."

"Well then, my dear love, that is just what I will say; and it sounds so very civil and kind, that I think he cannot be offended."

"Quite impossible, dear papa!" replied Gertrude, moving towards the door with a quick step. "Good bye!"

But before she had passed through the said door, she was recalled by the voice of the baron, who, in rather a loud key, articulated:—

"Come back, Gertrude! Come back for one short moment, my dear love, I must beg of you! That won't quite do, either, Gertrude! It is so very abrupt, my dear child! So very much like what any other person might say—any ordinary person I mean—and, therefore, you see, my dear, I don't think it can be quite the proper thing for me to say."

Gertrude, of course, stepped back, as in duty bound; but she looked exceedingly vexed.

"Then if you cannot find words to refuse him, papa, I suppose I *must* marry him, notwithstanding all the reasons I have assigned against it."

And again she turned to leave the room.

"No, Gertrude! No!" said the baron, in his most pompous tone. "It shall never be said, that I gave my daughter and sole heiress to a man I did not approve, solely because I did not know how to refuse him. Give me that little book, if you please. My best answer will be, the holding this book in my hand, and saying (after I have expressed a great deal of personal regard for him): *No man, Count Adolphe, can become the husband of my daughter with my consent, whose family have not yet found a place here.*"

Gertrude blushed to the very roots of her hair, as she listened to him; and for some seconds she remained perfectly silent. She then drew a long breath, as if she had struggled with herself, and had conquered some feeling which had impeded her reply; and then she said, "Yes, papa. Perhaps that would be the best answer you could give."

And having said this, she waited for no farther rejoinder, but hastened back to the door, and left the room.

<hr>

CHAPTER XVIII.

Before that eventful day was over, Count Adolphe contrived to seek, and to find his friend Rupert.

The painful state of suspense in which the reply of Gertrude, and her reference to her father, had left him, could in no direction have found anything so nearly approaching relief and consolation, as in the long walk through the neighbouring forest, which they then took together. Rupert was still sanguine as to the answer he was likely to receive; but the lover himself was much less so.

"In some respects you ought to know her a great deal better than I do," said the anxious Adolphe; "and yet I think, that as concerns the all-important question, it is I who am right, and you who are wrong."

"It may be so, dear Count," replied Rupert, gravely; "for most surely I have little, or rather no means of judging correctly on such a subject. What I told you, however, was perfectly true. I can, at least, be certain, as far as having accurately repeated the words I heard her say about you. Farther, dear friend, I cannot go; for if words are uttered with two meanings, I think I am quite as likely as you can be to give them the wrong interpretation, instead of the right."

The most anxious hours, however, pass away as rapidly as the most delightful ones, if we could but teach ourselves to believe it; and though the interval appeared immeasurably long, the moment for appearing before the august Baron von Schwanberg seemed to have come all too soon, when it arrived at last. Count Adolphe was, upon most occasions, a very fearless, stout-hearted young man; but, despite his valour, he was very considerably agitated when the moment arrived at which he was to request admission to the presence of the always sublime, but now positively awful, Baron von Schwanberg.

But having made this request, he was at least spared all farther waiting; for he was at once shown into the room in which stood the most luxurious arm-chair which the mansion could boast, and which, therefore, had long become the favourite dozing room of its master.

He rose from his chair as his young visitor approached, and extended a hand to him with so very condescending a bow, that the Count Adolphe felt his hopes most agreeably strengthened; and it was, therefore, with more firmness and courage than he had himself dared to hope for, that he avowed his attachment, and besought permission to offer his hand to the young baroness.

Nobody who had been half-a-dozen times in the company of the Baron von Schwanberg, could doubt that the first words he uttered would be prefaced by a sonorous " he-hem!" and the sound of this, on the present occasion, though it had, perhaps, something rather more than usually solemn in it, did not, therefore, greatly dismay the young suitor; but when it was followed by the drawing from his pocket a richly bound little book, which he held between his hands, and bowed over, with a sort of mysterious reverence, the young man knew not what to think, and almost began to doubt whether he had made himself clearly understood.

At last, however, the great man spoke, and uttered these words :

"No man, Count Adolphe, can become the husband of my daughter, with my consent, whose family have not yet found a place here."

Now, it is certainly extremely probable that the majority of highly-born young Germans know the Almanack de Gotha by sight, for it is, in its ordinary form, a queer-shaped little book, and easily recognised ; but it so happened, that Adolphe Steinfeld did not recognise it; and he stared at this strange, and to him perfectly unintelligible appeal, very much as if the noble baron had answered him in Greek.

9—2

A silence, which appeared alarmingly long to the lover, followed; but as he happened to have so expressive a countenance that even the slow baron perceived that he had not been understood, this silence rather assisted the *dénouement* than delayed it.

"Is it possible, young man," said he, "that you do not understand me? Is it possible that you do not know this book when you see it? This book, sir, is the 'Almanack de Gotha!'"

"Oh, yes, sir!" replied Adolphe, "I have often seen it. But what has that book to do with the business which has brought me here? Surely I have not made myself understood."

"Pardon me, Count Adolphe von Steinfeld! You have made yourself very clearly understood; and it is now necessary that I should make myself equally intelligible. Perhaps you are not aware that this volume, small as it is, contains not only the pedigrees of all the reigning dynasties of the earth, but records also the names of all those noble persons who are in any way connected with them? Both my own family, and that of the noble lady my wife, may boast of this honour; and no man, as I had the honour of telling you before, can become the husband of my daughter, with my consent, whose family have not found a place HERE."

Count Adolphe looked at him steadily for a moment. Perhaps he was speculating upon the possibility of his being in jest; but if this idea occurred, it did not last; for this moment being past, the young man thanked him for having spared him the annoyance of uncertainty, by the unconquerable nature of the obstacle to which he had referred; and then, taking his hat from the table on which he had placed it, he made a low bow, and left the room.

He paused for a moment in the great hall, to decide whether he should ask for his horse . . . or for his friend, Rupert. At length, however, he decided upon the latter; and having made his presence known by aid of the door-bell, he said he should be glad to see Mr. Rupert Odenthal, if he were at leisure to come to him.

"The Herr Rupert is in the library, my Lord Count," replied the servant; "shall I show your Lordship thither?"

"No!" replied the rejected lover, rather abruptly. "I wish to see him here, if he can come to me."

On this, the servant disappeared, and Rupert obeyed the summons which had been conveyed to him, with as little delay as possible.

"Can you walk with me part of my way home, Rupert?" said Count Adolphe. "If you can, I shall prefer walking, and will send a servant hither for my horse."

"Certainly, I think I can walk with you," replied his friend; "but wait a moment, while I say one word to the baroness."

"I had rather *not* wait here, my good friend," replied the Count, with a smile. "I will go walking on slowly towards home, and you will follow me, if you can."

Whereupon Rupert gave an assenting nod, and they parted; but, within five minutes after, Adolphe heard a step behind him, whereupon he turned round, and in another moment the two friends were slowly proceeding together, linked arm-in-arm, the one speaking, and the other listening, in a way that showed them both to be very deeply interested in the subject-matter of the discourse.

"Good day, Rupert!" were Adolphe's first words.

Rupert nodded his head in reply.

"I am cured, Rupert," was Adolphe's second speech.

"The devil you are!" was Rupert's reception of this, uttered in a tone of dismay.

"How much the devil may have to do with it, my good friend, I am not certain; but not much, I should think, for, altogether, the work is a good work, and I am my own man again."

"Explain! dear Adolphe, explain! Do you mean to say that you are no longer in love with the Baroness Gertrude?"

"Perhaps I begin to doubt if I ever was very much in love with the daughter of our thrice-noble neighbour; perhaps you are right, and that the fact of this unfortunate young lady's being the daughter of that insane old booby, is, and ought to be, reason good against any one being in love with her."

"I never said so, Count," replied Rupert, in a tone of indignation. "I think her very charming, and I know her to be very excellent; but one cannot—at least, *I* cannot—fall in love with the first pretty and good young lady that one sees. But this is all idle wandering. Do tell me, and in an intelligible manner, if you can, what has happened to you."

"I will, *if I can*," replied the Count; "and the condition is but reasonable; for how is a man to make that appear intelligible in relation, which, when it occurred, had the very closest resemblance to a sort of obscure insanity? . . . But wait a moment, Rupert, and I will act the scene, and this will give you a clearer idea of what has just passed, than any narration of mine could do. . . . Now, then, just sit you down there, upon that fallen tree, and I will sit down upon this one. . . . You don't happen to have a book in your pocket, do you, Rupert?"

"The chances are in favour of it," replied the young librarian, laughing. "You know my vocation, Count! Some of them generally stick to me, if they happen to be small;" and, so saying, he thrust his hand into his pocket, and drew thence a miniature edition of "La Fontaine's Fables."

"Selected by Fate, on purpose to assist my exhibition!" cried Adolphe, seizing it. "Only you must be pleased to fancy it a great deal more thick, and a good deal more stumpy. So! Now, then, remember, if you please, that you are the enamoured Adolphe von Steinfeld, and that I am the noble Baron von Schwanberg."

"Go on!" said Rupert, placing himself in the most touching attitude which the seat assigned him would permit, and assuming an expression of countenance admirably calculated to suggest the idea of a mental struggle between Love and Reverence, Hope and Fear.

"Yes!" exclaimed Adolphe, "that is the way I looked at him —at least, I hope so—for that is the way I intended to look. But, now, mark me! I flatter myself that you perceive at once my utter contempt and indifference for you and your looks. My thoughts are here, sir; here, in this sacred little stumpy volume, which is neither more, nor less, than the 'Almanack de Gotha,' and thus I declare my will. . . . *No man shall ever marry my daughter, with my consent, whose family have not found a place here.*"

Rupert sprung from his pathetic attitude, and indulged in a hearty burst of genuine laughter.

"Are you in earnest, Count?" he said, when he recovered the power of speaking.

"Most perfectly in earnest, my dear friend," replied Adolphe; "and now, I presume," he added, "that you will not wonder at my not wishing to delay my departure from the castle longer than was absolutely necessary."

"That you should wish to get out of his way, if only to enjoy the laugh which I have enjoyed now, I can easily understand; but not that you should so suddenly have recovered from your tender passion as to run away from the object of it."

"My dear Rupert!" replied the young nobleman, very gravely, "I certainly think the Baroness Gertrude von Schwanberg a very beautiful girl; and moreover, I have fancied, right or wrong I scarcely know, that she was more really intellectual, and more capable of being a rational companion, than any young lady I have yet seen. . . . But, be she what she may, my good friend, I would not take the daughter of that noble owl for my wife, if she were ten times more beautiful, and ten times more intelligent, than I thought her, when I galloped, with a lover's speed, towards Schloss Schwanberg this morning."

"You rather surprise me, Count Adolphe," replied Rupert, looking at him with very genuine astonishment. "I must confess that I am, except in theory, extremely ignorant of such matters; but I certainly had fancied that a disappointment in love, was a much more serious affair than you seem to make of it."

"Well then, I suppose it was only a fancy, and not a passion. But, at any rate, it works me and irks me no longer. I tell you I am cured, Rupert, and I am thankful! All I regret is the sort of shyness which I fear may arise between me and that dear library yonder; which means, being interpreted, that I shall not see so much of you, that I shall not be able to borrow so many books, and that I shall no longer have the refreshment of having freedom of thought justified, and made manifest, as you all seem to enjoy it there, without having the fear of priestly interference before your eyes. I am afraid I must lose all this, and I shall miss it greatly."

"I do not see the necessity for your losing it," replied Rupert. "Were I in your place, I should recount the whole affair to the young lady's mamma, with precisely the same frankness that you have recounted it to me. She is a sort of second providence, in my estimation; and I do not much think that anything could go on well, in our region, without her advice and assistance."

"Do you not think that Gertrude must have told her what passed between us?"

"She may have done so, but I do not feel certain of it. The young baroness only referred you to her father, I think?"

"Exactly so. She made no allusion to her mother," replied Adolphe.

"And how do you mean to communicate to the young lady the rejection you have received from her father?" said Rupert.

"I don't very well know," replied his friend. "I am half inclined to think," he added, "that she guessed what the result would be when she sent me to him."

"And even if she did," replied Rupert, "I do not see that you can blame her for it. She would not have been acting properly, according to all your noble notions, if she had taken it upon herself to reply either yes or no. Neither would she have mended the matter if she had referred you to her mother, for she would have known perfectly well that in that case her mother must have handed you to her father. Such being the immutable ultimatum in all such affairs."

"Yes, Rupert, I know it as well as you do, and I am a fool in affecting to believe that the poor girl had any alternative. Nevertheless, I am a true man, and a wise one too, when I tell you that I am cured of my love-fit; for I swear to you, by all that is beautiful, and all that is good, I would not consent to become the thrall and the son-in-law of this old Almanack, for all the pleasure that beauty and wit united could bestow on me."

"I am by no means surprised to hear you say so," returned Rupert, laughing, "for methinks I can understand your feelings as well as if I were a Count myself. Nevertheless, dear Adolphe, I still abide by my opinion, that in order to make this queer little affair of love, and the Almanack de Gotha pass off without any ulterior bad consequences, your best adviser will be found in the Baroness von Schwanberg. But here we must part, my good friend, or I shall leave myself no time to perform any part of the duty for which I receive wages, lodgings, and sustenance. But if you will come to the castle to-morrow morning, and enquire for the lady of the castle, I will undertake so to arrange matters, as may enable you to tell her all that has passed, and receive counsel from her unerring judgment as to the best method to be pursued in order to leave things as if the events of to-day and yesterday had not passed at all."

"I will in all my best obey you, sir," said Adolphe, gaily. "Contrive to manage this for me, Rupert, and you shall be my great Apollo, for most truly can I assure you that I wish for nothing more."

Rupert had not undertaken more than he was able to perform. His ever-kind patroness never threw any difficulties in his way when she perceived that he wished to consult her; and within a couple of hours after the deeply-offended Count Adolphe had received his dismissal from the baron, the baron's lady was made acquainted with all that had passed, save and except the private interview which had taken place between Gertrude and her father. But, as it happened, the omission of that one little scene produced neither obscurity nor uncertainty in the mind of Madame von Schwanberg. The drama went on perfectly well to its catastrophe without it. It certainly required some little effort on the part of the baroness to preserve her gravity as she listened to the description of the almanack scene; and no little praise was merited on the part of Rupert, for the tone of respectful solemnity with which he narrated it. But this moment of danger being happily got over by both parties, no difficulty whatever seemed to rest on the mind of the lady, as to the manner of bringing this foolish little affair to a conclusion, without leaving any very painful recollections of it behind.

"If I understand you rightly, Rupert," said she, "Count Adolphe will be made aware, before I next see him, that you have acquainted me with all that has passed?"

"Assuredly," replied Rupert. "It is by his express desire that I have made this communication to you, madam."

"And the advice which I shall give him will be this," returned the baroness; "I shall advise him immediately to obtain his very indulgent father's permission to travel for a month or two; and, if he follow my advice, he will visit us all after he returns, as if he had totally forgotten that anything of the kind had passed. Of course, Gertrude has told me of his abrupt proposal to her, and of the very proper manner in which she referred him to her father. It is evident to me, that she is much more disposed to forget, than to remember this silly fancy of our young friend; and I flatter myself, that Adolphe will easily be brought to follow her example."

"Indeed, I hope so," said Rupert, very honestly, but without deeming it proper to avow his knowledge that such was already the state of his mind.

Nothing, in short, could be more rational on all sides than the manner in which this juvenile fancy was permitted to evaporate and be forgotten. There was but one feature in the business which at all puzzled the sagacity of Madame von Schwanberg; she was a good deal perplexed to account for the baron's silence on the subject, and for some time she lived in daily dread of being summoned to a private interview, for the purpose of hearing of the very magnificent manner in which he had thought proper to reject the splendid proposal which he had received from their high-born and very wealthy neighbour.

Had she been aware that he avoided the subject himself, and had commanded his daughter to avoid it, from the fear that any discussion on the subject might have led to the discovery that the noble refusal, and still nobler manner of it, had not originally been his own suggestion, she would have understood his silence concerning it much better.

CHAPTER XIX.

THE conversation between the Baroness von Schwanberg and the Frau Odenthal, which was recorded some chapters back, had been forgotten by neither of them; nor was it likely that it should be; for they had both of them been deeply in earnest in the opinions they had then expressed; and though the subject had not been fully, nor even openly discussed, they had both made themselves sufficiently understood to have each created a lasting feeling of sympathy and esteem in the other.

But, to the regret of both, the intercourse so auspiciously began, and which seemed to promise so much mutual gratification and comfort, was suddenly and painfully checked by the earnest entreaty of Madame Odenthal's last surviving sister, that, as her son no longer required her presence in order to ensure him a comfortable home, she would make her long-talked-of visit to England.

As this letter, in addition to its earnest entreaties, brought also the pecuniary means of complying with them; the good woman aroused her courage, and set off for England.

Once there, she soon reaped the reward of her exertions, by perceiving that her presence was indeed a comfort to the affectionate relative she went to visit, and whose failing health certainly made her presence more useful there, than it could have been in the house of her brother Alaric, who since his nephew had been domiciled at the castle, had greatly less need of her *usefulness* than her invalid sister.

The letters which passed between her and her son, were long and frequent; and it was so evident from those of the young man, that the home he had found in the castle was in every way more advantageous than it could ever be in her power to make that of Father Alaric, that the idea that it *might be* necessary for her to return for Rupert's sake, soon died away, and was forgotten.

But though, in the case of her son, the weeks, months, and years, wore away without bringing any probability that he was likely to lose his present asylum, and return to the humble roof of his uncle, the case was different with herself; the sister of Madame Odenthal died, bequeathing to her all she possessed,

which, although amounting to no very large revenue, was enough
to ensure her the same peaceful home which she had so long
enjoyed under the roof of Father Alaric, and with the additional
comfort of being able to remunerate him for it.

The return of this very unassuming, but very excellent woman,
was hailed with joy, not only by her brother and her son, but by
that son's discerning patroness also, who welcomed her rather as
a greatly valued equal, and friend, than as the mother of a
dependent.

Nor did Gertrude appear in any degree to have forgotten her;
they had been great friends before the departure of Madame
Odenthal, and they became great friends again, immediately after
her return.

The situation of Madame de Schwanberg was in many respects
a very singular one. She was a very great lady; the mistress of
a magnificent residence, of a large, attached, and profoundly
obedient household; and her noble lord and master was almost
obsequious in his manners and address to her. Moreover, her
highly-favoured and highly-esteemed protegé, Rupert, contemplated her as the most admirable human being that it was possible
for nature to produce; and better still, her dearly-loved child
loved her in return, even as she deserved to be loved

Yet, with all this, the Baroness von Schwanberg had not one
single human being within reach of conversation, to whom she
did, or could with propriety, open her heart, upon subjects of the
greatest importance and highest interest.

Though of a Roman Catholic family, and, until the period at
which her early marriage took place, brought up according to the
usual routine and discipline of that church, the Baroness von
Schwanberg, in common with a vast number of quiet, meditative,
reading people, was no more a believer in the Roman Catholic
religion, than in that of Johanna Southcote.

But to a woman of sane judgment, placed in such a position as
I have described hers to have been, the idea of proclaiming, and
preaching a faith, in opposition to that professed by all around
her, would have been a mischievous, as well as a vain attempt.
She might have disturbed many spirits, without enlightening one;
and if this very rational decision had not sufficed to keep her
quiet, she would probably have been so from the habit she had
naturally fallen into, from the peculiarities of her noble husband's
conversational tone, of never uttering any opinions at all.

She had indeed much to make this quiet course easy to her;
for in the first place she was a very great lady, and in the next,

she was rather a sickly lady; and for one or both of these reasons, no one who had ever held the situation of confessor at Schloss Schwanberg, from the time she was installed as its mistress, had ever troubled her about any ceremonies either irregularly performed, or altogether forgotten.

And, indeed, upon the doctrine that man and wife are one, it would not have been reasonable for the spiritual director of the castle to complain; for its master delighted in ceremonies, as sincerely as its mistress contemned them; and as her offences were only those of very unostentatious omission, while his merits were of a nature and style precisely the reverse, it had never been considered necessary to take any notice of her peculiarities.

But although thus quietly permitted to think and to believe for herself, she had often wished to find some friend who could think and believe with her; and one great reason for her so wishing, arose from her doubts respecting the propriety of teaching Gertrude to feel the fallacy of the religion, to the ceremonies of which she had been accustomed.

The Baroness Schwanberg was perfectly aware, that, despite the unity of truth, and the ever clear difference between right and wrong, there might be such a dilemma as a divided duty; and, in truth, she felt that her own theories on the subject of religion were much better calculated to satisfy her own honest conscience, than to furnish a ritual for the guidance of her daughter. She was aware, too, that she was herself very profoundly ignorant of the value of the respective authorities upon which her own faith, and that of her husband, was founded; and she shrunk from the awful responsibility of deciding for her child on so very momentous a subject.

It is necessary so far to describe the state of Madame de Schwanberg's feelings on this subject, in order to make the pleasure she had felt from her brief communion with Madame Odenthal at all intelligible. She had no difficulty in perceiving that she was neither an ignorant, nor an ordinary-minded woman, and moreover it was very evident that she was an ENGLISH Protestant; and all this was quite enough to make the solitary-hearted lady of the castle look forward to frequent companionship with her, with a degree of satisfaction which, considering her station, would have appeared to the baron, could he have been made aware of it, as an unmistakable symptom of insanity.

But, unfortunately for his deeply disappointed wife, Madame Odenthal was summoned to her sick sister within so short a time after this promising conversation had taken place, that all hopes of renewing it seemed at an end.

Her absence had lasted nearly four years, nevertheless the interval had not been long enough to have caused her to be forgotten; and it was with very genuine and cordial satisfaction that she was welcomed by the baroness when she came to enquire for her health, and to thank her for all the kindness which had been bestowed upon Rupert.

There was now, to say the least of it, quite as earnest a wish on the part of the lady of the castle to converse freely with the mother of its librarian, as there had ever been ; but even now this was not to be achieved without difficulty; for, excepting when Gertrude was riding with her father, the mother and daughter were rarely separated; and as she might wish to converse on many points with her humble counsellor in a manner which might startle the still (ostensibly) Roman Catholic Gertrude, it was quite necessary to her purpose that they should be *tête-à-tête*.

It was not long, however, before a severe illness which attacked the baroness, furnished only too good a reason for her entreating Madame Odenthal to make the castle her principle abode. A violent cold, caught while taking shelter from a sudden storm in a barn, where she was exposed to a strong current of air, had attacked her chest; and she was ordered by her medical attendants to confine herself during the winter to the warm dressing-room, upon which her own apartment opened.

While submitting to this discipline, her malady seemed to abate, her cough become less troublesome, and the feverish symptoms less alarming; but although by no means of a complaining temper, she could not but confess, that the confinement was very irksome to her.

Gertrude implored very earnestly that she might share her mother's retreat; but as both father and mother declared that this could, on no account, be permitted, excepting for a stipulated length of time every day; she consented to the regulation, on condition that Madame Odenthal were invited to take her place in the sick room, when she was herself absent.

"If your papa approves it, my dear Gertrude, I will very willingly consent to this condition," replied the baroness; "she is very kind, and very gentle, and I shall like to have her with me extremely."

"Then that settles the thing at once," replied the baron, with an air of great satisfaction. "It is a very remarkable thing, my dear lady," he continued, addressing the baroness, with a very condescending smile ; " but by some extraordinary peculiarity of character, our daughter never does propose anything which does not, on examination, prove to be exactly the best thing, under the circumstances, that could be proposed. I have no doubt, that *race*, and *inherited* talent, have a good deal to do with this ; and it is a species of especial blessing, for which we ought to be exceedingly thankful. Indeed, I am by no means certain that it would not be proper to cause Father Alaric to make allusion to it, either on the *fête* day of our daughter, or any other solemnity which—"

"Indeed, papa, you do not know half Madame Odenthal's good qualities yet!" exclaimed Gertrude, (who, like a "chartered libertine" as she was, scrupled not to interrupt her grandiloquent papa now and then, when she fancied her mother would be spared something she did not like to hear thereby). "She knows so much! And then her being an Englishwoman is such a great advantage to me ; for though mamma speaks it, I believe, quite as well as a native, I do not profit by it half so much as I ought to do. But it is more polite, you know, to address Madame Odenthal in her native language."

"There again!" exclaimed the proud father ; "that is an idea quite worthy of a reigning prince, receiving an ambassador! "

"Oh! my dear papa! That is exactly what I should like to do!" cried Gertrude, clasping her hands, and speaking with great energy.

It would be impossible to do justice by description to the look of the baron as he gazed at her while she uttered this tirade. The reader may easily understand what was passing in her mind better than her mother could do ; for she, good lady, had never been initiated into Gertrude's mysterious passion for royalty, and for everything connected with, or approaching it. But her father, notwithstanding his constitutional slowness of comprehension, understood her thoughts perfectly, and in his heart of hearts, he breathed "Amen!"

CHAPTER XX.

THE proposal made by Gertrude, that Madame Odenthal should take up her residence at the castle, was immediately acted upon; and evidently to the great satisfaction of all the persons concerned. The idea of being useful to the benefactors of her son, would have made a much less agreeable proposal welcome to Madame Odenthal herself; and as to Rupert, he only felt that the state of things thus suddenly brought about, so completely realized all his fancy could have suggested, had that faculty been taxed to sketch what he could have most desired; that he almost feared he was dreaming, and should wake, and find that " there was no such thing."

Gertrude, of course, was pleased, for the scheme was her own; and as for the poor baroness, she felt that the gratification of the wish, so long delayed had come to her at a time when it was infinitely more valuable than it could have been at any other.

But, notwithstanding all this measureless content on all sides, an event was threatening, and even fast approaching, which was prognosticated by none, save Madame Odenthal; and even by her it was anticipated as a calamity by no means likely to occur soon, but only as a too certain termination of the insidious malady she was watching.

But it was the baron, whose astonishment appeared to be as great as it was possible his grief to be, at hearing that the consort of the reigning Schwanberg had actually departed this life before she had fully accomplished two-thirds of the age which he had already reached!

The only relief he found in this amazed state of mind, was from the conviction, which was the result of long meditation on the subject, that it was greatly more likely that his daughter, who so strikingly resembled him in the powers of her intellect, should resemble him also in longevity, than that she should unite her mother's physical weakness to his own intellectual strength.

Having, by the force of reasoning, brought himself to this conclusion, he determined to bear—and he did bear—his loss with every appearance of the most heroic philosophy.

The brave-hearted, stalwart Rupert wept secretly, as even a

stout man may weep, who feels that he has lost a friend to whom the whole world could never, in his estimation, show an equal; and the young man's mother forgot her own grief, as she watched and comprehended his.

But who can paint the feelings of the miserable Gertrude? She meditated, day and night, upon her own condition, and felt that she was a wreck.

The contrast between the characters of her father and her mother, would have taught her to feel, if nothing else had done so, the beautiful, the brilliant, the estimable, and the loveable qualities of the latter. She felt too, that in her own nature, there was a leaven that might be likely enough, now she had lost her, to change all that was good within her, to something greatly the reverse. These were points in her character which the influence of her mother had rendered comparatively harmless, but which poor Gertrude felt might master her, now that the restraint was removed which had come in a shape too dear to be resisted; for she had loved, and hugged, the chain which had restrained her wilfulness, with too deep and true affection to render it at all likely that she would ever break it.

But now! . . . . . .

Without a metaphor, the poor girl trembled as she looked forward, and thought of all the perils which were likely to beset her.

Her adoring father, her watchful companion, Madame Odenthal, her kind friend Rupert, ay, and every servant in the castle, looked at her pale cheek and altered eye, and pitied her.

But there was not one among them who had any true notion of the real state of her mind, or the degree in which she suffered. They were, however, all right in one opinion, which the experience (greater or less) of each enabled them all to form; for they all consoled themselves by the conviction that this depth of sorrow could not last for ever . . . "for, if it did," as the old housekeeper very justly observed, "the young lady must needs follow her mother to the family vault; for nobody who knows anything about what could kill, or what could cure, would be fool enough to doubt that die she must, if she went on long in that fashion."

And Gertrude did not die; for harvest does not follow seed-time with more benignant certainty, than that mysterious process takes place by which the suffering caused by the death of those we love, is healed.

There was, too, another power in action, by which Gertrude

was greatly assisted in her efforts to resume her former occupations; and this was a sort of self-esteem, or rather a longing for self-esteem, which she knew she could only obtain by conquering the heart-sinking despondency which had beset her; for, as her solitary musings most truly told her, it was not only the piercing grief for her mother's loss which had thus broken her spirit, but a selfish and cowardly feeling about her own welfare.

"If, indeed," she inwardly exclaimed, "I am so utterly incapable of guiding myself, I am both unworthy to live, and unworthy to call myself her child. But, God help me! I sometimes think that I hardly know right from wrong!"

Once awakened, however, to the necessity of deciding this tremendous question for herself, her energy and her health returned; and whatever blunders she might make, or whatever other risks she might run, that of prematurely entering the family vault was not among them.

This amendment in her health and spirits did not take place without her being fully conscious of it; and she rejoiced at it, not only as a relief from suffering, but as a proof that she was neither too weak nor too wilful to conquer a state of mind which she knew was pernicious to her welfare.

Pretty nearly the first use that she made of her recovered activity of mind, was to set about arranging such a scheme for her domestic life as might ensure her that nearly first of blessings, a perfect command of her time, and yet surround her with such an appearance of domestic surveillance as might set gossip at defiance.

But how was this to be achieved? How was she to obtain the personal and intellectual freedom so indispensable to the happiness of such a mind as hers, and yet preserve the external appearance of living under the influence of such authority as a young girl of seventeen ought to acknowledge and submit to?

But, difficult as the question certainly was, her first thought solved it, though in a way that few besides herself, if placed in the same situation, would have ventured to propose.

Her first thought suggested the idea that, of all the persons she had ever seen, Madame Odenthal was the only one whom she should like to have with her, in the three-fold capacity of governess, companion, and chaperon.

When the humble position in which she had been accustomed to see Father Alaric's sister was considered on the one side, and the inordinate love of everything precisely the reverse which

10

constituted the master-passion of her father, was contemplated on the other, it is difficult to understand how she ever found courage to attempt so desperate an undertaking as the convincing the Baron von Schwanberg that the most proper person he could select to superintend the important business of completing her education, and, subsequently, the more important business still, of acting as her chaperon in society, was the quiet-looking Madame Odenthal.

But the young Baroness Gertrude being very decidedly of opinion that she should prefer this arrangement to any other that suggested itself to her, she determined, without a moment's hesitation, that the attempt should be made.

Whether the confidence she felt that she should succeed arose chiefly from her knowledge of her father's character, or from the consciousness of her own, may be doubtful.

It would be long to tell, and needless too, how she contrived to place the question before him, so as to make all that was really in favour of it convey to his mind not only its own rational weight, but with it an ingenious superstructure, speedily constructed after such a fashion as to touch his monomaniacal passion for being supreme.

She painted, with an eloquence which positively made him shudder, the possible, nay, the probable airs of authority which such persons as were usually selected for such a situation were likely to assume; and, at length, summed up her pleadings by saying, "If you and I, my dearest father, were, in our characters and views of life, more like the generality of those we see around us, it would be well for us to select for this situation a person who might be supposed capable of adding dignity to our establishment; but, as it is, it appears to me that all our dignity must emanate from OURSELVES."

There was something in the manner in which the young baroness spoke these words, as well as in the words themselves, which completely overpowered every objection. They seemed to find a thrice-repeating echo in his heart.

In short, the cause was won; and all that Gertrude had left to do, in order to have this important affair settled exactly in her own way, was to persuade Madame Odenthal to undertake the performance of duties for which she knew herself, poor, dear woman, to be most particularly unfit.

But here again Gertrude proved herself equal to the performance of a very difficult task, and she set about it, too, with considerable ingenuity, and with a variation in her method which proved her to possess considerable insight into other characters besides that of her father.

Nor was she, on this occasion, under any necessity of affecting what she did not feel, which, to do her justice, was a great relief to her. She painted her own situation very nearly such as it really was, described the heavy charge which the loss of her mother had brought upon her, with equal truth and feeling, and concluded her appeal by quietly desiring her humble, but sympathising friend, to paint to herself what her condition would be, if, upon her refusing the situation thus offered to her, her father should take upon himself the task of choosing another to fulfil it.

Both Gertrude and Madame Odenthal, with equal propriety and good feeling, avoided all broad allusions to the peculiarities which might be likely to render his selection a source of suffering; but she ended this appeal by saying, "Remember what my mother was! Remember how she loved me!—and remember, too, as freshly as I do, how she loved you! And having dwelt a little on these thoughts, refuse, if you can, to come between me and the suffering which must fall upon me, as the inevitable consequence of such refusal."

The eyes of Madame Odenthal filled with tears, as she looked at, and listened to, her.

"I am afraid you know, my dear," she replied, "that I have not strength of mind enough to refuse you; and, in truth, it is only my belief in your having greater firmness than myself, which can at all justify my yielding. It is you, dear child, who must teach me the way I am to go, and not I who must teach you. Of course, I am not alluding to any matters of importance, for, on such points, I do truly believe that there can never be any difference of opinion between us. But it is concerning all matters of etiquette that you will find me so utterly ignorant as may, I fear, be very inconvenient to you."

"I have no doubt you are right, Madame Odenthal," replied Gertrude, very frankly. "The probability of this inconvenience has not escaped me; but having been very ceremoniously brought up myself, I have all the routine of ceremony at my fingers' ends; and if you, my dear Madame Odenthal, will condescend to learn from me the recondite mysteries of entrances and exits, and when to walk forward, and when to walk backwards, and all the ingenious varieties of bowings and bendings, from the angle which threatens absolute prostration, to the rapid little miniature dip, skilfully imitated from the graceful curtsey of a jointed doll,—if

10—2

you will first give your whole heart and intellect to this branch
of aristocratic learning, you will find all the rest extremely easy.
You will have, indeed, to put your fingers in a particular angle
at the distance of about an inch from your lips, and make them
perform a sort of pantomimic manœuvre, which means, by being
interpreted, a vast variety of both courteous and affectionate
greetings. But, in short, my dear, kind friend, if you do but
love me well enough to put your common sense upon the shelf
for a few moments, now and then, while I am exerting my somewhat dormant energies in giving you lessons in the *fine* arts, I
have not the slightest doubt that we shall both of us be admired
as most distinguished individuals, wherever we go."

There was really as much truth as playfulness in all this; and
when the grateful and kind-hearted Madame Odenthal had once
made up her mind to believe that by accepting the situation
offered to her, she might really contribute to the comfort of the
motherless Gertrude, there were no more difficulties to be conquered.

Gertrude very faithfully kept her promise, and became an
admirable mistress of forms and ceremonies; and, as the tall
slight form of Madame Odenthal, and her fine features, were
happily the reverse of everything described by the tremendous
epithet, *vulgar-looking*, the wilful heiress not seldom congratulated
herself upon the undaunted courage she had displayed in venturing
to select for her chaperon, one of the very last people in the
world, whom any one living in the world (but herself,) would
have thought of installing in such an office. And yet, it is very
possible that she selected the only person who could have filled
it, without becoming, in some way or other, an annoyance to
her.

<hr>

CHAPTER XXI.

The clever train of argument by which the young baroness had
contrived to convince her father that he assuredly had the power
of making any one great, whom it was his will to declare so, had
proved very perfectly satisfactory; but nevertheless he was, as
he privately confessed to his daughter, a good deal surprised at

the appearance of Madame Odenthal, on the first occasion that he saw her officiate in full dress, as her companion and *dame de compagnie.*

The mournful period of strict domestic seclusion being over, Gertrude, who knew her father well, had determined to profit by this first occasion, in order at once to produce the effect which she felt might be of so much serious importance to her future comfort.

The baron had invited a rather large party of noble neighbours, in honour of the highly distinguished guest of one of them, who had favoured the neighbourhood with his presence, for the purpose of enjoying the field sports for which it was celebrated.

As Gertrude had no intention of introducing Madame Odenthal as a relative, there was no occasion for her being in mourning; but nevertheless the young lady in selecting her dress, the choice of which was referred with laughing indifference wholly to her, decided that she should wear black velvet, which, though not mourning, might pass as that of a distant connection, or very intimate family friend.

If Gertrude had been an artist, she could not have dressed her friend with more successful effect.

In a word, the wilful girl being determined that nothing should be wanting to produce the effect she desired, had contrived to make the poor, but still very handsome widow, look exceedingly like a somewhat reserved, but very pleasing woman of fashion.

In order to avoid the possibility of her father's betraying any inconvenient feeling of astonishment on first beholding the metamorphosis thus produced, Gertrude had contrived that the baron should be in her dressing-room when Madame Odenthal, according to promise, entered it in full costume, in order to know if the final arrangements of Teresa were approved.

The old gentleman's first movement was to rise from his chair, and make her a profound bow; but his next, which was produced by her venturing to smile as she perceived his mistake, was to stagger back to his chair, very much as he might have done if she had pushed him into it.

He speedily recovered himself, however, and as he was not a man to be long awed by the aspect of any nobility only accorded by Heaven, he said to his daughter, without any sort of ceremony, "I should wish to speak with you alone, my dear Gertrude."

Whereupon Madame Odenthal glided from the room with the very least delay possible.

"Upon my word, my love, this is one of the most extraordinary things that I ever remember to have witnessed," said he. "It certainly is *very* extraordinary! Very extraordinary indeed! I am quite aware that I *have* influence, my dear Gertrude, but I will frankly confess to you, my child, that I had no idea, till you pointed it out to me, of the sort of influence which it is evident I possess upon the appearance and manners of those who approach me."

"You see then, that I was right, papa, about Madame Odenthal. I felt quite sure that if you placed her in the situation she now holds in your family, a very short time would suffice to make her, both in manner and appearance, all that you would wish her to be."

"You were right in so thinking, Gertrude," he replied, with great solemnity; "and I have no doubt, my dear," he added, "that you were also right in the reason you gave for thinking so. You said, as I well remember, that I ought to be the source of dignity to those around me, and not to receive it from them."

"Yes, papa, and I think so still," replied his daughter, gravely.

Thus far everything had succeeded so perfectly according to the wishes of the young lady, that there really seemed to be some danger of her following her father's example, and fancying that her will was to be law in all things.

There was still, however, one more experiment to be made, before she could feel quite certain that her self-willed contrivances respecting the station which she wished Madame Odenthal to fill, would be approved by her son.

Rupert had never yet seen his gentle mother robed in black velvet, and looking like a duchess; and she had some slight doubts as to his approving for her, what seemed to have so near an approach to child's play. It was therefore not quite without a little nervous agitation that she awaited an occasion of this first dinner party, the moment of his entering the drawing-room.

She might have spared herself this annoyance, if it was one, by having contrived that he, as well as the baron, should see her in her robes of office in private. But, for some fanciful reason or other, Gertrude did not choose this, and, on the contrary, had made Madame Odenthal promise that she would carefully avoid his doing so.

It was not therefore till he entered the drawing-room, after the last guest had arrived, on the day I am describing, that this wonderful metamorphosis met his eye.

At the first glance he positively did not know her. He only

saw before him a very handsome, middle-aged lady of fashion; but when she met his gaze, he felt that it was his mother who smiled upon him, and he certainly felt also, that any man might be proud of such a mother.

And then his eye glanced, almost involuntarily, from her to the young baroness.

The glance which he met in return, seemed sparkling with a sort of happy triumph which was quite unintelligible, unless this wondrous change was her own work.

Gertrude had not intended that he should discover this, and had hinted as much to Madame Odenthal, who, on her part, had kept her promise of secrecy very faithfully, considering it only as a playful whim.

But though Madame Odenthal was faithful to her, she was not faithful to herself; for her sparkling eye, her brilliant colour, and her involuntary, but most radiant smile, revealed the secret.

Thus much it is easy to tell; but it is less so to explain why his discovery of its being the will, or whim, of the heiress of Schwanberg, to render his mother the most distinguished-looking person in the society, should produce so great a change in all his own feelings towards her.

The philosophical part of the world tell us, that we are all of us what circumstances make us; and this is true, if we go far enough back to look for the circumstances: but in the case of Gertrude, it was scarcely needful to go farther back than her own birth. Her mother was a very admirable person in many ways; and Rupert was quite sufficiently aware of this, to think it highly probable that Gertrude, also, would turn out to be an admirable person in many ways.

But, on the other hand, he was equally well aware of what her father was; and the occasional uncertainty of temper and demeanour, which he had for some time remarked in the great man's heiress, was easily, he thought, accounted for, by her equally near relationship to him.

But he found it very difficult to bring this theory to bear upon the whim which had now seized her.

That there was a strong mutual attachment between Gertrude and his mother, there could be no doubt. During the whole period of the baroness's illness, the thoughtful kindness with which each had sought to spare fatigue and suffering to the other, had been marked by him with equal pleasure and admiration. But her insisting upon it, that his mother should be made to look like a duchess, could have nothing to do with such feelings as were manifested then.

This new whim, certainly, was very puzzling; nor was the effect upon himself less so.

Why did he now, for the first time, discover that his friend, Adolphe Steinfeld, was right, in thinking the eyes of Gertrude not only more beautiful than those of her lovely mother, but very decidedly more beautiful, also, than those of the nymph of the fountain, or of any other nymph that benignant nature had ever created to embellish the earth?

It was a thrilling, and a very strange sort of sensation which shot though his heart, as the new-born doubt arose in his mind as to his long established belief, that Gertrude *inherited her father's pride.*

" Can I have been mistaken?   Can I always and for ever have been mistaken ? " was a question which, though only propounded by himself, produced a very powerful effect upon his spirits.

The party which was assembled that day at Schloss Schwanberg was rather a brighter one than usual ; for it so chanced that one of the baron's noble neighbours had with him a newly-married young couple, as guests, who were well calculated to embellish and enliven any party. The bridegroom was French, and the bride English ; and it had but seldom happened in that very noble neighbourhood that an evening was passed with so near an approach to social enjoyment.

Though the English bride spoke French with tolerable facility, she freely confessed, that she greatly preferred speaking English ; and upon hearing Madame Odenthal address her son in that language, she immediately placed herself beside her, and smilingly hailed her as a country-woman.

It is probable that people of all lands speak their own language more gracefully than any other ; and the English stranger, who was herself too lovely not to be an object of attention, soon made Madame Odenthal share this honour with her ; for the bride seemed very greatly to enjoy the pleasant *lang syne* recollections of her early English days, concerning scenes which the elder lady could report of quite freshly, from having visited them more recently.

While this was going on in one part of the room, the husband of the beautiful bride was vaunting with great energy in another, the extraordinary beauty of his lady's voice, boldly declaring, that she had no reason to shrink from competition either with the voices of Germany or of Italy. Whereupon, the young baroness

Gertrude so earnestly expressed her hope that she would kindly place herself at the excellent pianoforte, which stood ready for use in the middle of the room, that the proud bridegroom could not resist the temptation of insisting upon it that she should do so, and sing a certain English song, which, as he said, had greatly contributed to the good work of converting her into a French wife.

The pretty bride, who was really as free from all sorts of affectation as it was well possible for a pretty bride to be, made but a feeble resistance, and concluded her smiling remonstrance by saying, that if Madame Odenthal would sit by her, she would consent; for that she had a sad trick of forgetting the words of a song, and that in such a case she could only hope for help from a country-woman.

So saying, she passed her arm under that of the *dame de compagnie*, and they proceeded together to the pianoforte.

Her enamoured young husband had really said very little more in praise of her singing than it deserved; and she performed the song he asked for, not only in very good style, but without requiring the aid of her country-woman to prompt her.

The usual effect of such a performance, of course, followed, and Madame de Hauteville was earnestly entreated to sing again; and then, the genuine love of music being strong within her, she declared herself quite ready to sing again, provided some one else would sing also. Whereupon, Gertrude playfully and gracefully offered her services; and though her performance was by no means equal in excellence to that of her guest, it was good enough to deserve, and receive applause, as well as to justify the eager claim for another song, from Madame de Hauteville.

"Do you ever sing English, dear baroness?" demanded the bride.

"Alas! no," answered Gertrude. "I wish I did!"

"I wish so too, my dear, as in that case we might manage a duet together," replied Madame de Hauteville. "Is there nobody," she added, turning to Madame Odenthal, who was standing near her; "is there nobody here who could manage to sing *this* with me?" pointing, as she spoke, to a page which she had opened in a miscellaneous volume of music, which lay on the pianoforte.

Gertrude only answered by dolefully shaking her head; but Madame Odenthal smiled, and looked towards her son, who, with several others, was standing near the instrument.

The lively English lady caught the smile, and immediately interpreted it.

"That gentleman sings, does he?" said she. "Then pray present him, and I will try to persuade him to sing this duet with me."

Now it so happened, that during the whole of Rupert's long residence at the castle, nobody in it had ever heard him sing—for nobody in it had ever asked him to do so; but the fact was, that he had not only great love for music, but he had also a very fine voice, and though with little science, possessed sufficient taste to enable him to sing very charmingly.

His priestly uncle was, in the sacred line, a very good musician also, and possessed, German-like, a very tolerable pianoforte, by the help of which, he had not only taught his young parishioners to sing abundance of canticles, but had made his nephew a very tolerable musician.

As neither his mother, however, his uncle, nor himself, had ever conceived the idea that this very ordinary rational faculty could be of any essential use to him, he had been rather permitted, than encouraged to indulge it; and excepting occasionally in the long-day season, when he rose with the lark, he had rarely profited by the remote situation of the library, in which Gertrude's practising piano stood, in order to indulge himself by the sound of it.

But, notwithstanding all this well-behaved prudence, Rupert loved music quite well enough to enjoy exceedingly this very novel mode of passing an evening in the stiff drawing-room of Schloss Schwanberg. Nevertheless, he was a good deal startled by Madame de Hauteville's abrupt demand upon him, and for a moment scarcely knew how to answer her. The baron, indeed, was so completely occupied in explaining to the nobleman of the highest rank in the company the manner in which he administered the territorial laws of the domain around him, that Rupert was quite aware that he ran no risk of offending him, either by granting or refusing the request so eagerly made to him.

But the idea that either his mother, or Gertrude, should think he blundered in his manner of replying to this very unexpected demand, was annoying.

If the thing had happened the day before, it would have been the eye of his mother that he would have sought, in order to ask for counsel; but now it was not to her, but to the young baroness that his first glance was directed; and the appeal was answered by a look of such radiant satisfaction, and bright encouragement, that he had bowed his consent almost before he knew what he was doing.

So no more time was lost; the duet was performed in very

spirited and excellent style, and rewarded by the applause it deserved.

There is nothing, perhaps, which in mixed society tends so promptly to produce a tone of intimacy between persons otherwise strangers to each other, as music. Where the love of it is genuine, its attraction is quite strong enough to overpower many of the little repulsive etiquettes which stand in the way of easy intercourse with new acquaintance; and such was decidedly, and very pleasantly, its effect on the present occasion.

The evening, instead of being extremely dull, was extremely agreeable. Carriages, greatly to the astonishment of their coachmen, were made to wait, nor did the party permit themselves to separate till arrangements had been made for their speedily coming together again.

The only effect which all this was likely to produce on the Baron von Schwanberg, was an unwonted degree of fatigue; and such would very decidedly have been the case, had not the sensation of sleepiness been overpowered by the astonishment he felt at being addressed by some of the most distinguished among his guests, with earnest petitions to name an early day for returning their visit, and doing them the especial favour of inducing Madame Odenthal and her son to accompany him and his daughter.

Had the astonishment of the baron been a little less overpowering, there can be little doubt that his reply would have politely, but solemnly, communicated the interesting information, that Madame Odenthal being his daughter's hired companion, would certainly (with their permission) accompany her; but that her son, Mr. Rupert, being only his librarian and secretary, he could not think of taking such a liberty.

But he was far from being sufficiently in possession of his usual share of comprehension, to be capable of saying anything of the kind; all he could do was to stand in an attitude of graceful dignity, with his heels together, and his right hand spread upon his breast.

His silence, however, was construed into a most amiable assent; one or two early days were named by the different petitioners, which the young baroness was eagerly entreated not to forget, and so they parted—the well-pleased guests declaring that it was the pleasantest day they had ever passed at Schloss Schwanberg, and the entertainers feeling more disposed to retire to their respective apartments than to remain together for the purpose of discussing all that had passed.

"Good night, papa!" was all that Gertrude said, preparatory to her leaving the room.

The words seemed to rouse the baron from a state that considerably resembled a dream; and being thus roused, he contrived to say, "Gertrude! come to me to-morrow morning, for a few minutes, before breakfast. I wish to speak to you."

"Yes, papa, I will," was her dutiful reply; and having uttered it she glided out of the room, followed by her *dame de compagnie*. Rupert had politely attended the departing ladies to their carriages, and did not again make his appearance in the drawing-room.

CHAPTER XXII.

FAITHFUL to her promise, Gertrude failed not to make her appearance on the following morning, precisely at the time and place at which she knew her father would be expecting her. His heavy, handsome features wore the look of firm-set self-importance, which was, indeed, the only expression, excepting that of weariness, which they were capable of assuming.

"Good morning, Baroness Gertrude," he said, awaiting her approach with an extended hand. "It is always a pleasure to me to see you, my dear, but particularly so just now, when so remarkable an instance has occurred to justify the opinion you lately expressed to me, concerning our present domestic arrangements in the drawing-room."

For a moment Gertrude employed herself in drawing forward a chair; an operation to which she gave too much attention to permit her looking in her father's face, as she replied, "I thought you would be pleased, papa, at the brilliant manner in which every thing went off yesterday."

"Of course, my dear, of course," he replied, with a stiff inclination of the head, that seemed intended for a complimentary bow. "There could be no doubt, I should hope," he continued, "that an entertainment given at my house, and at which myself and my daughter presided, would be a brilliant one. But the subject upon which I particularly wished to speak to you *now*, relates to other matters. You are certainly a very clever young lady, and possess a power of observation which I have no doubt is hereditary. But nevertheless it is scarcely possible, my dear, that you can, at your age, have arrived at that steady sort of observation which I now possess, and which you yourself already possess in no common degree, as you proved to me a month or two ago, upon an occasion which has, in fact, led to the results upon which I now wish to speak to you."

Gertrude was sitting at no great distance from the fire, the heat of which appeared to be oppressive to her; for almost without waiting till her father reached a full stop, she left her chair, in order to take from a distant table a newspaper, which she seemed to fancy would be useful to her as a screen.

"Pray, my dear, sit still!" said the baron. "I should not have desired you to come to me at so early an hour, had I not something of importance to say to you . . . . Do you remember telling me, Gertrude, at the time to which I allude, that the persons whom I permit to be habitually about me, ought to be such as would derive distinction from me, and not such as could, or might fancy they could, bestow it?"

"Oh! yes, papa! I remember our conversation quite well," replied Gertrude, appearing to find great relief from her newspaper.

"And yet, my dear, though this very just and proper way of thinking must have come into your head naturally, and merely, as I take it, on account of your being my daughter, I don't believe that your thoughts, clever as they were, ever made you expect to see what you witnessed yesterday. Did they, Gertrude?"

"Not exactly, papa," she replied. "But you know," she added, after the pause of a moment, "you know that when one mentions an idea, as I did to you in the conversation you refer to, it is only for the sake of expressing an opinion, and can have no reference to any particular circumstance."

"Of course, my dear, of course. I don't mean to say that you could have known beforehand anything about Madame de Hauteville. What I mean is, that, with all your natural family cleverness, I don't think you could have ever expected to witness such a strange scene as you beheld at the pianoforte yesterday. Did you, my dear?" said the baron, looking at her very earnestly.

Gertrude was at that moment in greater danger of seriously offending her father than she had ever been before in the whole course of her life, for she certainly did appear to be reading something in the newspaper. Fortunately, however, she raised her eyes, and perceived the indignant look that was fixed upon her, and which, doubtless, was like the lightning which precedes thunder—only a prelude to the voice of the storm.

"You puzzle me by your question, dear papa!" she exclaimed, with great quickness; "and I really scarcely know how to answer you. How could I, you know, before I had ever seen Madame de Hauteville—how could I guess the sort of impression the manners and appearance of Madame Odenthal were likely to produce upon her? Nevertheless, I certainly had a general idea, that if you chose to patronise your secretary's mother, all your acquaintance would think they were doing themselves honour by following your example."

These calming words produced the desired effect; the baron not only bent his head as a token that he acquiesced in her theory, but he almost smiled, as he added: "And not only his mother, but himself too, my dear Gertrude. Did you ever see anything so ridiculous as the fuss they made about him? However, *that* is *their* affair, you know, and not mine; and I cannot deny that there is something very agreeable in seeing such really distinguished people as those who were here last night, one and all of them, ready to fight for the honour and gratification of receiving a poor unknown boy at their houses, and his mother too, merely because I have thought fit to patronise them!"

"Yes, papa, it is gratifying," replied Gertrude, with that sort of quiet earnestness with which we acknowledge the feelings of which we may justly feel proud.

"I do assure you, my dear," resumed the baron, very solemnly, "that nothing can be farther from my heart, and from my character, than any wish to tyrannise over the society around me, many of whom, I am quite ready to allow, are of very true and pure nobility; but, nevertheless, I see no reason whatever why I should disdain the sort of homage which they all seem ready to pay me; and it is, therefore, my decided purpose to accept the earnest invitations we received last night, including in our family party, those, whose abode in my mansion has apparently ennobled, sufficiently to justify their being included in it."

In this, Gertrude very quietly acquiesced, merely observing that it was exactly what she expected from him, and that she quite agreed with him in thinking that he owed it to himself to sustain the dignity of the position in which it was evident his neighbours considered him to stand.

The immediate consequence of all this was, a few weeks of more frequent and more lively meetings than had recently taken place in the neighbourhood; and when the conclusion of the sporting season arrived, and dispersed them nearly all in search of metropolitan gaiety, in some land or other, the Baron von Schwanberg had acquired such a decided relish for the enlarged field of influence which, he fully believed, he had been enjoying, that, after secretly ruminating upon the subject for a quiet (not to say dull) week or two, he suddenly told his daughter that, having deeply considered the subject, he had come to the resolution of taking her to Paris.

The first effect of this very unexpected news on the heiress of Schwanberg was to make her suddenly look very pale; but before her father had time to be alarmed at this, her varying complexion changed again, and her colour became much brighter than usual; but she remained silent.

"Why do you not reply to what I have said to you, Gertrude?" said the baron, somewhat sternly.

"Because I was too much surprised, I believe, papa," she said; but she said it with so bright a smile, that he smiled too, as he added: "But I flatter myself that you are as much pleased as surprised, my dear."

"And more too, papa, if such a scheme should be really possible!" she replied.

"And why should you feel any doubt on the subject, Baroness Gertrude? Am I not generally found to be capable of doing whatever it is my will to do?" said he, with a sort of stern dignity, which made her feel that the subject was not a jocose one.

"Oh, yes! dear papa," she replied, with eagerness; "I am quite sure that if you choose to execute such a scheme, you will not only do it, but do it well. But, of course, there will be a great many things to be thought of and arranged, before such a journey can be taken. It won't do for you, papa," she continued, very gravely, and fixing her eyes upon the ground, "it will not do for you and me to go flying about the country quite like ordinary people. We must, of course, be attended by something like a *suite*."

"Of course we must, Baroness Gertrude," he replied, raising himself into the most dignified of sitting attitudes. "You cannot suppose that I have forgotten this. It may do very well for the De Hautevilles, who really are very elegant, fashionable-looking young people, to travel about, as I dare say they do, with a lady's-maid for his wife, and a valet for himself; but that won't do for *us*, Gertrude."

"Certainly not, sir," returned the young lady, with a look almost as dignified as his own.

"As to your personal attendants," he continued, "I shall make no objection whatever to your taking a second, if you think Teresa alone will not be sufficient."

"Thank you, dear papa! Teresa is a very good girl, but I don't want two of them," replied Gertrude, endeavouring not to smile; "but when you talk of a suite, I am sure you do not mean ladies'-maids and footmen."

"Oh dear, no!—certainly not—certainly not!" returned the baron, eagerly. "Madame Odenthal, of course, will be one of our suite, my dear."

"Of course, papa," she replied, quietly; "for, at my age, it would be quite impossible that I should appear in company without her."

"Obviously so—obviously!" returned the baron, raising his hand with an action which was meant to signify that this question was settled, and might be dismissed.

Gertrude bent her head in acquiescence, and said no more.

The baron, too, was silent; but it was evident that he intended to say more upon some subject or other, because, upon his daughter's making a slight movement, which he thought indicated an intention of leaving him, he shook his head, and made an expressive signal to her with his forefinger, which evidently meant that she was to stay where she was.

After this, her moving was, of course, out of the question, and she prepared herself to wait patiently for what was to follow.

The interval was not a very long one, though it seemed so, for he presently said: "And about myself, Gertrude. I really want your opinion, my dear, as to whom it would be most proper for me to take, by way of a *gentleman* attending upon my person. I will confess to you that I should not like this office to be filled by a mere stranger, for I have constantly observed through life, that the deference and respect which I wish to inspire, and which are so unquestionably my right, are not always felt *at once* by strangers when they first approach me. Such feelings are naturally the result of knowing me as I really am."

"I can understand that, papa, perfectly," replied Gertrude.

"I have no doubt you do. You are too clever, too much a Schwanberg, too much my own dear child, to be at a loss how to interpret it," replied her father, affectionately. "And this being the case," he continued, "it makes the task of obtaining such a person as I want rather difficult. It is absolutely necessary, you know, that he should have the appearance of a gentleman, as otherwise I should not be able, or, at any rate, I should not be willing, to let him follow me into the salons of any noble persons with whom we may become acquainted."

"Certainly not," replied Gertrude, with decision, and in the tone of one who knew perfectly well what they were talking about.

"I was sure you would agree with me, my dear, quite sure of it. But now then, you will observe," pursued the baron, "that our power of choice is very limited. In fact, my dear child, I can at this moment recollect only two persons who would be in any way proper to fill the office."

"Two?" repeated Gertrude, looking up at him with an aspect of considerable astonishment.

"You misunderstand me, my dear," resumed her father. "I do not mean that I wish to have two gentlemen following me everywhere, as a necessary part of my suite, but that I know only of two from which my selection can be made."

Gertrude bowed, in token that she understood him.

"Now the first who presents himself to my mind, is my confessor."

"Father Alaric!" exclaimed Gertrude, almost with a voice of dismay.

"Yes, my dear. I think Father Alaric would do extremely well. A priest, you know, is, or ought to be, always a gentleman; and Father Alaric is both too observant of my wishes, and too quiet in manner, to be likely to expose himself to any unpleasant observations."

Gertrude remained silent for a moment, and then replied; "What you say of Father Alaric personally, is perfectly just, dear papa. But do you not think, that your thus keeping your confessor in constant personal attendance, may suggest a suspicion that you may be one of the busy noblemen who wish to meddle too much with the subject of religious doctrine? If you were the Pope himself, you could hardly do more; and even if you were a Cardinal, I think such very close attendance of your confessor, might create more attention, and more suspicion, too, in a foreign court, than I think you would find convenient."

"Mercy on me!" exclaimed the terrified baron, his face becoming crimson; "how on earth could I for a single moment overlook so obvious an objection? Of course, my darling child, you are right! A man of my rank and station, will be watched as keenly as a reigning prince. No, no, I will have no priest in

11 ·

my train. You are quite right, Gertrude; I might have the eyes
of all Europe upon me, while I was only thinking of your amusement, my dear child, and of the best way of finding a suitable
alliance for you."

"Indeed, my dear father, I very truly rejoice at your having
avoided this peril," returned Gertrude, rising. "But I dare say
you have many other things to think of, and I shall only interrupt
you by staying here."

"But, Gertrude! you forget that we have not yet settled who
is to be my suite. Pray don't go away till that point is decided."

Gertrude quietly reseated herself, and sat in act to hear.
"Cannot *you* think of any body, my dear child, who might be
able to fill this office, and yet give us no trouble whatever? I do
assure you it would be a great relief to me, if you *could* think of
such a person."

"Indeed, papa," she replied, "I would, with the greatest
readiness, immediately endeavour to do so, did I not feel that no
one but yourself could name him with propriety. Who is there
but yourself, dear papa, who could at once be a judge whether
the person and manners of any one proposed, were such as could
justify your permitting him to attend upon you in society? And
also, which is equally important, whether you can yourself submit
to his attendance upon you without experiencing any feeling of
annoyance."

"Right again, my dear!" returned her father, looking highly
pleased; "I really think that, somehow or other, you are always
right, Gertrude. It certainly is quite true, my dear child, that
nobody can judge of my own comfort so well as I can myself;
and I don't scruple to say, that the handsome, well-behaved young
fellow, who saved your life about half-a-dozen years ago, by
dragging you out of the water, is just about the best-behaved
and least disagreeable sort of young man that I ever remember
to have seen. But nevertheless, my dear child, though young
Rupert was certainly one of the two that I just now mentioned
as the most eligible I could think of, I would by no means insist
upon it, if any other person occurred to you whom you thought
more fitting."

Gertrude listened to him very attentively, and after silently
meditating on the question for a minute or two, replied; "I really
doubt if you could choose better, sir. He has turned to very good
account the opportunities which your patronage has afforded him,
and I should suppose that he would be considered in any good
society as a well-behaved and well-informed young man."

"You have expressed yourself extremely well, Gertrude, as indeed you always do. He certainly is an exceedingly well-behaved young man. Nor can we be much surprised at that, my dear, when we recollect how frequently he has been permitted to converse with me, I may almost say with familiarity. In short, upon the whole, I doubt, as you say, whether I could choose better. And then we have the advantage of already knowing that he is one of those who is capable of being in some sort ennobled, as it were, by my influence. It is quite certain, as I am fully aware, as well as yourself, my dear child, that I cannot receive honour from those about me, although I can, fortunately, confer it; and therefore his being of humble birth is really of no consequence."

"None," said Gertrude, with an acquiescent bow.

"Well then, my dear," resumed the baron, evidently relieved from considerable anxiety, "all that remains for us to do now, I think, is to decide upon what office I can assign him. We must not call him Rupert any more, you must remember that; he must always be Monsieur Odenthal; and I think it would be as well to insert *de* before it, Gertrude, both for him and his mother. Madame de Odenthal, and Monsieur de Odenthal, really sound very well, and they, of course, could make no objection."

"On this point, I think you may do exactly what you like, papa," replied Gertrude, gravely. "To them the difference would not appear very material."

"Less so, than to us, I dare say, poor things!" returned the baron, gently shaking his head. "But we have not yet settled," he resumed, "what office we are to assign him, my dear Gertrude. It will be necessary, will it not, to explain why he is in my suite?"

"He is your secretary, papa," replied his daughter, looking as if a little surprised at the question. "I believe few persons in your distinguished position, ever travel without a secretary."

The baron gazed at her, as he very often did, with a mixture of surprise and admiration, and after the silence of a moment, he said, "I know that it is quite a common observation to say, that children resemble their parents, but I really do think, my dear, that your resemblance to me, has something more than common in it; I mean in the way in which you understand everything, more even than in your fine regular features. But then, there is another observation that I make too, Gertrude," he added, with a paternal smile, "and it is that, though your thoughts and mine almost always turn out to be the same in the end, they always

11—2

come into your head first. But I suppose, my dear, this is owing
to your being younger. It is, I dare say, just the same thing as
if we were running down the terrace walk together; you would
be sure to do it quickest, you know."

"At least we have the comfort of knowing, dear papa, that we
shall arrive at the same point at last," she replied. But now she
had gone too fast for him, for he looked puzzled, as he said,
"about getting to the end of the terrace, do you mean, my
dear?"

Gertrude bent her beautiful head in reply, and after the silence
of a moment, said, "Now then I think we have settled everything. I must go and talk to Madame Odenthal about it."

"*De* Odenthal, if you please, Gertrude," returned the baron,
very solemnly; "I really must insist upon the persons of my
suite being treated with the respect which ought to attach to
them."

<hr>

CHAPTER XXIII.

It is quite unnecessary to linger any more on the preliminaries
of this spirited expedition, the suddenness of which seemed somewhat startling to Madame Odenthal; but for some reason or other,
which it might be difficult very clearly to explain, the sort of endearing and almost filial confidence with which Gertrude treated
her well-beloved companion, was not quite unlimited. Nay,
occasionally, there was something so like caprice in the young
lady's manner of treating her, that it required all the genuine
affection which Madame Odenthal felt for the motherless girl, to
prevent her feeling estranged and offended.

But it was no very easy thing for Madame Odenthal to remain
long offended with Gertrude. There was so much that was essentially good, and so much that was irresistibly attaching about her,
at least, in her intercourse with her chaperon, that, despite all
her little mysterious caprices, this kind-hearted *dame de compagnie* loved her very affectionately.

Nevertheless, the worthy governante could not well help contemplating with something like astonishment, the extreme

indifference with which this young girl appeared to contemplate the change which awaited her, from the stiff, unchanging stateliness of her father's remote castle, to the brilliant and dazzling dissipation of the French capital.

This indifference would have been much less surprising, had Gertrude been ignorant of the vast difference between the life she had hitherto led, and that upon which she was about to enter; but, as Madame Odenthal well knew, it would have been difficult to find among the most diligent readers of Paris and London, any young lady better acquainted with the most lively representations of their manners, than Gertrude.

No indecencies of any kind, either social or religious, had ever been permitted to find their way into the library of the truly refined Madame de Schwanberg; but, excepting on these points, no restraint had ever been put upon the reading of Gertrude; and as her appetite for reading was much on a par with what a healthy mouse may be supposed to feel when left in perfect liberty within a favourite cheese, it was pretty evident to those who knew her as well as Madame Odenthal, that she was not unaware of the change which awaited her. But although it was impossible to suppose her ignorant of this, it was equally so to believe that it excited any very lively sensations, either of pleasure or distaste. As a companion, she was more than usually silent, and as a student, less than usually diligent. In short, her affectionate, but greatly puzzled friend, was totally at a loss as to the state of her young companion's mind respecting this unexpected event.

It was natural enough, that in this state of things, she should ask her son, during a *tête-à-tête* walk with him in the garden, whether he thought the young baroness liked the idea of this journey, or not.

His answer was: "Upon my word, dear mother, I can't tell."

"It certainly is not very likely that you should know, Rupert," she rejoined; "for I presume that I know her thoughts on most subjects better than you can do; and yet, strange to say, I really have not been able to discover what her feelings are about it. Nevertheless, it is impossible she can be really indifferent about it."

Rupert nodded his head, and said: "Certainly. One should think so."

"In some things she is very like her mother," resumed Madame Odenthal, musingly; "but in others quite the reverse. When the late baroness once knew she could trust a friend, she had no longer any reserve with them. But it is not so with Gertrude. Do you not think that there is a great deal of singularity about her, Rupert?"

The young man did not immediately reply, which caused his mother to look up at him. His eyes were fixed upon the ground, but his mother's question had caused a great change in his complexion. His face was scarlet. But after the delay of a moment, he very composedly replied to it, by pronouncing, with great distinctness, the word "YES."

"She is an admirable creature, nevertheless," returned his mother, earnestly; "and it is hardly fair, perhaps, for me, or for you either, to sit in judgment upon her, because she does not open her heart to us with as much freedom as if we were in all respects her equal."

"You think then," said the young man, with sudden vehemence, "that she is as proud as her father?"

"I have not said *that*, Rupert," replied his mother, quietly. "She has too large and too clear a mind to render that possible; nay, I am not sure that it would be fair to call her proud at all; but without her being so, I think it very likely that custom, and perhaps something like a feeling of propriety, may render it almost impossible for her to forget the difference of rank between us, entirely."

"Could she have acquired such a feeling from her mother, think you?" said Rupert, with something very like a sneer.

"No!" was the decided reply of Madame Odenthal to this question.

"The mind of her mother," she added, with the tone of deep feeling which the mention of her lost friend always produced, "was both too lofty, and too bright, to admit any shadow of prejudice, however slight, to tarnish it."

"I do not admire minds that are tarnished by prejudice," replied Rupert.

"Nor should I," returned his mother, shaking her head reproachfully. "You are so sudden, so vehement in your interpretations, that it is difficult to talk to you, Rupert. However, I do not deny that there are contradictory qualities in the mind of Gertrude, which often puzzle me. I very much doubt, if we either of us understand her perfectly."

"Nay, for that matter, my dear mother," returned her son, pettishly, "I freely confess that I do not understand her at all. But my dulness on this subject can be of no great consequence to anybody."

And with these words the young man took an agile leap over the low fence, which divided the flower-garden from the vineyard; and left his mother to her meditations.

*   *   *   *   *

When Rupert Odenthal declared that the character of Gertrude was a mystery to him, he not only spoke with perfect sincerity, but he said no more than Gertrude herself might have echoed, had she been questioned on the same subject. Again, and again, and again, the harassed girl had endeavoured to arrange her thoughts, and regulate her feelings, but for a long, long time, her efforts were utterly in vain; and the severest self-examination to which she could submit herself, only left her with the renewed conviction, that she knew not right from wrong.

The unfortunate blindness of her mother to the probability that two young people, thrown together as Rupert and Gertrude had been, might find at length that they each liked the society of the other better than all that the earth had to offer them besides, was the root and origin of all they had suffered, and were about to suffer.

Had their intercourse been only the ordinary intercourse of society, the danger arising from it would have been infinitely less.

In that case, each might, perhaps, have learnt to think the other charming, fascinating, admirable; but each might not have learned to think the other the only human being extant, whose affection and companionship were worth living for.

For a considerable time Rupert had very greatly the advantage; for the idea of his falling in love with the heiress of Schwanberg, was too preposterous to find a place in his imagination; and moreover, he looked at her and considered her as a child, long after she had learned to think him the most admirable of men.

He had, besides, the great advantage of being guarded from the danger of discovering how well she deserved to be loved, by the captiousness and caprice which ever accompanies such feelings as she had for him, when unrequited. It was upon these caprices, and the strange inequality of manner which they led to, which had suggested to him—the idea that she inherited her father's pride.

And then came the interlude of his friend Adolphe's proposal, and rejection; the manner of which naturally increased his belief in her abounding pride. . . . And so matters went on for a few months longer, with very little change.

Then came the fatal illness of Gertrude's mother, which led to Rupert's mother becoming one of the family; and then it was that the heart's ease of the young man became seriously endangered.

Guarded by the immense distance between them, the attractions of the beautiful Gertrude had hitherto been contemplated by him as something to wonder at, rather than to love; but the presence of his mother in the family had not only brought them more together, but had betrayed many traits in her character for which he had never before given her credit.

Yet still he was, comparatively speaking, safe; for, while he never lost sight of the immense distance which their respective stations really placed between them, he contrived to make it greater still, by persuading himself that the brilliant Gertrude as surely inherited her father's pride, as she could ever inherit his estates. And this persuasion served him for a considerable time as *armour of proof*. Neither beauty, talent, temper, nor even her tender watchfulness over her sinking mother, could find a crevice at which to enter his heart; and she had loved him (ten thousand times better than she loved herself) for many months before it had ever entered his head to believe it possible that any clear-sighted man could love her.

Love her! The idea seemed absolutely monstrous. Love a woman who submitted with evident approbation to select her husband from the pages of the Gotha Almanack—rejecting all whose name could not be found in its pages!

No other absurdity could have produced so strong an effect on the mind of Rupert as this, for it seemed to identify the father and daughter, in his fancy; and, most assuredly, of all the human beings with whom his uneventful life had brought him in contact, the Baron von Schwanberg appeared to him the most little-minded and contemptible.

And thus it was with him till the eventful dinner-party, which has been described, when the sight of Gertrude, radiant with delight at her own success in her endeavour to place his mother beside her, as an equal, instead of a dependant, so completely overturned all his foregone conclusions respecting her pride, and the inherited similarity of her character to that of her father, that he at once fell into the other extreme, and would have given half his future life to prove to her that *now*, at least, he did her justice.

But though he would have given half his life to prove this to her, without forfeiting his own esteem by abusing the confidence which was placed in him, he would not, by his own good will, have gone one inch farther; and sharp must have been the ear, and keen the eye, which could have detected the removal of the prejudices which had hitherto protected him.

But what ear so sharp, what eye so keen, as those of a young girl in the position of Gertrude? Alas! she knew what love was too well, to make any mistake as to the foregone heart-whole indifference of Rupert.

His kindling enthusiasm for everything that was great and good, his ardent appreciation of everything sublime in poetry or exalted in moral worth, were not more clearly seen, or more deeply impressed upon her heart, than was her conviction of his utter indifference to herself.

But she had made up her mind to endure it, with the stern courage with which a high-toned spirit almost always resists injustice. This must not be construed into meaning that Gertrude thought she had a right to the admiration and the love of every man who approached her. Nothing could be farther from the fact—nothing more repugnant to her character. On the contrary, if there was any trait,—any feeling,—which could, in the least degree, justify the idea which Rupert had conceived of her inordinate pride, it must be found in the utter indifference in which she held the opinions concerning her, which were experienced by all the individuals with whom she had hitherto made acquaintance.

But there was a feeling at the very bottom of her heart, that Rupert *ought* to love her; for, had she not waited for his opinions, and accepted his judgment, day by day, almost from the first hour that she had known him? Had they not soared and dived together to all the heights and depths of human thought, as registered in the volumes among which they lived?

The leading axiom which had pervaded the system upon which Madame de Schwanberg had educated her daughter, was, that she should never permit a fallacy, which she knew to be such, to take root in her mind, nor conceal from her any historical, moral, or religious truth, which she herself recognised to be such.

It seems difficult (considering that Madame de Schwanberg was a well-informed and right-thinking woman) to discover any objection to such a system of education as this; but, nevertheless, under all the circumstances, it was far from being quite as safe as it might be supposed to be; for, though it can scarcely be said that Madame de Schwanberg, upon any important point, halted between two opinions, the tone of her mind, and of her teaching too, was weakened by a sort of timid consciousness that the turning her daughter away from the faith of her ancestors, was a daring deed.

And yet it was her most earnest wish that Gertrude should not be a Romanist; and it was, therefore, that she not only clung to Madame Odenthal, as a better-taught Christian than herself, but that she encouraged the freedom with which Rupert canvassed the subject in the presence of her eagerly-listening Gertrude.

That he was to her not only a great Apollo, but a great divine, long before any dream of love had mixed itself with her feelings, is most certain; and knowing how completely her confidence, her judgment, and her taste hung upon him, as an authority even superior to that of her mother, it did seem cruel and unjust on his part, that he should always and for ever treat her as if it were impossible that anything like real sympathy could exist between them.

But such was very decidedly the case, as far as he was concerned; for so deeply was he persuaded that the Gertrude of the library was only the obedient pupil of her amiable mother, while the Gertrude of the drawing-room was the sympathising inheritor of all her father's pride, as well as of all his acres, that whatever he might occasionally have been tempted to think of her talents, or her beauty, he accounted her as one so much out of the reach of affection, that he would have been quite as likely to sigh for the happiness and honour of becoming a cardinal, as of being the chosen partner of her heart.

It was indeed a strange caprice of fortune which caused the demolition of all the prejudice within which Rupert had entrenched himself; but, slight as seemed the cause, and sudden the effect, it may be doubted if all the arts which ever woman used could have been put in practice with so much success as attended the almost childish caprice by which poor Gertrude, at length, found her way to his heart.

This uneventful, though not unimportant retrospect, was necessary to make what follows, intelligible; but the web is not unravelled yet, for the struggle was not yet over in the heart of Rupert. The sort of mist through which he had been wont to look at her, and which had made her appear so far unlike what she really was, had, it is true, fallen from his eyes, and Gertrude felt in every move that it was so. But nevertheless their position relatively to each other, was still a very puzzling, and by no means a very happy one. The misery of doubt and uncertainty, however, was all on one side. The feelings of doubt had little

or no share in the emotions which were at work in the breast of
Rupert. Had he been asked to explain them, he could scarcely
have done it better, or more correctly, than in the words of the
well-known song,

"But if she is not for me,
What care I how fair she be?"

And he laboured so hard, poor youth, to keep this thought for
ever awake within him, that no sensation deserving the name of
Hope, had as yet been suffered to embellish his waking dreams.

From time to time, however, he endeavoured to assist the process of curing himself, which he was desperately determined to
effect, by labouring to persuade himself, as may be seen in the
sample given of his conversation with his mother, that the character of Gertrude was capricious and contradictory.

Such, with the exception of some few occasional fits of unchecked passionate adoration, was the condition of the unfortunate
Rupert, when the Baron von Schwanberg, his daughter, and suite
took their departure from the heavy walls within which the
proud owner was born, for the purpose of visiting the light and
glittering salons of Paris.

It would be difficult to say whether the heightened colour and
flashing eye, which was marked by other eyes than those of his
mother, should have been considered as indications of pain or of
pleasure; it was evidently not with indifference, however, that
he took his place in the vehicle which was to convey him to
Paris.

Neither would it have been easy to analyze the secret feelings
of the superb baron himself, at the moment he was preparing to
exchange his time-honoured authority at Schloss Schwanberg, for
the less assured, but more widely-extended influence, which he
hoped, with his fair daughter's assistance, to exercise in the gayest
capital in Europe.

But however widely extended was the sphere of this new-born
ambition, it was evident to his daughter, that his eye was still
steadily fixed upon one pre-eminently important object as the
great crowning glory of his ambition, for the last words he
addressed to her, before quitting his home, were these: "Gertrude!
you have, of course, packed up with your hands the Almanack
de Gotha?"

CHAPTER XXIV.

THOUGH the Baron von Schwanberg was perfectly correct in his estimates of the financial value of his own property, he was a good deal mistaken as to the proportion which his own wealth bore to that of many individuals with whom he was likely to be brought into collision in the course of his present expedition.

He set out, however, with a very noble "*sheaf of bills*" on a substantial Paris banker; and not only was his mode of travelling almost stately in its style, but his choice of a residence, on arriving at Paris, was more in keeping with his own ideas of his personal importance, than in exact proportion to his rent-roll. Moreover, to do him justice, it had never occurred to him that one means by which the travelling magnates of most countries contrive to sustain their lofty flight, while on the wing, is by not troubling themselves to look back to their forsaken nests at home.

Now this mode of relieving himself from the burden of two establishments, had never occurred to him. He neither dismissed servants, nor sold horses, and had never made any very close calculations as to how much, or how little, his absence from home would enable him to save towards defraying the expenses of his foreign residence.

That no such calculations should ever suggest themselves as necessary to Gertrude, may be easily believed; for her father would have thought it equally degrading and unnecessary, had he ever attempted to draw her attention to the details of finance.

The young heiress, therefore, could scarcely have failed of being a very happy young heiress, as she took possession of a very elegant hotel in the Fauxbourg St. Honoré, all the principal apartments of which had been engaged for their use, *had she not* unfortunately fallen in love with a youth, who, in addition to a good many other disqualifications for being a fitting object for her devoted attachment, had as yet betrayed no signs whatever of having any propensity to return it.

Nevertheless, the misery which certainly seemed likely to arise from this untoward state of affairs, was, for the time at least, almost forgotten, in the novelty and the brilliance of the scenes to which she was immediately introduced. How matters might have been managed for her if she had not previously made the acquaintance of M. and Madame de Hauteville, it is difficult to guess ; but the cordial liking which had sprung up between the two ladies in the country, had been sustained by a very brisk correspondence since they parted ; and it was the De Hautevilles who had selected this charming apartment for them, the De Hautevilles who had taken care that everything necessary to their comfort awaited them on their arrival, and it was the De Hautevilles who had made their joyous appearance at an early hour on the following morning, to welcome them on their arrival, and to offer their services in every possible way that could secure to the strangers all the pleasures of novelty without any of its embarrassments. It is needless to dwell upon the facilities which such assistance afforded for establishing the noble strangers as welcome guests in every salon most desirable to enter, from the Bourbon sovereign to the banker millionaire ; and in the case of our "baron," ignorance was most decidedly bliss, for having been once assured upon unimpeachable authority, that the De Hautevilles were noble, it never entered his head to suspect that some of the most splendid salons which were opened to him, owed their gold and their damask to revenues which he would have considered as scarcely more illustrious in their origin, than those accruing from the dust-cart.

Not having been long accustomed, however, to the dignity of being attended by any gentleman of "his suite" either at home or abroad, he felt at first a little embarrassed by the necessity which he was assured there existed for his taking Rupert with him everywhere.

Having once assured him that it was right and proper that he should be so attended, Gertrude did not again condescend to allude to the subject. Nor was there, as she perhaps foresaw, any occasion that she should do so ; for not only did the baron himself find an immense relief from always having at least one person born for his will, within easy reach of him, but the *succés du salon*, which the fine voice and good mien of the young man speedily obtained, aided as it most cordially was, by the zealous efforts of the De Hautevilles, would have rendered it much more difficult to have kept him out of society, than to have introduced him into it.

Nothing, in short, could apparently be more successful than this expedition. It was not that the baron felt his consequence increase—that, perhaps, was impossible—but he had the delightful consciousness that it was witnessed by a very considerably larger number of distinguished personages than he could even have hoped to assemble round him at Schloss Schwanberg.

Even the remarkable success of his secretary in every salon they entered, caused him but little surprise, and no annoyance, for he attributed it wholly to his own influence; and when, upon the first meeting between Madame de Hauteville and Gertrude's humble *dame de compagnie*, he saw the arms of the French *elegante* literally open to receive her, he took the opportunity, the very first time he found himself alone with his daughter, of "improving the occasion," by pointing out to her the great importance to persons in his exalted station, of permitting none but estimable individuals to appear under their patronage.

"It is perfectly evident, my dear Gertrude," he said, with great solemnity, "that persons like ourselves might do incalculable injury to the morals of society, did we not carefully select the individuals whom, for our own pleasure, or convenience, we place near us, from among the most estimable portion of our inferiors. It must be as evident to you, my dear, as it is to me, that if this very useful mother and son, whom we have attached to our service, were as worthless, as we happily know them to be the reverse, their being presented by ME, would be quite enough to ensure their being received in the manner you now witness. This is certainly a great privilege, one of the greatest, perhaps, belonging to our rank; but, of course, we must take care not to abuse it."

Gertrude listened to this, as she did to all his pompous harangues, with a sort of fixed and mute attention, which she flattered herself was as far from hypocrisy as the circumstances of the case permitted, but still she felt that it *was* hypocrisy; yet, alas! was it not a deeper hypocrisy still, to hide in her heart all that nestled there? Had it not been for this bitter thought, her present situation would often have been one of very great enjoyment. The gaiety, the animation, the bright variety of everything around her, so perfectly new, and so perfectly unlike the manner of life to which she had been accustomed, would have had great charms for her, had her heart been more at ease; nay, there were certainly moments during which all her secret anxieties seemed forgotten, and when life appeared to her as a state of existence capable of more enjoyment than she had ever before thought it calculated to bestow.

The first serious misfortune, in truth, which befel her in Paris, was occasioned by her being seen at a ball at the Tuileries by an Hungarian nobleman of high birth and large possessions, who very speedily became convinced that she was in all respects precisely the individual intended by special providence to assume his name and share his honours.

It was not to herself, but, according to long-established continental fashion, to her father, that he communicated this important opinion. Nothing could be more dignified than the manner in which he made this communication, unless, indeed, it were the manner in which it was received; and never, perhaps, could any two gentlemen of their class have been seen to exhibit themselves to greater advantage, than they both did during this interview.

This splendid proposal was a very welcome one, even to the Baron von Schwanberg; for he was himself aware of being so very nearly dazzled by the constantly brilliant, yet constantly changing scene which surrounded him, that he had more than once become conscious of a painfully anxious feeling, lest the great object of his existence might be lost merely from the difficulty of selecting the best, amid so much that was desirable.

"Ja!" was the syllable which his heart ejaculated in reply to the noble Count Hernwold's dignified, and in every way flattering proposal; and "ja!" already trembled on his lips, when, by a sudden expansion of intellect, which he immediately felt to be providential, he recollected the solemn condition which must be fulfilled before such a proposal could be accepted.

It would have been difficult, however, for any man to have brought a greater number of stately words together, than the baron contrived to do before he concluded the harangue by which he contrived to make the Count understand, not without some little difficulty, however, that it was not in his power to respond to his polite proposal definitely at that moment.

"How, my Lord Baron?" returned the astonished suitor, waxing wrath and red; "I am not to receive an answer?"

"I must implore you, my Lord Count," returned the flattered father, in a tone so meek and gracious, that a stranger to him might almost have been beguiled into believing that he considered himself of very little more consequence than all the other great men in the world, "I do beseech you," said he, "to believe, what, in fact, it is quite impossible to doubt, namely, that no father living, except, perhaps, the few who are crowned kings, could listen to such a proposal as you have now done me the honour to make, without feeling themselves gratified, both as fathers and as nobles, in the very highest degree. Nevertheless, my Lord Count, I trust that I shall stand excused in your eyes, if I venture to repeat that I must petition for as much delay as may be required to announce your magnificent proposals to my daughter."

Count Hernwold had risen from his chair upon hearing the unpalatable words which informed him that he must wait awhile before he could receive an answer; and he stood face to face before the baron, with an aspect still more haughty than his own; but no sooner did the well-pleased father give him to understand that the delay required, was only for the purpose of making the lady of his choice acquainted with the honour done her, than the whole of the lover's ample visage became radiant with satisfaction.

Count Hernwold was, beyond all question, a very handsome man, though somewhat approaching to heaviness, both in feature and stature. His age was that which, in the male, must be considered as the meridian of human life, having just completed his fortieth year; and the smile with which he reseated himself, upon becoming aware that his proposals were to be referred to no harsher tribunal than that of the fair lady's will, made him look younger and handsomer still.

The interview ended by the most dignified and courteous assurances on both sides, that the cementing the friendly relations which already existed between them, by the union proposed, would be ever considered as the most happy event of their respective lives.

During the time that the unfortunate Gertrude had been making this involuntary conquest, she might fairly have been considered as one of the most unhappy young ladies in Paris.

The first few weeks being over, during which a ceaseless succession of engagements had sometimes amused, and sometimes bewildered her, she first felt weary, very heavily weary, and then very profoundly miserable.

In truth, the self-examination to which she frequently subjected herself, could not well lead to any other result. She would sometimes sit for hours in the well-guarded solitude of her own chamber, and meditate upon her own position, and more minutely still, upon her own conduct.

The writing she read upon the wall was certainly neither flattering, nor consolatory.

Her conscience told her, that let the fruits or the follies of her father be what they might, he was still a loving and most devoted father to her. There was no hollow deception in *his* love, no mixture of falsehood in any demonstration of it. And having come to this conclusion, she turned her eyes to examine the sketch which her conscience proceeded to draw of herself.

In return for true affection, she paid a heartless seeming of deference, which, cold and the very reverse of loving (as at the best, it must be), had not in her case, even the merit of being sincere; for she felt no real deference for him; nor had she, at the bottom of her heart, the most remote intention of obeying him on any single point of sufficient importance to affect either his happiness, or her own.

Yet though she had courage enough, and truth enough, to enable her to finish this sketch, without leaving out a single fact, or a single thought, that tended to complete it, there was no feeling awakened by it which might lead her to atone for her deficiencies.

"I hate myself!" she murmured to her own ears in contrite bitterness of spirit; but it was a species of contrition that brought more of despair than of repentance with it.

And having reached this point of misery, she started from her chair, paced with a passionate and hasty step the noble room that was appropriated for her private use—examined anew the fastening which ensured her privacy, and then, throwing herself upon her knees, implored Heaven to grant her strength to conquer the fatal passion which had made her such a wretch.

She felt as if her desperate prayer was heard; when she suddenly resolved to tax her memory through the long portion of her past existence, during which her love for Rupert had influenced her every feeling and her every thought, in order to revive the bitter memory of all the proofs which he had demonstrated, that *he shared not* the madness which destroyed her.

It would have been difficult for her self-accusing spirit to have hit upon a severer penance for her faults.

Rare indeed were the traces left upon her memory of any word, or any look, that could be fairly construed as betraying LOVE; and of such love as she felt for him—not one.

"Is such a life worth having?" she exclaimed. "WORTH HAVING!" she repeated, bitterly. "Is not *endurable*, the better word? *Why* should any human being submit to the endurance of prolonged life, when conscious that every new day which dawns upon them can only bring a renewal of misery?

"Nature," she whispered to herself, "Nature has not endowed us with the power to prolong our days, but she has bestowed upon us the power of shortening them. . . . Why should this power

12

be left us, but for our use and benefit, as all other power is?
Oh! what a luxury would it be, to lay my head upon my pillow,
knowing that I should sleep, and never wake again to the misery
of seeing his cold indifference!"

For a few guilty, dreadful moments, the miserable Gertrude
remained with her eyes closed in very frightful reverie; but
passion is as sudden in transition, as vehement in demonstration;
and the next sob that relieved her throbbing heart, was given to
repentance.

Poor girl! with all her vehemence, and all her faults, she was,
perhaps, still more deserving of pity than of blame; she was still
very young, and most unhappily situated. Madame Odenthal
would assuredly have been the confidante of *all* her feelings, *had
she not been Rupert's mother;* but such confidence was now impossible. Would it not have been like pleading her cause to HIM,
and imploring his love?

"Alas!" sighed poor Gertrude, as she meditated upon the impossibility of confiding her sorrows to this dear and only friend;
"I feel at times as if I were mad enough for anything. And
perhaps I am—mad enough for anything but *that!*"

She wanted, however, no right-minded confessor to tell her,
that in her bold longing for death, she had sinned against the
benign law of nature, which teaches us, till reason itself is shaken,
that the consciousness of existence *is* a blessing, and that it is the
will of our Creator that it should be so.

This truth soon rushed back upon her heart, and brought repentance with it; and then she set herself to think deliberately
of her position, and patiently endeavoured, as far as her agitated
spirits would permit her to do so, to discover, amidst a choice of
evils, what line of conduct she could pursue which would be the
most likely to reconcile herself to her own conscience, and most
contribute to the happiness of her father.

It had so happened that on that evening, at a ball given by one
of the magnates of the Paris season, Rupert had for more than
one dance become the partner of one of the loveliest girls in the
room. It had happened, too, that he had not once asked *her* to
dance; a liberty which had become almost a usage, *once* in the
course of every evening that they met in a ball-room.

This omission on his part was by no means accidental, having
been occasioned by his over-hearing a royal duke declare, that he
must contrive to get one waltz with the beautiful Baroness de
Schwanberg, as there was no Frenchwoman who could compete
with her in her national dance.

On hearing this, the discreet Rupert determined that his modest claim should not be made till this dance with the noble duke had been performed; but some accident or other prevented its ever being performed at all; and the consequence of this was, that the ball began, and ended, without poor Gertrude's having received the anxiously-looked-for invitation from her father's modest secretary, to take the accustomed "*tour de waltz.*"— "What great events from little causes spring!"

The bitterness of Gertrude's disappointment certainly bore no reasonable proportion to its importance; but it may be said in her defence, that she had long been kept in a state of very torturing uncertainty, and her mind harassed; and her spirits weakened by this, had left her unable to judge fairly either of his conduct, or her own.

She retired to her room that night in the full persuasion that she was not only an object of perfect indifference to him, but that he had seen—or suspected—what her feelings were for him; and that his neglect of her throughout the evening proceeded from a friendly and honourable wish to cure her of a folly which he did not share, and which could only be productive of misery to her.

Yet, in the midst of the agony produced by this persuasion, she did him justice; nay, she did him more than justice; for she not only gave him credit for the honourable discretion which had dictated the cautious reserve with which he always treated her; but for the absence of all such weakness on his part as *might* have led him to *wish* that they had been differently situated.

That night, or, at least, all that was left of it, was passed by the unhappy girl in very earnest and very praiseworthy efforts to take such a review of her own position, and the duties which it reasonably imposed on her, as might enable her so to act, as in some degree to reconcile her to herself.

Nor was this truly conscientious effort made in vain—such efforts rarely are; and just as the sun began to peep through the crevices of her window shutters, she fell into a peaceful sleep, which lasted till Teresa thought "it would be quite nonsense to let it last any longer."

CHAPTER XXV.

THE results of that night's meditation were more enduring than the sweet sleep which followed it. Gertrude's first sensation on awaking was, that she had undergone some violent change; nor were the more deliberate thoughts which followed, at all calculated to remove this impression. If she had herself described this change, it is probable that she might have said: "I had lost my senses before it, but now I have recovered them."

Were I to attempt giving a detailed description of the state of Gertrude's mental condition, as it had been when she awoke on the previous day, and as she felt it to be now, the discrepancy would appear too strong to be rationally accounted for; but those who have studied the strange varieties of human character, know that what might be truly termed unnatural in one, may, with equal justice, be pronounced essentially natural in another.

There was so much of the earnestness of truth in the character of Gertrude, that, whatever she felt, she felt deeply; and whatever she purposed to do, she purposed firmly. Nor, on the present occasion, were reasons wanting to justify the change which she resolved to achieve, not only in her future conduct, but her future feelings.

"The madness has lasted long enough," she murmured. "Young as I am, I have already spent whole years of life in doteing upon one who doted not on me; and, more sinful still, I have been hardening my heart during the whole of this ill-spent time against my own father. Alas! alas! Of how much finer a quality is the love of his heart than the love of mine! And yet, have I ever for a moment ceased to consider myself as his superior in all intellectual, ay, and in all moral qualities? 'Take physic, vanity,' clear your vision a little before you repose on your own view of the case, with such perfect satisfaction."

It would be difficult to imagine any state of things more favourable for the gracious reception of Count Hernwold's proposals than was thus produced.

Gertrude had breakfasted in her own dressing-room—an arrangement by no means uncommon with her since her abode in

Paris—as her own hours of rising had become later, while those of her father had remained unchanged. Madame Odenthal had been her companion at breakfast, but had left the room when her father entered it. She perceived, the moment he entered the room, that some great event had happened, and was not left long in doubt as to the nature of it. The "Almanack de Gotha" was in his hand, and he flourished it triumphantly over his head as he approached her.

Gertrude was very pale when the door opened upon her, but before the baron and his Almanack had reached her table, she was red enough.

"You were inspired, Gertrude! My noble-hearted Gertrude, you were, you must have been inspired, when the admirable idea occurred to you of consulting this precious volume as a preservative against every wish of contaminating the purity of your race, by uniting yourself with any whose ancestors or connections are not found to have their names enrolled in this invaluable volume!"

These words were quite enough to enlighten her upon the nature of the errand which had brought her father to visit her, instead of his waiting for her to make a visit to him, as was her daily usage.

Her feelings would have been vastly different had a similar circumstance occurred to her on the preceding day. The sight of her father and his Almanack then, would have roused within her a spirit of resistance which might have led to very painful domestic results; but now the case was very different. For one short moment, for half a moment perhaps, she again felt her wicked wish to die. . . . But in the next, she positively breathed a silent, desperate exclamation, which, if it had been expressed in words, must have been rendered, "Thank God!"

Her noble father, however, was much too full of the business which brought him there, to have any speculation to bestow upon her manner of receiving it. The fact that the high-born, wealthy, and illustrious Count Hernwold had asked for the honour and happiness of her hand in marriage, was uttered once, twice, thrice, before he dreamed of pausing to ascertain what her answer might be.

But was he not justified in this? Did he not carry his justification in his hand? So, no less than three different pages did his well-taught fingers turn, and on each did the name and title of Count Hernwold meet his search.

"We have not waited for nothing, have we, my Gertrude?

These alliances are all but royal, and nowhere, I will be bold to say, could a man so allied have made a better choice."

While this happy rhapsody was pronounced again, again, and again, with but little variation either in words or tone, the bride-elect was occupied in recalling her meditations of the preceding night, and again she inwardly breathed, "Thank God!"

Nor was she far wrong in thinking that such a termination would be better than the continuation of the lamentable state in which she had already passed what ought to be the brightest, if not the happiest years of life. To love, and love, and love in vain, with the additional misery of knowing that her love was both sinful, as an act of disobedience to her father's will, and contemptible in her own eyes, from the thought that it had been never solicited, was surely more dreadful still.

It was not many hours since she had arrived at the full conviction that this last crowning misery of Rupert's indifference had been proved beyond the reach of hope to contradict it; and if it had been her habit, as it was that of her father, to persuade herself that everything which befel her was in consequence of a deviation from the laws of nature, permitted for her particular gratification and advantage, she would assuredly have believed that this opportune proposal of marriage from a person whose name was to be found in the "Almanack de Gotha," was the result of a special dispensation of Providence.

Her manner of receiving the intelligence thus brought, was, therefore, not exactly triumphant; but, though she again became, for a few moments, extremely pale, she displayed no indication of repugnance.

"Was it not a blessed dispensation that brought us here, Gertrude?" he said, clasping his hands together, in an attitude of devotion. "Our thanks must be rendered in our own chapel, Gertrude; and Father Alaric must be instructed to select proper services for the occasion. And now tell me, my dear love," he continued, "in what apartment you would wish to receive my Lord Count, when he waits upon you to offer his personal homage? Will you admit him here, Gertrude?"

The wretched girl half rose from her chair; but, fortunately, she did not raise her eyes from the floor; if she *had*, not even the baron's seven-fold shield of dulness could have prevented him from seeing something there which would have startled him.

In that short moment, however, Gertrude found time to resolve that all she had already suffered, should not have been suffered in vain, and that the fate she had decided upon for herself should not be rendered more lingering, and more bitter still, by any wavering feebleness in her manner of meeting it.

She instantly reseated herself, and replied, in a tone which had perhaps a touch of haughtiness in its dignity: "No, Sir, if you please; not here. In my estimation, there would be greatly too much familiarity in receiving such a visit here. Let him find me in the great drawing-room, if you please."

The baron clasped his hands, raised his eyes to Heaven, and whispered, quite audibly, his fervent thanks to the Virgin Mary, for having inspired the heart of his child with such noble feelings!

There are, probably, many causes, none of them very strictly philosophical, which may enable a woman—and even a young one—to assume an aspect of composure, when her pulses may not be making very healthful movements. Some such must have been at work at the heart of Gertrude during this tremendous visit from Count Hernwold; for it would have been difficult for any young lady to have displayed more perfect self-possession.

The interview, however, did not last long; but when, exactly at the moment when everything desirable upon the occasion had been uttered, Gertrude rose to leave the room, the Count, as he handed her to the door, declared, with no faltering accent, that he considered himself at that moment to be, beyond any possible reach of comparison, the happiest man upon the surface of the globe called earth.

CHAPTER XXVI.

As Rupert Odenthal had lived for several years of his life without being at all certain what his own feelings were with respect to the Baroness Gertrude von Schwanberg, it would be hardly fair to expect that the faithful chronicler who has undertaken to relate his adventures, should venture to state any positive opinion on the subject at this very particularly perplexed period of his existence.

Let it suffice to say, that whatever his feelings were, on hearing that the young lady was about to be married immediately to the Count Hernwold, he never uttered a single word expressive of them, to any one.

His mother once touched upon the subject, upon finding herself *tête-à-tête* with him, shortly after the important news had been announced throughout the family, but the conversation was cut short very abruptly by his starting up and leaving the room; but ere he passed through the door, he turned to her, and said, "For mercy's sake, my dearest mother, do not begin haranguing me on this subject! I hear of it from every soul in the house, and out of it, till I am positively sick of the pompous old fool's name! Just fancy what it must be for me to have my lord, the baron, rehearsing the titles and alliances of his strutting son-in-law from morning to night! Don't *you* begin on the same theme, or I really shall be tempted to run away."

His mother smiled, and nodded very good-humouredly, fairly confessing, as she said, that they were likely to hear enough of my Lord the Count, without entertaining each other on the subject.

And so they parted, and Madame Odenthal kept her promise, and did not trouble her son with any further observations on the subject.

But she did not promise that she would not herself, when in silence and in solitude, dwell upon this subject with the most heartfelt satisfaction.

Though far, very far, from knowing, or even suspecting the whole truth as to the feelings of Gertrude or of Rupert for each other, she had, nevertheless, often spent anxious hours, both by night and by day, lest these two young people, so perilously thrown together, might learn at last to love each other too well.

To have become a spy upon both, or either of them, would have been repugnant to her nature; and her disposition in this respect had, doubtless, kept her ignorant of much that might have been very obviously evident to one of a different temper. However, there was much that was very puzzling and contradictory in the conduct of both; so that what she half made up her mind to believe one day, she rejected as perfectly untenable the next.

But, for all that, she could not be said to be at all easy in her mind upon the subject, and most assuredly it was a great relief to her to hear that her beautiful Gertrude was about to become Countess of Hernwold.

But the silence of Madame Odenthal on the subject, or the silence of her son either, mattered little, and was noticed less; for so many, both in the house and out of it, appeared to talk of nothing else, that their voices on the subject could scarcely have been heard, and were certainly not missed.

It is not my fault, if my readers are not already aware, that the Baron von Schwanberg was a very pompous gentleman; and with so very splendid a marriage in prospect for his daughter, they need scarcely be told now that his preparations for it were made to ring, not only through his own abode, and those of all his numerous fine friends and acquaintance, but that the most fashionable tradesmen in Paris soon became aware, that if they knew their own interest, they would speedily set every available agent at work, in order to secure a share of the golden harvest which this union of wealth with wealth, seemed to promise them.

But though the Count Hernwold was a very pompous man, on some points perhaps almost as pompous as his magnificent intended father-in-law, he had the discretion to give vent to his own overwhelming consciousness of superiority, less in words than in actions.

He had informed this delighted father-in-law, that he conceived it would be absolutely necessary for sustaining properly the position of himself and his noble bride, that, in addition to their various country residences, they should have a permanent hôtel in the most distinguished quarter of Paris.

Now if, instead of concluding this dignified announcement by the word PARIS, Count Hernwold had named PERU, the baron would scarcely have had sufficient presence of mind to testify, or even to feel astonishment; for the Baron von Schwanberg knew that there might be some few who were superior on *some* points. Great as he was, he was not, for instance, one of the Heaven-elected few, destined to wear a regal crown; and he could hardly be said to have ever expressed any positive discontent at this dispensation of Providence. He knew perfectly well that the earth contained but very few crowned heads; and it was, doubtless, this consideration which had enabled him to reconcile himself with so little difficulty to not being one of the number.

But, this class set aside, he certainly had a most comfortable conviction, that he had an exceedingly good right to compete with all the rest of the human race, without running any great risk of finding a superior, or even an equal, among them.

Yet, greatly as he gloried in his noble pedigree and his large possessions, he was quite aware that he could not hold the superior station assigned him by Providence, had he no other claim to pre-eminence.

He knew that there were pedigrees as ancient, and races as pure as his own, and that there were sundry estates as large, or larger. But he had, certainly, never yet made up his mind to believe that, take him for all in all, there *could* be found another individual equal to himself in all respects.

He probably never had asked himself whether he thought that any other man living could stand as upright, or balance himself as securely upon his legs, as he could do; but, on the other hand, it is pretty certain, that if he had asked himself such a question, he would have answered, to the best of his knowledge and belief, No.

On one point, and one point ONLY, had he as yet brought himself to believe that he might meet a superior; and it so happened that the Count Hernwold was one of the distinguished personages to whom he was willing to accord this superiority.

In short, the Baron von Schwanberg felt that his destined son-in-law was more a man of the world, that is to say, of the fashionable world, than himself. This superiority was, of course, the more readily accorded by the baron, from the obvious fact, that no man can be in two places at once; and therefore it was impossible that he could, while passing his days in the stately dignity of his own castle, be enabled to become a well-known and distinguished member of the fashionable world in Paris.

Had his daughter been a son, it is likely enough that he would have preferred a continuation of the same remote dignity for him, to every other; but since his arrival at Paris, he seemed somehow or other to have become aware that there was more fuss made about a well-born woman of *fashion*, than even about a stiff-backed old baron, of sixteen quarters.

Moreover, he had acquired a sort of dim consciousness that his own departed lady, notwithstanding her close alliance with the Gotha Almanack, would have been a more brilliant and a more renowned personage in the salons of Paris, than she had ever been within the venerable walls of Schloss Schwanberg.

Such thoughts as these had naturally prepared him to listen to whatever Count Hernwold proposed, with a very decided conviction that he must be right; and the Count, with all his conscious superiority in such matters, had no great difficulty in persuading the wealthy father of his beautiful *fiancée*, that however costly his plans for their future *ménage* might appear, the birth, the station, the beauty, and the future fortune of his peerless daughter, rendered it no more than she had a right to expect.

What lavish expenditure was it possible he could propose, which would not have appeared a positive duty under such circumstances?

Upon one or two occasions, soon after this brilliant marriage had been proposed and accepted, it happened that a sort of generous rivalship displayed itself between the two gentlemen, as to which of them should manifest the most profuse generosity in the preparations that were making for its celebration; and there was certainly more than one Parisian tradesman who profited largely by this magnificent spirit of emulation.

As to the fair idol who received the offerings, had she been formed of wood or stone, she could scarcely have been more indifferent as to the beauty or the value of all that was thus laid upon her altar.

There was one point, however, on which, as the preparations went on, she soon ceased to be indifferent; and this variation from the dignified tranquillity with which she heard of, or received all the various offerings and preparations which marked the progress of the great affair of which all Paris was talking, arose upon the subject of the house that was about to be prepared for her reception in this gayest of cities.

When it was definitely settled between the baron and the Count that Gertrude *was* to have a mansion fitted up for her in Paris, it was Count Hernwold who, having convinced the baron of the necessity of it, seemed naturally enough to think that the pleasant task of selecting and embellishing it, devolved on him; and of course the execution of this task was rendered more agreeable still, by the necessity it occasioned of very frequent reference and consultation to, and with, the lovely lady in whose service he was employed.

Now this, after being exposed to it for a short time, became too great an annoyance to Gertrude to be endured.

Since the tremendous hour of self-examination which led to the atonement she was now making for all the disobedient feelings of her past life, she had persevered in the resolution then taken with unflinching constancy; feeling, perhaps, that any and every misery was preferable to what she had endured, when writhing, during the long hours of that dreadful night, under the intolerable weight of a self-accusing conscience.

But it appeared to her, that the sitting to listen to Count Hernwold's pompous boastings of all the expense, as well as all the trouble he meant to bestow upon the mansion which it was his purpose to purchase, and decorate expressly for her, was a penance that no duty called upon her to endure. There was something too in her manner of discussing the subject, which seemed perpetually calling for her gratitude; and as she felt none, she did not think it a part of her duty to affect it.

Why should she feel grateful?

She knew perfectly well that she was heiress to a very large fortune; for alas! poor girl, the knowledge of this fact had been the source of all the misery of her life.

But hateful as the consciousness of this had so often been to her, it might at least, she thought, save her from any feeling of *gratitude* for having a suitable house prepared for her.

"Gratitude should be a delightful feeling!" thought the melancholy girl. "It should be such as I used to feel for my dear mother, every day, and all day long. . . . Such as I have felt, and must ever feel, for Rupert, though he does not love me! But before he knew what love meant, he saved my life at the risk of his own. I can feel grateful for that . . . but I cannot, and will not, feel grateful because a man thinks it proper to prepare a fine house for himself and his family to live in. Count Hernwold is quite aware of the large fortune which must eventually be mine, and the fine house will some day or other be paid for by my father."

There was no form of words, however, that she could hit upon, by which she could civilly remind her noble lover of this fact; and at length it occurred to her, that the only means by which she could escape his annoyance, which she shrank from as a very painful addition to the various other miserable feelings which beset her, was by suggesting to her father, that it would be more accordant to the dignity of her position, as his daughter and his heiress, that the house preparing for her should be prepared by him, and not by the Count.

When she began her harangue, her father prepared to listen to her with a smiling countenance, his hands cosily folded over each other, and with the self-satisfied look which he generally wore, when she was talking to him, and which indicated that he was sure of being pleased—as, of course, he could not fail to be— as he considered every word she uttered, was spoken, as it were, by inheritance, and therefore, in fact, emitted by himself.

It was probably this persuasion which at once reconciled him to her proposal, which, to say the truth, was extremely far from being a rational one, and could only be excused in the poor captious bride-elect, by her profound ignorance of the ordinary usages of the world in matters of business.

The superb baron himself, however, was certainly not much more familiar with such matters than she was; but, nevertheless, it is possible he might have demurred a little at hearing this unexpected proposal, even though it proceeded from her, had it not been that it touched directly upon his ruling passion for being the first, and, in fact, the only very important person, in every business that was going on.

This was quite enough to procure his consent, and ensure his perfect happiness, as long as the bustling business lasted.

Of course, the first thing to be done, was to write to Count Hernwold, informing him of his paternal wish to be himself the purchaser, and the arranger of all the domestic elegancies and comforts which were to make the splendid dwelling provided for his daughter, worthy of the highly-honoured lady who had been selected as its mistress.

The Count was a good deal surprised by the receipt of this epistle, as he had certainly expected that the furnishing the elegant dwelling he had chosen was to be done at his expense, as well as the purchasing it. However, he was not a person to be at all likely to quarrel with such an arrangement as that now proposed. He was certainly possessed of a large landed property, but being one of those self-indulgent individuals who never refuse themselves any gratification as long as it is in their power to obtain it, he was as little desirous of spending money, when the doing so would not increase his gratification, as of sparing it when it would.

He wrote, therefore, a sort of playful answer to the baron's pompous announcement of his intentions, declaring that to him, and to him only, would he have yielded the delightful task of decorating the palace of his future sovereign.

Count Hernwold, in fact, was one of those gentlemen who, as the saying goes, had lived all the days of his life; and the consequence of so doing was, that, beautiful as he thought the Baroness Gertrude von Schwanberg, he would no more have thought of marrying her, than of marrying her maid Teresa, had he not known her to be an heiress, as well as a beauty.

It is certain, however, that it had never entered his head as a thing possible, that he might immediately turn her wealth to account, by getting her father to furnish his house for him; and the proposition afforded him all the pleasure of a most agreeable surprise, as well as being extremely convenient.

Not indeed that Count Hernwold contemplated any difficulty in achieving this necessary work himself, for his estate was large,

and his credit good; but, nevertheless, like most other men of
fashion, he would occasionally have been well pleased to have
found a little more ready money at his bankers than he had been
able to leave there. For, though by no means deserving the
epithet of *gambler*, Count Hernwold liked play, and would at any
time have considered himself as being in an extremely disagreeable position had he entered a salon where this pleasant excitement was to be found, with the consciousness that he had better
not play, because it would be inconvenient to him to lose.

Nor was he by any means sufficiently in love to prevent his
still wishing to pass the last animating hour or two of the day,
where play, in a gentlemanlike and honourable style, was going
on.

But since the important affair of his marriage had been arranged, he had been rather shy of risking the price even of a
bracelet or a mirror, for a certain degree of inconvenience would
have been the consequence, had he lost it; and Count Hernwold
detested inconveniences of all kinds, as heartily as we are assured
the evil spirit hates holy water.

The having his fine house furnished for him, without his producing a single rap to pay for it, was, therefore, an accident quite
as welcome as it appeared to him whimsical, and he became
gayer and more *debonair* than ever.

But the relief which this arrangement produced to Gertrude,
was great indeed; for not only did it exonerate her from the
necessity of listening to daily statements of the gallant and tender
anxiety with which the Count was decorating their future blissful
abode; but she was relieved also from the heavy necessity of
hearing her father rehearse, in his most oppressive style of eloquence, her extreme good fortune in having captivated a nobleman, whose personal merits, and high connections, rendered him,
in every way, so suitable an alliance for the heiress of Schwanberg.

That her aching, weary heart felt this relief, and that she was
thankful for it, is most certain; but she scarcely allowed herself
to dwell upon the consolation, greater still, of being left *alone*,
positively alone, for several hours in every day; for the baron,
though deeply conscious that he was the source and head-spring
of everything that influenced the destiny of his family, had never
been a busy-body, and would at the present crisis have felt
greatly at a loss how to perform the task he had undertaken, had
he not enlisted Madame Odenthal as his assistant.

The time had been, when Gertrude would have very painfully

missed the society of this long-tried and much-loved friend during the many hours of the day that she was driving about with the baron, from shop to shop, and from warehouse to warehouse, in order to assist him in selecting the vast variety of articles necessary for completing the task he had undertaken; but now the case was different.

Excepting Rupert himself, his mother was the person with whom she most dreaded to be *tête-à-tête*.

It is true, that from the time of her engagement to Count Hernwold, Gertrude had become a very altered person to her. She was, indeed, still observant, still gentle, still careful of her accommodation and comfort; but the tone of loving familiarity was gone.

Had Madame Odenthal believed such a change possible, she would have thought that Gertrude no longer considered her as a person with whom she could converse in a tone of perfect equality; but as often as this obvious idea suggested itself, it was *very nearly* rejected, both by the clear head and the warm heart of the affectionate Englishwoman.

Had she not known her from a child? And was it possible that such a nature as she had watched in Gertrude for long years of the most familiar union, could be suddenly changed in every feeling of the heart, and every process of the understanding, because she was about to be married to a middle-aged gentleman, whom her father had chosen for her husband?

The answer to this questioning would have been a decisive and indignant negative, had not facts occurred too strong to be set aside by any foregone conclusions.

Gertrude contrived, without any very positive breach of civility, however, to keep out of her way; and from the very day that her engagement to Count Hernwold was announced, the good woman had never found herself *tête-à-tête* with for her five minutes together, without the occurrence of something or other which was converted into an excuse for their being separated.

The position of Madame Odenthal in the family, where for the last year or two she had found so comfortable a home, was indeed strangely altered in more ways than one, for within a week or so of the painful change she had remarked in the manners of Gertrude towards her, she endured the great additional sorrow of being informed that her worthy brother, Father Alaric, had been suffering from a severe illness, and that he expressed so earnest a wish for the immediate return of Rupert, as to leave no possibility of refusing it.

Rupert himself, though so long an alien from the little vicarage which had been his early home, testified as much eagerness to comply with this request, as the good priest in making it; and within twenty-four hours after receiving the letter which summoned him, Rupert had taken a hurried and agitated leave of his mother, and of the family of which he had so long been a member, and was on his road to his former humble dwelling at Francberg.

CHAPTER XXVII.

Good Madame Odenthal was sorry for the illness of her brother, and sorry for the absence of her son; but she was considerably comforted, especially for the last-mentioned misfortune, by the marked change which again became visible in the manner of the capricious Gertrude towards herself.

Whether it were occasioned by the pity she felt for her, for having lost the society of her son, who was so justly beloved, or from a feeling that, perforce, she must be well-nigh weary of the assiduous attendance required of her by the indefatigable baron; in short, whatever might be the cause, it very speedily became evident to Madame Odenthal that there was no longer to be any estrangement between her and her long-loved Gertrude.

Now then, that they were again on their former confidential terms together, her *dame de compagnie* ventured to hint to her that she thought the baron was going to greater expense than could be necessary in furnishing and decorating a house which was to be her residence for only a third part of every year.

"If I mistake not," she added, "you are to pass four months out of every twelve at your own beautiful Schloss Schwanberg, four at Count Hernwold's fine place in Hungary, and the remaining four—merely the winter season, you know—in Paris."

Gertrude appeared to listen to her very attentively, and she had taken the hand of her old friend in hers, and fixed her loving eyes upon her face, in a way that could not leave any doubt as to her being fully engrossed by what she was saying; and yet there was something absent and vague in the tone in which she replied—"I suppose papa thinks that I shall like to have fine furniture, and, if so, it is very good-natured of him to take so much trouble about it."

"And is he right, Gertrude?" returned Madame Odenthal, looking anxiously at her. "Will it give you great pleasure to have all this fine, costly furniture?"

Gertrude withdrew her eyes from the examining glance of her companion, but she did not withdraw her hand, sitting for a minute or two motionless and silent. "Answer me, dear love!" said Madame Odenthal.

"What was your question, dear?" returned Gertrude, shaking her head, as if to rouse herself from the fit of absence into which she seemed to have fallen.

"I asked you, dear Gertrude, whether your father was right in thinking that it will give you pleasure to have your house so splendidly furnished?"

Gertrude was again silent for a few seconds, and then replied, in a voice that expressed anything rather than anticipated pleasure, "If the house, and all that he is putting into it, were more splendid than any other in Paris, or in the world, it would not, and could not, create in me the slightest sensation of satisfaction."

The delicate complexion of Madame Odenthal turned from pale to red, and from red to pale again. The gloomy words, and still more gloomy manner in which the unfortunate Gertrude made this declaration, seemed in an instant to remove everything like doubt from the mind of her truly unhappy friend, and to realise all the miserable suspicions which had long haunted her respecting the real state of poor Gertrude's feeling on the subject of her approaching marriage.

Madame Odenthal had been long debating with herself as to whether it would be most kind or most cruel to encourage the poor girl in opening her heart to her on the subject; and it is probable the decision would have been in favour of confidence, instead of reserve, had it not been for the again-and-again rejected, and the again-and-again returning, suspicion of the real object of the unfortunate heiress's affection. It was this which prevented her from seeking a confidence which she dreaded to receive; and even now, when the avowal of her repugnance to the marriage seemed more than half made, she affected to misunderstand the feeling she expressed, and replied, "I quite agree with you, my dear, in thinking that many people waste both time and money very idly in the decoration of their dwell-

13

iugs. Comfort is, in my opinion, much more essential than splendour."

"Comfort, Madame Odenthal? Comfort for me? Where am I to look for it? In uniting myself to such a man as Count Hernwold?"

Relieved by these words, melancholy as they were, from the dread which haunted her of hearing the name of the man she preferred to him, Madame Odenthal felt her courage revive, and, after giving a moment's rapid reflection to the subject, replied: "If you do not love him, Gertrude, it is not yet too late to say so. Your father's love for you is unbounded; and did he know that you disliked Count Hernwold, he would speedily find means to break the engagement."

"No, Madame Odenthal!" replied Gertrude, gently; "my father's love for me is not unbounded; but, even if it were so, it might not be in his power to make me happy. But this is idle talking. Your observation would not be useless, if you were to say that my good father loves me dearly. I know he does; I know that he loves me so dearly, as well to merit that I should love him a little in return. But I fear I have never yet loved him as I ought to do. My spirit is a perverse spirit. There is something within me that will not let me act as I would wish to do. But hitherto, perhaps, he has never had the misfortune to discover how very far I am from being what he wishes me to be . . . and from what he believes I am! He may be dead, and I too, my dear old friend, before I shall find so good an opportunity of pleasing him. I am quite determined to marry Count Hernwold. You must see, as plainly as I do, that papa is perfectly delighted—perfectly happy—at the idea of my doing so. It can make very little difference to me who it is I marry; and I do not mean that you, or anybody else, should ever hear me complain about it. Only I don't see any reason why I should add to my sins by pretending to love the carpets and curtains."

Madame Odenthal felt relieved. She plainly perceived that Gertrude had no intention of so completely taking her into her confidence as to allude to any other attachment; and whether she were right or wrong in suspecting that her own son was the object of it, she being left in apparent ignorance, was, on every account, most desirable.

Gertrude had, fortunately, not been looking at her; indeed, she evidently avoided doing so, fixing her eyes immovably upon a fragment of silk which she was unravelling.

Lightly, therefore, and with no appearance of suspecting that more was meant than met the ear, Madame Odenthal acquitted her of all blame for not being more in love with her fine furniture, and even ventured to say that she began to wish the baron himself had a less violent passion for it.

"I am certainly very ignorant in all such matters," said the good woman; "but it seems to me that your papa must be spending a very large sum of money. Did he ever tell you, my dear, the amount of the sum which it was his purpose to expend on your furniture?"

Gertrude smiled.

"I thought you knew my father better than you now appear to do," said she. "I can no more fancy that he would condescend to name a limit to the sum he destined for such a purpose, than that he would inquire how much the dinner of to-morrow would cost, before he sat down to it. Nor do I suppose that there is any reason in the world why he should do so." Madame Odenthal did not immediately reply to this; and, indeed, her silence lasted so long, that Gertrude, looking up from her ravellings, said, with some quickness, "What are you thinking of, dear friend?"

"You will laugh at me again, if I tell you," replied Madame Odenthal, shaking her head.

"And if I do, you ought to be glad of it. I was afraid that I had left off laughing. I suppose it is the near approach of all the prodigious splendour which is awaiting me, that has made me so grave. I really wish you would say something to make me laugh."

"But perhaps it may be less at my wit, than my folly, that you will feel inclined to do so," said the good woman, colouring; "but I will boldly tell you my thoughts for all that. My opinion is, dear Gertrude, that your papa is scarcely aware of the large amount of debts that he has already contracted. We are all so accustomed, you know, to consider his great estates as bringing him a revenue beyond what he can wish to spend, that I should not wonder if he had adopted the same idea himself; and that he may hardly be aware of the great difference of going on as he did at Schloss Schwanberg, and as he is doing now, at Paris."

Gertrude listened to this very unexpected statement with all the attention it deserved, and certainly felt no inclination to laugh at it; but nevertheless, she was so nearly in the state of mind which Madame Odenthal attributed to her father, that her words produced surprise, rather than alarm.

After silently pondering for a minute or two upon what she

13—2

had heard, she replied, "I am very glad you have thus spoken to me, my dear friend, because the mere possibility of such a want of thought and calculation on the part of my dear, generous father, is quite enough to make me anxious to know whether there is any, even a remote, possibility that such may be the case. It really never occurred to me to think of such a possibility before ; but now that the thought has been awakened, you may depend upon it, that it shall not be permitted to go to sleep again till you and I are both of us quite sure that it may slumber and sleep in safety ! "

What Gertrude thus promised, she speedily performed ; and it was by no means very difficult to find an opportunity for doing so ; for the very next time she saw her father, he was, if possible, more than usually full of his new-found occupation, and more than usually earnest in his declaration, that the mansion of Madame la Comtesse de Hernwold should be one of the most splendidly furnished in Paris.

Upon this hint she spoke, smilingly asking him if he had ever calculated what the amount of the entire cost would be, when the whole of his plans were completed.

He stared at her in return to this question with the most genuine astonishment, not altogether unmixed with displeasure.

"Is it possible, Baroness Gertrude," he said, "that the approaching change in your situation can have inspired you already so much with the spirit of a thrifty housewife, as to render such an inquiry on your part serious ? I flatter myself that my daughter has never yet had occasion to trouble herself by calculating the expense of any purchase which it may have been her pleasure to make ; and I conceive myself fully justified in assuring her that the nobleman who has been accepted as the future husband of my heiress, is by no means likely to be so sordid in his motives as to render any such anxieties needful, or, in fact, in any way proper, for the future. Never again, Gertrude, let me hear you express an idea so every way unbecoming your station ; and, at the same time, so every way unnecessary superfluous, and, in fact, ridiculous."

This speech was certainly the nearest approach to real scolding that had ever been addressed to Gertrude, and for a minute or two she felt rather at a loss how to receive it. But it required no longer interval to bring to her heart the conviction, that whether scolded or not, it was her duty to listen to him with respectful attention, and not to permit herself to be too certain that the baron might not be right in his estimates, and herself and Madame Odenthal wrong.

At the present moment, however, all she could do was to mollify the angry nobleman's offended feelings by the frank confession that she certainly was much too ignorant of the subject they had been discussing, to give any opinion upon it; and finally restored his good humour, by impressing a gentle kiss upon his forehead, and assuring him that she was only afraid of his being too generous.

CHAPTER XXVIII.

Notwithstanding the indignation both experienced and expressed by the baron at listening to this unexpected remonstrance from his daughter, the said remonstrance did not altogether fall to the ground.

It is, nevertheless, certain that the Baron von Schwanberg said no more than he felt, when he pronounced that such fears as his daughter had expressed, were alike unfounded as to fact, and injurious as to the imputation they cast upon his discretion.

But the baron was a great smoker, and ere he laid aside, that night, the splendid apparatus by means of which he indulged this habit, the idea occurred to him, that although Gertrude had talked not only like a child, but a silly one, it certainly was not impossible that among the vast variety of things which he had ordered, there might be some of a higher value, or, at any rate, of a higher price than he was aware of. He was ready to confess, too—at least to himself and his meerschaum—that he had never made himself very familiar with the price of ornamental furniture in any land, and that it was not unlikely that it might be rather particularly costly at Paris.

All the sage reflections brought him at length to the conviction, that it might be as well to order some few of the tradesmen he had employed to send in their accounts. And as one wise thought very often begets another, he also determined, just before he settled himself to sleep that night, that he would also send to the banker, with whom, on his arrival, he deposited the *sheaf* of bills which he had brought with him on arriving at Paris, and which had been since augmented by rents transmitted to him by his tenants in the country, in order to learn what balance he had in their hands.

The good-natured reader could only be pained were I to attempt entering into particulars either respecting tradesmen's accounts, or the banker's either. Suffice it to say, that the discrepancy between the amount of what he owed, and what was due to him, was great indeed! It was so great, in fact, as for a long time to appear to him absolutely incredible; and the terrible process of proving to him that a hundred thousand taken from eighty thousand, left, or rather *found*, a deficit of twenty thousand, was not performed by the unfortunate Madame Odenthal, without a degree of difficulty which amounted to very positive suffering.

Gertrude was not permitted to be present at any of the painful scenes which preceded his final conviction, that he actually owed, after a three months' residence in Paris, twenty thousand francs more than he had, at the moment, ready money to pay.

It was in vain that Madame Odenthal pointed out to him the very consolatory fact, that the deficiency was by no means large enough to occasion him any permanent inconvenience; and that if he would please to write a letter to Rupert, directing him what tenants to apply to, and furnishing him with the necessary authority for collecting the sum required, he would be sure to transmit the money to the Paris banker long before any of the tradesmen he employed would think of troubling him about the payment of their accounts.

The baron listened to her with a countenance that became redder and fiercer with every word she spoke; so much so, indeed, that she became frightened, and stopped short, long before she had said all that it was in her power to say, respecting the perfect facility with which a gentleman in his position might obtain what he wanted without the slightest difficulty of any kind.

"What!" he exclaimed, in the very loudest tone to which his very loud voice could be raised; "what! do you suppose I am going to send about begging petitions to my tenants, imploring them, for charity, to pay me my rents before they are due? Woman! are you mad? What have you ever seen in my conduct, or in my character, which can justify your holding so base an opinion of me? *I* go begging to my tenants? I? And which among them do you think would do me the great wrong of believing that such a message could come from me? Your son is a very worthy, respectable youth, my good woman, and the manner in which I have permitted him to domesticate himself with me, has conferred upon him a degree of distinction which nothing else could have done; and, as you must have observed both in his case and your own, has induced that distinguished portion of society to which I belong, to permit his approach to them, as if, in some mysterious manner, he really belonged to their class. I am as much aware the effect my patronage has produced, as either you or he can be; but I am not so bewildered in intellect as to suppose that if he were to be the bearer of such a message to my tenants, as you have named, they would any one of them believe that such a message ever came from me."

Being here somewhat out of breath, from the extreme vehemence with which he had spoken, the baron paused; and poor Madame Odenthal took advantage of the interval to say, that though quite aware that nothing but his great and most condescending kindness had enabled her son Rupert to enter into such society as that to which he had been introduced by his generous master; yet still she thought that his character for truth in the neighbourhood where he was best known, would ensure his being believed, let him deliver to the good people whatever message he was charged with.

The interval during which she had pronounced these few words, and which was accorded to her by the absolute necessity of breathing, in which the baron had found himself, had so far enabled him to subdue the first emotions of the anger she had excited, as to enable him to reply to her in a tone of comparative tranquillity.

"And do you really believe, my good woman," he began: "do you really believe that there is any man, woman, or child (above babyhood,) residing upon my estates, who could be persuaded by your son, let his reputation for truth be what it may, that I could have been guilty of such conduct as you now propose to me?" And here the baron positively showed his teeth, as if he were really laughing. It is said that the merely placing the features in this position, will often restore the feeling of good humour, as well as the appearance of it, and it might have been so on the present occasion, in the case of the baron, for it is certain that the extremity of his wrath against Madame Odenthal seemed to have relaxed, and he dismissed her, rather stiffly it must be confessed, but without any further appearance of positive anger, saying, "There! you may go now, my good woman. You have been useful to me in going through these long accounts, and I am no longer displeased with you. Indeed, I feel that it would be a great folly in me to feel any lasting displeasure, merely because

MY ideas of what is right and honourable, differ from those of a person in so very different a situation. Go, my good Madame Odenthal, but remember that you are not, on any account, to inform my daughter of the unpleasant discovery which I have made. If I have got in a scrape, I know perfectly well how to get out of it; but I will not permit the tranquillity of the Baroness Gertrude to be disturbed for a moment. You understand me?"

"Certainly," replied the good woman, still looking somewhat frightened. "The Baroness Gertrude," she added very earnestly, "shall never become acquainted with what has occurred through me."

"Very well, then," was the rejoinder, uttered in a much more condescending tone than was usual with him on any occasion; "if you will faithfully keep that promise to me, I will, on my side, promise you to forget the offence your strange proposal of my begging assistance from my own tenants, occasioned me."

And so they parted; the baron, with the appearance of being suddenly restored to good humour, and Madame Odenthal, with a very painful burden of sadness at her heart, from the persuasion that his profound ignorance, both on the subject of buying the things, and on the subject of paying for them, could scarcely fail of producing painful consequences for her beloved Gertrude, who she was only too sure was in no condition to endure new sorrows of any kind.

This melancholy insight, however, into her state of mind, was the result of no confidential disclosures on the part of Gertrude; but, in truth, no one, excepting her blind father, could have known her as she had been, and seen her as she was now, without perceiving that she was in no condition to endure any new anxiety well.

But if he had marked her pale cheek and heavy eye, he would have thought but little about it, and that little would only have gone to interpret the change into a sympathetic feeling with what he had experienced himself. His head was giddy with all the splendid predictions with which he was perpetually regaling himself; and if he had thought about it at all, he would assuredly have accounted for the alteration, by telling himself that it was very natural, and that any girl might feel a little nervous and overcome, at the idea of being the mistress of such a house as he was preparing for her.

But, notwithstanding all this, he was sufficiently awake to the necessity of paying his debts, to prevent his losing any time in commencing the operations by which it was his purpose to achieve this desirable object.

His first step was to write the following concise epistle to his intended son-in-law :—

"MY DEAR COUNT,

"Will you have the kindness to bestow an early visit upon me to-morrow morning? I will not beguile you with any hope of beholding the young lady who is so soon to have the honour of becoming Countess of Hernwold, for the visit I ask for is for myself, and not for her.

"Believe me, dear Count,
"Your truly attached, and
"Very devoted friend,
"VON SCHWANBERG."

This epistle was immediately dispatched by the hands of an intelligent messenger, with strict orders not to return till he had himself placed it in the hands of Count Hernwold.

This command was both speedily and accurately executed; and the messenger brought back a verbal, but very courteous reply, that the Count would wait upon him at an early hour on the following morning.

This was performed to the letter; for Baron von Schwanberg had but just quitted the breakfast-table, when his expected visitor was announced.

The meeting was exactly everything that a meeting should be between two noble gentlemen about to be so closely united. It was more than merely cordial—it was really affectionate. As soon as they were seated, the baron said, with the very slightest shade of embarrassment imaginable, " I am afraid you will accuse me of being a very careless father-in-law when I tell you, my dear Count, that I find I have not cash enough at my bankers to pay for the furniture I have been purchasing as a present to you and Gertrude."

Count Hernwold very perceptibly changed colour, but answered, with a bow and something like a smile, " There are many persons in Paris to whom such a discovery might be very disagreeable; but it is impossible I can believe, for a moment, that you are one of them. The Baron von Schwanberg is not likely to find any great difficulty in bringing his banker's account into good order again."

" I wish I could tell you that you were right in thinking so, my good friend; but, unfortunately, my case is exactly the reverse. Instead of my not finding any difficulty in setting this matter right, I am extremely sorry to say that I know it to be impossible that I should do so.

"Impossible, Sir, that you should be able to settle your account satisfactorily with your banker?" responded the astonished Count, with a look of unmistakable dismay. "I must suppose that you are jesting with me."

"Pray do not adopt such an idea as that," replied the baron, with considerable dignity. "I should be extremely sorry, Count, that you should suppose me capable of such idle levity as jesting upon a matter of business. I desired you to call upon me this morning expressly for the purpose of telling you of the foolish blunder I have made in buying more furniture for the house than I have money to pay for, and also to beg of you to help me out of the scrape. I presume, my dear Sir, that you will have no objection to my ordering some of the heavier bills to be sent in to you? I hate the notion of being in debt to these people, and, therefore, I sent to you as soon as ever I found out how the case stood."

Had the astonishment of Count Hernwold been less on hearing this most unexpected declaration, it is probable that he would have interrupted the august speaker before he had concluded his harangue; but, for a moment, he really looked and felt as if he had been thunder-struck. He speedily recovered himself, however, sufficiently at least, to rise from his chair, which he almost threw across the room in the unbounded vehemence of his indignation, and to say: "I presume, Sir, that you trust to your age as your protection against my just indignation. I have every reason to be thankful to your creditors for the impatience of their demands upon you. Had it not been for this, I might have been the victim of the plot so infamously laid for entrapping me into a marriage with your daughter, under the scandalous pretence of her having a large fortune. Thank heaven, I *have* escaped!—and I shall thank *you*, perhaps, for giving me a lesson, which I am not likely to forget to the latest hour of my existence."

Having pronounced these words with a vehemence that seemed for a moment positively to stun the astonished baron, he rushed out of the room, without deigning to close the door after him, and screamed the word "CORDON" in such an accent, as he passed the *porte cochere*, that the porter came forth from his lodge, and looked after him with a very strong persuasion that he had lost his senses.

The poor baron, meantime, sat for a few moments immovably fixed in his chair, and in a state of indescribable bewilderment. The intellect of the baron was not a very bright, and not a very rapid intellect; and he had to shut his eyes, and meditate very profoundly for a minute or two, before it occurred to him that the extraordinary scene he had just witnessed might . . . nay *must*, from the impossibility of finding any other cause, have been occasioned by his believing that he, the Baron von Schwanberg, intended to defraud him of the money he had proposed to borrow of him! Such a suspicion might certainly have been offensive to any gentleman; but upon the Baron von Schwanberg, it seemed to fall with a sort of preternatural violence sufficient to justify his following the base offender, and trampling him under his feet.

And, in truth, he rose from his chair, his face the colour of the crimson hangings that adorned his room, and his limbs trembling in every joint, but greatly more from rage than age.

It was, perhaps, fortunate for him that he felt conscious he could not stand, and he, therefore reseated himself; for, had he at that moment possessed the power of overtaking the man who had offended him, such a scene might have ensued as would not greatly have redounded to the credit of either of the noble gentlemen.

The first moments which followed his reseating himself were passed in a state of agitation much too violent for his mind, such as it was—poor old gentleman!—to decide upon the line of conduct which it would be best for him to pursue under the circumstances; and, in fact, the first symptom he gave of having, in some degree, recovered his startled wits, was his pulling the bell-rope which was ever and always attached to his own particular chair.

It was not, however, so much the act of ringing the bell which proved his recovery from bewilderment, as the use he made of the assistance it brought him.

"Desire Madame de Odenthal to come to me immediately," was the command he gave.

And, accordingly, Madame de Odenthal appeared before him with as little delay as possible.

"Sit down, my good friend; I wish to speak to you," were the words with which he greeted her.

Now, most assuredly, the Baron von Schwanberg had ever behaved with the most perfect civility to Rupert's mother; nay, since, by the agency of Gertrude's lace and velvet, he had made the remarkable discovery that her near approach to his own greatness had in some degree infected her with greatness also, he had often treated her with some small degree of ceremony and politeness; but he had never before called her his " good friend."

She was immediately conscious that something extraordinary must have occurred to produce so remarkable an effect, and her woman's wit immediately suggested the probability that this *something* was connected with the unexpected pecuniary difficulties with which she had been made acquainted.

She was too discreet, however, to utter a word of any kind, and silently obeyed his command, by placing herself in the chair to which he had pointed.

It would have been a great relief to the baron if she had been a little less profoundly respectful.   If she would only have asked him what he was pleased to want, it would have been a help to him.

But after they had both sat profoundly silent for several seconds, the proud old man was obliged to commence the history of the insult to which he had been exposed, without the assistance of any preface whatever.

The first sound he uttered was again a groan; and then he began as follows :

" Did I not know, Madame de Odenthal, that it is impossible you should for a moment believe that I should mistake, misrepresent, or in any way exaggerate, any fact which I take the trouble of relating, I should doubt your power of receiving, as credible, the statement I am now about to make to you."

" Indeed, Sir, you are right in thinking that your word cannot be doubted by me.   Whatever you state as a fact, must, I know, be considered as such by you."

" Considered ?   Considered so by me ?   Do you suppose I do not know a fact from a falsehood, my good woman ?   But this is only nonsense and idle talking.   Listen to me, and you shall hear what you must believe to be credible, only because I state it."

Madame Odenthal meekly bowed her head, and the baron resumed.

" Madame de Odenthal!   I have been insulted! grossly insulted !   HERE, in my own dwelling, where no man could mistake me for another, I have been insulted ! "

And having said these terrific words, he again emitted a groan, which seemed not only to proceed from his mouth, but from his whole large person, so deep and so awful was the sound.

Madame Odenthal looked, and certainly felt, frightened; and would probably have both looked, and felt, more frightened still, had she not been aware of the magnifying medium through which the Baron von Schwanberg looked at everything which concerned himself.

She clasped her hands, however, threw up her eyes, and listened to him altogether in a manner which led him to think that it was very probable the statement he had already made would have been too much for her, and that she might have fainted at his feet, had not her profound respect for him, acted as an antidote, if not positively as a restorative.

From this point, however, the discourse between them went on with a much nearer approximation to common sense, than was often to be found in the conversation of the baron, when either himself, or anything belonging to him, was the theme; and as no other themes possessed much interest for him, Madame Odenthal had great reason to be satisfied at the effect which her gentle commentaries on the actual state of his affairs produced.

As her genuine indignation at Count Hernwold's conduct was quite as sincere as that of the baron himself, they had the advantage of standing side by side, instead of face to face, during the discussion which followed; and the consequence of this favourable position was, that before the baron returned her parting salutation, she had succeeded in convincing him that the best, and, in fact, the only way of punishing the recreant suitor as he deserved, was by making him clearly understand that the suspicions he had expressed respecting the state of the baron's finances, were as false as they were sordid.

So soothing, in fact, and so delightful, was the picture she drew of the false noble's discomfiture, upon discovering that the trifling embarrassment which the baron had mentioned to him, arose solely from the *extreme* liberality which which he was accustomed to treat his tenants, that she carried with her, on leaving him, his full permission to write to Rupert, authorising him to apply to one or two notoriously wealthy individuals among his tenants, desiring them to accommodate him, by forestalling their rent-day by a few weeks.

This important point settled, the greatly comforted Madame Odenthal proposed to take her leave; but ere she had reached the door, she was recalled by the voice of the baron, who fixing his eyes on her as she again approached him, said with a very piteous expression, and heaving a profound sigh—" But how shall I break this dreadful news to my unhappy daughter?"

The thoughtful, meditative, quietly-observing Madame Odenthal, had never obtruded herself on the confidence of Gertrude, and no single syllable had ever passed between them which might justify the mother of Rupert in believing that the heart of the resolutely-silent heiress was too irrevocably his, to permit her ever being the wife of another, without much great and lasting misery. But nevertheless she did believe it.

Had the object of this secret preference been any other but her own son, the high moral rectitude of Madame Odenthal, as well as her fond, womanly heart, would have revolted against witnessing her union with another; but as it was, she felt that she could in no possible way interfere to prevent it, without a species of treachery, and breach of trust, which she could not contemplate for a moment, without rejecting it as impossible.

Respecting the feelings of Gertrude, she had no doubt; but the case was very different respecting the feelings of her son.

There certainly had been moments when neither his habitual reserve, nor the real wavering of his doubting and capricious heart, could prevent her suspecting that he had known Gertrude too long and too well, to see her become the wife of another, without suffering; but, either from the uncertainty in which she still remained as to his real feelings, or because her woman's heart taught her to *know*, that let the sentiments of her son be what they might, the misery which threatened Gertrude outweighed a thousand-fold any that threatened him, she felt infinitely more pleased by this rupture on her account, than on his.

At the moment when the voice of the baron called her back, she was (perhaps unconsciously) hastening her steps, in order to enjoy the unhoped-for happiness of seeing Gertrude's sweet face again turned towards her with a genuine smile ; and she herself, good lady, was for one short moment in great danger of smiling too, as the words of the dismal-looking baron reached her ear.

But she had not been so long domesticated with the Baron von Schwanberg, without being able to check an ill-timed smile, and it was with a countenance of very suitable gravity, that she again approached his chair.

" How will she ever get over it ? " resumed the baron, clasping his hands, and looking the very picture of woe.

Madame Odenthal gently shook her head, and looked very grave.

" Why do you not answer me ? " cried the impatient and imperious baron. "How is it to be done? How is it to be broken to her?"

"If I might take the liberty of advising," replied the *dame de compagnie*, in the gentlest of all possible voices, "I would say that it might be safer for her to learn this sudden and very startling information from me, than from your Lordship."

"Safer?" repeated the baron, in an accent of great alarm. "Safer? Do you really think that this frightful news will endanger her health? . . . . Madame Odenthal! I will challenge the villain! My hand, old as it is, can still handle a sword! My child, my daughter, my heiress, shall not die unavenged."

Madame Odenthal deserved great credit for the manner in which she listened to this heroic burst of paternal feeling. For one short moment she very wisely remained silent, to give him time to recover himself, so that he might comprehend her words; and then she said, "No, my lord baron, I apprehend no danger to her life from this disclosure, nor even to her health ; provided the intelligence be communicated with caution. Women are, of course, better able to judge than any man can be, how far a painful fact should be softened, or revealed by degrees. Let me undertake this painful task, Sir! Much, and deeply, as I feel upon this most extraordinary occasion, it is impossible but that you, Sir, must feel still more. I know that I can trust myself; and that should the news I bring affect her nerves, I am well experienced in the best and safest methods of restoring her."

The poor baron looked very greatly relieved.

"You are right, my good woman! Quite right! Perfectly right!

"Go then at once, and be sure to make her understand that her feelings shall be treated with the very greatest consideration on my part; and that I shall even be ready to allow her the interval of several hours to recover herself before we meet."

Madame Odenthal waited for no further orders, but glided out of the room with very considerable rapidity.

CHAPTER XXIX.

She found Gertrude, as she usually found her *now*, upon entering her morning sitting-room, with much goodly preparation made for sundry sorts of rational occupation.

There was a pretty little embroidering-frame on one side of the table, and an exquisitely perfect writing-desk on the other. A little work-box too, which might have served as pattern for that of a notable fairy queen, found room to display itself to great advantage, although the said table had also to accommodate a very miscellaneous and not very sparing collection of books.

There were among them, French reviews and English reviews, and rather a queer mixture of philosophical essays, and modern novels in German, French, and English. And in front of all this, on a sofa, precisely the same length as the table, as if they were formed to take care of one another, and resolved to let nobody in between them save their sovereign lady, sat the pale and heavy-eyed Gertrude, with a countenance indicating as little either of the activity or the intelligence which could have profited by all this elaborate preparation, as it is well possible to imagine.

She received her old friend, however, with a smile, though a languid one ; and raising herself from the indolent position which she had chosen in defiance of all the elaborate preparations for industry which were before her, she said, " Have you seen my father yet, dear friend? Do you think he will come here this morning, to talk again about that weary house? Oh! I am so tired of it. And then, dear, kind man, he *will* ask, you know, whether I like the things ; and the real truth is, I don't like any of them ! And besides, I happen to have a headache, this morning. Dear, dear Madame Odenthal! don't you think I might take a drive with you in the Bois de Boulogne, instead of talking about the house? I do assure you, it will do my head good."

" Yes, my dear, I do not see any reason why you should not do so. I will, if you please, ring and order the carriage directly."

" Oh! thank you, dearest! it will be such a relief! I will get ready, instantly ! "

And so saying, Gertrude pushed away her beautiful table, and stood up.

"Sit down again, my dear, for one moment, for I want to speak to you. We shall not lose time, for I have rang the bell, and it must take a few minutes, you know, before the carriage can come round."

Gertrude reseated herself, poor girl! very meekly, saying, with a sigh, "And you, too, have *something to say to me.* You cannot think how I hate those words! It is what papa, and Teresa, and . . . . . . everybody says, when they are going to plague me about the house, and all the rest of it."

The door was here opened by a servant, and the carriage ordered.

"Is it to come round directly, Madame?" inquired the man.

"We shall be ready in half-an-hour," replied Madame Odenthal.

"Now then, begin!" said Gertrude, with another languid smile. "You must not keep the carriage waiting, you know; and you must remember the bonnets, and the boots too, for I think I shall get out, and walk."

"You shall do that, and everything else you like, if you will but listen to me patiently for a minute or two; but I cannot promise that my talk shall keep quite clear of the *house*."

Gertrude looked at the cheerful face of her friend as she said this; and sighed to think how very little of sympathy there existed between them. She uttered no observation upon it, however, but prepared to listen, with the patience she had learned from necessity, to details concerning a future that her soul abhorred.

There was something in the subdued and patient expression of Gertrude's pale face, that touched Madame Odenthal to the quick. To relieve her from the misery she was suffering, became her first object; and setting aside all dignity and decorum as completely as if she had never beheld the Baron von Schwanberg in her life, she seized the listless hands of Gertrude, which lay crossed upon the table, and pressed them almost passionately, as she exclaimed: "You are not going to have any fine house at all, my dearest Gertrude! You are not going to have either the house or the husband. Your father and Count Hernwold have had a tremendous quarrel, in which his Countship behaved most scandalously, and there is not the slightest chance that you will ever set eyes on him again."

"Out of the fulness of the heart the mouth speaketh," is, for

14

the most part, a saw carrying a very respectable degree of truth
with it; but on the present occasion it proved unsound. Tears, in
like manner, are pretty generally considered as a proof of sorrow;
but to this also, as a general law, the conduct of my heroine
gave a very decided contradiction; for although the information
thus communicated by her *dame de compagnie* was unquestionably
of a nature to fill her heart with various feelings of one sort or
another, she did not utter a single word; and although all foregone conclusions would lead to the supposition that the news she
thus received must be very particularly agreeable to her, the
feelings it produced were demonstrated only by a violent flood of
tears. The loving friend, however, whose news had been thus
strangely received, seemed in no way either offended or greatly
surprised, by the effect they had produced; neither had she recourse to the ordinary formula usually resorted to on such occasions, consisting of the oft-repeated phrase, "Compose yourself!"

Madame Odenthal did not seem even to wish that she should
compose herself; but after looking at her and her streaming tears
with very evident gratification to her own feelings, for a minute
or two, she gently walked round both the table and the sofa, and
as all access to the young lady was precluded *en face*, she placed
her hands upon her shoulders behind, and drawing her head back
against her bosom, impressed once, twice, thrice, a loving kiss
upon her forehead.

Gertrude twisted herself round by a sudden movement, and
laying her head upon the maternal bosom of the friend who bent
over her, uttered the emphatic words, "Thank God!" and then
closed her eyes, not as if she were about to faint, or to sleep
either; but as if to indulge for a few delicious moments in some
waking dream, that this strange news had suggested to her.

"It is a great delight to have you thus, and to see you thus
looking the very *beau ideal* of heart-felt happiness!" said Madame
Odenthal, gazing fondly in her beautiful face; "but I must not
indulge myself in looking at you, Gertrude," she added, "for I
only obtained the baron's permission to break this tremendous
news to you, on condition of letting him know without delay how
you bore it."

"Poor, dear papa!" exclaimed Gertrude, with a more playful
smile than had curled her lips for many a month. "Indeed, and
indeed, I am sorry that he should have anything to vex him;
but this, thank Heaven! comes by no fault of mine! Go to him,
dearest, and tell him that I cannot lament the loss of a man so

unworthy in every way of the honour of being allied to him.
Say this, and say it very earnestly. . . . And then come back to
me, my own dear friend, and let us see whether we cannot once
more enjoy a drive in the Bois de Boulogne!"

It was impossible that an embassy could have been more faithfully or more ably performed; and Madame Odenthal returned
with the welcome assurance, that her report of the high-minded
dignity which Gertrude had displayed, had so greatly delighted her
anxious father, that he really seemed very cordially to agree with
her, in thinking the rupture of her marriage a subject rather of
joy than of sorrow; "and I rather think," she added, "that my
good brother Alaric will receive instructions for returning thanks
in the chapel, for this new mark of the especial intervention of
Providence in your favour."

Gertrude shook her head, and tried to look demure; but, in
truth, not only her own heart, but that of her *dame de compagnie*
also, felt so wonderfully lightened by this unexpected rescue
from the splendid marriage, which had been contemplated with
almost equal aversion by both, that neither of them should be too
severely censured, if they betrayed a little more gaiety on the
occasion than befitted so solemn an affair.

Most true is the saying, "everything is comparative;" and
what is felt to be happiness at one moment, might be justly held
to be the reverse at another, where the circumstances in which it
came upon us altered. How else can be explained the buoyant
light-heartedness of Gertrude, while conscious that she had fixed
a life-long attachment upon one who never did, and never would
return it? Or how can we comprehend the measureless content
of her companion, who believed, in her inmost heart (though she
had never breathed her miserable conviction to any one), that
her dear and only son was, and most probably ever would be, the
victim of an attachment which never could, and never ought to
be successful; and which would, in all probability, as far as his
happiness was concerned, neutralize all the great and unhoped-
for success which his worth and talents had achieved?

Yet, in despite of all this, Madame Odenthal felt as light-
hearted as if her age had been about one-fifth of its actual sum,
and she had been setting forth upon an expedition to gather cow-
slips for the formation of cool, sweet-scented balls, wherewith to
storm the eyes and noses of her vengeance-vowing companions.
Whilst Gertrude, the long-struggling, yet hopeless victim of a
passionate attachment as ill-requited as it it was imprudently
placed, even more than shared the gay hilarity of her companion;

14—2

for she not only felt as if she were once more at liberty to enjoy the bright sunshine, and the balmy air, but she felt also that she was relieved from a weight of hopeless and endless misery, which neither earth nor sky could have power to make her forget for a moment.

But in spite of all this giddy enjoyment, the two friends had wisdom enough left between them, to recollect before the end of their expedition, that the poor, dear, disappointed baron must be immediately relieved from his pecuniary scrape; and on this point, Madame Odenthal, notwithstanding her usual modesty of demeanour, presumed so far as to assure Gertrude, that to her very certain knowledge, there would not be the slightest difficulty in obtaining from among his wealthy tenants, enough to relieve him from the difficulty he had got into, half-a-dozen times over.

"And herein," she added, with an involuntary sigh, "my poor Rupert may really be of some use, although removed, by his duty to his uncle, from his personal attendance upon his generous patron. My brother, and Rupert also, know much better than your noble father seems to do, that the tenants of Schwanberg are among the most wealthy individuals of the district; and, if I mistake not, the only objection to applying to any of them in this manner, arises from the danger of inspiring envy and jealousy in those *not* applied to."

"Decidedly, my good friend," said Gertrude, laughing, "you are a very agreeable companion, especially to a forsaken young woman, whose papa believes himself on the eve of a very disgraceful bankruptcy. Were I to consult my own feelings only," she added, "I think I should like to prolong our *tête-à-tête* in this delicious Bois de Boulogne till the sun was down, and the moon up. But let us be virtuous! Let us remember how very different our condition is from that of poor dear papa!"

"Well, then, we will return to the carriage, and drive home; and greatly as I have enjoyed our excursion, I approve the doing so, most sincerely," returned her companion. "But what are we to do, dear Gertrude," she added, "about the notice which must be immediately dispatched to the tenants? I wish Rupert were here! He might be secretary in this business to some purpose."

Gertrude did not immediately answer; she even turned her head away for a moment, as if some distant object occupied her attention, and then her parasol fell to the ground, and she had to pick it up; but when this was accomplished, she said with very irreproachable composure and sedateness, "Notwithstanding the absence of Rupert, I think this business must be transacted by him. My father has never, since I was born, spoken to me on the subject of his domestic finances, though he has often alluded to the large extent of his property, and, therefore, I should not like, just now, to talk to him on the subject; but *you* may, dear friend, with the certainty of being listened to without any painful feeling on his part. If I were you, I should tell him that as his secretary is on the spot, the application for the money had better be made by him; and all my father need trouble himself to do, is to sign his name to the instructions which you must convey to your son. His signature, without his troubling himself to write a word more, will be quite sufficient, you know, to give authority to the document."

Madame Odenthal not only nodded her head in token of approval, but pronounced the words, " Yes, that will be the best way," with a decision of tone that left no room for further discussion. Not a word more, therefore, was said on the subject; they mounted the carriage and drove home in excellent spirits, discussing the beauties and deformities of the gay streets through which they drove, with a vivacity which pretty clearly proved that at that moment, at least, they were neither of them very unhappy.

<p style="text-align:center">~~~~~~~~~~~~~~~~~~~~~~~~~~</p>

CHAPTER XXX.

Madame Odenthal wasted not a moment after her return before she waited upon the baron, whom she found seated exactly in the same place in which she had left him, and evidently not at all the better off for the various newspapers which had been placed on the table beside him.

She had scarcely entered the door, before he exclaimed in a plaintive voice, " How is she, Madame Odenthal ? How does my insulted daughter endure this indignity ? "

" Indeed, Sir, she bears it exactly as your daughter should do," was her prompt and cheerful reply. " Her drive has done her much good, she is come back in excellent spirits; and though she is now lying down, to restore her strength after the shock of so very sudden a surprise, she bids me to say to you, that she hopes when you meet, you will both feel inclined most cordially to wish each other joy of the fortunate escape you have had.

"Madame de Odenthal!" returned the baron, with great solemnity, "you have expressed yourself with the greatest propriety, in saying that your noble and high-minded young lady had conducted herself in a manner exactly and most admirably becoming my daughter. I own that I am proud of her. The manner in which she seems to have endured this almost incredible outrage, is the result, as I feel deeply convinced, of a further special interposition of Providence in her behalf. But although I am fully aware of this, my good friend, and (crossing himself) duly grateful for this renewed demonstration of the remarkable interposition of Heaven in her favour, yet still my heart is heavy when I think of the difficulties which lie before me! In what way am I to address myself to the unsuspecting individuals from whom I am to ask the FAVOUR of a loan? I protest to you, that I almost doubt whether I shall have sufficient command of my feelings to write the necessary document."

"And why should you write it, Sir?" said Madame Odenthal, earnestly, but with an air of the very deepest respect. "My son," she continued, "has still the honour of being your secretary, although the illness of his uncle has made it his duty to absent himself for a time. If you will permit me to write, from your dictation, the amount of money which you require for your accommodation at this moment, Rupert, on receiving this document, will immediately apply in person to the individuals you may be pleased to name; and, if this be done by this day's post, I will venture to promise you, Sir, that an order to the amount will be transmitted to your Paris banker before the week is out."

The baron's eyes opened themselves to the very widest extent of their capacity, and he stared at the good widow in a manner that very nearly overset her gravity—nearly, but, very fortunately, not quite; for had she smiled at such a moment, the consequences might have been very serious indeed.

Having finished his astonished survey of her quiet face, he said, not without a little satirical bitterness, "May I take the liberty of asking you, Madame Odenthal, by what means you have made yourself so strangely familiar with the affairs of my tenants, as to enable you to say that such and such among them will, to a certainty, be able and willing to make this partial payment of their rents before they are due?"

"Indeed, Sir, I must be bold enough to say that I think I am able to answer your question without any risk of leading you into error. I have lived for many years among the worthy people who have the happiness of being your tenants, and so has my son, Rupert, also; and we both know, from our long familiarity with them, and with their prosperous agricultural concerns, both what they would wish to do under such circumstances, and what they are capable of doing, without the slightest inconvenience to themselves."

The baron listened to her with a heavy countenance—poor man!—which at first expressed nothing but anxiety; but, ere she had finished her speech, some bright idea seemed to have suggested itself, and he replied, in a tone infinitely less gloomy than before, "What you say, Madame de Odenthal, certainly appears to have great probability in it. You *must* be likely to know more about these worthy people than I can do. And, moreover, Madame de Odenthal, a thought came into my head while you were speaking, which makes me feel a good deal less uneasy about it than I did before. It is quite certain, you know, that neither the Baroness Gertrude nor myself can desire to remain any longer in this extremely dirty and disagreeable city, than may be absolutely necessary for the settling these troublesome bills; and if, as soon as we return to Schloss Schwanberg, I were to invite the tenants that your son, Rupert, may have applied to, as guests to dine at my own table, it strikes me that they may think themselves not badly requited for the service."

The countenance of the worthy nobleman had become very radiantly red as he pronounced these words, partly, probably, from a really generous feeling of pleasure at having hit upon so satisfactory a mode of requiting the obligation to which he was obliged to submit, and partly from some little latent doubt whether such a remuneration might not exceed the bounds of propriety.

But the very cordial smile with which Madame Odenthal listened to this proposal, soothed and comforted him considerably more than he would have chosen to confess, even to himself; and, after the pause of a moment, he positively returned her smile, and said, "I am not quite sure, Madame de Odenthal, whether, under such very particular circumstances, I might not, with great propriety, shake hands with my guests."

"And if you do, my lord baron," she eagerly replied, "I will venture to say, they will consider the whole transaction as one of the most gratifying events that ever occured to them."

And here again the baron rewarded her with a very gracious

smile, and said, in an accent as nearly approaching the jocose as it was possible for him to assume, "I shall begin to think, Madame de Odenthal, that you have been learning somewhat from my daughter, at the same time that she has been, doubtless, learning much from you ; for you have expressed, during the present conversation, sentiments and opinions very much in accordance with those which she has, naturally, inherited from her ancestors. And now then, my good friend," he added, with more condescension of manner and aspect than he had ever manifested to her before, "you had better return to your young lady. Give her to understand that I no longer feel any embarrassment about the debts I alluded to, and that I flatter myself we shall very speedily set off on our return to Schloss Schwanberg. I have little doubt, Madame de Odenthal, that she will agree with me in thinking that, when the 'Almanack de Gotha' records the name of a noble as honourable in character as in rank, the fittest residence for him must ever be on his own long-descended property. The busy cities of the earth, Madame de Odenthal, are only suited, as homes, for the dissolute and necessitous."

Madame Odenthal listened most attentively to his words, then curtsied, and prepared to depart ; but, before she reached the door, he recalled her, by saying, "Do not, in your statement of what has passed between us, to my daughter, mention my suggestion respecting the propriety of my shaking hands with such tenants as may have advanced my next rents for me. She is a person likely to be very greatly shocked at the idea of any unbecoming degree of familiarity between persons of different stations in life, and I should not wish her to know that I had entertained any such idea, till we have had an opportunity of talking the matter over together in private."

Madame Odenthal repeated her reverence, and respectfully pledged her word that his having given utterance to this generous and most condescending idea should for ever remain in secret, till such time as it was his pleasure to refer to it himself.

The long interview having at length reached this satisfactory conclusion, Madame Odenthal, at length, made her escape, and returned to Gertrude, not without some slight expectation of being scolded for the length of her absence ; but Gertrude was evidently in no humour to scold anybody. She playfully received her *dame de compagnie* with outstretched arms, and, in answer to her apology, said, with great *naïveté*, "Have you been very long, my dear, kind friend? I have taken a cup of chocolate, my dear

Madame Odenthal, and there stands a cup ready for you. But I am not quite certain that I would advise you to take it. I suspect that it is drugged."

"Drugged, my dear child!" exclaimed her friend. "What can you mean?"

"Do not look so frightened, dearest! I do not absolutely mean that it is poisoned. I do not even suspect my *ci-devant* lover, Monsieur le Comte de Hernwold, of having anything whatever to do with the beverage; but I cannot help having some slight suspicion that I am intoxicated. How do people feel when they are tipsy, Madame Odenthal? They feel inclined to laugh, and dance, and sing, don't they? . . . Well! do you know, that is exactly what I feel now."

Madame Odenthal behaved admirably. It can scarcely be doubted, that a woman possessed in no common degree both of deep feeling and acute intelligence, must, in the course of the weeks, months, and years, which she had lived in the closest intercourse with Gertrude, have discovered, or, at least, suspected, her secret; but neither on the present occasion, nor on any other, had she ever permitted the slightest symptom of this suspicion to appear. And now, when the bright laughing eyes of Gertrude evidently sought hers, as if to read there more of unreserved sympathy than she had yet expressed, her searching glance was only met by the cordial smile of affectionate pleasure at seeing her look so well and so happy.

When the certain and perfectly uncontrolled independence which must devolve on Gertrude, ere very long, (for the baron was an aged father for so young a daughter), and the splendid property which this independence would place at her disposal; when all this is considered, the conduct of Madame Odenthal may well be called admirable. For if she entertained any suspicion of the truth at all, and that she should not was, in fact, impossible, she must have been aware that one leading word from her would have sufficed to make poor Gertrude pour out every secret of her heart before her. But by uttering this word, Madame Odenthal would have betrayed her trust—and it was not uttered.

Madame Odenthal was, in truth, an excellent and high-principled woman; but, nevertheless, it is certainly possible that she would have found her task a more difficult one, had the judgment which she had formed respecting the feelings of her son, been as correct as that at which she had arrived respecting the young baroness.

But she did *not* believe that Rupert loved Gertrude.

Whether it were that he had more power over himself, and was thereby enabled more effectually to conceal his feelings, or that the wish to do so was in him more earnest, it is certain that, in point of fact, his mother had been kept as completely in doubt, or rather, in ignorance, of his real feelings, as Gertrude herself; and this want of discernment was so far fortunate, that it made the strict performance of her duty not only more easy, but, in all probability, more effectual also; for if Madame Odenthal had known all that was struggling at his heart, and all that he was suffering from self-delusion respecting the real feelings of Gertrude, it would, indeed, have been a difficult task for his mother to have refrained from uttering one single word which might have turned all his sorrow into joy.

But in truth, poor Rupert had perfectly succeeded in persuading everybody, except himself, that, as far as love was concerned, he was still completely "fancy free."

It is certain, that in some of her "night thoughts," the watchful *dame de compagnie* wondered that it could be so; but such thoughts did not influence her conduct, or demeanour, in any respect; and when poor Gertrude sometimes paused in the midst of one of her playful sallies, and said, with her speaking eyes still-fixed on the face of her friend, "Can you not fancy, Madame Odenthal, how very dreadful it must be, to be married to a man one hates?" The only answer she received was a quiet acquiescence, accompanied by the expression of affectionate hope, that such would never be the fate of her dear Gertrude.

But this delightful conversation—for delightful it was—notwithstanding the reserve of Madame Odenthal, was not permitted to last very long, before that truly excellent person hinted that she ought not any longer to delay seeing her father.

"Believe me, my dear child, he has suffered very severely," she said; "and although I have the pleasure of knowing that I left him less unhappy than I found him, he is, I doubt not, still in a state of mind to make a cheerful visit from you very desirable."

"Then he shall have it, my dear friend!" replied Gertrude, springing gaily from the seat which she had lately occupied with such supine languor. "I suppose he is seated in state, as usual at this hour, in the little drawing-room, with as many newspapers of all nations around him as would keep him hard at work for a month, dear man! were he to condescend to read them."

And then, without waiting for an answer, she bounded, rather than walked, out of the room, singing the very gayest song she could remember from the last comic opera.

"Poor dear! poor dear!" murmured Madame Odenthal; "and what is to happen to her next?"

But this murmur did not reach the ear of the heiress, and therefore the only sedative she had to bring her to a proper degree of gravity and discretion, was her own good filial heart, which caused her with all sincerity to breathe a sigh, because her poor, dear father could not share the delicious feeling of light-heartedness which made it so difficult for her to walk, instead of dance, as she approached him.

There, in truth, he sat, poor stricken, proud, old man, struggling to do battle to the feeling which oppressed him; but having neither sufficient energy of intellect, or of animal spirits to attempt it.

On hearing the door open, he felt quite sure that it must be Gertrude who was come to visit him; and being very deeply impressed with the persuasion that her pride of place was at least equal to his own, he scarcely dared to turn his eyes towards her, lest he should see her bright beauty blighted by the grievous insult he had received!

But before he could fix his eyes on her, she had sprung to him, and dropping on her knees, she threw her arms round him, and exclaimed, "Join with me, my dearest father, in thankfulness for the chance which has happened to us! I do not mean," she added, with great animation, "I do not merely mean my having escaped an union with so contemptible a being, though you will easily believe, my dearest father, that it is not likely your daughter should be insensible to that; but what my thoughts chiefly dwell upon at the present moment is, the opportunity afforded you of humbling his unworthy spirit to the dust!"

"What is it that you mean, my poor, dear Gertrude?" returned her father, in a very piteous voice. "That he has humbled *me*, and, alas! my dearest child, that he has humbled you also, is but too certain; but what you mean by my humbling him, I cannot even guess."

"But you will do more than guess, you will see the whole truth at once, when I point out to you the effect of the step you have so wisely decided upon, as to your manner of paying these paltry debts. Trust me, dearest father, it would have been less injurious to your dignity if you had sold the last diamond from the rich casket of your family, than if you had permitted this man to assist you for a single hour by a loan."

"My dearest Gertrude!" returned the old man, gazing at her with the most profound admiration; "most truly may I say that no son could better deserve to inherit my honours, and my wealth, than you do; for I must confess, though I should be sorry to awaken a feeling of vanity in your young heart by saying so, that you inherit also the power, of which I am certainly conscious in myself, of expressing well the noble feelings of our race. But, alas! my child, though these feelings belong to us by the right of birth, and are, and must for ever be, our own inheritance, this is no moment in which to boast of them; for must they not for a short, but most miserable interval, be laid aside, while I become the creditor of some of my own tenants?"

"Laid aside, my dearest father? Laid aside at the very moment when there is such especial reason for blessing Heaven that they are awake within us? Believe me, father, it is the noble feeling of which you speak, that, after a moment's reflection, will teach you to rejoice, not only at having escaped the danger which threatened us, of forming an alliance with one so every way unworthy to approach you; but also for the gratifying manner in which you are enabled to thrust him and his vulgar insolence from you."

"Gratifying? Oh, Gertrude!" murmured the still crest-fallen baron, with a groan.

"Yes, papa! Gratifying in the very highest degree. I have listened in a manner that could not, perhaps, be considered as dignifying in you, to my excellent companion and friend, Madame de Odenthal, while she described the pride and joy which she knew would be felt by those whom her son should select as the honoured individuals from whom this trifling and temporary accommodation would be accepted. It is delightful, papa, to know that the same act which will afford accommodation to you, will be productive of such heartfelt pride and pleasure to them."

"It *is* delightful, my dear child!" replied the baron, seizing, as was his wont, upon every suggestion calculated to gratify his master-passion. "I really believe that you, and your very intelligent *dame de compagnie*, take a more correct view of the subject than I permitted myself to do in the first instance. But even so, my dear Gertrude," he continued, "I do not well perceive how my being made aware of these excellent feelings on the part of my tenants, can humble this insolent Count Hernwold."

"Do you not, dear papa?" replied Gertrude, laughing. "I think I do. There can be no doubt that when he left you in the insolent manner you have described, he felt persuaded that some difficulties would arise in the final settlement of these furnishing accounts ; because, as you will remember, everything was in the first instance ordered by him, and for everything he ordered himself, he is, of course, answerable. Depend upon it, therefore, that he will not rest till he has announced to the tradesmen you have both employed, the difficulty which might attend your immediately paying their bills, in the amiable hope and expectation that they will immediately become troublesome to you."

The baron, who was listening to every word she uttered, as if an oracle was proclaiming his destiny, here uttered a piteous groan. To which his daughter replied, by taking his hand, kissing it, and looking into his face with a smile.

"Wait a moment, papa!" she resumed ; "I have not come to the conclusion of my prophecy yet. While our noble Count is meditating on the best means of tormenting us, you will be engaged in writing an epistle to him."

"I, Gertrude?" exclaimed her father, colouring violently. "I write a letter to the man who told me that I wanted to entrap him into a marriage with my daughter? Child! child! you know not what you say! Notwithstanding my age, and that my hand is no longer as steady as it was wont to be, I may be tempted yet, to send him a challenge to mortal combat; but in no other way will I communicate with him."

"Nor will I ask you to do so, dear papa," returned Gertrude, gently ; "unless you should think it worth while to humble him in the manner I propose. What I wish is, that you should write to him as if his rude manner of leaving you had made little or no impression upon your memory, and tell him that you write merely to inform him that he need not feel any uneasiness respecting the unpaid bills, for that you should settle them all immediately, having discovered that you had ready money at your command greatly beyond the amount required, and that your mistake had arisen from the accidental absence of your secretary, who is in attendance upon a sick relation in the country."

Gertrude here ceased speaking ; but her eyes were still fixed upon the baron's face, and she had the extreme satisfaction of perceiving that the contraction of his brow relaxed as she proceeded, and then that he smiled at her with a look of inexpressible satisfaction. But this happy state of things only lasted for a moment. His countenance was again over-clouded by heavy gloom, as he said, "Such a letter, Gertrude, would be excellent, most excellent, and I should certainly write it with more pleasure than I ever wrote anything in my life; but how can I be quite certain, Gertrude, that Madame Odenthal is right about the tenants? Just think, my dearest child, what my feelings would be, if, after writing such a letter to Count Hernwold, I should get a letter from Rupert, telling me that the persons to whom he had applied, were either unable, or unwilling to assist me."

"Depend upon it, papa," replied Gertrude, looking very gaily at him; "depend upon it, our Madame de Odenthal would not speak with so much confidence on the subject, if she had not very good reason for doing so. But I will not deny, papa, that the very same idea occurred to me, and I told her frankly, that if this should happen, your position would be greatly more painful than it is now; for that you would have committed yourself, by stating to the Count what was not true."

The poor baron again became as red as fire, and exclaimed, in no very gentle accents, "Nothing on earth, Gertrude, shall induce me to run such a risk."

"I quite agree with you, dearest papa," she replied, "and so did Madame Odenthal also; but having acknowledged that the doing this would be worse than all the debts in the world, she quietly left the room, but returned to it a moment afterwards, with the casket containing my dear mother's magnificent pearls, which, with their superb settings, are, we all know, worth very considerably more than the thirty thousand francs. 'Here, Gertrude,' she said, 'is a guarantee which will effectually protect your father from the possibility of any such disaster; nor is this all,' she added, 'as my lord the baron well knows; for I have heard him say, that the family diamonds are of much higher value still, to say nothing of the massive plate, which would furnish the sum required half-a-dozen times over.' "

The baron breathed again. "Yes; I see, I see, my dear! That Madame de Odenthal is decidedly a very clear-headed woman," he replied, after meditating for a minute or two. "I understand her argument perfectly, Gertrude. It is not that she has any thought of proposing to me that I should sell my family jewels or plate. She is a bold woman, but not quite bold enough to propose *that*. I suspect," (and these words were accompanied by a very pleasant smile,) "her meaning is to show, by reminding me, very properly, of my various resources of family wealth, that I may write to this audacious Count, in such a manner as to make him most miserably conscious of the insolent blunder he has made, without my running any risk of pledging my noble word to a statement which might by any possibility be untrue, or in the very slightest degree inexact."

"You have stated the case exactly, my dearest father!" returned Gertrude, looking greatly relieved; for she had, not without reason, began to fear some Quixotic blunder on the part of her father. But now he had every appearance of being quite as well pleased as herself, and she therefore ventured to add, "Now then, dear papa, you will write the letter we were talking about, to this blundering lover of mine. Oh! what an escape you and I have both had, my dearest father."

"We have indeed, my Gertrude!" replied the old man, looking at her very fondly; "and if I should indeed manage to get through these troublesome embarrassments, and find myself once more with you and the good Odenthals, at Schloss Schwanberg, I really think I shall feel happier than I ever did before in my life."

There was something in these words which seemed to have a very decidedly pleasurable effect upon Gertrude, for they caused her to clasp her beautiful little hands, as if she had achieved a victory, and inspired her with courage to say, " Now then, papa, let me write the letter to Count Hernwold, just as if I were your secretary, as Rupert used to be, and you shall sign your name to it. Will you?"

It was evident that the baron was at that moment too happy to be dignified, for he positively laughed, as he replied: " Yes, my dear, I will let you do that, or anything else you please, provided, you know, that you consult your *dame de compagnie*, as all young ladies ought to do. I dare say that, between you both, the letter will be everything that the Baron von Schwanberg could wish it to be."

Gertrude waited for no further compliments, but springing from her chair, she gaily kissed her hand to him, and vanished.

<p style="text-align:center">~~~~~~~~~~</p>

CHAPTER XXXI.

LADIES have, doubtless, written letters to lovers under a vast variety of circumstances, but, for the most part, they may be easily classed under one of three heads—the hard, the soft, and the indifferent. But the letter which Gertrude had obtained permission to compose for her lover, did not exactly belong to either.; moreover, it was to be written in the name of her father, and not in her own ; but, nevertheless, she left the baron's presence with such a degree of excitement and animation visible on her countenance, as clearly demonstrated that her heart was deeply interested in the epistle she was about to indite.

Luckily for her feelings, she found that her *dame de compagnie* was not in their morning sitting-room, and she, therefore, sat down with the pleasant consciousness that she might indulge in the delightful emotion that was palpitating at her heart, without any restraint being put upon it by her *governess*.

Poor Gertrude! If there was a little merry mischief in that heart, as she sat down to perform the task she had undertaken, and which had been so solemnly entrusted to her, it must be remembered that she was still very young, and that it was very long since any merry thought of any kind had crossed her fancy. It may also be fairly stated in her defence, that she had always believed the addresses of Count Hernwold to be interested. This belief had certainly never been a source of pain to her; but, in fact, from the terrible hour in which she had determined to atone for all her past offences, by yielding herself implicitly to the wishes of her father, it had been only too decidedly the reverse. Yet, even on this point, excuses might be found for her.

"Surely," thought she, "our union will be less hateful, if it be formed on both sides upon motives which have no mixture of love in them, than if one were actuated by such a feeling, and the other not."

And in so thinking, she was surely right, although she was as surely wrong in believing such a union could be justifiable at all.

As it was, however, neither her tender conscience, nor her tender heart, troubled her with any reproaches; and it was, therefore, with a strange mixture of satisfaction and amusement, that she penned the following epistle :—

"The Baron von Schwanberg presents his compliments to the Count Hernwold, and begs him, in all courtesy, and without any mixture of jesting, to explain to him the real cause of the abrupt departure by which he concluded his late visit.

"The Baron von Schwanberg is aware that younger men than himself often find, and often make, amusement, from a playful pretence of being serious, when, in truth, they are only jesting; and, on the other hand, the Baron von Schwanberg flatters himself that Count Hernwold must, in like manner, be aware that persons of a more advanced age than himself, are more slow in perceiving a jest than in resenting an offence, which may be grave. On the present occasion, however, the Baron von Schwanberg is in no way disposed to resent, as gravely as it *might* be resented, the indiscreet burst of hilarity with which the Count Hernwold received the confidential communication which had been made to him relative to the state of the baron's banking account. Nevertheless, the baron must be excused for saying, that this feeling of forbearance, on his own part, does not go far enough to enable him to overlook the offensive freedom, and forgetfulness of proper deference, displayed in the mode of Count Hernwold's departure from his presence. Baron von Schwanberg, therefore, takes this opportunity of announcing to Count Hernwold that the projected alliance between their houses can no longer be thought of. This is decidedly a very grave termination to an ill-timed jest, but it is inevitable. As a proof, however, that the Baron von Schwanberg retains no harsher feeling towards Count Hernwold than the respect which he owes to himself renders absolutely necessary, he takes this opportunity of informing him that the hurried statement which he had made respecting his temporary deficiency of ready money, arose from a mistake, which, being now rectified, leaves his affairs in the same unembarrassed condition as they have ever been."

This epistle was so rapidly written, that, upon Gertrude's returning to her father with the open sheet of paper in her hand, he greeted her with a deep sigh, and said, very despondingly, "Ah! my poor dear Gertrude! you have found the task too difficult for you and the good Odenthal together! I am not at all surprised, my dear. It is no easy matter to write such a letter as we ought to send. Nothing was ever so unfortunate as Rupert's absence! He is so used to pen-work, that everything of the kind seems easy to him; but, to persons in our condition of life, it is quite a different thing."

Whilst he was thus speaking, Gertrude had approached his chair, holding her letter in one hand, while the other was laid affectionately on his shoulder. But the disappointed baron was much less inclined than usual to return her caress. He first shook his head, in a helpless way, from side to side, and then turned it fairly away from her, saying as he did so, "It certainly was rather foolish, my dear, to fancy you could do it, when I myself confessed that I saw considerable difficulty in it. You

15

had better send Madame Odenthal to me. Perhaps, after all, the best thing we can do is to make Rupert come back again immediately. He would find no difficulty at all."

"Don't do that, papa, till you have just looked at what I have written," said Gertrude, placing her production in his hands, and conscious, perhaps, that her father's proposal had brought a deeper glow to her cheeks than she would like to hear any commentaries upon.

"Have you, then, really written something already, my dear child?" cried the delighted old gentleman, adjusting his spectacles.

"Let me read it to you—shall I, papa?" said Gertrude, rather eagerly; for, in truth, she was rather proud of her composition, and fancied, perhaps, that her manner of reading it might be more advantageous than his.

"To be sure you shall, dearest!" he replied. "I know you can read well, Gertrude; and, I daresay, I shall find that you can write well also," he added, with recovered spirits. "Now, then, my dear, begin!"

"Yes, papa. I will only keep you waiting one moment, just to remind you that, angry as you justly are with him, this letter must not express it, because, you know, the real reason of our writing it is, that he may learn by it, what a blunder his impertinent suspicions led him into; and we could not do this, if we did not express the intelligence we wish to convey, in a civil form. I think he will be vexed, papa, at losing the fortune, though he may not care much about the lady."

"If I thought THAT, my darling Gertrude," replied the father, in very vehement anger, "I do not think that it would be proper to write anything to him, except a challenge!"

"I think this letter will vex him more than a challenge would have done," replied Gertrude, laughing.

"Read it, then! Read it, Gertrude!" cried the old man, rubbing his hands with every appearance of satisfaction.

And she did read it; and, moreover, she certainly did her own composition justice, for she contrived to make even our baron comprehend that there was a mixture of wormwood in it. But if the ceremonious wording of the epistle made him wince a little, from the doubt it engendered in his mind as to the possibility of its being too civil, the concluding sentence set it all right. She had never seen him so pleasurably excited before. He threw his arms round her, kissed her hands, patted her hair, and at last exclaimed, as a sort of summing up of every delightful feeling in one, " Gertrude! if you had been a son ten times over, instead of a daughter, you could not have done anything which would more clearly have marked the race from which you are descended. If my own hand had written every line, it could not more clearly have borne the mark of SCHWANBERG upon it, than it does now! But it is not every name in the Almanack de Gotha, my beloved Gertrude, the representative of which, whether male or female, could produce such a letter as this!"

And then, after silently meditating on the subject for a minute or two, he added, "It strikes me, Gertrude, that the very remarkable perfection of your character and abilities, must arise from the fact that both your parents . . . . observe what I say, my dear girl, I think it is because both your parents, female as well as male, are to be found, and repeatedly found, as you know, in that extraordinary and most precious volume (the like to which cannot, as I have been assured, be found in any other country of the known world); I think, I say, that this must be the reason why you are so very decidedly superior to every one else, whether male or female."

Poor Gertrude had been accustomed for so many years to the being assured by her father that she was superior to every one else in the world, that though very weary of hearing it, she had become in some degree indifferent to the sound; but at this moment she could not resist the temptation of saying, "At any rate, dear papa, the Count Hernwold cannot agree with you in opinion, on this point."

But she would not have uttered the idle jest, had she been at all aware of the effect it was likely to produce. It was upon her saying this, that he now for the first time seemed to be aware of the personal affront to her; and so vehement was the irritation produced by it, that she bitterly lamented her imprudence.

It was during one of the very violent bursts of indignation which recurred from time to time upon this theme during the course of the day, that a servant entered the saloon in which the baron, his daughter, and Madame Odenthal were sitting after dinner, and delivered a letter to his master.

The poor baron was, in truth, so completely worn out and exhausted, by the unusually vehement emotions which he had experienced and displayed during this suffering day, that he uttered another of his dismal groans, as the the silver waiter was most respectfully presented to him, with what looked an immensely voluminous letter deposited upon it.

15—2

The tired old man looked, and felt, as if he were afraid to touch it; and so very intelligible was the mute eloquence of his weary glance, that his daughter, who seemed to have gained by the events of the day all the energy which he had lost, sprung to his rescue, and taking the voluminous-looking dispatch from the footman, drew a chair close to him, and with a look which might have inspired hope and joy in any being capable of receiving either, she said, "May I break the seal of this magnificent-looking dispatch, papa? Let me open it, and read it to you, shall I?"

It is by no means quite impossible, that the Baroness Gertrude (though not quite such a phenomenon as her papa believed her to be) might have conceived some slight suspicion as to the contents of the dispatch she held in her hand, for she really was an intelligent and quick-witted young lady. Moreover, she had recognised the seal of her quondam lover, though her father had not, and she certainly anticipated considerable amusement from a perusal of the contents.

The reply of her father was, as she anticipated, a ready acquiescence; on receiving which she broke the splendid seal, detached the ample cover, and read as follows:—

"My Dear Lord Baron,
    "I have to acknowledge a weakness both of character and conduct, of which I honestly and honourably assure you, I am most heartily ashamed. Permit me to recapitulate to you, the very foolish circumstance which led to the folly, the worse than folly, which I committed in our last hurried interview. At the last ball, at which I enjoyed the exquisite happiness of meeting that loveliest of all created beings, your unequalled daughter, I tortured myself during the course of the evening by fancying that she looked coldly on me, nay, that she spoke more coldly still. My brain was on fire! I dared not trust my feelings, but retired at an early hour to my sleepless pillow. The mental agonies which I endured during that terrific night can never be forgotten while I live! It was within a few short hours of this dreadful paroxysm of jealousy and despair, that I received from you information, which would at once have appeared incredible from every other human being, namely, that your pecuniary affairs were in disorder. Nay, my dear and honoured friend, you must excuse me for saying, that not even from you would such a statement have appeared serious, had not my tortured mind been so frightfully harassed by the ideas which had

haunted me through the preceding night, as to be incapable of forming a rational judgment on any subject.

"But, as it was, I listened like a madman, believed like a madman, and acted like a madman!   And what remains for me now, but to throw myself at your feet, and at the feet of your angelic daughter, and implore you both to forgive, or rather, to forget the conduct which was dictated by insanity, and to receive again the homage and the adoration of one, who would shed his heart's blood to prove his devotion to the noble Baron von Schwanberg, and his adored and too lovely daughter.

"I remain, my ever honoured friend, in the ardent hope of being permitted, at no distant day, to substitute the more precious name of son, ever and for ever,

"Your devoted Servant,
"JOACHIM FECKLENBORG ALEXANDRE
"COMPTE D'HERNWOLD."

Gertrude read this letter, from the address to "My dear Lord Baron," to the signature of the devoted "Count Hernwold," with a well sustained dignity of voice and tone which might have done honour to the town-crier; and when she had finished the perusal, she re-enveloped it in its ample cover, closed it carefully, so as to make it look almost as splendid as it did before she opened it, and then, rising, presented it to her father with a very low and ceremonious curtsey.   If she hoped to obtain a smile from him by this, she was disappointed, for as he held out his hand to receive the letter she presented, he looked considerably more puzzled than amused.

"What does it mean, Gertrude?" said the poor baron, looking at her very much as if she had been an oracle.

"This Count Hernwold," he continued, "is a man of very high rank, and certainly very nobly connected; and I would on no account, either to him, or to any other nobleman, give way to any feeling of unjust anger; but surely, my judgment cannot have deceived me, can it, Gertrude?   Surely this letter of his to-day, is not at all consistent with his conduct to me, when I mentioned the embarrassment I was under about the tradesmen, you know, and the mistake I made about the banker.   I can't understand it, Gertrude.   I don't know what he means.   Do you think he is in earnest, my dear?"

"Yes, papa," replied Gertrude, "I have no doubt that he is quite in earnest."

"Then I suppose you wish him to come here directly. . . . Do you, Gertrude?"

"My dearest, dearest papa!" exclaimed Gertrude, fondly embracing him; "can you suppose for a moment that I can wish ever again to see a man who has insulted you?—First, by daring to treat you with indignity, when you stated to him your mistaken belief that your affairs were embarrassed; and then again, by daring to offer the renewal of his odious addresses, when he discovered that your noble property was *not* embarrassed at all! Never, never let me see him again, papa! if you love me!"

"I do love you, my darling child! And you never shall see him again, Gertrude!" exclaimed her delighted father; who, till she had uttered this consoling address to him, had positively trembled as if he had been seized with palsy, from the terrible idea that she was, perhaps, too much in love with the man who had insulted him, to bear the thought of refusing him, now that he was come forward again to offer himself.

Gertrude, meanwhile, on her side, was quite as much relieved as himself; for most assuredly she had begun to conjure up in her long-harassed mind, the frightful idea that she was not even yet safe from him. His large estate, his lying, but seemingly-humble apology, and that terrible page full of him in the Almanack de Gotha, might altogether, she thought, have power to destroy all the happiness which had gleamed upon her during the last few hours.

But this frightful vision, which seemed to turn her hands and feet to ice, and her cheeks to burning coals, vanished into something better than thin air, as the blessed words, "You never shall see him again," reached her ear.

"And now for the answer, my Gertrude," said the happy-looking baron, in a tone of light-hearted cheerfulness, which seemed for a moment to conquer even his dignity; "what answer are we to send him?"

"Let me send it! Pray, papa, let me send it! May I?" said Gertrude, coaxingly.

"Yes, my dear," he replied, after meditating for a minute or two, with his accustomed look of solemnity; "yes. I feel sure that I may trust you. But remember, my dear love, it must be very decisive."

"It shall," said Gertrude.

"Must it be written, Gertrude?" rejoined her father, anxiously. "Be very, very careful what you say to him."

"No, dear papa! I think we have had writing enough," was

her answer; and then she added, "Have the kindness, dearest Madame Odenthal, to recal Hans. I daresay he is in waiting, on the landing-place."

Madame Odenthal, who had been listening to all this with almost as much amusement as interest, lost no time in complying with this request; and on opening the door which communicated with the ante-room, she found that Gertrude's judgment as to the servant's probable vicinity, was perfectly correct, for there stood Hans, at the distance of about six inches from the key-hole.

"Come in, Hans," said the baron, with great solemnity. "Come in, and shut the door. The Baroness Gertrude will give a verbal reply to this dispatch."

Hans did as he was bid; that is to say, he closed the door behind him, and advanced two paces into the room.

Gertrude looked rather embarrassed, and approaching her father, whispered in his ear, "Don't you think, papa, that the best reply will be simply to say, that the letter does not require an answer?"

"Why, then he will come here at once, if you say that, Gertrude!" said the baron, looking perfectly confounded.

"I think not, dear papa," she replied, in a whisper; adding, in the same tone, "ask Madame Odenthal what she thinks."

"No! Baroness Gertrude!" returned the old man, proudly; "I will ask no one. Your judgment deserves to be trusted. Besides, my dear, we know," he added, touching his forehead with his forefinger, "where all your opinions *really* come from, in some way or other, and therefore I shall make no further difficulty about it . . . Tell the Count Hernwold's servant," he said, turning to Hans, with an air of peculiar dignity; "tell the Count Hernwold's servant, THAT THERE IS NO ANSWER."

It really seemed as if the grandiose tone of his own voice had acted as a commentary on the message, and enabled him to understand the spirit of it; for no sooner had the servant closed the door behind him, than the baron said, addressing Madame Odenthal, "I really think, my good friend, that our young baroness is as right upon this point, as I have ever found her upon every other. I really think, though it did not strike me so, quite at first, that the sending no answer, says more in the way of expressing contempt, you know, than almost anything that could have been written. If a person speaks to you, Madame de Odenthal, and you don't choose to answer, I should say that it was just about the most affronting thing you could do."

As Madame Odenthal very cordially expressed her conviction that the longest letter that ever was written could not by possibility express so much contempt as the sending no answer at all, the remaining hours of that happy day were passed in "measureless content by them all;" and certain it is, that had not my heroine's sublime father been just about as dull-witted as he believed himself to be the reverse, he could not have failed to discover now, though he had never dreamed such a thing possible before, that the heiress of his wealth, and the glory of his house, had been within a hair's breadth of sacrificing the happiness of her whole life, in order to gratify his blind ambition.

CHAPTER XXXII.

It would have been a difficult task to have induced the baron to believe, before he had made the experiment, how very easy a thing it is for a wealthy man to get into a scrape, and out of it again, if he does but set to work at both processes in a spirited way.

There was just delay enough occasioned by the negotiation entrusted to Rupert, to prevent the "De Schwanbergs" from running away from Paris so suddenly as to create gossip by their departure; and this was an advantage which nothing short of absolute necessity would have obtained for them, for it might be difficult to say whether the father or the daughter were the most impatient to quit it.

This piece of good luck, however, was only appreciated by Madame Odenthal; for from the day that their prompt return to the country was decided on, every moment of delay seemed only a lengthened torment, both to the father and daughter.

Gertrude had been very much admired, and very much courted, during her four months' residence in Paris; but she had formed no new friendships. Madame de Hauteville had retained her place, not only as her favourite friend, but as the only one from whose intimate society she found any real gratification.

No one, I believe, who has had a fair opportunity of forming an opinion on the subject, can fail to have observed that there is much more sympathy of character between the women of Germany and the women of England, than between those of France with either. The effect of our Norman mixture is much more easily traced among our high-born men, than among any class of English females; and my heroine found herself much more at home with her English friend, than with any one else whom she chanced to meet with in Paris.

But Madame de Hauteville had left Paris, in order to visit her own family in England, a week or two before this sudden breaking-up of the Baron von Schwanberg's Paris establishment; and the business of taking leave of her Parisian acquaintance was therefore very easily performed, and without the cost of either much time, or much sentiment.

There might be read in the countenances of both father and daughter, such an expression of "measureless content," as they drew near the noble mansion in which they both were born, that there might have been supposed to exist between them very perfect sympathy of feeling; but Madame Odenthal, as she looked from the one to the other, made no such mistake. She understood them both perfectly well; and as each familiar object met their eyes as they advanced, and was gazed at with a more or less lingering look, as the case might be, she would have run but little risk of blundering, had she undertaken to describe the thoughts of both; and the result of such a disclosure would have shown, at least, as little real sympathy of feeling as there was (though without intended delusion on either side) a striking appearance of it.

But not even in appearance was there any further similarity, when at length the carriage entered the spacious courtyard of the castle, and stopped before its lofty gates; for at that moment the dignified demeanour of the pompous baron relaxed in so unusual a degree as to cause him not only to smile, but to nod his sublime head, quite in a familiar way, to an individual who stood on the steps leading to them; while Gertrude, far from following his example, turned as white as a sheet, and altogether looked very much as if she were going to faint.

Madame Odenthal, however, was not looking about her, and making her observations for nothing; but, on the contrary, continued with very considerable cleverness to render it apparently impossible for the Baroness Gertrude to descend from the carriage till several books, which happened just then to fall on the floor and steps of the vehicle, had been removed.

Moreover, she managed, with great dexterity, to interpose her own person between poor Gertrude and the servants, who were employed in picking up the said books; and even to apply a bottle of salts in a most judicious and effectual manner, without being observed by anybody save the grateful girl herself.

Nor were either her kindness or her cleverness in vain. Gertrude was quite as anxious to conceal the weakness, for which she sometimes felt as if she hated herself, as Madame Odenthal could be, that it should be hid; and matters were so well managed between them, that Gertrude not only got out of the carriage, and mounted the castle steps very much as anybody else might have done, but she positively shook hands with Rupert before she attempted to totter through the hall, and get out of sight.

A small parlour, which was appropriated to the use of Madame Odenthal, was the room nearest the door, and there the suffering and self-reproaching Gertrude took refuge; her watchful friend entering with her for a moment, and then returning to embrace her son, and to assure the baron that Gertrude was perfectly well, and only feeling a little over-fatigued by her journey.

"I hope that is all, my good Madame Odenthal," replied the baron, rather dolefully; "but neither of us can be very much surprised if she should appear a little overcome on returning to her home, when we remember all she has suffered since she left it!"

As Madame Odenthal thought it would be best to avoid discussion on the nature and amount of the misery which Gertrude was enduring on account of leaving Paris, she only replied, "I think, my lord baron, that you will find the health and spirits of the Baroness Gertrude greatly improved after she has been for a few weeks restored to her favourite residence, and to her native air."

"Madame de Odenthal!" returned the baron very solemnly, but looking at her, nevertheless, with very condescending kindness; "Madame de Odenthal! I really believe that you are one of the most sensible and right-thinking females that ever was born. I cannot remember ever hearing you say a foolish thing in my life. I am not, indeed, altogether at a loss as to the cause of this peculiar superiority on your part; for the Baroness Gertrude herself (who you know, as well as I do, is never mistaken) pointed out to me the cause of it, several months ago. I shall, therefore, rest perfectly satisfied by what you say respecting my daughter's health, and only observe, that if she and you both think it will be best for her, after her long journey, to retire to her own room,

I shall say not a single word against her doing so, but only remark, that I shall be rather pleased than otherwise, if the people of my establishment can contrive to let me have my dinner somewhat before the hour at which it was ordered; for, although I am certainly not conscious of any weakness, either of body or of mind, I feel that my journey has rather increased my appetite."

Of course, the usual degree of attention and obedience was paid to the hint, and the dinner was hastened; but either in consequence of this change in the hour, or from some other cause, Gertrude did not appear at table; the message, however, by which she excused herself from doing so, and which was delivered by Madame Odenthal to the baron, concluded by a little whisper, hinting at the many subjects connected with *business*, which he would have to discuss with his secretary.

Nothing could have been more judicious than this message. The baron nodded his head as he listened, and he replied, "Just like her, Madame Odenthal! Quite right! Perfectly right!" And then he added, with a gracious little tap upon her shoulder, "There will be no objection whatever, to your taking your dinner with us, as usual, my good woman; but I should wish you to take the hint that the young baroness has given you, and must desire that I may be left alone with my secretary as soon as possible after the dinner is over."

The reply to this was, of course, received with the accustomed mute inclination of the head; and then the baron walked on with a stately step towards the dining-hall, too happy—much too happy—in finding himself restored to a position, far, far removed from all possible approach of equality, to suffer much annoyance even from the absence of his daughter.

As the dinner was a very excellent dinner, and the baron's appetite a very excellent appetite, the repast was by no means hurried, and by no means a very short one; so that, when Madame Odenthal returned to the quiet room where, at Gertrude's earnest desire, she had left her, to take her repast alone, she was by no means surprised to find that she had already left it.

Her first idea was that she should follow, and find her; but, as she mounted the great staircase, in order to reach the young lady's morning sitting-room, she passed a window which commanded an extensive view of the gardens, and as she paused for a moment to regale her eyes with a view of many pleasant objects from which she had long been separated, she perceived the dress of Gertrude, rather than Gertrude herself, floating gently along, amidst the trees of a distant shrubbery.

The meditation of a moment made her decide that she would not follow her.

"Poor young thing! She has great need of meditation," thought she. "She has been miserably unhappy for months past, and if there be any chance of her being less so now, it must be in herself that she must seek for it. This is no case for advice, and, least of all, from me. My best hope is, that she shall never discover that I have guessed her secret. Were she aware of it, I must, and would, leave her, for it would be treason and treachery to listen to her!"

CHAPTER XXXIII.

But although Madame Odenthal did not think it proper to follow poor Gertrude, I am conscious of no feeling which should prevent my doing so, or which should dictate my abstaining from inviting my gentle reader to go with me.

The sheltered walk which she had chosen, in which to enjoy the luxury of being alone, was one that she had much frequented, and much loved, from her very earliest childhood; and it was, moreover, endeared to her, almost solemnly, by having been the favourite promenade of her mother.

But the feeling which caused her to seek it now, proceeded not from any motive more sentimental than a very earnest desire to be alone.

She had left Paris with a feeling of joy which amounted very nearly to happiness; and though her spirits sometimes drooped as she meditated on the probable difficulties which might be in store for her, there was a very comfortable conviction at her heart, that she could never again be so exceedingly miserable as while watching the preparation of the fine house in which she was to live with the Count Hernwold as her companion and her husband!

There had been, too, a consciousness, not of happiness, certainly, but of something like enjoyment, in knowing that every mile she travelled brought her nearer and more near to Schloss

Schwanberg—that haven of rest, where she so earnestly wished to be.

But, alas!—the long journey accomplished, and the wished-for home opening its doors to receive her—how death-like was the pang which seized upon her heart!

She had not fainted; no such moment of relief was even for a moment hers; but she felt lost, bewildered, and terrified, when her eyes fixed themselves, for one short moment, on the face of Rupert, and she remembered that the wild pleasure which throbbed at her heart as she did so, was still a sin!

There is certainly nothing which so effectually strengthens our powers of endurance as the process of enduring. Gertrude was a much stronger-minded person now than before she had passed that dreadful night of self-condemnation, during which she had resolved to sacrifice herself, rather than betray the hopes and the confiding confidence of her father.

What she had endured from that frightful hour, to the happy moment at which she learnt that she was again free, might give her a fair claim to the courage of martyrdom; and the reward she now reaped for having endured it with so much faithful resolution, was found in the quiet reasonableness with which she was able to compare her present situation, with that which it had been when she was the affianced wife of Count Hernwold.

Yes! The difference was enormous! And even while tears rolled down her blushing cheeks, as she remembered the joyous feeling produced by the one short glance which she had dared to fix upon Rupert, as he stood waiting for them on the steps of the castle, she fervently thanked Heaven for the happy change which had taken place in her condition.

But her reverie did not end here.

Never were truer words written than those of the immortal line, which says, "Sweet are the uses of adversity." There is scarcely more difference between joy and sorrow than between the state of feeling into which Gertrude had been thrown when her conscience dictated to her, as a holy, filial duty, the compliance with her father's wishes, and which had so nearly made her the wife of Count Hernwold, and that to which she was resolved to resign herself.

And yet this latter, and comparatively happy state, involved the absolute necessity of abandoning every hope of being beloved by the only individual she had ever seen, who appeared to her capable of inspiring love in return!

And she *did* resign herself to the deliberate conviction of

Rupert's indifference, with a degree of gentle firmness, and uncomplaining hopelessness, which proved plainly enough that the uses of adversity had been beneficial.

"What should I say, what should I think, of any woman who declared that she had made up her mind to be miserable for life, because the man upon whom, unsolicited, she had fixed her affections, had not fixed his affections upon her in return?"

This was the plain question she asked herself; and the answer was such as to be well qualified to restore her to such a degree of philosophic indifference as might last her through life, by way of an antidote to all moaning misery from unrequited love.

This was decidedly a great step gained, and she felt it to be so.

Her beautiful head was shaken back; her eye lost its heavy gloom; her thoughts betook themselves to the well-filled shelves of her noble library; and then she thought of the cottages, and the cottage children, and of all the good she might do among them; and, finally, as she bent her lightened steps towards the house, she looked cheerfully about her to the right and to the left, and decided upon multiplying her flowers, and upon making herself extremely learned about everything that concerned them.

The last hours of this chequered day were far—very far—from being unhappy. On joining her father, she found him in excellent spirits, for Rupert had been a most agreeable companion. The young man himself was certainly in no unhappy frame of mind. My heroine, however much she might have been mistaken on other points, had made no blunder in attributing both great ability, and great elevation of character, to Rupert. He *had* loved, nay, he still loved, Gertrude with all the devotion of a high-minded and enthusiastic character; but he had seen, as clearly as he had seen the sun in the heavens, that he ought not to wish that she should love him in return.

He knew the baron, and all his follies, well; but he knew, also, how much he owed him. All that he might be said to value in *himself*, he had acquired by the kindly and confiding shelter which had been afforded him by this proud old man; and Rupert had not the bad courage to return all this, by seeking to undermine and destroy the dearest hope of his existence.

If he had ever been certain that he could have won Gertrude by such domestic treachery, he could have seen no hope of happiness in his success; and although it certainly had been with an emotion of almost overwhelming pleasure that he discovered, by her treatment of his mother, that she did not, as he had most falsely imagined, share the overweening pride of her father, the joy occasioned by this discovery was neither assumed or lasting.

He would, perhaps, have suffered more, had he hoped more.

And then came the journey to Paris, and the acknowledged admiration of the brilliant world they found there. . . . And then, the acceptance of Count Hernwold's proposals for her hand.

And so ended, and closed for ever, what poor Rupert considered as the only possible romance of his life!

The return of the family to Schloss Schwanberg was, however, not announced without causing him some slight emotion; and the intelligence of Gertrude's broken engagement was not learned with quite as much philosophical indifference as he could himself have wished. But he schooled himself into a very rational condition of spirits before the party arrived; and the very pleasant account which he had to report to the baron respecting the feelings and the conduct of his tenants, rendered their dinner a very pleasant one.

Rupert and his mother had found time to exchange a few words before this dinner began; and when the baron and his secretary adjourned to the family drawing-room to take their coffee, they found Gertrude and her *dame de compagnie* already there; and the evening was passed in a way that was extremely satisfactory to the two young hearts, both of which had been tormented by anticipating embarrassments and difficulties which, happily, did *not* arise, to destroy the enjoyment of finding themselves (one and all of them) exactly where they most wished to be.

Gertrude was the first who ventured, when the whole party were thus assembled together, to lead the conversation to the subject which, a short time before, had been so very painful, namely, the borrowing money from the tenants. But she was encouraged to break through all reserve upon the subject, by knowing that the negotiation had terminated in the most satisfactory manner possible; and she trusted, moreover, to the *savoir faire* of Rupert for detailing everything which it would be pleasant for her father to hear, and nothing which it would not.

Her confidence was certainly not misplaced; for Rupert knew his patron well, and was as little likely to say anything which had any chance of being painful to him, as Gertrude herself could have been.

In fact, the result of this conversation was the reverse of painful in every way; and not only was it gratifying to the old man, at the time it took place, but it opened the way to many pleasant feelings which he had never experienced before.

He knew himself to be an immensely great man, and assuredly enjoyed the consciousness of being so not a little; but he really did not know that he was, moreover, a very kind and liberal one, into the bargain.

But his prosperous tenants knew it, if he did not; and the lively description which Rupert gave of the delight, ay, and the gratitude also, with which his application to them had been received, awakened such a pleasant consciousness of this truth also, in the mind of the worthy baron, that he was evidently more touched at heart by it, than he had ever before been seen to be, by anything in which his daughter was not personally concerned.

Gertrude watched all this with a sort of pleasure that was quite new to her; and when a quiet smile, having no reference whatever to his grandeur, softened his proud features as he listened to Rupert's very graphic narrative, Gertrude was so touched by it, that she sprang from her chair, and impressed a kiss of very genuine fondness on his forehead.

"It pleases you to hear all this, my dear child!" said her father, throwing his arm round her. "And so it does me, Gertrude," he added with great simplicity. "I am sure I don't know how it has happened that it never came into my head before, that they might feel that sort of love for me that Rupert describes. I have never done anything for them except just not using them ill, but I really like to hear that they take it so kindly."

"But everybody else knows how justly, and how truly, you are beloved by these worthy people," said Madame Odenthal, respectfully; "and that is the reason, my lord baron," she added with a smile, "that I felt so very sure that there would be no difficulty in the way of Rupert when he applied to them."

"I remember it, I remember it, my good friend! Your conduct upon that occasion does you great honour!" returned the baron, with a degree of condescension that was almost affectionate. "You are a very excellent and a very valuable person, my good Madame de Odenthal; and both I and my daughter value you accordingly."

To this very flattering testimony of approval, Madame Odenthal made a most respectful reply; whereupon, the baron reiterated his compliment, and then added, with a sort of gay excitement, which was very unusual to him, "But there was one thing we talked about, my good friend, which you seem to have forgotten, but I have not, Madame de Odenthal. I have not forgotten what I said about inviting these worthy people to dinner . . . . to dine at my own table, you know. Have you really forgotten this?"

"No, indeed, Sir," said she, "I have not forgotten it. I had too much pleasure at hearing you propose it. I knew perfectly well that it was not very likely, or rather, I believe, I might say it was impossible. But we must not be over-hasty, my good friend. It is quite out of the question that I should do anything of the kind, without first consulting the Baroness Gertrude. So now we will hear what she says to it."

"What is it, papa?" said Gertrude, who had placed herself in a chair beside him. "What is the question which I am to decide?"

The baron rubbed his chin, and smiled with very perfect good humour; but yet he looked as if he were half-afraid that the frankly acknowledged pride of his nobly-born and nobly-minded daughter might be aroused, and shocked at the proposition he was about to make.

He took courage, however, and said, "The question, Gertrude, is this. Will it, in your estimation, be in any way indecorous or improper, if I were, in consequence of the attachment and affection of the excellent men, my tenants, of whom we have been speaking,—would it, in your opinion, Gertrude, be in any degree wrong, if I were to invite them to dine with us . . . . at our own table, Gertrude?"

"Wrong, dearest father?" she replied with considerable emotion. "Instead of its being wrong, I should consider it as one of the very best and most amiable acts that it would be possible for you to perform!"

"Then it shall be done, Gertrude!" returned her father, rather solemnly. "I know," he added, "what your feelings are on certain subjects, and that I shall run no risk of infringing the respect due to ourselves, if I have your sanction for doing what I propose."

After this, there was no further doubt or difficulty as to the invitation that was to be given to the good men and true, who had done them more than yeoman service; nay, Gertrude herself was permitted to be the bearer of it; and it may be doubted if the baron ever felt himself a greater man, than when he looked at the happy faces of his grateful tenants, who seemed to have quite forgotten that he was their creditor, as they sat around him at their splendid repast.

16

CHAPTER XXXIV.

NOTHING could have happened more calculated to ensure the peace of Gertrude, and the tranquil duration of the rational and improving life she was now leading, than the adventure which had befallen her at Paris.

When the baron had decided upon making his excursion thither, his head had been as full of grand matrimonial schemes as that of the most ambitious beauty could have been, on first emerging from her native shades.

But few young beauties ever received a more effectual check to their hopes, or a more mortifying blow to their vanity, than he had done.

Instead of studying the Almanack de Gotha, and dreaming both by day and by night of great alliances, he now shrunk from every allusion of the kind with a sort of sensitive aversion, which seemed to promise Gertrude much lasting peace. And with this very precious portion of happiness, she resolutely determined to be content. Had she never known the bitterness of such real mental anguish as she had endured during the time that she considered herself as bound to become the wife of Count Hernwold, she would have been far less sensible of the blessings she was now enjoying.

And, in truth, these blessings were manifold.

As soon as she became sufficiently tranquillised after the turmoil of emotions she had passed through while in Paris, to permit her common sense to have fair play, she made the notable discovery (which many others might make also, if they would submit themselves to the same process) that there was much more of good than of evil in her destiny. She positively brought herself to smile at last, and not in "*bitter scorn*," either at the idea of a girl under twenty, with health and wealth, an affectionate father willing to indulge her in every whim that could enter her head, the command of an excellent library, and the government of an excellent garden, making herself miserable, with a deliberate intention of remaining so for life, because she had fallen in love with a person who had not fallen in love with her!

This was the statement of her case which she drew up with all truth and sincerity; and then, after contemplating the picture it exhibited, she smiled, less, perhaps, at the picture itself, than at the idea that she, Gertrude, the daughter of her high-minded and philosophical mother, should submit her spirit to such thraldom.

The hours occupied by this mental process were not many; but the effect of them was both important and durable.

The first outward and visible sign of this, was the regularity of her daily occupations. There were, moreover, one or two changes which were so quietly brought about, that it was only by degrees that even Madame Odenthal herself became aware that they were not accidental; and that they were, moreover, intended to be lasting.

During by far the greater portion of Gertrude's life, the library had been the room in which she had chiefly lived; but now it was so no longer. Not that she had by any means given it up as a sitting-room; on the contrary, she had induced her father to repair thither regularly every evening, after he had finished his coffee and his pipe, instead of seeking his daughter and his tea (which he had learned to love as well as if he had been an Englishman) in the drawing-room.

It was, also, in the library that her favourite pianoforte was now placed, and it was there that her embroidery-frame ever stood ready, in case any book was in progress among them, deemed worthy of being read aloud by Rupert during the last hours of the evening. But before dinner the library now appeared to be exclusively the domain of the librarian; and although his mother occasionally passed an hour with him there, Gertrude never did.

Perhaps she was wise enough to recognize the truth of the adage, that "it is easier to abstain, than refrain." Had she permitted herself to pass any portion of her mornings in the library, as in her mother's lifetime it had been their constant habit to do, she might have remained there longer than would have been consistent with the plan and manner of life which she had now laid down for herself.

Rupert Odenthal was very decidedly a reading man, and, doubtless, profited by the uninterrupted opportunities thus afforded him of becoming acquainted with the literature of Europe and America; both ancient, as regarded Europe, and modern, as regarded all the rest of the world; for no change had been made in the long-established custom of permitting the mistress of the house to augment the Schloss Schwanberg library *à discretion.*

16—2

But notwithstanding his strongly-developed literary propensities, Rupert happened to be an accomplished gardener also, and
very particularly fond of flowers, and the scientific cultivation of
them. But although he had never made a mystery of this, it
seemed as if the young mistress of the Schloss Schwanberg
gardens did not wish to consult any one's taste and science in the
art of gardening, besides her own and her gardeners; for although
she rarely failed to pass some hours every day in the garden, for
not even bad weather prevented this, she never seemed to remember that there was such a place as the said garden, or such
a treasury of beauty and fragrance as her conservatories contained,
when Rupert was present.

What the young librarian might have thought of so strange a
peculiarity, it would be difficult to say; but with all his deference for the young heiress, he did not permit this apparent caprice on her part, to interfere with his love of beautiful flowers,
or his scientific cultivation of them; for he made it a daily habit
to pass the very first hour of daylight in the society of the head
gardener, who happened to be a familiar friend of long standing,
and who by no means seemed to be so adverse as his young mistress, to profiting by the aid of the scientific young amateur; and
little as the Baroness Gertrude might be aware of it, she owed
some of her rarest and most precious specimens to his persevering
researches, and his learned skill.

But notwithstanding the abundance of domestic occupation
and amusement which Gertrude contrived to provide for herself,
and her well-beloved *dame de compagnie* also, she did not appear
at all disposed to neglect any opportunities for social intercourse
which the neighbourhood afforded; this was not indeed very
much, for as the properties in their neighbourhood were large,
the proprietors were, of course, few; but fortunately the young
Baroness of Schloss Schwanberg was not the only individual
among them inclined to be sociable, and their retirement was by
no means deserving the name of seclusion.

The ridiculous affair of Adolphe von Steinfeld's sudden passion,
offer, and rejection, was remembered by his own family as a mere
boyish whim on his part, and had produced no subsequent cool-
ness between the respective families; and now the news of his
speedy return, after the absence of nearly three years of far-and-
wide wanderings, was anticipated with pleasure at Schloss
Schwanberg, as well as by the rest of the neighbourhood.

It may be that both the Baroness Gertrude and her librarian,.
heard the additional news, of his bringing home a young wife

with him, with more pleasure than surprise; but the community
of feeling between them, on this point, as well as on many others,
was never alluded to by either.

This expected addition to the somewhat monotonous society
of the neighbourhood, was, however, a theme freely discussed by
them all, as well as by every one else in the neighbourhood; and
it was welcomed by all, as likely to produce a great many gay
parties.

The marriage of Adolphe was nevertheless not thoroughly
approved by his father, for though the lady was rich, she was
English; and though she had the reputation of being highly accomplished, it was feared that she might not be able to converse
in German.

But, despite these little drawbacks to the complete satisfaction
of the Steinfeld family, they were prepared to welcome the fair
stranger most cordially; for the very fact of her being the cause
of bringing the wandering Adolphe home again, was quite enough
to ensure her a gracious, nay, an affectionate reception.

Adolphe had announced that they were to be accompanied by
the unmarried sister of his bride; and as he had taken care in
announcing this, to mention that the young lady was extremely
rich, extremely beautiful, and extremely accomplished, this
addition to their society was also joyfully hailed by all to whom
it was made known.

Even the Baron de Schwauberg, notwithstanding his usual
sublime indifference to most passing events, heard of this marriage
with satisfaction, as being a proof that the young man whom he
had always considered as a very promising youth, notwithstanding his unfortunate exclusion from the Almanack de Gotha, had
recovered from the disappointment which he must have experienced from the rejection of his hand by Gertrude.

On the very first occasion that he had found himself alone with
his daughter after hearing this news, he expressed himself much
pleased by the event.

"The Von Steinfeld family are not only extremely good and
amiable, my dear Gertrude, but, notwithstanding their unfortunate deficiencies in point of alliances, they really are of very
respectable nobility; and I sincerely rejoice to find that the son
has had the good sense to conquer his early, and perhaps somewhat presumptuous, attachment to you."

"His attachment to me, my dear father," replied Gertrude,
" was the fancy of a mere boy, and not very likely to be remembered long. But I too am very much pleased to hear of his

having formed a marriage with a young lady so highly spoken
of, for I have always thought that the De Steinfeld family have
behaved very kindly, in never showing any symptom of resent-
ment on account of the abrupt dismissal of their son; and with
your permission, I shall wish to pay every attention to the wife
of Adolphe."

"You will please me by doing so, Gertrude," replied the
baron, in a tone of very amiable condescension. "But yet," he
continued, with a smile, which was perhaps a little sarcastic;
"it is probable, my dear, from the country whence he has selected
his bride, that the unreflecting character which seems to have
marked his race in their former alliances, is still perceptible in
him. Not that I mean absolutely to deny that there may be
found races of every respectable antiquity of descent, even in
England; but, comparatively speaking, they are, I believe, very
few; and you may depend upon it, that this young bride has *not*
been chosen from among them, or the father of young Adolphe
would have stated this, when he communicated to us the fact of
his marriage."

"No, papa," replied Gertrude, with less apparent astonishment than the statement seemed to call for. "No, I do not
believe that Madame Adolphe de Steinfeld is of a noble family."

"You state this, my dear Gertrude," returned the baron, with
a frown, which evidently betokened a disagreeable surprise;
"you state this fact with a degree of indifference, which shows
that you feel less interest than I do for our very estimable and
very well-born neighbours. Perhaps it is not your purpose,
Gertrude, to honour her by any very intimate degree of acquaintance?"

"Indeed, papa, I have no such feeling!" she replied, very
earnestly; "on the contrary, I looked forward with much
pleasure to the chance of finding another English friend whom I
may love almost as much as I do Madame de Hauteville."

Nothing could have been more likely to promote the rapid
growth of intimacy between Gertrude and her new neighbours,
than this conversation; for in the first place it at once removed
any doubts she might have had respecting her father's approval
of it; and in the next, it suggested the idea that she might be
really useful to the wife of Rupert's highly valued friend,
Adolphe, by showing the neighbourhood that the heiress of
Schwanberg did not consider her deficiency of noble descent, as
any impediment to friendship.

CHAPTER XXXV.

It is pretty nearly impossible that any bride should make her first appearance in a country neighbourhood, without becoming an object of considerable curiosity to every individual who makes a part of it; but when the lady is young, handsome, rich, and a foreigner, this feeling is naturally heightened to a degree, that makes the first sight of her a matter of real importance. In the case of Madame Adolphe von Steinfeld, this feeling was rendered more active still, by the long absence of the bridegroom from the neighbourhood. Adolphe had been a very popular personage among them, and his return after so long an absence, was of itself enough to produce a great activity of visiting; no wonder then that his arrival, accompanied by a beautiful young wife, should be the signal for a great deal of neighbourly and hospitable intercourse. Nor was the additional circumstance of the newly-married pair being accompanied by a splendidly beautiful sister of the bride, to be considered as a matter of trifling importance.

Both the ladies were the daughters of a wealthy London banker, but by different mothers; the unmarried sister being the elder of the two, and in possession not only of the handsome fortune bequeathed to her by her recently deceased father, but of her mother's still larger property, of which she was the sole heiress.

Adolphe de Steinfeld was wise enough to say little or nothing concerning the defunct banker; for he well knew that the fact of his having passed the last years of his very respectable life amidst the best society that our humble island can boast, would do but little to redeem his memory from the odium of having *"been in business,"* in the judgment of the rustic magnates among whom his daughters were now welcomed as beauties, and heiresses of high degree.

Adolphe, however, had not married his wife because she was rich; he really was very sincerely in love with her, though she was as little like the object of his first love, as it was well possible for a pretty young woman to be.

Madame Adolphe de Steinfeld was a bright little creature, that at twenty-two, scarcely looked more than fifteen. She was *mignonne* in the fullest sense of that very expressive epithet. Moreover, she had untamable animal spirits; and rather than not be amused, she would have had recourse to the tricks of a monkey, or the frolics of a kitten.

She certainly was good-humoured; for she was not only laughter-loving herself, but rather than not see those around her laughing also, she would put in action, without scruple, any and every species of playful mischief in order to produce it.

Her unmarried sister was a very different sort of person. She was six years the senior of Madame Adolphe de Steinfeld; but from the beauty and delicacy of her complexion, looked considerably younger than she was. Her eyes were large, blue, and of the most languishing softness; and her abounding hair, which descended in long natural ringlets to her shoulders, was almost flaxen. In person she was tall and beautifully formed, but beginning to show slight symptoms of becoming a little more plump than was consistent with that exquisite perfection of youthful beauty of which she had been justly considered, in her own particular style, as a model.

How it happened that this beautiful Arabella Morrison, with a fortune of several thousands a year, over which no human being had any control but herself—how she had contrived to reach the age of twenty-eight years, without being tempted to bestow herself and her thousands upon some one of the very many who had smiled and mourned, knelt and prayed, in the hope of being taken into life-long partnership by the banker's fair daughter, was a mystery to many.

The answer which perhaps most nearly approached the solution of it, was given by her giddy young sister Lucy, when she was questioned on the subject by the nurse, who had been very much like a mother to her since the early death of her real parent. "What can be the reason, Miss Lucy, that your sister, with all her beauty, and all her money, has never got a husband yet? Why, my dear, she is going on very fast for thirty."

This speech from Nurse Norris produced the following reply from Lucy, who was at the moment very busily engaged in examining some part of her own bridal paraphernalia.

"I think I can tell you the reason, Nurse Norris," she said. "She admires and adores her beautiful rich self too much, to think that any one who has yet asked her to bestow herself upon him is worthy of such a treasure."

"Why, then, in that case, Lucy dear," returned Nurse Norris, "it is likely she will die an old maid at last, notwithstanding her being such a beauty and heiress."

"No!—not if she has the luck of ever seeing any one sufficiently worth having, to make her pay a good price for him."

"But if she goes on much longer," rejoined Nurse Norris, "she may have to ask the question her own self, Miss Lucy; for those that the like of Miss Morrison would call good matches, generally like something young, as well as rich."

"Well!—we shall see, Goody!" returned the busy bride-elect. "All I know is, that she has made Count Adolphe promise to take her to Germany with us; and so now you may go on with your packing, without wasting any more time in gossip. . . . And if I do not find everything in the most beautiful apple-pie order for starting by the day after to-morrow, I will leave you behind me, as sure as your name is Nurse Norris!"

The only reply to this threat was given by a very fond nurse-like kiss upon the forehead of the pretty threatener.

But we must leap the gulf between this threat and the safe establishment of the bridal party, of which Nurse Norris made an important part, at the far-away German castle of Count Steinfeld.

It may easily be imagined that Schloss Schwanberg was not the last of the noble mansions in the neighbourhood whose gates were opened to receive the gay bridal party which it was expected would so greatly enliven the society.

The meeting between the bridegroom and his affectionately-remembered friend, Rupert, was as cordially friendly as their parting had been.

Had Adolphe not returned as a married man, it is possible that Rupert, notwithstanding all his deep resolves to retain to his dying day his passionless respect for Gertrude, might have felt, in spite of himself, that the renewal of acquaintance between her, and her former adorer, might produce a change in the present even tenor of their life at Schloss Schwanberg, which would not tend to the general happiness of its inhabitants.

But, as the case stood now, the pleasure of the meeting was equal on both sides, and unmixed with any drawback whatever. Even the sort of embarrassment which might have arisen, either from an awkward allusion, or from no allusion at all, to this violent first-love fit of the bridegroom, was effectually prevented by the light and frolicsome tone in which Adolphe himself now recurred to it.

"Do you remember how distractedly I behaved about that nice, good, quiet girl at Schwanberg, Rupert?" said he. "How on earth I ever came to take it into my head that I was in love with her, I shall never be able to comprehend, if I were to live a thousand years; for, the real fact is, she was by no means the sort of girl I admire. As I think of her now, it really seems to me that I must have pretended to be in love, in order to amuse myself. Do you remember all about it, Rupert?"

"Yes; perfectly," replied Rupert with a quiet smile.

"Oh! I don't wonder at your laughing, for I perfectly well remember, too, that you told me at the time, that you did not see any beauty in her. . . . And, I daresay, you were very right. But do you also remember the 'Almanack de Gotha?' How many a good laugh have I had, from remembering that scene with the stiff-backed old baron! Has she ever had any offers since, Rupert?"

"Oh, yes! I believe so. She was very much admired at Paris," was Rupert's discreet reply.

"Perhaps the tender-hearted Parisians found out that she was an heiress?" returned Adolphe. "But the warlike Gauls would have no chance whatever with the baron and his 'Almanack.'"

"Probably not," returned Rupert; "and so little, on the whole, did the baron like his Parisian campaign, that I advise you, Count, not to allude to it, if you wish to keep him in good humour."

"If you call me COUNT, I will shoot you, Rupert. So you had better keep me, too, in good humour, I promise you. And if you *could* contrive to make the baron talk a little about the 'Almanack de Gotha' before my wife, I should really take it as a very particular kindness, my dear friend, for she is the most laughter-loving little animal that ever was born."

Rupert answered him very gravely, that if he, *Rupert*, was to be kept in good humour, it could only be done by *not* laughing at the baron at all.

"If your young wife, my dear Adolphe, deserves the happiness of being your wife, as much as I hope and trust she does," continued Rupert, earnestly, "she will soon learn to value his daughter too highly to find food for mirth in anything that would be painful to her."

"Be not too serious with me, my dear old friend!" returned Adolphe, with a feeling that was anything rather than jocose. "If I, indeed, thought my dear laughing little wife was really capable of wounding the feelings of a good daughter, for the sake of a joke which might amuse herself, I should be very likely to run away from her. I daresay you do not know yourself as well as I know you, Rupert, or you might give me credit for sounder · judgment than you are now, perhaps, likely to attribute to me, when I tell you that I have never, since we parted in the forest yonder, met with any one whom I could consider as worthy to rival *you* as my chosen friend. I must have recourse, I believe, to that delightful entreaty—pardon me for being jocular—which we enjoyed so heartily together some half-dozen years ago; but, notwithstanding this dangerous propensity, which has certainly been greatly increased by my union with Madame la Contessa Adolphe Steinfeld, I am quite aware, Rupert, that I have not yet met with any man whom I considered as your equal; and as long as I feel this, you need not fear that I should do or say anything that could pain you, for the sake of a jest."

This conversation was of considerable importance in fostering the intimacy between the noble houses of Schwanberg and Steinfeld; for Gertrude would never have endured the seeing her father made an object of ridicule, or even of playful sport, by the young English stranger, although she was well inclined to profit by her vicinity, and to assist her own schemes for the arrangement of a very cheerful and happy existence, without running the risks which might perhaps be incurred by any more visits to gay capitals.

The amusement of the neighbourhood, when welcoming and fêting the fair strangers, was probably not a little increased by watching the remarkable contrast between them.

It took Rupert but little time to arrive at a tolerably decided conclusion respecting both the ladies, and he rejoiced with very affectionate sincerity that the choice of his friend Rupert had fallen on the younger sister. Towards *her*, he felt disposed to feel, and to cherish, very friendly sentiments; for, amidst all her wild rattle, he discerned considerable shrewdness of observation, and, what was better still, a cheerful temper and a loving heart. Moreover, it was easy enough for an observer less interested on the subject than himself, to see that she was devoted, heart and soul, to her husband; and that, in the midst of all her frolics, the idea of amusing and pleasing him was the prevailing thought, and the inspiring motive.

Of the elder sister, Gertrude, at least, formed a very different judgment. In point of personal beauty, indeed, she thought that there could be no second opinion; for, in her estimation, Miss Morrison was the most beautiful woman she had ever seen; while, to the miniature bride, she could not accord any epithet more flattering than "*pretty*." Beyond this opinion respecting her beauty, however, not even her very sincere wish to like her new neighbours, could enable her to add a single word that betokened either admiration or approval of the elder. She thought her imperious, affected, vain, and capricious; and there was something in her manner of attracting and receiving the attentions of every man whom she thought it worth her while to notice at all, which was so totally unlike anything Gertrude had ever seen before, as to puzzle as well as disconcert her.

Probably, however, neither her liking for the younger sister, nor her disliking of the elder, had much immediate influence on the intercourse which followed. It was speedily a settled point in the neighbourhood, that the English ladies were to be welcomed among them by every possible species of hospitality; and for several weeks this amiable project prospered in every direction. The old became young, and the young became brilliant; and a somewhat remote province of Germany seemed in a fair way of rivalling the memories of Brighton and Ryde, in the judgment of the English sisters.

But, decidedly, the individual who enjoyed all this the most, was the Baroness Gertrude.

She had, indeed, previously pretty well made up her mind to the belief that she not only was, but she was sure to continue so, exceedingly happy in the mode of life which she had arranged for herself, that nothing more was, or could be, wished for. But when she perceived the marked change which the return of Count Adolphe made in the existence of Rupert, she began to think differently.

That Rupert was as much superior in mind and information to all her noble friends and acquaintances, as he was inferior to them in rank and fortune, was a truth that was too deeply impressed upon her mind to be ever overlooked or forgotten; and notwithstanding her resolute spirit of content, she did sometimes sigh in secret, as she remembered how completely he was shut out from all intercourse with that stirring world, of whose marvellously rapid onward movement she was made tolerably well aware by the *unbound* compartment of her library.

Her mother's often-expressed opinion of Rupert's intellectual superiority, had certainly left a deep impression on her memory; and this, together with her own consciousness that it had never yet been her lot to meet any one else whose mind seemed in harmony with her own, or could be in harmony with his, made her often sigh in secret that there were no means within her reach, by which she could assist him to break through the barrier that seemed to separate him from all whose talents and acquirements could render them fitting companions for him.

The mistake which Rupert had fallen into, of fancying that the young Gertrude beheld Count Adolphe with especial favour, originated solely in her almost unconscious gratitude to that highly-talented young noble for having selected their obscure librarian as his favourite companion and most intimate friend; and the evident and eager pleasure with which this intimacy was now renewed by the travelled bridegroom, and welcomed by the remote and almost solitary scholar, again caused Gertrude (who was in no danger *now* of being so inconveniently mistaken) to profit by every possible opportunity of bringing the families together.

In this object she certainly succeeded to the utmost extent of her wishes; for scarcely a day passed without their meeting. But as Count Adolphe was no longer a single man, who could, without impediment, trot over the three miles which divided them, either with or without the assistance of his horse; their almost constant companionship could not have been achieved, had not Gertrude encouraged his young bride to accompany him, both on foot and on horseback.

Fortunately, this young bride was really a very charming little girl; and having wisely made up her mind that somehow or other she must, and would, learn to talk German, she speedily discovered that the Baroness Gertrude was the only individual she had yet met with, who at all understood how to teach her.

This would all have gone on very completely to Gertrude's satisfaction, had this extreme intimacy of intercourse been confined to Count Adolphe and his gay little wife; but, unfortunately, the beautiful Miss Morrison did not permit it to continue long, before she gave her sister to understand that it was her will and pleasure to be included in the horse and foot expeditions to Schloss Schwanberg, which were of such constant recurrence.

"But you cannot go there every morning, as I do, Arabella, unless the Baroness Gertrude invites you," remonstrated the young Countess Adolphe.

"Do not give yourself any trouble on that account, Lucy," was Miss Morrison's reply; "only let me know at what hour you mean to set off to-morrow morning, and I will manage about the invitation for myself."

"What nonsense!" exclaimed Lucy, shrugging her shoulders.

"You could not walk there, and back again, as I do, without fancying yourself half killed; and as to your riding! Mercy on me! Just fancy yourself and your ringlets trotting away upon such a pony as Adolphe has got for me!"

These remonstrances were very reasonable, and founded on truths incontrovertible. But women are wilful—pretty women particularly so; and when wealth is added, without either father, mother, brother, or husband to control the wishes and whims of the fair possessor, this wilfulness sometimes assumes a degree of power and activity that becomes troublesome to those within its influence.

～～～～～～～～～～～

CHAPTER XXXVI.

"Use lessens marvel." It would have been considered as a strange and portentous spectacle a year or two before, if Schloss Schwanberg had been seen any single day of the year, under the same aspect as it might now be contemplated every day, and sometimes all day long.

The hall-door seemed now to be always standing open, instead of being always solemnly shut. The library was no longer sacred to Rupert and his catalogue; but Adolphe von Steinfeld might be seen, stretched at easy, if not at lazy length upon the sofas of this noble apartment, with more than one precious volume within easy reach of his hand there, though he might have sought for such in vain for many an Austrian mile around him.

And Rupert was there too, but no longer like the deeply-read and careful librarian, gravely, in youthful earnestness inhaling, as it seemed, the atmosphere around him, and thankful to Heaven in his very soul, that if shut out by destiny from free communion with human hearts, he was thus enabled to exercise his intellect, side by side as it were, with the highest order of human minds. Rupert no longer passed his long mornings in solitude; nor was his free and easy friend Adolphe his only companion. For the pretty little Lucy had a great notion that she too had a taste for books; and in order to prove this to the entire satisfaction of her dearly beloved Adolphe, she rarely, or rather never suffered any of their long lounging morning visits to be brought to a conclusion without insisting upon it, that Gertrude should go with her into the library, not exactly for the purpose of reading, but in order to look at all the beautiful books, and make her clever husband, and his first-rate learned friend Rupert, talk about them.

In all this literary lounging the beautiful Arabella took her part, although the doing so, was so striking an innovation upon her usual habits, that her sister, naturally enough, remarked upon it; and had more than once asked her what pleasure she could possibly find in sitting, or in lounging about for hours together, in a great big room, without a single looking-glass in it.

"I suppose I find the same kind of pleasure that you and Gertrude do," was once her reply.

"Oh! dear no, Arabella! that is quite impossible!" returned the indignant bride. "Without ever saying a word about Gertrude, although she certainly is *my* very particular friend, I have, I should hope, reason enough to like to be there. If you could but be so lucky, Arabella, as to find some one handsome enough, and grand enough, to give yourself and your fortune to, you would know, without my telling you, *what* it is that makes me so fond of the Schwanberg library."

"Upon my word, my dear child, you make yourself as great a fool about your husband, as you do about everything else. If I were in your place, Lucy, I should be positively ashamed of showing such excessive fondness for any man. If Adolphe were ten times my husband, I would not follow him about as you do."

"You do not know what you are talking about, Arabella! When you are married yourself, my dear, I shall be much more inclined to listen to your opinion."

"And in that case it is most probable that my opinion would not be so much worth having," replied the beauty. "However, while things remain as they are," she added, "I shall do all I can to prevent your making yourself appear *too* ridiculous in the eyes of the Baroness Gertrude, and, it may be, of your husband, also; and of course, my taking care to be always with you, will be the most effectual way of achieving this important object."

Lucy looked in her face and laughed, but said nothing. It was a saucy look, and might have said, being interpreted, "do not trouble yourself!" The baron, meanwhile, had every appearance of being in better health and spirits than his daughter ever remembered to have seen him enjoy. Nor was she at all mistaken in this opinion; Baron von Schwanberg never had felt himself so happy before.

It had certainly been with the expectation of finding a more illustrious son-in-law among the numerous admirers who were sure to crowd round his heiress in the splendid salons of Paris, than he could hope to meet with in the retirement of his noble, but remote castle, that he had made the joyless excursion which, in every sense, had cost him so dear; and it is highly probable that he would have sunk into very hopeless dejection, in consequence of what befel him in the course of it, had he not been sustained by firmer spirits than his own. But now, instead of this, he really felt himself a happier man than he had ever been in his whole life before. In the first place he had inflicted indignity in the very hour when he was tortured by the idea of receiving it. In the next, he felt, on returning to his own isolated baronial greatness, that no other greatness could bear a comparison with it in real dignity. And then came the agreeable surprise of finding that he was beloved, as well as reverenced, by those whose industry furnished his revenues; and last, but not least among the subjects he found for self-gratulation, was the discovery that he had not offended his good and noble neighbours of Steinfeld, by pointing out to them the lamentable fact, that their names were not to be found in the " Almanack de Gotha."

All this, joined to the unhoped-for blessing of seeing his heiress apparently as happy as himself, might well account for the fact that the stately baron condescended to give symptoms of being a very contented, as well as a very dignified old man.

Had the case been otherwise, Gertrude would never have ventured, nay, she would never have wished to promote this daily and familiar intercourse with their neighbours, as cordially as she now did; nor was there any great self-delusion in her believing that she did so as much for her father's sake, as for Rupert's.

But assuredly Rupert's share in the matter was not trifling. No woman, perhaps, ever believed herself more sincerely in earnest than Gertrude did, when she made up her mind to renounce, at once and for ever, every hope, every dream, of Rupert Odenthal's ever becoming attached to her. But this was, in her estimation, a reason for, rather than against, the doing everything which was in her power for his permanent advantage.

"Had Rupert loved me," thought she, "I could have passed many happy years of life in quietly watching the development of his admirable mind, and in teaching myself to become in some degree worthy of being the companion of his life . . . . The happiness of my dear father would still have been the first and holiest of my daily cares; and when he should have been taken from me, I would have become the wife of Rupert, with no fear that the spirit of my father, if removed to a higher sphere, would contemplate with displeasure my uniting myself to the most exalted being I have ever met with in this. . . . But now my object must be different. Rupert loves me not. But shall I withdraw my aid from him for this? Rupert must be as a brother to me; and I have only to fancy myself a few years older than I am, and that I am his elder sister (somewhat unjustly made my father's heiress), in order to render all that I intend to do as easy as it will be righteous. But it would be very sad, should he be forced by his position here, to pass years of solitary thought, and solitary study, without any companion capable of doing him justice. Adolphe de Steinfeld is full of bright intelligence, and *he* does Rupert justice. Accident has thrown them into great intimacy, and it shall not be my fault if this ripen not into close and life-long friendship."

It was thus she reasoned, and upon this reasoning she acted. In one respect, at least, this scheme worked pleasantly, and succeeded well; for no day passed without bringing the two young men together, and no sorrow followed without the feelings of mutual sympathy and esteem between them being increased.

Had the share which the English sisters took in this intimacy been more annoying than it really was, Gertrude would very resignedly have submitted to it. But she really liked the young bride exceedingly; and though the addition of the beautiful Arabella to the *coterie* was not felt as an improvement by any of them, it was too inevitable to provoke either resistance or complaint.

The young Countess Adolphe, however, did at length relieve her mind upon the subject, by setting Nurse Norris to talk about it.

"I wish I knew what it was induced Arabella to follow Adolphe and me so, when we go to Schloss Schwanberg," said the bride, as her loving tire-woman was arranging her beautiful hair. "Does her gossiping maid, Susan, never make any of her sage remarks upon it, Norris?"

Norris continued for a minute or two to brush the silken tresses which hung over her hand, without making any reply to this question; and then Lucy turned suddenly round upon her, at the risk of deranging all this beautifying brushing, and exclaimed, "Now, then, I am sure there is some mystery about it, Norris, or else you would have answered me directly. Tell me, this very moment, all about it, or I will send you home in a Dutch waggon to-morrow!"

"Well now, Miss Lucy . . . . I beg your pardon, my Lady Countess! . . . . be so kind as to let me bide with you a little longer, and I will tell you all I know about it; but that is so little, that if I don't add a small bit of guess-work to it, I don't think it will be worth your ladyship's hearing . . . But, Susan certainly *does* say, that she thinks Miss Arabella has fallen in love again."

"And I should not be the least surprised if she had," replied the Countess Adolphe; "if it were not that the only man she sees, except the old baron, takes no more notice of her than if she were made of wax. Does Susan say, or think, or guess, or whatever you call it, that Arabella has fallen in love with the Baron von Schwanberg?"

"No, Miss! No, my lady! I do beg your pardon, my darling, but you do look so very young, that I can't get myself to remember that you are married, and a Countess."

"Never mind about that, you foolish old woman. I forgive you now, once and for ever, and you may call me baby if you will, till I am as old as the beautiful Arabella herself, if you will only go on with your story. *Has* my magnificent sister set her heart upon being Baroness von Schwanberg? Upon my word and honour, Goody, I should be delighted to hear it. Only just think of the fun!"

"Yes, Miss . . . . yes, my lady. I have seen the tears come into your eyes with laughing at things she has done not half so funny. But that is not it," replied Nurse Norris.

"Then what is it, you silly old woman?" resumed her impatient young mistress. "There certainly *is* a person at the castle, that though, of course, not half-a-quarter so charming in my eyes, is quite as handsome, and I daresay some might say still handsomer, than my beautiful Count Adolphe; but I tell you, nurse, that he takes no more notice of her than if she were a stick. You won't tell me, I suppose, that Arabella has fallen in love with him?"

"I don't speak of my own knowledge, my dear," replied Norris, "for how should I? Miss Arabella never tells any of her secrets to me. But Susan says, that this great beauty and fortune that you have got the happiness of having for your sister, is fallen so over head and ears with that handsome young gentleman at the castle, that she thinks she will be after poisoning herself, or may be jumping into the river yonder, if she don't get him."

The young Countess remained silent for a minute or two, and

it was certainly a wicked thought that occupied her during this interval. Her rich and beautiful elder sister was an immense bore. She had bored Lucy from the very earliest moment at which she could remember her own existence; she had bored the beloved Adolphe very grievously during the earlier months of their acquaintance, and before his engagement to herself had given her a right to take possession of him . . . And now she was, most unquestionably, a terrible bore to them both. "What a relief it would be, if that handsome Rupert Odenthal would marry her!" That was the thought which had entered her head; and certainly it was, considering her own opinion of her beautiful sister, a wicked thought.

But it would have been more wicked still, if the Countess Adolphe had not been the daughter of a rich English banker.

The idea that wealth was the most important ingredient in the earthly destiny of a human being, had grown with her growth, and strengthened with her strength; and it should be stated in her defence, that if half the wicked thought was suggested by the consciousness of the immense relief which it would be to get rid of her sister; the other half arose from the simultaneous recollection that Rupert was only librarian to the Baron von Schwanberg, although the great learning and cleverness of her beloved Adolphe had selected him as his chosen friend, on account of his wonderful intellectual superiority.

But weighty, and mighty, and important as these thoughts were, they did their work so rapidly, that there was but a short interval of silence between the young Countess and her aged attendant, before the meditative bride said, turning sharply round to the old woman, who had resumed her hair-brush: "And pray, goody wise-woman, what has Susan seen, or heard, to put such stuff into her head?"

"Oh! lor! my dear young lady, if I was to set about repeating one-half of Susan's long stories, it would be time for you to go to bed before I had done."

"Well then, just pick out a few as quick as you can, there's a dear old darling, and you shall tell me the rest another time. I just want to see if there is anything at all like common sense in what she says."

"Why, first and foremost, my dear, Susan says, that she is got back to the old way which she always takes to, in all her love fits; that is, you know, she will sometimes dress herself two or three times over in different styles, as she calls it, and then stands

17—2

before the glass, and practises, like, half shutting her eyes, and hanging her head on one side, and leaning upon her fine white arm with I don't know how many bracelets on it, sitting before the glass all the time, and looking at her own face as if she was longing to kiss it. And this is the way, Susan says, that she always goes on when she is in love; and you know, my dear, Susan must know a little about it, because she has seen it over and over again, so very often. Well, and then she has been at the old work of flower-keeping, till the leaves all fall upon the carpet, day after day, as she presses them to her heart. And then she brought home a gentleman's glove with her one night, when you had all been dining at the castle; and this glove she goes on sticking in under her pillow every night. But all this would be nothing, you know, my lady, in anybody else; but Miss Arabella has been going on now so many years in the same way, and we always are so sure to hear that she is going to be married after every new beginning of this sort; that, bless you, my dear, Susan knows the signs, she says, as well as she knows the figures on her sampler. And all this began, my lady, when you was a little girl at school."

"And pray, my good Nurse Norris, if Susan is so very observing, can she not tell us why none of all these fifty thousand love affairs ever ended in marriage? With Arabella's fine fortune, to say nothing of her beauty, it is quite impossible that all the men who have offered to her, and been accepted too, should all turn out traitors, and forsake her."

"Yes, to be sure, my dear, it would be impossible to believe it; and that's the reason, I suppose, why it never happened. Susan says, that she don't believe that any one of all her lovers ever played her false in any way. . . . The fortune, you see, Miss Lucy, is such a hold-fast. No! my dear, it was none of all the gentlemen, nor was it your poor, dear papa either; for she soon gave him to understand, good, quiet gentleman, that she was independent of him. No, my dear child! It was nobody in the wide world but her own self who ever broke off any of the marriages. But Susan says, that it was no sooner settled that she was really to be married to a gentleman, till little by little, day after day, she seemed to get tired of him, and began taking to somebody else; and she knew well enough that her money always made her sure of her work. She knew, Miss Lucy, that she might play as many queer tricks as she liked, without the least bit of danger that she would be left in the lurch to die an old maid. She is quite up to that, my dear! . . . Nobody ever says, or sings either, to a lady with eighty thousand pounds in her pocket,

'If you will not when you may,
When you will, you shall have nay.'

She knows as well as everybody else, that gentlemen never do say 'nay' to that."

"You are a very wise old woman, Goody Norris," said her young mistress, laughing heartily; "and as I don't think this love-making sister of mine will ever fail, in some way or other, to take good care of herself, I certainly do not mean to give myself any trouble about her. It will be funny enough, to be sure, if all this English banking money should settle down at last into the pocket of a German baron's library! But, upon my word, my greatest objection to it would be, that I think he is a great deal too good for her."

"Well, my lady, of course you know best," returned the old woman, demurely. "But if the young gentleman is as wise as we hear he is handsome, he might manage, I should think, to be the last of her lovers, and the first of her husbands, without troubling himself much about her goodness. Money is a very fine thing, my lady!"

The effect of this conversation on the young bride was not, perhaps, exactly what it ought to have been. The state of affairs, as described by her sagacious old nurse, appeared to her to promise a very considerable portion of fun; and her imagination immediately set to work to devise scenes, and arrange circumstances, in the best possible manner, for the purpose of extracting amusement from this new *amourette* of her fair inflammable sister.

Her firm conviction that the object of this tender passion did not, in the very slightest degree, return it, only added zest to the jest; and there would be novelty, too, in seeing how the beauteous Arabella would contrive to render herself a bright example of persevering study, and, in short, altogether devoted to literature!"

She had already seen her, upon one occasion, become so devoted to art, that the Royal Academy was, for several months, the only place in London where real enjoyment could be tasted. At another, her whole soul was, as she declared, absorbed in music. At one time, she was so enthusiastic a Puseyite, that the majority of her acquaintance did not scruple to declare that she had evidently made up her mind to become a member of the church of Rome; as she had, in fact, been heard to say, that Dr. P. had but one fault . . . "he did not go far enough!" But from this peril of perversion, she had been saved by the excessively fine eyes of a young man who, as he said, gloried in confessing that he, at least, was not ashamed of avowing himself to be purely evangelical.

The next aspirant for the safely-funded eighty thousand, was a man of fashion; and while his reign lasted, all memory of the banking concern was ungratefully forgotten, and the Peerage was never, by any chance, permitted to be beyond reach of her hand. . . .

All these had, in their day, afforded infinite amusement to the saucy young Lucy; and she now recollected, with great satisfaction, that she had never as yet enjoyed the gratification of seeing her beautiful sister devoted to literature.

Notwithstanding her own very great felicity as a wife, and the genuine pleasure she took in the society of her new friend Gertrude, she now became conscious that her happiness would very decidedly be greater still, if she could but have the fun of watching one of Arabella's tender passions, with her beloved Adolphe at her side to enjoy the joke with her! Nay, she was not without hope that she might manage to inspire her dear, darling, sober Gertrude, with a sufficient spirit of fun also, to make her capable of enjoying the scenes she was quite sure she should be able to get up for her amusement. Nor did her plot end here; for being, in truth, despite a great deal of childish, mad-cap nonsense, a kind-hearted little personage; she bethought her that she might really do a very good thing, if she could manage to keep alive this new passion of Arabella's long enough to bring it to the old-fashioned conclusion of marriage.

She had not witnessed the great delight which Adolphe had testified upon meeting again the only companion and friend to whom he had ever strongly attached himself, without feeling sufficiently interested about him to lead her to find out, as nearly as might be, who, and what he was; and this had, naturally enough, led to the conviction, that it would be a monstrous good thing for him if he could marry such a fortune as Arabella's!"

She only wondered she had never thought of it before Nurse Norris had put it into her head! But she supposed that her dulness on the subject had been caused by the unmistakable indifference of the young man. . . . And this thought caused her to pause, and think a little, if thought it might be called; which led her to decide at last, that the less Rupert liked Arabella, the more fun there would in getting him to marry her; and that as, of course, Arabella must at last marry somebody or other, her money could not be better disposed of, than in making Adolphe's particular friend a rich man!

This last decisive thought being, decidedly, a very important thought, was digested in silence; that is to say, she did not then and there communicate to Nurse Norris the conclusion at which she had arrived; but having, rather more quietly than usual, awaited the skilful old woman's assurance, that her beautiful head was quite perfect, she descended to the drawing-room with the comfortable assurance that she might set to work upon her scheme immediately, as the Schloss Schwanberg family were a part of the company expected at dinner.

Fortunately for the gratification of Count Adolphe, and the fair ladies he had attached to him, the Baron de Schwanberg had not abandoned the idea that it was necessary, or, at least, highly desirable, that he should be always attended by his *suite;* and Rupert, therefore, as well as his mother, in her capacity of *dame de compagnie,* accompanied him on the present occasion.

The Countess Adolphe watched their entry with a sort of sparkling satisfaction, which made her look extremely pretty; while her Venus-like sister, draped, as to the ivory shoulders, in transparent lace, and eyes melting with a sort of dreamy softness, that caused the wicked Lucy to rub her little hands with uncontrolable glee, seemed to see only one of the group which entered; but that one received a smile which the Baroness Gertrude saw, though it is highly probable that the baron's librarian did not.

CHAPTER XXXVII.

WHATEVER varieties may be found in the social habits and manners of the various drawing-rooms of Europe, there is at least one hour in every day, during a portion of which it would be difficult to find any external variety at all.

When a mixed party are assembled in a drawing-room, awaiting a summons to the dinner-table, I believe that it will invariably be found that the gentlemen separate themselves from the ladies, and stand chatting together in groups till the welcome summons arrives which unites them together in pairs, in the order that etiquette or inclination may dictate.

The party assembled at this hour in Count Steinfeld's drawing-room, on the day that his son's bride had held at her toilet the conversation with her attendant which was related in the last chapter, consisted of about a score of persons, among whom were the Baron von Schwanberg, his daughter, and *suite*.

The gentlemen of the party had grouped themselves at two of the windows, for the purpose of chatting at their ease, and of admiring the beautiful garden upon which the said windows opened.

Gertrude, as usual, had placed herself beside the young Countess Adolphe; but did not, as usual, find her full of gay spirits and laughing chit chat. On the contrary, she not only seemed incapable of replying to what was said to her, but it appeared very doubtful whether she had heard a single word of it.

Puzzled to account for this unusual want of attention in her new friend, Gertrude ceased to address her, and turned her attention to other individuals in the apartment.

It did not take her long to discover the cause of the volatile Lucy's pre-occupation.

On the opposite side of the room to that now occupied by the gentlemen, stood a richly-carpeted oval table, almost covered with books and engravings; and around, or near this table, were congregated the sofas and easy chairs on which the ladies were seated.

One fair deserter from this group, had, for some reason or other (perhaps to examine the dimensions of some particularly fine tree), stationed herself in a graceful attitude of meditation at one of the windows.

It required no second glance to show Gertrude that this solitary fair one was Miss Morrison. There was, indeed, no chance that any other could be mistaken for her; for who else could have found so beautiful an attitude in which to place themselves, merely for the sake of looking out of a window?

From the picturesque individual who had thus withdrawn from the female group, Gertrude's eyes wandered back again to the friend who sat beside her; and then she discovered why it was that Lucy had paid so very little attention to all she had said to her.

Lucy's eyes were not so large, nor so meltingly soft as those of her elder sister, but there was no want of speculation in those laughing eyes of hers; and a less intelligent observer than Gertrude, would have found no difficulty in discovering that their merry mistress was at that moment very particularly amused by the discoveries they were making for her.

And then, of course, Gertrude's eyes took the same direction as those of her friend; and truly she found that there was wherewithal to be amused by what they looked upon.

The groups which occupied the window at which the beautiful Arabella had stationed herself, consisted of Count Adolphe, his friend Rupert, and two gentlemen of the neighbourhood, who were discussing with them the details of a tremendous thunderstorm which had occurred in a distant part of the country; an account of which had reached them by the newspapers of the morning. Miss Morrison, of course, clasped her beautiful, ungloved hands, and she listened; and every soft feature seemed to express to the utmost extent of its power, both the agitation of terror, and the sympathy of pity.

Her brother-in-law was the person standing next to her; but though she anxiously addressed repeated questions to him, respecting the melancholy particulars of the catastrophe, it was evident that he was paying too earnest a degree of attention to the gentleman who seemed to know most on the subject, to be able to listen to her plaintive voice with the attention which it of course deserved.

But this state of affairs did not last long. The gentle creature was far too deeply interested by the melancholy catastrophe of which they were speaking, to endure such heartless indifference; and therefore, crossing her ivory arms upon her bosom, and raising her eyes to Heaven, as an appeal either against the cruel severity of the elements, or the hard indifference of her brother-in-law, she glided across the window to the spot where Rupert stood, and gently laying her fingers on the arm of the almost unconscious young librarian, she murmured her gentle inquiries; first, in French, which she spoke with an accent which rendered it pretty nearly intelligible, and then in English, which, as she well knew, was his mother-tongue.

"Tell me," said she, "for the love of Heaven, how much of this terrible story is true! I am not made to endure these horrors with indifference! Life lost! Human life! And so utterly without preparation! Oh tell me, Monsieur Rupert! Tell me that it is *not* true!"

To this pathetic appeal, the hard-hearted Rupert only replied by the unfeeling words, "I beg your pardon, madame, but I did not exactly hear what you said;" and then, abruptly turning to the individual he had been listening to, he appeared, and probably really was, utterly forgetful of her presence.

Gertrude watched all this, and smiled, for she could not help it, at the *minauderies* of the beauty; but as tricks such as she was now displaying were with her of every-day recurrence, she found nothing in them to account for Lucy's air of extreme amusement.

"What is there, Lucy, in the dismal history they are giving there, that makes you look so mischievously merry?" said Gertrude, turning to her, after watching the group for a minute or two.

"My dear, darling girl, you must be the very dullest soul alive, if you find nothing to amuse you in what is going on there! . . . . But perhaps you do not comprehend it, Gertrude? Perhaps you never before saw a lady pay her addresses to a gentleman?"

Gertrude coloured. She felt that she did comprehend it, and would gladly have lost her usually delicate bloom for a month, could she thereby have avoided betraying emotion at that moment.

The Countess Adolphe looked at her archly, and laughed. "You look absolutely shocked, my dear! It *is* rather a particular manner of making a conquest, but I am so used to it, that I don't mind it at all. Arabella has not fallen in love for nearly three months, I think, and upon my word, upon this occasion, she has, in my opinion, chosen a charming subject; for Mr. Rupert is not only the handsomest man I ever saw (excepting Adolphe, of course), but he *must* be a charming person, or he could not be Adolphe's dear friend. And moreover, my dear girl," continued the chattering little bride, "I shall really approve her marrying this young man excessively. Of course he can't have much money of his own, or he would not be living with your papa as his librarian; and Arabella's eighty thousand pounds sterling will be a very good catch for him, won't it?"

The Baroness Gertrude, young as she still was, had been too long accustomed to the necessity of maintaining an appearance of composure, while every pulse was throbbing with painful emotion, to betray the feelings which this startling speech occasioned; and it was perhaps because she was accustomed to this painful task, that she now performed it so well. She had neither recourse to looking at the carpet, or at her fan; but quietly turning her eyes towards the group at the window, she said, " What can have put so strange an idea into your head, dear Lucy ? "

" Exactly what must put it into your head too, my dear, if you are not blind," replied the laughing bride.

" You need not be afraid to look at her, Gertrude," she continued; " for when she is in this condition, she neither knows nor cares who looks at her, nor what they may think of her proceedings. I certainly never did see anybody quite like her, in this respect; but I suppose that is because it is so very seldom, you know, that one does see a girl with eighty thousand pounds sterling, entirely and altogether her own mistress. Why, you know, if she chose to marry Mr. Rupert's servant, if he happens to have one, there is no one in the wide world that could prevent her. She knows this as well as I do, and that's the reason that she seems to care so little what people may think of her. As to Adolphe and me, I give you my word and honour, Gertrude, that we would not take the trouble of walking across the room to prevent her marrying a shoe-black, if she took it into her head. We are quite rich enough, and I believe we shall both of us be monstrously glad when she takes herself off. And then, as to this young man, it would, of course, be a very pleasant thing to dear Adolphe to see him so well provided for. I really believe that he loves him as well as if he were his own brother."

During this long speech, Gertrude remained with her eyes pretty steadily fixed upon the speaker; so steadily, indeed, that Lucy at last exclaimed, " Why do you look at me, Gertrude ? You might have the fun of watching them, without losing a word that I am saying. Do just look their way for one moment, Gertrude. There is nothing ridiculous in him, I don't mean that. He is looking as grave as a judge all the time. But it is a perfect treat to watch Arabella ! Do you think, my dear, that any woman ever did actually melt, and dissolve herself into a dew by the mere influence of the tender passion ? Because if such a catastrophe ever could happen, depend upon it, Gertrude, it is going to happen now."

The Baroness Gertrude smiled, but it was a grave, proud sort of smile, and by no means satisfied Lucy.

" Do you mean never to laugh again, that you miss so glorious an opportunity ? " said she, again fixing her eyes upon the group at the window; and then, as if words were inadequate to express her enjoyment, she inflicted a merry pinch upon the arm of her resolute quite neighbour, murmuring in her ear at the same time,

"Upon my honour, I think she will kiss him! I do, upon my word and honour, Gertrude; and if you will not look at them this moment, I don't think that I will ever speak to you again!"

What might have happened next, either to the observers or the observed, had the dinner not been announced at that moment, it is impossible to say; but at this critical juncture the master of the house stepped forward, and presenting his arm to the most nobly allied married lady in the party, led the way to the dining-room.

Gertrude was so placed at the long table, around which the company were marshalled, that she could not see the pair who had afforded her friend such exquisite amusement; she only knew that they must be seated together, because she happened to turn her head as she crossed the hall, and perceived that the beautiful Arabella was hanging on the arm of Rupert.

But had she not seen this, she would have been aware of the fact from the numerous glances cast by the young Countess, who sat opposite to her, towards the lower end at the same side at which Gertrude herself was seated. As each of these somewhat indiscreetly long glances produced a smile on the saucy face of Lucy, which she took no pains to conceal, there could be little doubt that the manœuvrings of her sister were proceeding in the same style which had afforded her so much amusement in the drawing-room.

But Gertrude had not so long endured the deep-seated persuasion that the affection which Rupert felt for her was that of a brother to his sister,—she had not so long meditated upon this conviction with the unshrinking resolution of a stoic, without having taught herself to expect that she should some time or other have to watch his becoming enamoured of some other woman. And now, it seemed that the time for this had come; and the desperate sort of courage with which she determined to *bear it well*, might have gone far towards assisting a martyr at the utmost need.

Had she yielded with a little more complaisance to the earnest entreaties of her friend Lucy, during the discussion of the thunder-storm at the window of the drawing-room, and watched the cold indifference, or rather the utter unconsciousness with which Rupert suffered the fair lady's glances and sighs to pass over him, she might have spared herself a great deal of very unnecessary suffering.

The evening of this day was, as usual, spent in music. Gertrude very rarely sang, and never in so large a party. The tone of her voice was deliciously sweet, but Madame Odenthal was the only one who was fully aware of this fact; for, conscious that she had little power, and less science, the act of singing in company was really painful to her; and with her usual quiet perseverance in doing what she thought rational, she had taught her friends and acquaintance to leave off asking her to sing.

But she played well, and had of late found solitary practice a great resource, as well as the means of great improvement. She therefore no longer declined to play when invited to do so; and she was, perhaps, proud to feel, that upon the present occasion she was as much mistress of her fingers, as if there were no such person as Arabella Morrison in the world. It so happened, that on the present occasion, one of Count Steinfeld's guests was a young man of very prepossessing appearance, who was a stranger in the neighbourhood, though his family were near neighbours to the Count; but the young Baron Nordorffe was an officer in the Austrian service, and having been more with his family at Vienna than in the country, was personally a stranger in the vicinity of his father's country residence. This young man had been amusing himself during the long interval passed at the dinner-table, in comparing the beauty of the English Arabella, with that of his countrywoman, Gertrude. They had both sat opposite to him, so he enjoyed a favourable opportunity for the study of both.

Under any and every imaginable circumstance, the marked contrast between them must have been striking to every one, but it was not well possible for this to have been displayed better than on the present occasion. The flaxen-haired Arabella rarely sat still for many seconds together. She had always too much to do, to permit this. She had to arrange her curls; she had to show off her hands and arms; she had to find or make opportunities for displaying her teeth; and, what was much more important than all the rest, she had to perform without ceasing, all those wonderful evolutions with her eyes, which she certainly considered as the most important of all her social duties.

The young Baron Nordorffe certainly thought her wonderfully beautiful, even before he found out that she was wonderfully amusing also; and for some time, he devoted to her pretty nearly all the attention which a young gentleman who had taken a good deal of active morning exercise, could spare from his dinner.

An object in perpetual movement when full in sight of us, is pretty sure to attract the eye; but sometimes it will also happen that the eye fixes itself upon an object because it is perfectly at rest; and thus it was, that after the young Baron Nordorffe had amused himself for some time by the ceaseless mobility of Arabella, he turned his eyes, as if for repose, on the quiet loveliness of Gertrude.

It was impossible, perhaps, that this loveliness could have been displayed with greater effect than it then was, most unconsciously to the pre-occupied girl herself. The contrast was in every way favourable to her; for not only was her beauty of a higher order, but the composure of her demeanour had as much of dignity as indifference in it. A waiting-maid, or a milliner, might have played all the tricks that Arabella was performing, without any difficulty whatever; but it is only a gentlewoman who can be sufficiently at ease in society to look as Gertrude did.

Baron Nordorffe was just then particularly unlikely to fall in love, because his head, and his heart too, were very fully occupied by a much more important affair. He had, in fact, very strong hopes of being appointed aide-de-camp to an amiable and highly fashionable general officer, and till this very interesting question was settled, he could not occupy himself seriously about anything else; nevertheless, he had certainly found considerable amusement from occasionally fixing his handsome eyes, first on the one fair lady, and then on the other; and, despite his preoccupation, he was sufficiently interested by the appearance and manner of Gertrude, to request his hostess to present him to her, when they returned to the drawing-room.

Baron Nordorffe, like the majority of his countrymen, was really fond of music, and he knew enough about it too, to be quite aware that the performance of the Baroness Gertrude was of no common order; and even if he had not thought her the handsomest woman in the room, he would probably have hovered near her with the same marked attention till the party separated.

His doing so produced, however, no very great impression upon her of any kind. He was a gentlemanlike and conversable young man, and she felt neither bored, nor even fatigued, by his talking to her; for it was by no means part of her system to have recourse to her own thoughts for amusement while in the company of others.

Whether on the present occasion these thoughts, less obedient than usual, might have wandered a little from the lively metropolitan gossip of her new acquaintance, to the information she had received from Lucy respecting the present tender passion of her sister, it would be hardly fair to inquire. If it were so, she gave no sympton that such thoughts had made any impression on her, for she returned home at night apparently in the same equable state of spirits as usual.

<center>~~~~~~~~~~~~~~~~</center>

CHAPTER XXXVIII.

But the events of the day had not passed over the mind of Rupert so lightly.

As to the beauteous Arabella, however, it would have been quite " all one that she should have loved some bright particular star, and thought to wed it," as that she should hope to make any impression upon the heart of the Baron von Schwanberg's librarian.

He certainly must have been rather a singular young man; for it is a positive fact, that neither upon this occasion nor upon any other which had preceded it, had she made more impression upon his heart, or even upon his memory, than her pet dog had done. Had he been urged to give an opinion upon the merits of either, he could only have complied by making an effort to think more on the subject than he had yet done; and then, if he had answered with perfect honesty, he must have replied that he thought them both rather troublesome.

But although the unfortunate young man had forgotten all about her eyes, and her arms, and all the rest of her numberless claims to admiration, he had not forgotten any of the manœuvres of Baron Nordorffe, by which he had contrived to occupy the attention of Gertrude during great part of the evening.

It would be an o'er long tale to tell how well the idle notion of her inherited pride had served him as a shield against all her beauty, all her sympathy of mind, and all her kindness to his mother. But the ill-supported fabric fell at last; and long, very long before he was himself aware of his own condition, he loved her with all the devotion of an ardent and powerfully developed character.

If Gertrude on her side had loved him less, he would have been more likely to discover that her feelings towards him offered no absolutely fatal barrier to his wishes,

It was the consciousness of her own unchangeable but unasked-for love, which had made her so strongly feel the necessity of reserve; nay, of more than reserve.

She felt the necessity of adopting a line of conduct which might not only prove her indifference to him, but give him reason to suppose, that either from love of power, or an extreme fastidiousness, she was extremely likely to remain unmarried.

As no hope of possessing her was ever permitted to cross his fancy, the idea of her remaining single, was the most fortunate for himself that could have entered his head; for it fostered all his habits of study, and often suggested the idea of their latter years being still passed in a community of literary occupation, which would place him about mid-way between misery and happiness.

It was in this state of mind that he went to Paris, and in this state of mind he continued till the acceptance of the Count Hernwold dispelled this (certainly) rather presumptuous hope.

But the mind of Rupert Odenthal was not fitted to be the receptacle of despair. He certainly abandoned this hope of remaining the librarian of Schloss Schwanberg to his dying day; but, after meditating through a few sleepless nights, he at length came to the conclusion that the approaching event would set his spirit more completely at rest, and more perfectly free, than it had ever been before; and the idea of becoming a solitary, undisturbed, literary man, and so remaining to his dying day, began to have charms for him.

At least he fancied so; but, altogether, it must be confessed that he occasionally felt a good deal like a man who had been suffering from delirium; and it was only when this doubtful, dreamy sort of sensation left him, that he became conscious of his still pitiable weakness. No sooner did this consciousness return, than his efforts to emancipate himself returned likewise. Without having any over-weening opinion of himself, he certainly felt that nature had designed him for something better than a love-lorn, hopeless swain, whose existence was to wear away in pining for a blessing that was beyond his reach.

"There is so much," thought he, "to which I may reasonably aspire, that the fixing my wishes upon what I can never obtain, would be acting considerably more like a spoiled child, than a reasonable man."

And fortified by this admirable philosophy, he was enabled to act, to speak, and even to look with such uniform forbearance and propriety, that a much vainer woman than Gertrude might have been led to the conclusion at which she had arrived respecting his constant and unchangeable indifference towards her.

During the visit at Count Steinfeld's, which has been described in the last chapter, he had, however, the mortification of fearing that he had not advanced so far towards real, genuine, and sincere indifference, as he had flattered himself. He was provoked and indignant at his own weakness, as he felt the hot blood mounting to his temples, while he marked the evident admiration of the young stranger, and on leaving his pillow on the following morning, whereon he had not dreamed, but meditated, he resolved, for the first time, to lead his mother into conversation on the subject of Gertrude, both as concerned the marriage which had been so abruptly broken off at Paris, and on the conquest which she had, in his opinion, so evidently made on the preceding evening.

Had Rupert been less uniformly successful in concealing from his mother the secret which he still intended should lie for ever buried in his heart, he would doubtless have found more difficulty than he now experienced in leading her to talk, almost without reserve, upon the subject.

So perfectly, indeed, was the good lady convinced that her son had never for a moment forgotten the distance between himself and the honoured heiress of his magnificent patron, that it had positively never occurred to her as a thing possible that he should love her, even as she too well knew the unfortunate heiress loved him. Had it been otherwise, no consideration whatever would have induced her to suffer their present manner of life to continue; for Madame Odenthal had a sensitive, nay, almost a timid, conscience; and not even the belief that she might ensure the life-long happiness of both, could have induced her to connive at keeping together those whom the "Almanack de Gotha" so evidently intended to keep asunder.

But her mind was perfectly at ease on this point, Both her knowledge of Gertrude, and of her own woman's heart, taught her to know that, as long as her son retained his indifference, there was no need for her to break up their comfortable establishment, in order to preserve her pupil from the danger of an unequal alliance. On the contrary, she thought, and certainly not without some show of reason, that her attachment was much more likely to wither quietly away, under the influence of Rupert's blighting indifference, than if he were separated from her by any will but his own.

Rupert, therefore, found his mother perfectly unprepared for

18

the examination to which it was his purpose to submit her, and her early entrance into the library, on the morning following the dinner party which has been described, afforded him an excellent opportunity for the purpose.

Madame Odenthal had entered the room in search of a volume which the young baroness had requested her to procure for her; and having impressed a loving mother's kiss on the forehead of the young man as she passed him, was about to leave it, when he recalled her, by saying, "Are you vanishing again, mother, without bestowing a word upon me? Come!—sit down quietly with me for five minutes, and tell me what you thought of the party yesterday."

His mother immediately complied with the request, and placed herself near him at his writing-table.

"The party was a very nice party. Did you not think so?" said she, smiling. "I am sure it was not the fault of Miss Morrison if you did not, for, most assuredly, Rupert, she looked beautiful with all her might. Did you not think so?"

"Certainly, I did," was his reply. "But she always does that, you know, so I am used to it, and quite hardened. But I saw, also, what is not quite of such constant recurrence, namely, a very evident approach to flirtation between your young baroness and the newly-imported Baron Nordorffe. I think you must have observed it, mother, as well as myself. Did you not?"

"No, Rupert," she gently replied; "I saw nothing of the sort. Flirtation cannot be performed as a solo, you know; and I am sure I saw nothing like flirtation in the manner of the Baroness Gertrude."

"Nay, mother, I did not mean to accuse her of the slightest impropriety," said he, gravely; "but if flirtation is not to be named, I think you will not deny that the young man was very evidently captivated?"

"Why, really, I think it did look a little like it, Rupert," she returned; "but Gertrude's manner is not calculated, I think, to give strangers much encouragement."

"At any rate, mother, she evidently gave this new man as much encouragement as was necessary," said Rupert, somewhat sarcastically. "How much will you bet me, mother," he added, "that the Baron Nordorffe does not propose for her before he leaves the country?"

"I shall think him a very presumptuous man if he does," was her reply. "I know little or nothing about him; but truly the heiress of Schwanberg—and *such* an heiress, too—deserves to be adored at a distance for at least a *little* while, before her fair self and her broad lands are asked for."

"You are as jealous of her greatness, my dear mother, as her father himself could be," replied Rupert, with a faint smile; "but, I presume," he added, "that you would be rather more indulgent than the loving father himself in such a matter as this."

"You mean to insinuate, then, that Gertrude has shown herself as inflammable on her side as the Baron Nordorffe on his? You are of opinion that the Baroness Gertrude is enamoured of this new gentleman, are you?"

"It may be so, mother," replied Rupert, looking earnestly at her.

"This may be your judgment respecting her," replied Madame Odenthal, gravely, "but it is not mine, Rupert."

"Do not be angry with me, dear mother!" said he. "I did not mean to say anything offensive. But it certainly appeared to me that she was by no means displeased by the attentions of this young man."

"Displeased? And why should she be displeased, Rupert? There was nothing offensive in her attentions."

"Evidently not," he replied. "But, nevertheless, it is very possible that you may be right, mother," he added. "It is very possible that, notwithstanding all that has passed, she may still retain too tender a recollection of Count Hernwold, to permit her, so very soon, to receive the addresses of another."

There was certainly something extremely far from amiable in the tone with which these words were spoken, and good Madame Odenthal was, perhaps, more seriously displeased with her son at that moment than she had ever been with him before, since the hour of his birth. The words were decidedly ungracious words, and very unjust when applied to Gertrude.

"I have never considered it as a part of my duty, as the salaried companion of the Baroness Gertrude, to explain to you, Rupert, or to any one else, what I considered to be real motives, and feelings, which induced her to receive the addresses of Count Hernwold," she said, with more sternness of manner than was at all usual with her: "nor shall I enter upon the subject now. I certainly should have thought that the most indifferent observer in the world, if gifted with common capacity, and having known her so long as you have done, might give her credit for better reasons for accepting a man whose highest merit was having the manners and appearance of a man of fashion, than, to use a vulgar phrase, having *fallen in love* with him. It never occurred to you, I suppose, that her earnest desire to gratify the wishes of her father was the cause of this acceptance?"

"Never!" replied Rupert, with emphasis.

For a moment Madame Odenthal was silent, but she looked at him very earnestly, and with an expression that perplexed him, for it spoke (unintentionally) surprise and curiosity, not wholly unmixed with doubt.

She waited in vain, however, for any further reply to her question, and, at length, said : "Let us not waste our time, Rupert, in idle speculations on the character of the Baroness Gertrude, which it is very evident you do not sufficiently comprehend to discuss with firmness; but I must confess that, great as your dulness appears to be on the subject, I could not have believed it possible that you should conceive her capable of retaining *tender recollections* of a man who has behaved to her father in the way which you know Count Hernwold has done?"

And having said this, she rose with rather a rapid movement, and left the room.

Her son remained very deeply absorbed in rumination.

What was there in that last glance which she cast upon him, to cause so strange a revulsion of feeling?

The countenance of Madame Odenthal was usually expressive of great gentleness, and she rarely parted from him without a kindly nod or smile, betokening affection. But now he could only remember her parting look as expressive both of anger and contempt.

He knew his mother well. He knew that no mere difference of opinion could have caused her to bestow such a glance upon him. He felt that he had been unjust to Gertrude. But his mother's words had accused him of more than that; she had spoken of dulness on his part, as well as of injustice.

But it would be easier to follow the movements of a vapoury cloud, and attempt to explain why at one moment it took this form, and at another that, than to attempt any intelligible description of the flitting thoughts, which passed across the brain of Rupert, after his mother had closed the library door upon him.

Perhaps it is impossible for any man to have been beloved as he had been, without a thought at some moment occurring to him, that was more or less tinctured with the truth. But, in his case, the impediments to his dwelling upon any such thoughts as deserving belief, were great indeed. The strong persuasion which had possessed him for years, that Gertrude inherited the absurd and very paltry pride of her father, had certainly gone far towards preventing his knowing, or even guessing, her to be the noble creature which she really was; and when at last this blundering delusion passed away, and he saw her with less of prejudice and more of truth, he had been struck with a feeling that almost resembled terror, from the idea of returning all the benefits he had received from his patron, by seeking to rob him of the treasure which he prized so dearly.

It is true, that day by day, he felt more strongly that not to love her was impossible; and though this conviction involved the necessity of his passing a life uncheered by hope and unblest by affection, he screwed his courage very resolutely to the endurance of it, cheered by the reflection that he might reasonably hope for her companionship for years to come; for he instinctively felt that if her father's authority did not interfere to force her inclination, she was not likely to be easily won.

The announcement of her intended marriage when they were at Paris, was certainly a tremendous shock to him, for he had not expected it; but this young and highly intellectual man had not loved for a year or two under the firm conviction that he loved in vain, without being in a great degree prepared to endure such a shock, without sinking under it.

And Rupert did not sink. He turned to the resources and consolations furnished by his own mind, and by the many opportunities afforded by his present position for enlarging his stores of knowledge, and increasing the sphere of his intelligence. Yet, nevertheless, as the preparations for the marriage of Gertrude proceeded, he felt conscious that it would be a great blessing if he could be out of sight of them; and, as we know, he paid a timely visit to his uncle Alaric.

It is unnecessary to trace what his feelings might have been upon learning the rupture of this marriage. Not all his prudence could prevent his hailing the return of the family to Schloss Schwanberg as something very like a restoration to life; and the subsequent return of his friend Adolphe (accompanied by his wife), rendered the weeks which followed decidedly the happiest he had ever known.

Far as he was from the truth respecting the real state of Gertrude's affections, there was something in the steady sedateness with which she arranged and regulated her manner of life, which not unnaturally suggested the idea that she meant it to continue. Even the circumstance of her ceasing to make the library her

morning sitting-room, and thereby leaving him in solitary possession of it, much as he would have wished to change this for the
habits of the good old times (when the bright and highly culti-
vated intelligence of his beloved patroness had helped to pioneer
his own active mind through the labrynth of accumulated thought
which was ranged around them); yet he found much to soften
his regret at having lost this, in the idea naturally suggested by
Gertrude's punctual adherence to her new arrangement, which
led to the obvious conclusion, that what had so evidently been
planned with deliberation, was intended to be lasting.

That the young and lovely Baroness Gertrude von Schwanberg
should have deliberately taken the resolution of remaining single
through life, was an idea that had certainly a good deal of im-
probability in it, and Rupert would have acknowledged this as
readily as anyone; but nevertheless there was a feeling, rather
than an opinion, which lay at the bottom of his heart, and which
whispered incessantly, that it was at least possible.

How much this soothing idea contributed to his enjoyment of
the life he was now leading, it might be difficult to say; but it
had received a rude shock while watching the attentions of the
handsome and graceful Baron Nordorffe; and the very decidedly
bad temper in which his mother had found him on the following
morning, was certainly attributed to this.

But she little guessed, good lady, how much more than sufficient to cure this was the scolding which she had given him.
That one word *dulness*, and the look which, quite unconsciously
on her part, accompanied it, had done more towards making him
feel it *possible* that he was beloved, than all the years that had
passed over them, every day of which might have given ample
proof of the fact, had he but read them right.

CHAPTER XXXIX.

THE evening of that day had been fixed upon by a noble lady
in the neighbourhood for giving—not a ball, that was quite out
of the question on so short a notice—but a dance, which she
assured the Steinfeld family was in honour of the beautiful Miss
Morrison; but nevertheless it may be doubtful if it would have

been given at all, had not the highly distinguished Baron Nordorffe been in the country.

But whatever might be the lady's motive, the act was hailed
as a benefaction by the whole neighbourhood.

By no one, however, was the invitation more joyfully welcomed than by Madame Adolphe de Steinfeld. "Now, then,"
thought that lively lady, "I shall have the exceeding delight of
once more seeing Arabella waltz with the hero of the hour!
And if Gertrude is too well behaved to enjoy it with me, I will
give her up at once, and she shall never be my particular friend
again."

The day and the hour for this gaily anticipated amusement
arrived accordingly, and in order to ensure herself from the possibility of disappointment, the laughter-loving Lucy commissioned
her husband to arrange the first dance according to her especial
will and pleasure. "Being a bride, I must, of course, dance
with the dashing young son and heir of the mansion; and you,
Adolphe, being a bridegroom, must, of course, dance with the not
very beautiful eldest daughter. I am sorry for you, my dear,"
she added, coaxingly, "but it cannot be helped. You may
have free choice afterwards. But you must observe," she continued, gravely, "that I make a particular point of Arabella's
dancing the first waltz with your friend Rupert. He is really a
most charming person, besides the being your most intimate
friend, and I like to show everybody that we all consider him as
a person of first-rate consequence."

"That is very sweet of you, my pretty Lucy; but are you
quite sure that your magnificent sister will approve your choice
for her?"

"Do not give yourself any anxiety on that point, my beloved,"
replied his wife. "I should be excessively stupid if I had not
found out by this time what my magnificent sister would approve,
and what she would not. I know her better than you do as yet,
Adolphe, dear, and I pledge you my word that she will not dislike dancing the first waltz with your friend Rupert—nor the
last, either."

As the latter part of this speech was uttered very decidedly,
avec intention (if I may borrow an expressive phrase from our
faithful allies), it aroused a greater degree of attention on the
part of Adolphe, than he was always in the habit of paying to
the lively sallies of his pretty bride.

"What do you mean, Lucy?" said he, very eagerly; "do
you think your sister has fallen in love with Rupert Odenthal?"

"Yes, husband," replied Lucy, very demurely placing her hands before her, with the air of a dutiful child who is about to be questioned.

"You think your sister Arabella has fallen in love with the baron's librarian?"

"Yes, husband," repeated Lucy, with a modest little courtesy.

"How can you talk such nonsense, my dear little angel!" said the fond husband, caressing her. "We never talk of unmarried ladies falling in love in our country, unless the parties are engaged to be married."

"That is a great deal better than our way," replied Lucy, gravely; "but with us," she added, "unmarried ladies very often do fall in love, without being able to manage the marrying part of the business at all to their satisfaction. But perhaps it is possible that our sister Arabella may be more fortunate."

"Do you mean to say, Lucy, that you think my friend Rupert is in love with your sister?" said Adolphe, thoughtfully; adding, in a half whisper, "I don't."

"No more do I," rejoined Lucy, holding up her finger playfully, and mimicking his tone. "But a man may be heart-whole one day, and in love the next; you can't deny that, Adolphe. My sister is very handsome, my good man, whatever you may think of the matter; and moreover, as I told you, my dear, when you offered to me, she has rather more than double my fortune."

"Rupert will never marry for money, Lucy," replied Adolphe, knitting his brow.

"Don't look so fierce, my dear," replied his wife, laughing. "I really like Rupert excessively, and perhaps, though he is only a librarian, I should think him too good for my ridiculous sister. . . . Only, you know, Arabella is really very rich. She would be a great match for him, in that point of view, and giddy as you think me, I have always been taught to know, and remember, that as long as we remain in this wicked world, money is, and ever must be, a very good thing."

Madame Adolphe von Steinfeld uttered these words so gravely, as to make her husband laugh.

"You may laugh, Adolphe, as much as you like," she added; "but you cannot deny the truth of what I say. But let us be quite serious, both of us, for one minute. I am quite in earnest when I say that I should be very glad to see my sister Arabella marry Rupert Odenthal. Now tell me, quite in earnest, too, how you should like it?"

Her husband did not immediately reply; but after a silence, during which his eyes were fixed on the floor, he said, "Your question is not an easy one to answer, Lucy. Trust me, I love you all the better for the feeling .which would reconcile you to becoming the sister of a man both poor and lowly born, because he is my friend; and it seems like an ungrateful return for this, to say that I do not think your sister worthy of the happiness of becoming Rupert's wife."

"Nay, dearest! Do not stand upon ceremony with me!" returned his gay little wife, bestowing a playful caress upon him. "Perhaps you have found out, you sharp-witted creature, that I have not the very highest possible opinion of Arabella myself. But it is possible, you know, that the becoming Rupert's wife may improve her. I have often thought that it would be a monstrous good thing for her if she were married, because it would be impossible for her to make such a fool of herself then as she does now. But on the other hand, it is quite certain that her money will remain the same; and just think, Adolphe, what is to become of your dear friend when the old baron dies! . . . . He cannot leave him that great grand room, and all the books in it, by way of a legacy; and if he did, the poor dear fellow would be obliged to sit and starve there, in the midst of them, for I am sure he would not sell one of the books to save his life."

"Lucy!" replied her husband, rather solemnly, "I think Rupert Odenthal would rather starve, than marry a woman he disliked."

"Disliked! Oh, Adolphe! What strong words you do use!" exclaimed his wife. "I can't think how you can talk of disliking such a beautiful creature as Arabella! It is very natural that *I* should not be very fond of Arabella, because she is so much older than I am, and has always wanted to tyrannize over me; but that is no reason at all why such a young man as Rupert should not both admire her beauty, and like her fortune."

"Perfectly true, my dear love," replied Adolphe, laughing; "and though I don't think I should like to propose the match to him, I promise you to do nothing to impede it. Heaven knows that if I did not think she would plague him, there is nothing I should like so much as seeing him placed in the possession of an independent fortune, and our both of us having, moreover, the privilege of calling him brother."

"Well, now! that is beautifully said, Adolphe!" exclaimed his wife, gaily. "And I may trust you then, may I not? I may trust, I mean, that you will say nothing to Rupert to set him against her?"

"Certainly you may," replied her husband. "Indeed, to say the truth," he added, "I do not feel at all disposed to speak otherwise than kindly of her; for if you are right, Lucy, in believing that she wishes to marry my friend Rupert, it proves her to be of a very noble and disinterested character, for she must be quite aware what his position is."

"Oh, yes! She is quite perfectly, and altogether aware, of what his position is," returned Lucy. "And the only thing necessary to render the marriage a happy one, is that Rupert too, after they are married, should be equally well aware what her position will be then. All wives, you know, my dear, are obliged to do exactly what their husbands choose; and as your friend Rupert is a very sensible man, he will not choose that his wife should behave like a fool; and that will make a great improvement in Arabella."

The conversation proceeded for some time longer, in a tone which seemed to hover between jest and earnest; but it ended, however, by Adolphe promising very seriously, that he would neither do, nor say anything, to prejudice his friend against Miss Morrison; nor, in short, do anything which might, in any way, impede the marriage which his wife so very greatly desired to bring about.

And in truth, Count Adolphe himself, when left to take a sober, solitary view of the affair, began to think that such a marriage as Lucy contemplated for Rupert, was perhaps the only means by which such a degree of independence could be secured to him as might enable him, when his present patron was no more, to indulge his studious habits, without running any risk of being starved by doing so.

Matters were in this state when the promised dancing party took place; and the whole neighbourhood, not a very large one, seemed assembled together with the pre-determination of being superlatively gay and happy.

The venerable Baron von Schwanberg did not always think it necessary to attend his daughter to the parties assembled for the express purpose of dancing; considering her *dame de compagnie* a sufficient chaperon, and his librarian and private secretary a sufficient *suite*. But upon this particular occasion, he proclaimed his intention of accompanying her party, stating his reason for doing so, to be his wish to see the beautiful English heiress, Miss Morrison, performing the national dance.

This exceedingly flattering compliment was felt as he intended it should be by the beauty, who prepared herself accordingly to be more captivating than ever.

It is possible, indeed, that the extreme care bestowed upon every part of her attire, might have had its origin in the silence of Rupert, rather than in the eloquence of his patron. In fact, Arabella began to feel a good deal surprised, and a little alarmed, at the *no progress* she had made in her resolutely-purposed conquest of Rupert : it was really the first time in her life that she had ever encountered so much difficulty in achieving this object ; for her beauty was precisely of the kind to produce a sudden fever of admiration, while her demeanour was precisely of the kind to encourage the most frank declaration of it.

It is likely enough, however, notwithstanding the intrinsic value of her fair hand, that many who had scrupled not to avow their adoration of her beauty, might have scrupled about giving their name in exchange for her wealth, even if her unbridled covetousness for new conquests had not led her to leave the victims she had subdued, for the sake of pursuing others who were still unscathed.

There could be no doubt, however, that during the last ten years she might have been married, at least, as many times, if such had been her will ; but hitherto she had evidently preferred hitting her game, to taking possession of it.

Upon the present occasion, however, her feelings were wholly different ; whether this difference arose from her having really received a deeper impression than she had ever felt before, or merely from the eagerness occasioned by the difficulty of obtaining her object, may be doubted. There might, perhaps, be a mixture of both ; and moreover, it is by no means impossible that her having listened to a conversation between the young ladies, in which one was almost convulsed with laughter herself, while reducing the other to the same extremity, by relating how she had positively heard an old maid talking of women who were at least *five-and-twenty*, and calling them GIRLS !

To an unmarried beauty of twenty-eight, there was a mixture of something terrific in this jest ; and it might certainly have some effect in producing the resolution which she speedily came to, of marrying Rupert, as well as falling in love with him.

She was not insensible to the fact, that Rupert had not as yet followed the example of all the other men on whom she had bestowed an equal degree of encouragement ; that is to say, he had not declared himself her adorer.

The anger which might have been created by this, was effectively checked by the persuasion, that his silence was occasioned by timidity, and not by indifference; and under the influence of this persuasion, she very deliberately made up her mind to let him understand that, in her estimation, love should for ever be "lord of all;" and that her beautifully fair hand, with her eighty thousand pounds sterling in it, were at his service.

CHAPTER XL.

If any kind dickey-bird, or prophetic mesmerising friend, had whispered in Rupert's ear, as he took his accustomed place, as *suite*, in the carriage which was to convey him to the promised waltzing party, "that a beautiful lady would very nearly make him an offer of marriage before he returned home," he would probably have been seized with such a fit of the tooth-ache, as might have sufficed to excuse his bolting out of the carriage, and hiding himself in his bed-room. But as no such miracle was performed in his favour, he drove on, poor, unconscious youth, and made his *entrée* very nearly at the same time as his self-destined bride. The scene was a very gay one, and as bright and beautiful as pretty women, flowering shrubs, and abundance of wax-lights could make it.

Adolphe had not forgotten the promise he had given his wife respecting the arrangements for the first waltz; and it was, therefore, as the partner of the Baron von Schwanberg's librarian, that the beautiful Arabella prepared to exhibit her unequalled loveliness, and her peculiarly bewitching style of dancing.

It was a searching glance that Rupert sent round the circle as he stood up with her. This glance was not in the hope of finding anything he wished to see, but precisely the contrary; and though carefully searching, it was perfectly satisfactory, for no Baron de Nordorffe was there. Poor Rupert was perhaps hardly conscious himself of the effect which this discovery produced on his spirits, but for the moment it was positively favourable to Arabella, for it caused him to dance with a much greater degree of animation than was usual to him.

Arabella was aware of the animation, but altogether mistook

the cause; and before the dance ended she had succeeded in fully persuading herself that all the coldness she had hitherto perceived in him, had arisen solely from his timidity, and the painful consciousness which accompanied it, that the librarian of Schloss Schwanberg must not lift his eyes with the audacity of love to the beautiful possessor of eighty thousand pounds sterling.

There are, doubtless, to be found, in these rapidly improving latter days, a multitude of highly-educated young ladies, who, although conscious that their respective papas have acquired colossal fortunes by a traffic in money, or money's worth, are yet aware that not quite every young man who dances with them, would be delighted to marry them, if he could.

But our Arabella Morrison was not one of these. Her father had spent his entire life in successful industry, and being by nature of a confiding domestic temperament, he had been in the constant habit of indulging himself, when in the bosom of his family, with a good deal of comfortable, confidential boasting, all tending to show, and to prove, that money formed not only the sinews of war, but of everything else in civilised human society . . . that the man, or woman, who possessed it might, if they knew how to use it, possess anything, and everything, they wished for, from one end of the earth to the other . . . and that only those who had it not, were in any danger of finding themselves obliged to sacrifice their own inclinations to those of other people.

"I could find in my heart something like pity," he was wont to say, "for any poor devils who had got into mischief by reason of their poverty; but I have no pity whatever for rich folks, who don't know the value of what they have got." The ideas thus impressed upon the minds of his daughters concerning the importance of the wealth which it was in his power and purpose to bestow on them, was, doubtless, influential in forming the characters of both, but in a very unequal degree.

Her own beauty, and her own fortune, filled the mind of the eldest too completely to leave room for any feelings not connected either with one or the other. But it was not so with the young Lucy. She was light-hearted and affectionate; and although her own large fortune, and her sister's still larger one, were oftener in her thoughts than might have been the case had she been accustomed to a higher class of ideas as the theme of daily domestic talk, she had still enough of unspoiled native material about her to love what was good, and hate what was bad, without any reference to her own particular interest.

It was this feeling which led her to wish very seriously, in the midst of all her fun and frolic, that Rupert might, in sober earnest, become the lover of her wealthy sister; and her inherited and habitual faith in the influence of wealth, led her to believe that there could be no difficulty whatever in bringing this about, provided the young man was made aware that the hand of her sister was really attainable.

Arabella, meanwhile, on her side was, at least, equally confident that either her beauty, or her wealth, was sufficient to make him her slave (or, in vulgar parlance, her husband), and that nothing but his respect for her superior station was likely to impede his throwing himself at her feet.

While the thoughts of the two English sisters were thus generously engrossed by this very obscure young man, he was, at the bottom of his ungrateful heart, as unmindful of them both, as if they had been a pair of pretty goldfinches, imported by his friend Adolphe, as specimens.

As such, however, he treated them both with the sort of consideration and attention which he would have bestowed on anything considered as valuable or interesting by this much-loved friend. But beyond this he certainly never bestowed a thought upon them; and upon this particular occasion, while one of these fair importations was bringing every faculty, and almost every muscle, into action in the hope of enchanting him, and the other generously working her active little brain to discover the best way of bringing a marriage between her wealthy sister, and his penniless self to a happy conclusion (before the fair Arabella changed her mind), he forgot as nearly as it was possible for him to do, that they existed.

It is true, indeed, that he danced with them both, but he danced with Gertrude likewise; and though there was certainly no perceptible change in her gentle, equable manner to him, he felt, from some cause or other, which it would be difficult very clearly to define, that he had never enjoyed a ball so much in his life.

The unhoped-for absence of the young Baron Nordorffe might have had something to do with it, or it might be that his recent conversation with his mother had made him conscious that he had indeed been unjust to Gertrude; and he was now, perhaps, feeling happy, because his heart told him that he was unjust to her no longer.

In truth, as he looked at her beautiful face, and read there the noble calmness, the thoughtful intelligence, and the gentle content, which it expressed, he felt that, in the words which he had spoken to his mother respecting her, he had, indeed, done her great injustice.

Nothing makes people so gracious and so agreeable as the sensation of happiness; and so gracious and so agreeable had Rupert been, that, far from feeling in despair, the beautiful Arabella laid her head that night upon her pillow, with the delightful conviction that the handsomest man her eyes had ever looked upon, only wanted a little more encouragement to throw himself at her feet.

And before she closed her eyes in sleep, she very solemnly told herself that he should have whatever degree of encouragement might be still required to bring him there. Whatever deficiency she had seen in his apparent admiration of her universally acknowledged beauty, she attributed with great satisfaction, and the most undoubting confidence, to the awe naturally inspired in his mind, by the inequality of their stations in life.

"Had he dared to make me an offer of marriage this evening, I should most assuredly have refused him." . . . Thus ran her mental soliloquy; "for it would have been a presumption unpardonable, even in him, unequalled as he is! Nothing—no—nothing but the most frank and generous encouragement on my part could justify such audacity on his. I am thankful that he has not been guilty of this; for I must, in justice to my own elevated position, have refused him, if he had done so, devotedly as I am attached to him. Noble-looking, graceful, enchanting Rupert! I have often fancied myself in love, but I never knew what love really is, till now! And shall I, then, refuse to make both him and myself happy for life, merely because circumstances oblige me to speak first, instead of him? Young as I still am, I have lived long enough to know the symptoms of love when I see them. No man's eyes ever sparkled and danced in his head as those of Rupert did to-night, without his being in love! Luckily for me, and my adored Rupert, there is no living soul in the whole wide world who has either the right or the power to control me! Our love shall be as faithful as it is fervent, for never can he, nor will he, forget the generosity which makes me indifferent to his total want of fortune; nor can I ever hope, or expect, or even wish, to see any other man looking so gloriously handsome as he did to-night!"

Such were the last waking thoughts of the beautiful Arabella on her return from the ball, which, in a greater or less degree, had proved so very agreeable to some others of the party; nor were her waking thoughts on the following morning at all less passionately tender, or less devotedly generous.

She had found the means of making herself a very decided favourite with the Baron von Schwanberg, probably because she had acted by him as her principles taught her to act by every created man. None were too young—none were too old—to be captivated; and the Baron von Schwanberg, like a great many other old gentlemen with whom she had made acquaintance, was ready to declare that she was by far the most charming young lady he had ever known.

And she, on her side, declared herself on this occasion, as on many former ones, to be very proud of the admiration which old gentlemen in general expressed for her; for it proved clearly, she said, that she had a great and praiseworthy respect for old age. Her saucy sister, indeed, puzzled her a little one day by asking her, when she was boasting of this amiable feeling, why old ladies did not seem to like her as much as old gentlemen?

It was from the stately Baron von Schwanberg himself that the invitation proceeded which led to the engagement, the remembrance of which so delightfully cheered the waking thoughts of Arabella. He had himself invited her and her sister to accompany Adolphe to the castle on that day, and to dine with them *sans ceremonie*. The two young men (Adolphe and Rupert) having previously made an arrangement to ride together to a little town at the distance of a dozen miles, where Rupert had some commission to execute for his patron.

The invitation had been as cordially accepted as it was given, and the enamoured beauty had decided upon a plan before she closed her eyes in sleep, by which she flattered herself she should at once bring affairs to the happy crisis at which she was impatient to see them arrive.

CHAPTER XLI.

Count Adolphe escorted the carriage which conveyed the fair sisters to Schloss Schwanberg, and then proceeded with his friend upon their proposed expedition.

Having paid their smiling compliments to the gracious baron, the ladies repaired with Gertrude to the library, where a portfolio of new caricatures, just arrived from Paris, promised to afford them considerable amusement.

Arabella beguiled an hour or so in laughing over these pictorial epigrams, in running her dainty fingers over the keys of the pianoforte, and then in looking at the backs of sundry volumes with as scrutinizing a glance as if she really wanted to ascertain their contents.

Having performed this ceremony, which she very cleverly felt to be appropriate to the place she was in, she suddenly exclaimed, "Where is your dear father, Gertrude?"

"In the breakfast-parlour, I believe," replied Gertrude. "The newspaper is always taken to him there."

"Then it is there I will go to look for him," returned the beauty. "Perhaps he would like to play a game of backgammon? I should be delighted to play with him!"

"Shall I take you to him?" returned the well-pleased Gertrude, whose rapid thoughts immediately suggested the possibility of reading something aloud to Lucy, instead of passing the whole morning in being jocular.

Miss Morrison immediately passed her arm under that of her young hostess, in token of assent; and in this manner they walked together to the breakfast-room, where they found the baron installed in his own particular chair, and with the newspaper on a small table before him; but it was very decidedly evident that his propensities at that moment were more in favour of dozing than reading.

After a most gracious salutation of welcome on the part of the old gentleman, which was quite affectionately received on the part of the young lady, the amiable backgammon proposal was made, and accepted with the best possible grace on both sides. The board was sought, found, and arranged by Gertrude, and then the stately Baron von Schwanberg and the lovely Arabella Morrison were left *téte-à-téte*.

The lady, certainly, did not appear to know much about the game—but this was of no great consequence; she blundered, and laughed, and looked beautiful; while he corrected, and smiled, and looked benignant.

But when this had gone on for one game, and the baron was arranging the board for another, Arabella suddenly extended her hand, and laying it gently on his, to stop his proceedings, she said, with her very sweetest smile, and in her very sweetest accents, "My dear, dear Baron von Schwanberg, tell me candidly

19

—have I deceived myself in thinking that you feel kindly towards me? If I have, tell me so candidly; but if I have not, I will open my whole heart to you, and ask your opinion, and perhaps your assistance, in an affair upon which the happiness of my future life entirely depends."

The old gentleman answered, as it is to be hoped the majority of old gentlemen would do, under similar circumstances, that there was nothing which would give him greater pleasure than the being able to promote her happiness in any way.

"I was sure that I could not be deceived in you, my dear Sir," returned the beautiful young lady, with her eyes imploringly fixed on his; "I was sure that in addressing myself to you, I should find as much kindness of heart as nobleness of feeling. But before I proceed to the matter in which I am bold enough to hope for your assistance, it is necessary that I should explain to you what my situation in life really is. I am not, like your charming daughter, my. dear Sir—I am not nobly born."

This was a fact which the baron was already perfectly aware; but as his very sincere admiration of her did not in any degree rest upon the antiquity of her race, or even upon the rank of her parentage, he was able to assure her, with the most perfect sincerity, that she need feel no scruple in avowing this, for that the really affectionate feelings with which he was disposed to regard her were produced by her own personal merits alone, and could be in no way affected by her pedigree.

She seized one of his hands in both hers, and having pressed it affectionately, ventured to impress a kiss upon it.

"What is there, my dear young lady, that I can do to assist you?" said the gentlemanlike old man, feeling a little embarrassed.

"I am older than my sister, my dear baron, and yet, as you are aware, I am still unmarried," said Arabella, with a gentle smile.

"Yes, my beautiful Miss Arabella, I am aware of it," returned the baron; "and as you have mentioned the subject yourself, I will confess to you that it has been a matter of great surprise to me."

"When you have known me longer, my dear Sir, your surprise will be less; for you will find that it is not in my nature to form hasty attachments, or to be very easily pleased. Quite the contrary, indeed. Few young ladies, I believe, have received as many offers of marriage as I have done. But I think that one reason why I am still single, is that I am aware that my fortune is so unusually large that there may be some danger of my falling into the hands of a mere fortune-hunter, which I assure you, my dear baron, is no small class in our country."

"Indeed, I have heard so, my dear," replied the baron ; "and a young lady cannot be too much commended for being on her guard against so contemptible and unprincipled a set of wretches."

"Indeed, I have always said so; and I am sure I would a great deal rather die without being married at all, than bestow my wealth upon any such person," returned Arabella, with a look of consummate discretion.

"But yet, my dear Sir," she continued, "now that my younger sister is married, I begin to feel that I want a home of my own ; and though nothing can be more kind and obliging than Count Adolphe, I cannot help feeling that there is something quite ridiculous in a young lady possessed of a fortune of eighty thousand pounds sterling, having no home of her own."

"You are certainly right, my dear," replied the baron, after a pause of some considerable duration, during which his mind was occupied by an attempt to calculate what the yearly amount of income produced by eighty thousand pounds sterling might be ; but this was beyond him. Had he asked his fair companion to solve the problem, she would have done it as correctly as if, instead of being a banker's daughter, she had been a banker herself.

"You are certainly right," he repeated, after this pause ; " and anything which it is in my power to do towards making so desirable an arrangement, you may most freely command."

Arabella thanked him by bestowing another gentle kiss upon his noble hand, not aware that what she intended as a mark of tender and familiar affection, he would interpret as a symptom of profound respect, arising from the imposing difference between her pedigree and his own.

Of such a misconstruction, however, she had not the least suspicion, and had even thrown somewhat of condescension into the expression of her charming eyes, to prevent the poor dear old gentleman from thinking he was a bore.

But this little bit of bye-play being performed, she determined to trifle no longer, but to get over the ground, which, even in her eyes, had some awkward points, as rapidly as possible.

"After what I have already said," she resumed, "you will probably not be greatly surprised to hear that my choice is already made."

Had not the young lady kissed his hand after the manner and

fashion of his domestic servants, both male and female, the Baron von Schwanberg might at this moment have experienced a painful feeling of alarm, lest his own name should be pronounced by the fair islander's rosy lips ; her beautiful and very graceful respect for him had, however, been too decidedly demonstrated to justify such fear, and he, therefore, ventured to encourage her by saying, "Go on, my dear! Be very sure that you will find an indulgent listener in me."

Thus encouraged, the beautiful Arabella clasped her hands together, and then raising them as if to hide her blushing face, she murmured the name of "Rupert Odenthal!"

For a few seconds the baron sat silently looking at her ; and she began to feel that he was too much shocked by the inequality of rank between herself and the Apollo of his library, to listen to her favourably, notwithstanding all the coaxing she had bestowed upon him.

But this painful state of mind did not last long. A very few minutes had sufficed to suggest to the baron the cause and source of the fascination which had made a beautiful young lady possessed of eighty thousand pounds sterling, fall in love with his librarian.

It was not very often that the intellectual workings of the baron's brain were of so active a nature as to break forth in soliloquy, but such was the case on the present occasion, for though his eyes were fixed on his fair companion as he spoke, it was with himself he held parley, and not with her.

"Most extraordinary! Most extraordinary indeed!" he exclaimed. "Gertrude will comprehend the whole affair in a moment!" Arabella was a good deal bewildered, and a good deal disturbed, by this allusion to the young baroness.

Why should she be able to comprehend the whole affair more than anyone else? Though they were apparently on very friendly terms together, she very particularly disliked Gertrude ; and she was, perhaps, the very last person in the world to whom she would have wished any reference to be made on the subject of her own attachment.

Under the influence of these feelings, she exclaimed, "Oh goodness, Sir! Do not say anything about it to your daughter."

The French of Arabella was sufficiently intelligible, though her accent was not very pure ; and the baron was at no loss to perceive that the idea of letting Gertrude into her confidence was by no means agreeable to her.

"You mistake me, my dear young lady!" said he, very

graciously. "Of course, I should never think of communicating to anybody, what you have confidentially confided to me. My allusion to my daughter, had reference to a totally different subject. Yet, nevertheless, it is a subject which must naturally be interesting to you, and I will explain the matter to you as shortly as I can, my dear young lady. This fortunate and very excellent young man, whom your admirable judgment has led you to distinguish in so generous and flattering a manner, was really little more than a peasant boy, before accident introduced him to my notice, in a manner which induced me to permit his introduction into my family in the capacity in which you now see him. But it was not to that introduction, but to its effect upon him, to which I alluded, when I pronounced the word *extraordinary*. I really find nothing, in all my experience, more extraordinary than the effect which his daily association with me has had upon him, and, indeed, upon his excellent mother likewise. This effect was first made evident to me, Miss Arabella, by the sort of notice which was taken of them both, by all the most distinguished members of the society to which they were introduced, when I attached them to me as a part of my suite. At first, the tone of equality upon which they appeared to be received, surprised me a good deal; but after my daughter, the Baroness Gertrude, and myself took the trouble of examining the real state of the case, it soon became very clearly evident to us both, that the station which it has pleased Providence I should hold in society, is one of sufficient dignity and importance to enable me to elevate those whom I permit to associate with me, and that I am, in like manner as my sovereign is in a still higher degree, the source of honour to those around me."

Having said this in the most meek and modest tone possible, and with the aspect of humble piety with which pre-eminently religious people express their submission to Providence when specially exerted for themselves, the baron fixed his eyes upon the ground, and remained silent, as if in the holy *recueillement* of thanksgiving.

During this picturesque interval, Arabella remained silent also, for she was puzzled.

Had the baron hinted that he paid to Rupert and his mother such an annual income as enabled them to live "*like gentlefolks*," she would have understood him considerably better, and have thought that the statement accounted very satisfactorily for the position which they appeared to hold; but having given a moment, in vain, to the finding out what he meant, she gave up the attempt, and the next words she uttered were, " Well, then, my dear Sir, you will be kind enough, will you, as you have been so much like a father to the young man, to continue in the same friendly way with him still, and make him understand, in the manner that these sort of things are managed here, that in addition to all the other favours you have conferred upon him, you have found him a wife with a fortune of eighty thousand pounds sterling ? "

In justice to the intellect of Miss Arabella Morrison, it must be confessed that no young lady upon her travels could have turned the information she acquired respecting men and manners more practically to account, than she did upon the present occasion. Having been very gravely assured that it was the continental fashion for the friends of the parties concerned to arrange all marriages, without any apparent interference whatever on the part of the lady (all love-making between people of fashion being performed afterwards), she certainly showed very considerable cleverness in having recourse to the baron, whose interference, she thought, would give both dignity and authority to the proposal.

As to the result of the negotiation, no thought in the slightest degree approaching to doubt annoyed her for a moment. She had been so long accustomed to hear herself called an angel, that she very sincerely took it for granted that she must be very like one ; and when it is remembered that, in addition to this, she was cheered by the ever-present recollection of her eighty thousand pounds sterling, it may easily be believed that she contemplated the happiest termination to this well-arranged affair.

The shy reserve which she could not but perceive in the manner of Rupert, she attributed wholly to his humility ; and she very delicately stated this to her venerable confidant, adding, with a bewitching smile, that she trusted to his influence for the remedy to this.

" And your trust shall not be in vain, my dear Miss Arabella," he replied.   " We should both of us have reason to be much less satisfied with the young man than we are at present, if his conduct had been at all different.   When I have spoken to him in the manner which I am now authorised to do, you may be very sure my dear, that this painful reserve will vanish."

" Yes, I hope it will ! " she replied, with a degree of *naïveté*, which must have produced a smile on any face less sublimely solemn than that of the Baron von Schwanberg.

As it was, however, the important interview proceeded without
any such indecorum, and before they parted, it was settled between them, that the young man should receive an intimation of
the happiness which awaited him on the following day. "And
after this intimation has reached him," added the old gentleman,
with a very gallant bow, "my office will be over, and the happy
young man, as we may easily believe, will become his own
advocate."

"Yes, I hope so!" again murmured Arabella; and then the
backgammon-board was restored to its place, and the beautiful
Arabella returned to the library.

CHAPTER XLII.

On the following morning the baron condescendingly laid his
hand on the arm of his secretary, as he was about to leave the
breakfast-room. "I have something to communicate to you, my
young friend," said he, in his most gracious manner, "so you
must leave my books to take care of themselves for a little while.
Reseat yourself, Rupert, reseat yourself."

Rupert obeyed. "I think you cannot doubt, my good Rupert,"
resumed the stately old man, "that I take a very great, I may
say a very affectionate interest in everything which concerns
you."

Rupert bowed with an air of deep respect, and replied, "Indeed, Sir, I believe it."

"Then you will believe also, my good friend, that it is with
great pleasure I announce to you a piece of good fortune which
almost any young man might welcome with joy, and which you,
my good Rupert, cannot fail to receive not only with joy, but
with the deepest gratitude. I am commissioned by an individual,
against whose wishes in the business there can be no appeal, to
inform you, that the fair hand of Miss Arabella Morrison, together with her vast fortune of eighty thousand pounds sterling,
are blessings not beyond your reach, however much they may
have been hitherto beyond your hopes."

The complexion of Rupert became crimson, which caused the
baron to smile, and ... [illegible]

"You are overpowered, my good lad! and it is very natural that you should be so. But you must recover yourself. I shall not have executed the commission with which I have been intrusted in a satisfactory manner, if I can only report as the result of it, that you coloured violently, and looked very greatly embarrassed."

This was said with a smile, and, considering the solemn dignity of the features which produced it, a gay smile. But no answering smile greeted him. Poor Rupert was not only embarrassed, but deeply pained. He fancied that he understood the whole business completely, and that the extremely unwelcome intimation he had now received had come from his friend Adolphe.

The fact that the friends had never discussed together either the good or the bad qualities of the lady, rendered this less improbable than it would have been, if either of them had freely expressed his opinion of her to the other.

Her beauty and her wealth were obvious facts and obvious advantages; and even in the first very painful moment of embarrassment, and almost of dismay, occasioned by the baron's communication, Rupert felt a movement of affection towards his strongly-suspected friend, as he remembered that it was probably the wish of being brought into closer connection with him, which had led to this deplorable blunder.

His reply, however, being evidently waited for with impatience, must be given immediately; and making a strong effort to recover the composure which had been so painfully shaken, he said, "I trust, my lord baron, that the sincerity with which it is my duty to answer this proposal will not displease you; but not even the fear of doing so must deter me from saying at once, and most decidedly, that the lady in question has not inspired me with any feeling which could lead me to make her my wife."

If the unlucky Rupert had studied for a month in order to find the mode of expression likely to be most offensive to his patron, he could not have produced a more vehement feeling of indignation.

The old gentleman was for a moment absolutely breathless; but no sooner had he recovered the power of speech, than he poured forth an absolute torrent of mingled contempt and anger.

The situation of the young man was at once too ridiculous and too painful to be endured; and accustomed, as for many years he had been, to the pompous assumption of superiority which formed the staple commodity of all the baron's harangues, he was too much chafed and vexed at that moment to endure it; and exclaiming, in an accent of more suffering than ceremony, " Excuse me, Sir, excuse me ! " he left the room.

That the old gentleman's predominating feeling at the moment was that of anger against his unlucky secretary, is certain ; but as he set himself to reflect upon the next step he had to make in the performance of the extremely disagreeable commission he had undertaken, the idea of having to announce to his petted favourite, the beautiful Arabella, that the offer of her lovely self, and her eighty thousand pounds sterling, had been refused by his penniless secretary in the most decided manner possible, perfectly overwhelmed him. How could he do it ? how was he to pronounce the words necessary to convey this insulting truth ? He ! he who had never uttered an uncivil word to any lady in his life !

It is highly probable that in the course of this long life he had never had so harassing an affair to discuss with a lady before in any way ; and the more he thought of it, the more intolerably disagreeable it became.

At length his spirits sunk so completely under the idea of what was before him, that he suddenly resolved to escape it, by commissioning his daughter to perform the task for him. He felt, indeed, that there certainly were some objections to thrusting his daughter into the secret confidence of the beautiful Arabella (especially as that young lady had particularly objected to anything of the kind); but every consideration gave way before the dreadful idea of having to face the beautiful Miss Arabella under such circumstances ; and having finally made up his mind that Gertrude was really and truly the most proper person to perform this terrible office—because Gertrude always did know how to do everything a great deal better than anybody else—he set off to look for her in the library, fully determined that if he did not find her there, he would follow her into her own room, or even into that of Madame Odenthal, rather than not relieve himself of the heavy burthen which so grievously tormented him.

Fortunately, however, Gertrude was in the library, and so was Madame Odenthal likewise. The reason for this departure from her recently-arranged manner of passing her mornings was, that she was expecting the arrival of Lucy ; it having been agreed between them when they parted the preceding night, that she should return in the morning, for the purpose of finishing the perusal of a newly-arrived English novel that they had been reading aloud to each other.

Rupert also was in the room. On leaving the presence of the

angry baron, he had naturally betaken himself to his usual resort, and had already seated himself in his accustomed nook in the recess of a large bow-window, before he became aware that Gertrude and his mother were in the room. They had recently parted at the breakfast-table, and no salutation was exchanged between them, save a slight bow; but as the new arrangement respecting the solitary occupation of the room by Rupert had been only tacitly established, they neither of them thought it necessary to retreat, and each of the trio very quietly addressed themselves to their respective occupations.

But this delusive tranquillity was of very short endurance; for scarcely had they all placed themselves in the position they intended to occupy, than the door of the room was thrown open with considerable violence, and the Baron von Schwanberg entered.

Gertrude looked up, and greeted him with a smile; Madame Odenthal respectfully bowed her head; but Rupert rose from his seat, and seemed uncertain whether to stay or go.

"Soh! you have taken refuge here, have you? Base, ungrateful boy! But I think that you will not dare to tell this young lady of your most insolent and infamous conduct!"

Such were the words with which the furious old gentleman assailed the startled ears of his daughter, her greatly shocked *dame de compagnie*, and the very indignant, but at the same time very miserable, Rupert.

Gertrude was the only one of the trio who appeared to retain the faculty of speech; but she felt extremely indignant as well as astonished, and with a degree of spirit which she might not have displayed if she had herself been the person who had offended, she rose, and with a rapid step approaching her father, she laid her hand upon his arm, and said, "My dear father, you are using language which I am quite sure you will be sorry for when you recover your composure. Though I know nothing as to the cause of this vehement agitation, I will venture to say that you are in some way or other mistaken. Rupert Odenthal cannot possibly have deserved the words you have addressed to him. He is neither base nor ungrateful."

"Not base! not ungrateful!" returned the baron, vehemently. "I have the very highest opinion of your judgment, Baroness Gertrude, but even you cannot form any accurate judgment concerning circumstances of which you are ignorant. Listen to what I have to tell you, Gertrude, and then you will find that upon this occasion, as upon every other, our opinions and feelings are exactly the same. I pity his very worthy and unhappy mother with all my heart; but nevertheless, she must submit to hear what it is absolutely necessary she should know, because I am not without hope that she may be able to make this very insolent young man repent, and reform his conduct."

This long speech, which was delivered with as much solemnity as indignation, was followed by a short pause, more solemn still; and then raising his right hand, and pointing with its fore-finger to the desperately embarrassed Rupert, the baron thus resumed : "That young man, Gertrude, has this day received the noblest proof of generous and devoted attachment that ever was bestowed upon a man. And how, think you, he has requited this? It has been requited by the deepest ingratitude, and the most bitter insult! But it is not by merely saying this, Gertrude, that I can give you a full and true idea of what his conduct has been . . . . it is absolutely necessary that I should state the particulars. This very presumptuous and most ungrateful young man has had the insolence to refuse the hand of that very beautiful and amiable young lady, the sister of the Countess Adolphe Steinfeld."

"Depend upon it, my lord baron," interposed Madame Odenthal, eagerly, "there has been some mistake,—some foolish joke, perhaps. I am quite sure, Sir, that nothing approaching such a subject has ever passed between them."

The baron turned towards her with a grim smile and mocking bow. "I should have thought that you must have known me long enough by this time, Madame Odenthal, to be aware that I never mistake," he said. "In the present case, the proof that I have not committed the very vulgar offence of blundering, is sufficiently clear, I presume, to satisfy even you. The amiable, lovely, and most generous young lady who has been thus unworthily treated by your ungrateful, and, I must say, very insolent son, has herself confided to me the secret of her noble and most generous affection for him. I presume you will confess there can be no mistake, when I tell you that she commissioned me to give your son the (doubtless unhoped-for) intelligence that she was willing to bestow upon him her hand in marriage. And what think you, madam, was the reply I received from your penniless son to this offer of a lovely bride, with a fortune of eighty thousand pounds sterling? The offer, too, being conveyed by ME. The answer, madam, was distinctly this ; *that he declined the proposal.* You still look incredulous, Madame Odenthal. Let me refer you then to the insolent young man himself."

As he uttered these last words, the baron waved his hand majestically towards the offender, and then dropped into a chair with an air of mingled contempt and indignation.

Why, or how, it came to pass that the eyes of Rupert and Gertrude met at that critical moment, for the first time since this extraordinary scene began, it is difficult to say. So it was, however; and thereupon the words of Claudio may be aptly quoted. He was quite right when he said, "Let every eye negotiate for itself, and trust no agent."

It might have been long, yea, very long, before the well-guarded secret of their respective hearts had been guessed at by either, had it not been for the gleam of light which seemed to flash at that moment both from, and to, the eyes of both.

CHAPTER XLIII.

Gertrude had changed colour so vehemently, and at the last change had become so suddenly pale, that the watchful Madame Odenthal became seriously alarmed for her; and with less of ceremony than she generally used when the baron was present, she left her place, threw a sustaining arm round Gertrude, and led her from the room.

"You see, young man, the light in which your conduct is considered by my daughter," said the baron, solemnly; "it is evident that she is shocked, very deeply shocked, by your conduct. Let me hope that the high respect which I cannot doubt you feel for her, will induce you to conduct yourself in this matter with more propriety than you seemed disposed to do when you first answered me."

Rupert, who, in fact, scarcely heard what he said, replied by bowing his head, and mechanically saying, "Yes, Sir."

"Very well, that is just as it ought to be, Rupert," returned the baron, very greatly relieved. "In the present state of affairs, by far the best arrangement will be, that you and your good and very condescending friend, Count Adolphe, should talk the matter over between you. Perhaps, my good Rupert, I was more displeased with you than you deserved, for it has just occurred to me, as very probable, that you might have thought your acceptance of this generous young lady's proposal might have been displeasing to me, as tending to lessen the distance which ought for ever to remain impassable between persons in different stations of life; and I will not deny, that if such be the case, you ought, by no means, to be too severely blamed for your refusal. In short, Rupert, it strikes me that it will, for very many reasons, be much better than you should talk over this affair confidentially with your good friend, Count Adolphe, than that I should interfere any further in the business. And it may be as well, my good lad, that you should hint to him that I shall greatly prefer his speaking to his sister-in-law on the subject, to my interfering any further with so very delicate an affair."

How much of this speech was either heard or understood by Rupert, it might be difficult to say; for again his only reply was, "Yes, Sir."

But this answer, such as it was, appeared perfectly to satisfy his patron, who, no longer under the influence of the beautiful Arabella's winning ways, began to see, in the very decided, not to say vehement, repugnance of Rupert to the proposal made him, more of prudence than he had himself manifested on the subject; for no sooner had he named the young Count as the most proper negotiator in the affair, than the idea that such a marriage must be extremely disagreeable to him, and to his noble family, occurred to him; so that on leaving the library (which he had entered with the decided intention of turning Rupert out of the house) he felt more disposed to favour him than ever, from the conviction, that his dread of offending him by for a moment forgetting his own inferiority, had been the real cause of his refusal.

And Rupert, too, if his thoughts could truly be described as being occupied by anything but Gertrude, was meditating an immediate interview with Adolphe. As to the beautiful Arabella, he certainly gave her credit for every possible degree of absurdity, and of fancying that she was in love with him, and he in love with her, among the rest. But such thoughts occupied him scarcely for an instant, nor did he deem it possible that the notion of a marriage between them had originated with her, and it was to Adolphe to whom he attributed this preposterous scheme.

He knew, and he knew with sincere pleasure, that this true and faithful friend was more than satisfied; he knew that he was happy in the choice he had made of the pretty, sweet-tempered Lucy; but he knew also that Adolphe's attachment to himself had never changed from the first hour of their boyish companionship to the present time, and he could, therefore, easily understand the possibility of his wishing for such a family connection between them as might, in a great degree, insure their never being long asunder.

Yet still it was difficult for him to comprehend how it was possible that Adolphe could so little appreciate his real character, as to believe him capable of uniting himself for life with such a woman as Arabella Morrison. But, notwithstanding this puzzling incongruity, it was upon Adolphe that his suspicion rested, and it was to Adolphe that he determined to address himself, for the purpose of being extricated from this very ridiculous dilemma.

No sooner, therefore, did he cease to hear the departing footsteps of his massive patron, than he rushed from the library to the stables, and startled the tranquil steadiness of the German grooms, by his vehement demand for "a horse! a horse!" without a moment's delay.

Rupert was well beloved, and his vehemence was only greeted by a smile, while as little delay as possible was permitted to occur before he was in the saddle and galloping rapidly towards the friend whom he intended so very heartily to scold.

All this was business-like and rational; yet, nevertheless, although he set his horse's head in the right direction, and took care to keep it so, his own head was unceasingly running back to Gertrude, and to the strange and inexplicable expression of her face at the moment their eyes met.

But it was in vain that he meditated upon it—and in vain that he strove to forget it; so that the business, by no means very pleasant in itself, upon which his rapid movements proved him to be so earnestly bent, was literally half-forgotten before he reached the presence of his friend.

Luckily for the dispatch of this very important business, however, he found Count Adolphe alone, in the snug little room which was appropriated to the especial use of himself, his books, his cigar, and occasionally of his little wife also.

"Welcome, dear Rupert!" said Adolphe, cordially, and with an extended hand.

Rupert looked at him for a moment without accepting this ever-cordial hand.

He seized upon it at last, however, and grasping it in his own, he exclaimed:

"Adolphe! I thought my heart was as open to you as this kind hand has ever been to me. . . . But it is not so, it seems, for you have most lamentably mistaken me!"

"As how, my dear fellow?" replied the Count, looking exceedingly puzzled. "I should be sorry to have mistaken you, Rupert," he continued, "because it is a positive fact, that I think so highly of you as to make it impossible I should change my opinion, without your losing something in my esteem. I hope it will not be much, Rupert! But go on and state the case. In what have I mistaken you?"

Rupert looked earnestly at him for a moment, as if to discover if there were any jest afoot; a solution which would not much have mended the matter, considering that his august patron, the baron, was one of the parties concerned in it.

"Speak! Explain yourself, Rupert!" again exclaimed Adolphe, impatiently.

"How is it possible, Adolphe," replied Rupert, gently, but very gravely, "how can it have been possible that you, who know me so well, should so greatly have mistaken me?"

"In what have I mistaken you, my good friend," returned the Count Adolphe, with a good-humoured smile. "I declare to you, that, with the exception of your mother, I think I am less likely to mistake you than any living mortal."

"And I should have thought so too," said Rupert, shaking his head, "if I had not just had such very painful proof of the contrary. How could you for a single moment persuade yourself that I could be tempted by my poverty to become the husband of Miss Morrison?"

"But you give me credit for having much greater power of persuasion over myself than I really possess," returned Adolphe, laughing. "I should as soon have thought," he added, "of persuading myself to marry her, instead of Lucy, for the sake of her extra thousands sterling."

"Then this preposterous idea had *not* its origin with you?" said Rupert, extending a hand of reconciliation towards his friend.

"It is a proof that I am of a very forgiving nature," returned Adolphe, as he gave the offered hand a friendly grasp; "that I should so readily, and without any explanation too, accept this repentant fist of yours. But even now, I feel a good deal disposed to make a quarrel of it. How dare you, young Sir, accuse me in your heart of such a vast amount of witless wickedness, as would be required in order to conceive such an idea?"

"Forgive me, Adolphe! I feel that you really have something to forgive," returned Rupert. "I ought not, even for a moment, to have believed it possible. And yet, when I was told

that such a marriage had been suggested, and had been consented
to by the young lady in question, how could I help falling into
this error? No one knows so well as yourself my dependent
condition, Adolphe; and I certainly believe that there is no one
who would be more glad to change it, if it were possible. But I
certainly was greatly annoyed when I fancied that you had hit
upon such a means for achieving it."

"Well, Rupert, I forgive you, which goes further to prove *my*
excessive amiability, than *your* innocence. I wonder now," he
continued, laughing, "whether you would have galloped over in
the same state of furious indignation in order to quarrel with my
wife, if you had happened to find out that within the last twenty-
four hours she has actually been committing the sin for which
you have been accusing me?"

"Do you mean, Count Adolphe," returned Rupert, looking
greatly distressed, "that your charming wife was the person
who wished to bring about a marriage between her sister and
myself?"

"Whether she ever wished this or not, I will not pretend to
say. She likes you very much, and might, perhaps, have been
vastly well pleased to have had you for a brother; but if any
such ridiculous project ever entered her head, she had not courage
sufficient to mention it to me. No. Her active imagination has
been employing itself in another direction. But for anything I
know, my dear Rupert, this may put you in as furious a rage as
the other; for I well remember the time when you declared that
a middle-aged matron on one side, and a young rustic, with a
pitcher on her head, on the other, were both, or either of them,
infinitely more attractive than the lady in question."

It really seemed as if this day had been set apart in the
calendar, as the epoch at which poor Rupert Odenthal's equa-
nimity was to be tried in almost every possible manner.

The words so lightly spoken by his friend, produced a degree
of agitation both in heart and head, which it required a very
strong effort to conceal; but the effort was made, and not in vain.
Where fortitude and self-command are imperatively called for,
from such a man as Rupert Odenthal, they are rarely found
wanting.

"May I ask you to explain yourself?" said Rupert, quietly.

"Yes, you may," replied his friend, with the same tone of
unsuspicious gaiety with which he had began the subject; "and
I will answer you, too, if you will promise not to shoot me, by
way of punishing the impertinence of my wife; she actually

offered me a bet the other day, with very long odds in my favour too, that you would be married to the Baroness Gertrude von Schwanberg before two years were over. Before I took the bet, however, I was generous enough to tell her that she was taking a leap in the dark, and that I was not; for that I happened to know, from the very best possible authority, that the Baroness Gertrude's style of beauty did not please your fancy."

" Such an assurance must have been sufficient, I should think, to convince the fair lady that she was wrong," replied Rupert, with a very masterly command of voice.

" Not a bit!" returned Adolphe, laughing; " my wife is the most resolute little creature I ever knew. Her only answer was, ' Will you take the bet, Adolphe? Ten English sovereigns against ten German thalers.' Excessively obstinate of the little creature, was it not ? "

" The Countess Adolphe looks upon sovereigns as we do upon counters," replied Rupert, with a somewhat unmeaning smile.

" No! that is not the right explanation, Rupert. English ladies, both young and old, know the value of sovereigns perfectly well. But the best part of the joke is, that with all the confidence she expresses about winning her bet, she declares that the love is altogether on the lady's side, and that, as yet, you are perfectly heart-whole. But she is, in truth, a most enthusiastic admirer of the Countess Gertrude, ten times more so than ever I was in my tenderest days, before I was choked with the Gotha Almanack; and she predicts that, despite the nymph of the fountain, and the middle-aged lady before mentioned, your hard heart will be melted at last, and that you will return her tender passion."

The very respectable degree of composure with which this prophecy was listened to, did Rupert Odenthal great credit; the only symptom he gave of not being in a state of perfect self-possession, was his attempting to take his leave immediately, without saying another word concerning the important business which had brought him there. Fortunately, however, Count Adolphe was less thoughtless.

" Do not go, Rupert!" said he, laughingly detaining him by the arm; " for pity's sake don't leave me without giving me some few instructions as to what is to be done or said to Arabella. . . . . . If I comprehend your modest hints aright, you have received from, by, or with the consent of my rich, fair, and rare, sister-in-law, an intimation that if you are in love with her,

20

you will find no reason either to hang or drown yourself. Is this, in sober earnest, the fact?"

"Unless the baron has mistaken her," replied Rupert (looking a good deal provoked at having such an avowal to make), "such is the case."

"And what answer to this delicate intimation do you mean to return?"

"I wish," replied Rupert, very coaxingly, "that the answer could be given in the shape of advice from her friends, without letting her know that I had ever been made acquainted with her generous condescension."

"Excellent!" cried the greatly-amused Adolphe; "and may I ask which of her friends you would select to perform this pleasant office?"

"Of course I cannot presume to give such a commission to any one," replied Rupert; "for as the person whom she selected as her ambassador evidently intends to have no more to do with her, there is no one from whom I have any right to ask such a service. But if Madame la Comtessa——"

"What! My poor dear little wife?" exclaimed Adolphe. "Have you really the cruelty to inflict such a task upon her? .... Why, it must be in revenge, I think, for her having hinted the disagreeable surmise about the Baroness Gertrude, which I mentioned to you just now. Fie, Rupert! Fie!"

The two young men stood looking at each other for a minute or two, with aspects as strongly contrasted as those of Tragedy and Comedy; till at length, the good-natured Adolphe took pity upon his really embarrassed friend, and said, "I cannot look quite so grave as you do about it, my dear Rupert, but the silly girl must be answered in some way. She has a faith absolutely fanatic in the power of her own beauty, and her own wealth; and I do verily believe that she thinks, in all sincerity, that any man, and every man, would be delighted to marry her, if he could. But, in this particular instance, I have no doubt that still another cause has helped to make a fool of her, and that she has taken this most absurd step in consequence of a conversation which took place among us the other day, respecting the different customs which prevail in different countries as to the mode of marrying, and giving in marriage. I observed at the time, that she listened very attentively to my father's statement concerning the manner in which the friends of the parties negotiate the affair for them; and you may depend upon it, that she thought, by employing the superb baron, she was commencing a negotiation in the most dignified and approved style possible."

"Very likely," replied Rupert, looking very little comforted by this suggestion; "but it really seems to me as if the baron thought so too."

"And if he does, I think you must get the Baroness Gertrude to talk to him," returned Adolphe. "Her influence over him, you know, is unbounded," he continued; "and if my sharp-witted little wife is right in the notion I have just mentioned to you respecting her, she will be sure of finding some way or other of convincing her noble papa that he must himself put an extinguisher on the tender passion of my admirable sister-in-law."

The kind-hearted Adolphe was one of the last men in the world to say, or to do, what might have given pain to any one; and so sincerely was he attached to Rupert, that he would willingly have endured much pain himself, rather than inflict it on him. But the impression which had been made upon him by the former declaration of his friend, "that he saw no great charm in Gertrude," was still so fresh in his memory, that it never occurred to him as a thing possible that he could have changed his mind upon the subject. Nor did any such possibility occur to him now. He only saw, in the heightened colour and agitated expression of Rupert's countenance that he was harassed and ill at ease; and seeing him suddenly preparing to depart, he said, "If you don't wish to see me quarrel outright with this absurd Arabella, you must snap your fingers at her, Rupert, instead of looking so profoundly miserable. Set your heart at rest, however, as to her doing anything further to annoy you. I did but jest when I exclaimed so loudly against Lucy's having anything to say to her on the subject. Depend upon it, that if we confide to her the task of informing your fair innamorata that her scheme has not answered, it will cause nothing but mirth to Lucy, and a good deal of impotent rage, perhaps, on the part of Arabella. So set your heart at rest, dear Rupert! If she is likely to be troublesome to any of us, Lucy shall give her a hint that there is some one dying for love of her, either in Paris, or London, or Jerusalem, and she will immediately discover that the climate of Germany does not agree with her."

It was but a languid sort of smile that poor Rupert bestowed upon his friend in return for the pleasant hopes of a speedy release from the beauty which he thus bestowed upon him; yet, such as they were, they, nevertheless, proved quite sufficient to

20—2

chase all annoyance on that score from his memory. It was not upon Arabella Morrison that his thoughts were fixed as he slowly rode back to Schloss Schwanberg.

CHAPTER XLIV.

HAD the climate in which the said Schloss Schwanberg was situated been suddenly changed either into that of Asia or of Siberia, the effect of the alteration, both upon Rupert and upon Gertrude, would have been very much less than that produced by the sort of glimmering light which the circumstances just related had caused to shine on both of them.

So much has already been said explanatory of what their respective feelings really were, that there is no need of repeating it here; and presuming the reader to understand perfectly that they were very devotedly attached to each other, despite the many very strong reasons existing to make such a state of things extremely inconvenient, all that is left for their historian to detail, is the result to which this strangely-assorted attachment eventually led.

It was pretty nearly impossible that such a woman as Madame Odenthal, deficient neither in natural acuteness nor natural affection, could long continue unaware of the complete revolution which had taken place in the state of mind, and, as it seemed, in the character of her son.

Little as she could ever have wished (reasonable and well-principled as she was) that the hardly-tried yet still-devoted love of the high-born heiress should end in a mutual attachment, it would have been unnatural, not to say impossible, for her not to feel pleasure in witnessing the obvious happiness which had quietly taken the place of the uncomplaining but melancholy resignation of Gertrude; while Rupert seemed suddenly endowed with a brilliancy of talent and an energy of character which she had never witnessed in him before, but which it was difficult to witness now without pleasure.

Yet these powerful though often-fluctuating feelings were entirely confined to her own bosom. The young people had already given sufficient proof of firmness of character, to convince her that no lecturing of hers could have any effect beyond that of paining them; and, therefore, after very deliberate consideration of the subject, she determined to let matters take their course; and, to all outward appearance, the relative position of the parties continued to be exactly the same as it ever had been.

Nevertheless, Gertrude had the very great satisfaction of understanding, from a multitude of seemingly trifling circumstances, that this dearly-beloved second mother was aware of the improvement which had taken place in the mental condition of her son. He was, in fact, no longer like the same being; and yet it was only to this mother and Gertrude that his change was perceptible.

To the baron he was, as he always had been, observant, yet unobtrusive; not appearing under embarrassment or restraint of any kind, yet never passing or forgetting the distance which the difference in rank placed between them.

That the baron, therefore, never found out that he was associating with an individual whom he had never known before, is not extraordinary; but such was, in truth, the case.

Not even to each other, however, did Rupert and Gertrude fully open their hearts upon the subject of the future. They scrupled not to deprecate the reserve which had thrown, for years, so deep a gloom over the hearts of both; but not even in the unbounded confidence to which such retrospection necessarily led, did they either of them venture to prophecy of the future.

The reason for this was obvious. As long as the baron lived, the idea of an union between them seemed about equally impossible to both; for Gertrude felt it to be impossible that she should cause her father such pain as this alliance would produce; while Rupert felt it to be equally impossible that he should urge her to do what it was evident her conscience pronounced to be wrong.

But the axiom of our French friends has all the truth of philosophy in it—everything is comparative; and in comparison to the state of mind in which Rupert and Gertrude had passed the last three years of their young lives, their present condition was one of great—of very great happiness.

The comic little embarrassment which the tender passion of the beautiful Arabella occasioned to the ungrateful Rupert, was not permitted to have any very great or lasting effect on this new-born happiness; but as the good feelings of Adolphe were soon awakened, notwithstanding the ceaseless jestings of his wife, to the consciousness that they were doing wrong in permitting her to persevere in her absurdity, he contrived, as gently as he could, to make her understand that Rupert was not at all a marrying man.

On his first using this strictly English phrase in speaking of him, Arabella looked at him with great contempt, and replied, "I don't think, Mr. Count, that you know much about the matter."

"At any rate, my dear Arabella," he replied, "I think I must know more about him than you can do . . . . I have known him far more years than you have known him months, my dear."

"That is very possible," she replied; "but I am a woman, and you are only a man; and everybody allows, you know, that we women understand all about the heart, a great deal better than you men do."

"And what do you think that you have found out respecting the heart of Rupert Odenthal?" returned her brother-in-law.

"You have no right to ask me any such question," she replied, with great dignity, adding with another toss of her handsome head; "and I thank God that there is nobody living who has such a right. However," she continued, "I have no sort of objection to answering you, and I think that I have found out that he would have no sort of objection to marrying me."

Count Adolphe felt that this sort of light skirmishing would not effect the purpose he had in view, and, therefore, he very courageously ventured to say, "My dear Arabella, I think it is my duty to tell you that you are mistaken."

She coloured violently, but remained silent for a minute or two, and then said, "On whose authority, Sir, do you tell me this?"

"It is the opinion of the Baron von Schwanberg, Arabella, and, therefore it is mine . . . . for he is a great deal too wise a man to be mistaken."

This very judicious answer seemed to have great effect, for she now remained silent for a much longer interval. In fact, she had been waiting with some anxiety for a message from her aged and noble confidant, and not receiving any, concluded, that, from some accident or other, the grand old gentleman had been too constantly engaged to see her in private.

Upon hearing her brother-in-law thus gravely assert, however, that this said grand old gentleman did not believe his librarian was inclined to marry her, every feeling of her heart was converted into absolute hatred towards the despicable individual, who might be the happiest of men, if he were not an idiot.

Could she have had the power of condemning this offending individual to immediate destruction, it is extremely likely that, in the frame of mind which she was in at that moment, she would have done it; but as, fortunately, this power was wanting, she sought the relief of solitude, and having reached her own apartment, she locked herself into it as carefully as if she expected to be besieged.

She had not, however, enjoyed this uninterrupted solitude long, before she had very resolutely determined the plan of conduct she should pursue.

It did not take her long to decide, that the low-born Rupert, notwithstanding his stately figure, and his handsome face, was neither more nor less than a clown and a fool; and as such, she threw all remembrance of him to the winds.

In fact, as she very vehemently told herself, he was not worth a thought, and she would not give him one. But her "little vixen of a sister" was not to escape so easily. Arabella felt strongly persuaded that she, and her Dutch husband (as she constantly called Adolphe when she was angry with him), had been in some way or other the cause of her noble and most generous feelings having been so basely requited; and it took her but a very short time to decide upon the mode of vengeance she would adopt, in order to be revenged.

"They think," she muttered, "that because I am still unmarried, I am in want of them, and their precious protection! They think that they are sure of carrying me about with them wherever they go, and of bringing themselves into notice by the brilliant effect which I am always sure to make in society . . . And no bad scheme, either! I will do them the justice to allow that my fortune and my face together, would be likely enough to atone for their own detestable folly and insignificance, if anything could do it. But I will teach them the difference. That giggling idiot, Lucy, has made the most detestable sort of marriage in the world! A title! A pretty title, without one atom of style or fashion belonging to it! They shan't be many months older, before they have both learned to know the difference between my presence and my absence."

These muttered meditations were far from being the mere idle ebullitions of transitory disappointment and ill-temper; on the contrary, they were the result of her deepest feelings, and most resolute purposes. And we may take our final leave of this beautiful creature at once, by stating, that by the help of her quick-witted and intriguing little waiting-maid, she contrived to get at a groom, who spoke French glibly, and took bribes with equal facility and intelligence. By his assistance she managed to convey herself, her wardrobe, her maid, and this said groom (suddenly promoted to the rank of *courier*), to an obscure exit from the castle court-yard, where her own fine travelling carriage, in which she had made her journey from England, awaited her, and at an hour so early in the morning as to secure her from the embarrassment of encountering any of the noble family of Steinfeld.

It was generally supposed that this well-managed elopement had been arranged by some fortunate individual, whom Lucy would be speedily informed had been added to her family connections, by way of a brother.

But Lucy herself knew her half-sister better. "No!" said she, when this very natural surmise was suggested; "no! Arabella will fall in love a great many more times yet, before she falls into marriage. She has always been very subject to love fits; but with all her folly in this way, she has always seemed clever enough to get out of an engagement as easily as she got into it; and I should not wonder, if she went on in the same way for years! Arabella is certainly very proud of her beauty, and is excessively fond of dressing herself, and of being told that she is an angel, and that one man after another is dying for her. But take my word for it, Adolphe, she loves her money still more tenderly than she loves her beauty."

This harangue, which was very kindly uttered in order to calm the useless activity of her husband (who seemed to think that it was his duty to look after the runaway, and induce her to return to them, if still unmarried), not only produced the effect for which it was spoken, but was often quoted by Adolphe afterwards, as having been perfectly prophetic.

The beautiful Arabella had reached the mature age of fifty-three, ere she finally consented to bind herself to one adorer, instead of remaining at liberty to receive the homage of many; nor did she marry then, without taking excellent good care of her darling money, keeping very nearly the whole of it at her own disposal, and bequeathing it, at last, to a frolicsome young gentleman of twenty-two, who assured her, that among his various whims and vagaries, the only one which was really a part of himself, was that which led him to prefer old ladies to young ones.

CHAPTER XLV.

But we must now resume the course of our narrative. The perfect and most happy understanding which, after long years of secrecy and suffering, was at last established between Rupert and Gertrude, for some time appeared perfectly sufficient to content the hearts of both; and no wonder that it should have been so, for the happiness it had brought to them both was in very bright contrast to the heavy hopeless gloom which had before enveloped them.

It had been mutually agreed between them, after a good deal of discussion, that Madame Odenthal should not be made acquainted with the secret of their attachment. This reserve, far from arising from any want of affection on the part of either of them towards this truly friendly mother and motherly friend, was the result of the most tender anxiety for her tranquillity. They both knew her too well, not to feel certain that were she made acquainted with their attachment, she could not fail to be unhappy, whether she kept their secret or betrayed it.

Such a confidence must, in fact, have placed her in a most embarrassing position. She was so implicitly trusted by the baron, that, to betray that trust by becoming an approving repository of such a secret, would doom her for ever, in her own eyes quite as much as in his, to the reproach of the very deepest treachery; while, on the other hand, if she returned their confidence, by betraying it to him, she must estrange herself for ever from all that was left her to love on earth.

All this was so obvious, that it took them not long to decide that neither of them could have any confidant, save the other.

Nor was there any great difficulty in strictly adhering to this resolution. Rupert was quite conscious that he had effectually succeeded hitherto in concealing from his mother all that he wished should be still concealed; and nothing, therefore, was necessary, but that he should persevere in the same line of conduct which he had so long and so successfully adopted.

With Gertrude, indeed, the case was different; but, nevertheless, the difficulty was not much greater; for though the suffering girl had often been conscious that Madame Odenthal suspected her attachment—an idea which she chiefly derived, perhaps, from the fact of Rupert never being made the subject of conversation between them—the habit of silence concerning him, when they were *tête-à-tête* together, was sufficiently established to prevent any feeling of embarrassment from being created by its careful continuance.

For several months after the long-delayed explanation took place, by which the mutual affection of these dangerously-placed young people was made known to each other, they both thought that they had attained a degree of happiness which greatly exceeded what usually falls to the lot of human beings during this imperfect stage of their existence.

Little or nothing was changed in their usual manner of existence; yet each day, and almost each hour of the day, seemed bright with new happiness. Had they never known the dreary misery of loving, without daring to hope, almost without daring to wish for a return, they would not now have enjoyed the fulness of happiness which seemed to awaken them into a new state of existence.

The very secrecy of this happiness seemed to increase its intensity. The sentiment which each was so delightfully conscious was reflected in the heart of the other, could not, they were quite certain, be understood by any but themselves; and, therefore, its being suspected by none, was a blessing inexpressibly precious.

The daily routine of their lives (totally as they were actually changed) seemed to go on without any variation; and, in fact, the very sharpest eye could have detected no alteration but one.

On returning from Paris, Gertrude had very discreetly made a law respecting the disposition of her time, which, according to the long-established habits of Rupert, prevented their ever occupying themselves in the garden at the same hour of the day. But this prudent regulation existed no longer; and they pruned trees, picked off dead leaves, and removed fading blossoms very often side by side, and even occasionally walked together from one end of the long shrubbery avenue to the other, without any qualms of conscience interfering on either side to prevent them.

It was during this very happy interval that the superb Arabella withdrew herself from the neighbourhood; and although her doing so was very decidedly a domestic blessing to her sister, and by no means very much regretted even by her sister's good-natured husband, the suddenness of her retreat, as well as the

mysterious manner of it, led to more gossiping in the neighbourhood than they either of them liked to encounter; and it was,
therefore, speedily decided between them, that the wisest thing
they could do, would be to see a little more of the world; the gay
little Lucy assuring her husband that, after she had seen Paris
and Vienna, and enjoyed a little dissipation at both, she should
be ready to come home, and be quiet for the rest of her life.

Schloss Schwanberg relapsed again, and very speedily, into its
former stately stillness after their departure. No more beautiful
young ladies arrived to persuade the baron that he was still a most
fascinating old gentleman; and the conclusion of his acquaintance
with the fair Arabella, had annoyed him too severely to leave him
with either courage or inclination to repeat the experiment of
making himself agreeable.

All this was extremely favourable to the establishment of such
a mode of life as Gertrude now looked forward to as the greatest
happiness within her reach; and, in truth, so great was the happiness it brought, when compared with the misery she had long
endured, that her enjoyment of it almost made her forget that she
might be happier still.

The health of her father was excellent, for he, too, felt that the
life he was now leading, suited him vastly better than either the
brilliant splendours of Paris or the flattering fatigue of becoming
the confidential friend of a beautiful Arabella.

To the final adventure, however, with that young lady, he
never alluded. The reason for which, probably, being that, even
he, would have found it impossible to discuss it with the degree
of solemn dignity which ought to belong to everything in which
he bore a part.

It was becoming very evident, also, to an eye as observant of
his likings and dislikings as that of Gertrude, that he was growing
every day more attached to his own arm-chair, and more reluctant
to leave it. He had married so late in life, that, young as his
daughter still was, he was an old man; and the habits of his
whole life having been uniformly self-indulgent, he felt more
disposed, than his still excellent health rendered necessary, to
yield to these unsocial propensities.

It would be doing the excellent Gertrude much less than
justice to suppose that she would have been likely, under any
circumstances, to have resisted his daily increasing attachment to
the stately solitude of his own abode, in order to procure amusement for herself elsewhere; but, as it happened, this very quiet
and retired mode of life was precisely what she would have

arranged for herself had her own enjoyment been the only object she had in view; and it would be difficult, perhaps, to imagine a situation in which lovers so imperatively separated by circumstances in one direction, could be so propitiously situated in another.

That there was a good deal of sympathy between the character of Rupert and that of Gertrude, in some respects, cannot be doubted. They could scarcely have loved each other so devotedly, had it been otherwise; but, had there been more still, they would have contemplated the happiness of their present condition with a greater equality of contentment.

The nature of Gertrude was as gentle as it was firm. During that most miserable period of her life which she had passed in Paris, even while believing it to be her duty to place herself in a condition more miserable still, the sweet gentleness of her temper had never given way. Not even Madame Odenthal, through all the dismal hours of that most wretched winter, so many of which had been passed by her *tête-à-tête* with poor Gertrude, had ever seen her give way to melancholy, or beheld her charming countenance disfigured by an aspect of discontent.

There had been, even then, through all the varied sorrows which pressed so heavily on her young heart, a patient sweetness, that had no mixture of complaint in its expression. And the same gentle philosophy might easily be recognised in her aspect now. While thankfully blessing the happy change from the anguish of thinking that she was doomed to pass her life in loving one who would never love her in return, she showed no symptom of lamenting that she was not happier still.

Nor was there the least mixture of affectation in this; she really was as contented, and happy as she appeared to be. Her first thought on waking was one of joy, for it brought the assurance of passing many hours of the coming day with Rupert, and the dearer assurance still, that Rupert loved her. And when she laid her head upon her pillow at night, the remembrance of that precious love, which had been seen by her, though by no one else, through every hour of the happy day, was the theme of her last waking thought.

But, alas! the case was widely different with Rupert. No sense of filial duty, no tender feeling of filial love, softened his heart, and enabled him to bear with the like resignation the dreadful impossibility of making the admirable creature, who so tenderly returned his love, the wife of his bosom, and the assured companion of his life.

He vainly pleaded to her, in the words of his own English church, "Those whom God has joined together, let no man put asunder." She could only shake her head, and say, "No Rupert! no! Those words cannot be applied to us! It cannot be the will of God that I should wound my father to the heart, and perhaps shorten his days, in order to ensure my own happiness. He gave me my life, dear Rupert, before you saved it. The first duty which heaven appoints us to perform, is that which we owe our parents. Let me not fail in that, for if I did, you would no longer see in me the same creature whom you have so long and faithfully loved. If I saw you do what would most deeply pain your mother, Rupert, should I still love you as perfectly as I do now? I do not think it."

And Rupert, to do him justice, did not listen to such language as this without feeling the deference it deserved; and that, in truth, was much, for it was the outpouring of a most true, pure, and loving heart. But the being very fully aware that it was so, did not greatly improve his condition, or lessen his regret at feeling that she could not, and ought not, be his.

This state of things went on, with little or no variation, for above a year, during which time poor Gertrude would really have been very happy, if the state of Rupert would have permitted her to be so. But this he could not, or, at any rate, he did not do. He was certainly not himself at all aware how much pain his languid eye, his unelastic step, and the evidently depressed state of his spirits, occasioned her, or he would not have suffered these painful symptoms to be so very visible. Yet, not even the seeing all this, could for a moment shake her resolute determination, that her father should not be made the victim of his unbounded confidence in her.

It is true, that her firm spirit would sometimes droop, when meditating on the hapless obstacles which kept them asunder; but all this resolute firmness of spirit returned, when she remembered that the bare mention of such an union as that which could alone ensure Rupert's happiness, would not only utterly, and as long as life was spared him, destroy his, but that the shock which such a proposal would occasion, might shorten the life which for so many years had been wholly occupied in loving, cherishing, and indulging her.

It so chanced that Rupert one day entered the library while she was sitting there alone, and weeping bitterly, as she meditated on the perversity of a destiny which only left her the power of choosing between the misery of dooming the man she loved to the dreary, lingering suffering of a hopeless attachment, and that of endangering the life of her doting father, by stabbing him to the heart in the point where she knew him to be most susceptible.

When Rupert questioned her as to the cause of this vehement burst of feeling, she only begged him to forgive her weakness, without insisting upon her explaining the cause of it. But he could not be so silenced, and the scene ended by her opening her whole heart to him, and making him understand the bitter suffering of such an alternative.

This painful scene was so far useful, that it put an effectual stop to the pleadings which had so often wrung her heart, when the only reply she could make to them was, "Rupert! It is impossible!"

Before they parted she made him feel and fully understand *why* it was impossible; and he promised, with all the solemnity of fervent truth, that she should never hear any pleading from him again, a compliance with which might lead her to deem herself a parricide.

And the unhappy Rupert Odenthal not only made this promise sincerely, but he kept it faithfully.

<center>~~~~~~~~~~~~~~~~~~~~~~~~</center>

CHAPTER XLVI.

IT is an excellent adage which says, "Never do wrong that right may come of it;" but it is sadly true, nevertheless, that by doing right at one moment, we may sometimes entail sad mischief on the future. There can be no doubt that the Baroness Gertrude acted according to her duty, when she resolutely refused to destroy her father's happiness for the sake of promoting her own; and yet this resolute adherence to duty probably occasioned more suffering than it saved.

Moreover, it is probable, that during the melancholy discussions that have been described, and which terminated by Rupert's pledging his word that he would not again urge her to avow her attachment to her father, there was one point upon which she would have been wiser, if she had yielded to his wishes.

Having promised that her father's days should never be embittered by a knowledge of this attachment, Rupert had ventured to ask for her promise that she would be his wife after the death of her father; and she certainly showed more of weakness than of wisdom, when she answered him by a passionate flood of tears, and declared, that dearly as she loved him, she would rather that they should part that moment, never to meet again, than give a promise which might, by slow and treacherous degrees, lead to her wishing for an event, which it had been the morning and evening prayer of her life might be far, far from her!

This feeling was a very natural one, but it led her wrong.

By the encouragement she had already given, she had so cherished and strengthened the attachment she had inspired, that by refusing to permit any positive promise of becoming his wife to pass her lips, she deprived him of the best, if not the only source of courage and consolation which it was in her power to bestow.

The effect was very melancholy, and it was not long in showing itself.

From being a most persevering reader, and a writer too—for the mind of Rupert was of too active a nature not to seek this indulgence—he became the very idlest, and most objectless of men.

It was in vain that poor Gertrude endeavoured to check this growing malady (for such, in truth, it was), by endeavouring to lead him into literary discussion, and to amuse his mind by suggesting thoughts, and speculations, less melancholy than his own. All such efforts were utterly useless.

And yet it was evident that he endeavoured to rally the sinking energies of his character, and to be to her the same inspiring companion he had ever been. But such efforts were perfectly in vain; he was no longer master of himself, and his faculties.

His position was, in truth, a very cruel one.

During several years he had baffled, by the efforts of a naturally vigorous mind, and the courageous animal spirits of early youth, the painful effects arising from the conviction that the high-placed beauty whom he had dared to love, did not, and could not, condescend to love him in return; and if this utter hopelessness had continued for a year or two longer, he would doubtless have outlived, and probably forgotten, the ardent dream of these almost boyish days.

But ere this sort of oblivion, or anything approaching it, had come upon him, he had the doubtful happiness of believing that this first and only love was not unrequited.

The effect of this discovery was as decisive as it was inevitable. The world no longer contained anything which appeared to his feelings worth living for, unless Gertrude and her love were blended with it.

The happiness which ensued from the first mutual and frank avowal of an attachment so natural, yet so long concealed, was great indeed, and it would be difficult to say which young heart derived the highest and most perfect felicity from it. But, unfortunately, the position of the parties was such, as to render it impossible that this feeling of happiness could last.

As long as Gertrude had remained hopelessly convinced that the devoted affection which she had bestowed on Rupert was unreturned, she had found very rational, and, to a certain degree, very effectual consolation, in such a constant occupation of her time as left her with few idle moments in which to indulge meditation, or the untowardness of her destiny; which, while seeming to place her in a position in many respects so enviable, denied the only blessing that in her estimation was really worthy of the name.

Very persevering and very meritorious were the efforts by which she had thus sought to emancipate herself from this vile thraldom of unrequited love; and had the love remained unrequited, they would probably have been crowned with the success they deserved.

But no sooner did she discover her mistake, no sooner did she feel

> "How sweet's the love that meets return,"

than all these efforts ceased, and for a time, she was, perhaps, one of the very happiest creatures in existence.

And so she might have continued, perhaps, if Rupert could have contemplated the situation in which they now stood to each other, with the same satisfaction as herself; but the first intoxicating joy of the explanation being over, he began to feel that if she had not courage enough to ask her father's consent to their union, and influence enough to obtain it, the consciousness of her devoted affection was rather a misery than a blessing . . . . and it can scarcely be denied that he was right in thinking so.

Up to this period, Madame Odenthal knew nothing of the explanation which had taken place between her son and Gertrude, beyond what her own sagacity had enabled her to discover. They both knew her too well, not to be aware, that they should be throwing a heavy load upon her conscience, by confiding to her the secret of their attachment; and their discretion certainly saved her, for some time, from a very painful embarrassment.

She could not, however, long remain blind to the marked change which had taken place in them both, nor could she long doubt the cause of it.

The affectionate discretion which prevented their avowing their mutual attachment to her, did not go the length of carefully concealing it; and the firmness of character which her son had displayed during all the misery she now felt sure he must have endured at Paris, convinced her that he would require no lecturing from her to prevent his returning all the generous kindness of the baron, by inducing his daughter to leave him; and she, therefore, felt herself justified in letting matters go on without any interference on her part, till the death of Gertrude's aged father should leave his daughter at liberty to act for herself.

But this very rational resolution was now shaken by the painful change which she witnessed in her son; and no sooner did she become aware of this, than she became fully as miserable as the lovers themselves.

To her son, however, she gave no hint either that she read his heart, or was aware of the ravages which the state of it had caused both in his mental and bodily health; but she could no longer retain the same reserve with Gertrude; and notwithstanding the obvious and very sad impossibility that either could help the other, the confidence thus established between them was certainly in some degree a relief to both.

Yet it would be difficult to imagine anything much more sad than the conversations they held together, when all the other inhabitants of the castle had retired for the night. The very perfect accordance, moreover, which existed between them on the subject of all their melancholy discussions, only served, in their case, to increase the pain of them. Had either of them sincerely differed from the other on any one point, it could scarcely have failed to be a comfort; but not only was there no contrariety of opinion, but there was scarcely a shade of difference between them; for the strong sense of duty which led both to resolve that the tranquil happiness of the old man's life should not be disturbed, was equally firm in both.

"Were we not so perfectly of the opinion that this unhappy love must be conquered," said Madame Odenthal, "these most melancholy, but most dear moments of confidence, my dearest Gertrude, would soon degenerate into a conspiracy, and a conspiracy against one who has been the fondest of fathers to you,

21

and the most generous of benefactors to me. Let us thank Heaven, dearest, that no selfish feeling has been powerful enough to beguile us into such sin!"

And this feeling did sustain them both; and the proud old man dozed on in his easy chair, firmly persuaded, that not even the "Almanack de Gotha" itself recorded many names, the dignity of which was sustained with such unspotted purity as his own.

Had the passive courage of Rupert been as well sustained as that of Gertrude, the destiny of both might have been very different. But it was not so. And yet neither his mother nor Gertrude could accuse him of failing in the promise he had given, of urging the latter no more to pledge herself to any engagement for the future. But ere many months had passed over them, so painful a change became evident in Rupert, as to suggest to them both the most terrible idea that could enter the mind of either. Health, both of mind and body, was evidently failing him.

It is only by degrees that such a fact is in any case considered as likely to become permanent by those watching it at the commencement; and both the loving hearts which were so tenderly devoted to him, were long sustained by the persuasion that accidental cold, and consequent fever, were the causes of the symptoms which alarmed them, in which persuasion they were strengthened by the assurances of the invalid himself, who, although he confessed that he was not quite well, reiterated his assurances that he should soon be better.

CHAPTER XLVII.

While everything was thus apparently stationary at Schloss Schwanberg, an important change took place in the family of their nearest and most estimable neighbour, Count Steinfeld.

His wife, who though not a very brilliant, was a very amiable woman, died from a fever caught by some imprudent exposure to cold, after active exercise. Her son and his wife, who

had been now absent for more than a year, were suddenly recalled, but arrived only in time to attend her funeral.

The only persons admitted to see them during the first month
or two which followed this melancholy event, were their
neighbours at Schloss Schwanberg, and Gertrude's society became
a blessing of no small importance to poor Lucy; for she had lost
much of her former gaiety since they parted, having become a
mother, and lost her child, just as she was made aware that life
had better pleasures to bestow than any which could be welcomed
by laughter.

She was now much more sedate, without being at all less
agreeable; for her quick faculties and charming good humour
were only the more endearing, from being no longer displayed in
the perpetual garb of jesting.

The return of Adolphe seemed, for a time, to produce a very
salutary effect on the health of Rupert; and the having remarked
this, caused Gertrude to promote, by every means in her power,
an almost daily intercourse between the two families, and this
intercourse certainly proved a most essential advantage to both
parties. The truly sorrowing widower, who was still almost a
young man, having some family arrangements to settle with the
brother of his deceased wife, was prevailed upon to change
the scene by transacting the business in person, at the distant
residence of this brother; and Count Adolphe and his young
wife were left in occupation of the family mansion, which being
"a world too wide" for the reduced household, was greatly
benefited by the frequent visits of the Schwanberg party.

The aged baron, indeed, had for some time been beginning to
feel that it was more agreeable to receive visits, than to make
them; but as Father Alaric had been of late taken into as great
favour as a backgammon player, as he still continued to be as a
confessor, he was always at hand to assist his sister Odenthal
in supplying the place both of his daughter and his secretary.

But although Rupert never met his friend Adolphe without
pleasure, the excitement caused by his return soon faded away;
and though he frequently, as in days of yore, brought over some
newly-arrived volume, or pungent pamphlet, upon which they
might compare criticisms, and philosophise on the onward movement of the age, it was often evident to the quick eye of Adolphe,
that his friend was no longer the same ardent thinker, or the
same animated companion, that he was wont to be.

Rupert could still talk, and talk well, on all the stirring themes
which science and philosophy suggested, but it was not without

21—3

effort that he did so; and this intimate and almost daily intercourse had not continued long, before Adolphe became convinced
that his friend was suffering from some malady, either mental or
bodily, or both.

It chanced that our old acquaintance, Dr. Nieper, who was
still the favourite Æsculapius of the neighbourhood, was making
a professional visit to Lucy, when Rupert arrived to keep an
appointment which he had made with Count Adolphe.

It was more than a year since the doctor had last seen his
former patient; and he was immediately struck by the alteration,
by no means for the better, which had taken place in his appearance during the interval.

"What have you been doing with yourself, my young friend,
since I had last the pleasure of seeing you?" said the sagacious
doctor. "You look as if you had been making a campaign in
Egypt, and that it had very particularly disagreed with you."

It was a very languid smile with which Rupert replied, "No,
doctor, I have not been campaigning in Egypt. Perhaps I have
not been campaigning enough, anywhere. I believe I am
gradually growing into the condition of the poor grub commonly
called a book-worm."

"Then I strongly recommend you to leave the Schwanberg
library to take care of itself for a little time, while you set forth
upon a scamper either north, south, west, or east, to amuse yourself. I would not have taken so much trouble as I did some
seven or eight years ago to keep you alive, after your heroic
adventure with the little baroness in the river, if I had thought
you would turn out nothing better than a grub."

While laughingly making this speech, Dr. Nieper had taken
the hand of Rupert in his, and with an air of very easy indifference was carefully feeling his pulse.

He made no observation, however, upon the condition in which
he found it, and almost immediately afterwards took his leave.
Rupert returned to the business upon which he and his friend
had been engaged before this interruption, and which consisted
in the examination of a very dusty collection of old coins which
Adolphe had discovered in some out-of-the-way corner, and
which he flattered himself the *savoir* of his friend Rupert might
enable him to arrange; but Adolphe pushed the table aside,
saying, "No, no, Rupert, if you are unwell, you shall not be
teased by such tiresome work as this. Let us take a stroll up
the long walk. It will do us both a great deal more good than
poring over these dirty coins."

Rupert offered no opposition to the proposal, and the two young men set off upon their lounging excursion.

This was certainly not the first time that Count Adolphe had been aware that his friend was looking unwell; but Rupert having replied to the affectionate inquiry on the subject which this observation led to, by saying, " I have had a bad cold, and that always makes one look half dead, I think," had received the explanation as perfectly satisfactory, and contented himself afterwards by occasionally reiterating the usual formula so constantly repeated upon similar occasions. " Do take care of yourself, Rupert. You do not look as if you had got rid of that abominable cold yet."

But the words, and still more the manner, of Dr. Nieper had alarmed Adolphe; and he determined to take advantage of the next opportunity which presented itself, to learn the skilful practitioner's real opinion.

He did not wait long for this, for Lucy was still under his care; and having waylaid the good doctor as he was making his retreat, the young Count asked him, with some anxiety, whether he thought his friend Odenthal had any complaint more serious than the " bad cold " which he complained of.

" If you had not asked me this question, Count Adolphe," replied the Doctor, " I think I should have addressed something like it to you. It is some months since I last saw this very magnificent young fellow, and the change which has taken place in him startles me. He is decidedly suffering under the treacherous influence of low fever. Is it long since you first remarked this painful change in him ? "

" No, not long," replied the Count. " When I did remark it, he told me that he had been suffering from a severe cold. Do you think, Dr. Nieper, that a cold is a malady of sufficient importance to account for the change which we both remark in him ? "

" *A cold ?* " repeated the Doctor, shaking his head; " a cold is a sort of nick-name for a multitude of maladies, which would sound a good deal worse, if described more accurately. He may have had a cold, and this cold may have been neglected, and it may, though I don't say it has, but it may have settled upon the chest, which would be quite enough to account for the very unsatisfactory state of his pulse. But it is just as likely that he may be suffering under the influence of some mental vexation, as from any other cause. It does sometimes happen, you know, at his age, that young people worry themselves into fevers, without

the help of any specific malady. Let it be what it may, I trust
he will do battle with it, and master it too, for he is one of the
finest young men I ever saw."

Adolphe neither liked these threatening words, nor the tone
in which they were spoken; for there was evidently some alarm,
as well as much kindness, in the good man's manner. He was
determined, however, if there was any serious malady, he would
find it out, and prevent its being neglected.

"He shall have change of air and scene, if that will do him
any good," thought the kind-hearted Adolphe. "I would travel
with him round the world, dear fellow! rather than lose him!"

The intercourse between the two families was too frequent to
leave any long interval before the young men again met; and
then, although Rupert's reply to his "How are you?" was a
very prompt "Very well, thank you," his appearance was by no
means accordant with it.

The dusty coins were again brought out, the occupation they
were likely to offer being more favourable, in the young Count's
opinion, to the cross-examination to which he fully intended to
submit him, than the absence of all employment for eyes and
hands.

Although the very happy husband of the pretty Lucy was as
free from all lover-like admiration for the stately Gertrude as it
was well possible for a man to be, he well remembered the time
when he had thought her very charming; and although he equally
remembered that Rupert was at that time very far from looking
at her with the same admiring eyes as himself, he thought it by
no means impossible, that during the years they had since passed
together, the judgment of the man might have corrected the
defective taste of the boy.

"Mercy on him, if this unfortunate change has actually taken
place!" mentally exclaimed Adolphe, as he recalled the result of
his own adventure. "If the 'Almanack de Gotha' rejected me,
how will it serve my unfortunate friend?"

But the obvious difficulties attending such an attachment, by
no means sufficed to convince Adolphe that it could not exist;
moreover, he very modestly remembered that it was possible the
young lady herself might be more inclined to throw over the
'Almanack' in this case than in his own; and if, indeed, Rupert
Odenthal loved Gertrude, and was loved by her in return, it was
not very improbable that the utter impossibility of obtaining the
baron's consent might occasion misery sufficient to break more
hearts than one.

Adolphe remembered, too, while ruminating on this very interesting possibility, that Lucy had long ago hinted a suspicion that Gertrude had feelings, even tenderer than a sister's love, for this companion of her youth, who had first saved her life, and then, beyond all doubt, very materially contributed to embellish it; for no one knew better than Adolphe, no, not even Gertrude herself, how very delightful, and how very attaching a companion Rupert would be.

"And must he die for it?" mentally exclaimed his friend, as this very probable state of things suggested itself.

"Yet who is to find out the real state of the case? and how is it possible that we can give counsel, or aid of any kind, without being in their confidence?"

But it was easier to see the truth of this, than to devise any plan by which the difficulty could be lessened. If this suspected attachment really existed, the impediments to any happy conclusion to such a romance were of much too stubborn a character to afford any reasonable hope of their yielding to any influence which could be put in action to remove them.

The bare idea of attacking the baron on the subject, so vividly recalled the scene of his own dismissal, that his active imagination immediately painted to him the sort of indignation which was likely to ensue, upon Rupert Odenthal's being proposed to him as a son-in-law, and he instantly decided that the experiment must not be made.

If Rupert had been his own brother, Adolphe Steinfeld could not have shrunk from the idea of his being treated with indignity, more sensitively than he did now; and, at length, he decided that, by far the best remedy which could be applied, if further observation tended to confirm the notion of this attachment, would be absence. "I will carry him off!" he mentally exclaimed. "We will together traverse this pretty little globe of ours, from east to west; and it may be, that when we return, we shall find this high-born heiress safely united in holy wedlock to some noble Von something, whose name glitters through half a dozen pages of the holy Almanack."

It was without the very slightest approach to satirical impertinence that La Fontaine's well-known words,

"On a souvent besoin d'un plus petit que soi,"

occurred to him. He felt conscious that, intimate as he was with Rupert, he should be greatly at a loss how to set to work in order to discover whether he was right or wrong in the guess he had made respecting the greatly-altered condition of his friend. "I know that, if I attempted to hint my suspicion to him, I should do it in so confoundedly awkward a manner, that I should be sure to give him pain, but not be so sure of obtaining his confidence," thought Adolphe, as he meditated long and anxiously on the subject. But, having come to this conclusion, he went on a little further, and then it occurred to him that, although he might fail in arriving at an exact knowledge of the state of Rupert's affections, by way of question and answer, Lucy might accomplish the same object, by means of her intimate intercourse with Gertrude.

And then it was that the saucy quotation about "*un plus petit*" suggested itself. But, truly, there was no offence in it, according to his interpretation; and any mind which could have followed his, as he dwelt upon the tender tact and loving gentleness with which he knew his Lucy would perform such a task, if hoping to serve her friend thereby, would have found only what was endearing in the word *petit*, and nothing at all approaching the more contemptible characteristics of a mouse.

CHAPTER XLVIII.

THE languid eye and feverish cheek of poor Rupert would not easily have passed from the mind of his friend, even if he had been surrounded by a host of the very gayest company; but, as it happened, he and his Lucy passed the evening of the day on which he had first felt seriously alarmed about him, in a perfectly undisturbed matrimonial *tête-à-tête*, and it was thus that the subject was discussed between them :—

"Lucy, dear," said Adolphe, as they sipped their evening coffee, "do you remember telling me, at least a year ago, I think it was, that you fancied the Baroness Gertrude was a little bit, or so, inclined to fall in love with my friend Odenthal?"

"Yes, husband," replied Lucy, very demurely; "I remember it very particularly well."

"But, as you have never said anything about it since, I presume you have changed your mind."

"I don't very clearly see why that should follow," returned

Lucy, rather gravely.   "But, I believe, I was only in jest when I said it."

"So I remember thinking at the time.   But tell me, Lucy, has no such idea about either of them ever come into your head since ?"

"Why do you ask me ?" was her rejoinder.

"Don't be mysterious, my dear, unless you have pledged your word to be so," returned her husband.

"I have certainly pledged my word to nothing in any degree connected with the subject; and if I have ever thought of it since, it has not been in the way of a jest, Adolphe," was her grave reply.

Her husband remained silent for a minute or two, and then said, "My dear Lucy, if you have ever had any confidential conversation with the Baroness Gertrude respecting her feelings towards Rupert, or his towards her, let me very earnestly beg you to believe that I would not for the world be the means of leading you to betray it."

"I am quite sure you would do no such thing," returned his wife.   "But I, on my side, am in no more danger of committing such treachery, than you are of tempting me to do it; for I never heard Gertrude allude to Rupert at all in any of the many *tête-à-tête* conversations which we have had together . . . so decidedly, indeed, has this been the case, Adolphe, that I own to you I have sometimes thought that she would not trust herself to talk of him."

"God grant it may be so !" cried Adolphe, fervently.

"What can you mean, dear husband ?" exclaimed Lucy, with surprise.   "Would you wish the Broness Gertrude to fall in love with Rupert Odenthal ?"

"I might form such a wish, Lucy, and very rationally, too, in my opinion (provided he returned her love), for I do not believe the whole world can contain any man more worthy of her.   I know him well, Lucy, and I know of no fine quality which he does not possess, nor of any evil one which he does."

"Oh, Adolphe ! what a dreadful misfortune it is that their respective stations should place them so far asunder !" exclaimed Lucy, with very genuine feeling.   "As I have received no confidence," she added, "I shall betray none by telling you, that in my heart I do believe Gertrude loves him."

"And I do believe in mine that he loves her !" returned Adolphe, with great energy; "and if we are both of us right in our conjectures, my dear wife, I know of no deed that I should consider it more righteous to perform than the removing all the doubts, difficulties, and obstacles which impede their becoming man and wife."

Lucy joyfully clapped her hands on hearing these very unexpected words, and bestowed a nod and smile of unmistakable approbation on her husband. But her glee did not last long; for after the meditation of a few minutes, every one of which, as they passed, caused her to look graver and graver, she heaved a very heavy sigh, and exclaimed, in a voice which sounded very like a groan, "Oh, Adolphe! the baron! the baron!"

Adolphe prefaced his reply, by seizing with one hand a piece of crumpled paper on which some idle characters had been scrawled, and then thrown aside, and with the other a volume of Tennyson's poems, which lay upon the table.

"Now, Lucy!" said he, almost solemnly, "look on this paper and on that. Which of these articles do you consider as the best deserving of preservation?"

Lucy looked puzzled for a moment, but her bright eye kindled as he went on. "That worn-out morsel of transmuted rag," said he, pointing to the crumpled paper, "may serve, not unaptly, to represent our right good friend the baron; and this," he added, taking the Tennyson volume in his hand, "as fitly represents our ardent-minded, philosophical Rupert. Now, Lucy, if you were obliged to decide that one of these two objects must of necessity be thrown aside and forgotten, in order to preserve the other in the highest possible preservation, the choice between them being left wholly to you, how should you decide?"

"I doubt not I should say on this occasion, as I should on most others, Adolphe . . . . You must decide for me. And as usual, dear husband, I should do so with very little fear that your fiat would run counter to my wishes."

"You are a darling wife, Lucy; and my friend Rupert shall have a darling wife too, if we can but find out some good way of conquering the difficulties that surround him."

"The only difficulty is the baron, dear Adolphe!" said Lucy, shaking her head in a very desponding style. "Your crumpled bit of paper does not represent him fairly. As far as his being rather useless goes, it might do very well; but you do not understand Gertrude as well as I do, if you fancy that she considers him as of little consequence, because he happens to be of little use. I do not believe that she would run the risk of making him unhappy during the few years of life which may remain to him, if she could ensure her own happiness by doing so to the end of a life as long as his own."

"I daresay you are right, Lucy; I do believe that there is an immense fund of devoted affection, and heroic self-denial, in the heart of every tolerably good woman. But she is not the first, you know, who has felt the inconvenience of a divided duty. If she performs her part as a good daughter, in such a manner as to send Rupert to an early grave, I shall not very easily forgive her," said Adolphe, somewhat sternly.

"Oh! as to that, my dear friend," returned Lucy gaily, "men have died and worms have eaten them . . . . You know the rest."

"I know the rest of your quotation, but you do not know the rest of my prophecy . . . ." And then, discarding all playfulness of manner, Adolphe related to her very exactly what had passed between himself and Doctor Nieper.

She was both pained and surprised at this, and for the first time, began to feel that Adolphe was very gravely in earnest.

Nor was it without reason that he was so. He had made no blunder either in the judgment he had himself passed on the painfully altered appearances of his friend, nor in the interpretation which he had given both to the words and the manner of Doctor Nieper.

But no sooner was the warm-hearted Lucy awakened to the fact that Adolphe really believed the tranquillity, nay, it might be, the life of his friend was endangered by this apparently desperately hopeless attachment, than she at once set herself very seriously to consider whether some way might not be found, ere the mischief had gone too far to be repaired, by which a *dénoue-ment* somewhat less terrible than death might be brought about.

No sooner had she expressed to Adolphe her ardent wish to make some effort, whether likely to be ultimately successful or not, by which a chance at least might be given of such hope for the future as might, in some degree cheer the present, than he eagerly accepted her proffered services.

"I am quite sure," he hopefully exclaimed, "that it is not in the nature of gentle, soft-hearted woman, to be so sternly stubborn in their secrecy, as it is evident my friend Rupert intends to be. He thinks that it is his duty to bury this miserable, hopeless attachment in eternal silence, and if once persuaded that it is his duty to die, and 'make no sign,' he will do it."

"He shall not do it if I can prevent it," exclaimed Lucy, eagerly.

"Dear wife!" said Adolphe, fondly kissing her; "I would give my little finger to ensure to poor pale Rupert a life-long companion as dear to him as you are to me!"

"Then let me have a long talk with Gertrude," said Lucy, very much in earnest, as was evident from her eyes as well as her voice.

"You shall, dearest!" replied her husband. "I have great faith in you, for your heart is in this business, my dear wife. You will make your approaches gently. Lead her to say ten words about Rupert, and I will trust to your sagacity for making out their meaning, assisted by the context you will find in her eyes."

No time was lost in putting this scheme in action, and it was with right good will that *la petite* set about it.

The minds of the two friends could scarcely admit of comparison, they were so widely different both in strength and in tone ; but the qualities of which the heart is considered as the home, had much more of sympathy. Lucy would have felt herself greatly more embarrassed had she been charged with a mission to discover Gertrude's opinion on any of the multitude of abstract points on which human minds seem "agreed to differ," (as if only for the purpose of displaying the endless variety of their fanciful workings) than she was now, that she had undertaken to dive into the depths of a woman's heart, which has been so very often described as unfathomable. But she felt, or fancied, that the way was both short and direct.

She made her first step towards the point she had in view, by saying, "How is our friend Rupert to-day, my dear Gertrude ?"

"Very well, I believe," replied Gertrude, occupying herself as she spoke, in looking for some object which she had, or had not, dropped upon the carpet. "But I have scarcely seen him to-day. I think he has gone to assist Count Adolphe in 'doing nothing,' as you sometimes saucily describe their learned avocations."

"Adolphe is uneasy about his health," said Lucy, gravely ; "and I must say I do not think he is looking well. Does not his mother feel uneasy at seeing him so evidently changed in appearance ?"

"Changed in appearance?" repeated Gertrude, so evidently changed in appearance herself, as she repeated the words, that Lucy felt her doubts, if she had any, as completely solved, as if the most explicit declaration on the point she wished to elucidate, had been uttered by the pale and trembling lips of poor Gertrude. She had, indeed, been taken entirely by surprise. Had it been otherwise, she might perhaps in some degree have avoided so very decided a demonstration of her feelings. For one short moment she struggled to recover herself, but the effort was in vain, and she burst into tears.

The eyes of pretty Lucy were dim, too, as she looked into the face of her friend, and perceived how painfully her burning blushes completed the story which her tears began.

"Why should you turn your eyes away from me, my sweet Gertrude!" she exclaimed. "Love me only half as well as I love you, and you will find comfort and not suffering, from perceiving that I read your heart."

"Spare me! spare me!" sobbed Gertrude.

"Spare you the comfort of knowing that your noble nature is understood by one whose greatest boast (next to possessing her husband's love) is, that she believes herself beloved by you? Fie, Gertrude! Fie! I know that Nature has not endowed me with such talents as she has bestowed on you. But you should not shrink from my true love on that account."

"Shrink from it?" said poor Gertrude, with clasped hands and streaming eyes. "Oh, Lucy! Lucy! could you but read all my heart as correctly as it seems you have read a part of it, you would know, that if my wretched, self-condemning spirit, could, or can, find comfort from anything, it must be from your indulgent affection. That you blame me, that you *must* blame me, for having in my heart of hearts so cruelly rebelled against the well-known and most earnest wishes of my dear, devoted father, is, I well know, as certain as that the light of heaven enables us to see each other! That you should still love me, Lucy, is indeed a balm to my heart, but I feel as if I had no right to apply it."

"And why not, my beautiful baroness?" said Lucy, smiling affectionately at her. "Perhaps you think that you shall be fixing a very heavy responsibility on Adolphe and on me, by opening your heart to us; but you will be exonerated from this now, dearest, by my having taken the initiative, and confessed, that, notwithstanding all your admirable discretion, we have discovered your secret. And how could it have been otherwise, dear Gertrude? The obvious probability of such an attachment, thrown together as you have been for so many years, could scarcely fail to strike friends who know you both so thoroughly well as we do. . . . . How could it have been possible, dearest, that you should not love one another?"

"God forbid that my poor father should ever be so quicksighted! I think it would kill him!" said Gertrude, with a groan.

"Fear nothing on that score," returned Lucy, laughing. "I am quite sure," she added, "that if I were to state the fact to him, he would think I was romancing."

"Yes. You are quite right!" said Gertrude, hiding her face with both hands. "I have so constantly and so carefully deceived him, and he has so frankly and so honourably believed my falsehoods, that it was certainly very nearly impossible that the truth could reach him. But what a picture is this giving of myself?" she added. "How can you fancy that you love me, Lucy?"

"There is no fancy in it, my dear friend," replied Lucy, gravely. "You have had a very difficult destiny to contend with. I can by no means blame your father, however, for having established Rupert Odenthal as a member of his family. I cannot blame him for it, because he felt grateful for an immense service, and hoped to requite it by giving him a happy position in his family. But you must excuse me if I say that his doing so, would have been utterly inexcusable, had not his inveterate prejudice of rank and birth rendered him totally blind to the probable consequences which were likely to ensue. . . . . Likely? . . . . Oh, much more than likely; the consequences, Gertrude, were inevitable. If you do not shut the eyes of your judgment, in order to give your terrified conscience *champ libre* to torment you, it is impossible but you must perceive the truth of this. Why has Adolphe selected Rupert as the chosen friend of his life? Is it not from the same cause which has led you to select him as the chosen friend of yours? Is it not because their frequent intercourse enabled them to know each well, and is not your attachment the consequence of the same process? That process, under the circumstances in which your father placed you, was inevitable, I tell you; and you might as reasonably blame yourself for being wet under a shower-bath, or scorched in the midst of a fire, as for loving such a being as Rupert, while constantly associating with him. It may, according to your notions, be a misfortune, but you will never persuade me that it is a sin."

Poor Gertrude's eyes had been full of tears when Lucy began her harangue, but it was with a very sweet smile that she repaid her eloquence.

"Lucy!" she said, after the silence of a minute or two, "I may perhaps have done Rupert no more than justice; but I have done less to you."

"How so, dear friend?" returned the young Countess, taking her hand, and looking at her very affectionately; "I would not hear your enemy say so," she added, with a loving kiss. "In what have you done me less than justice?"

"I have never given you credit for one half so much eloquence as you have now displayed," replied Gertrude. "But alas! alas!" she added; "how dare I trust my judgment upon such a theme? There is one point, however, upon which I am quite sure you are right. You cannot estimate the worth of Rupert Odenthal more highly than it deserves. My preference of him beyond all others whom I have known, may, therefore, be reasonably defended, and conscientiously excused. But I doubt if this can in any degree absolve me from the duty I owe to my dear father. I think, Lucy, that if I were to marry Rupert Odenthal, I should break my father's heart. I think it would kill him, Lucy;" and as she said this, tears again started to the eyes of Gertrude.

Lucy did not immediately answer her. It was, indeed, not easy to do it, if she expressed her opinion honestly, without doing more harm than good to the cause which she wished to advocate; for she really thought it by no means improbable that if the experiment were tried, the result might prove Gertrude to be right; the Countess Adolphe really thought it very possible that such an event might endanger the life of the baron.

In short, she fixed her eyes upon the carpet, and looked very grave; and as a further proof that her admired eloquence had failed her, she got up to take her leave.

Gertrude rose too, and held out her hand. Lucy received it, and for a moment held it silently between her own, and then said, "I must leave you now, my dearest Gertrude, because I feel that my remaining with you must do you more harm than good. It is your own heart must be your counsellor, and it is a difficult case upon which that dear aching heart has to plead . . . for it is retained on both sides of the question. But I will not leave you without one other word; more, however, in the shape of commentary than of counsel. I think you are right in believing that the effect of hearing that you were attached to Rupert, might be very seriously injurious to the health of your father; but neither will I conceal from you, that the health of Rupert gives us great uneasiness. Dr. Nieper has seen him accidentally, at our house, and thinks him far from well. Your

position, Gertrude, is a very difficult one, but we shall do each
other no good by talking of it.   I confess I see but one means of
escaping from it . . . and that will not, most assuredly, be aided
by discussing the subject with anyone.   The only safety must be
found in exactly a contrary course.   Consult your own heart as
well as your own conscience, Gertrude, and if both the lives
which seem to hang on your decision can be cared for, as they
ought to be, it must be achieved by the *secret* decision of your
own heart, and your own judgment.   You need no confidential
advisers, Gertrude, and it is far better that you should have
none."

Lucy waited for no reply, but kissed the pale cheek of her
friend, and left her.

<center>~~~~~~~~~~~~~~~~</center>

CHAPTER XLIX.

Lucy had not set off on her charitable visit to Schloss Schwanberg, without giving her husband a hint that she intended to find
out, if possible, the terms upon which his friend, and her friend,
stood together; and he watched for her return with some impatience.   But she brought him considerably less intelligence
than he had hoped to receive.

On one point, however, and that certainly, a very important
one, she made a report which he was glad to receive, although it
went no further than to confirm the opinion he had already
formed on the subject.

"Yes, Adolphe!" was her prompt reply to the first question
he asked her.   "Yes! We make no mistake about *that*.   Let
Rupert love Gertrude as devotedly as heart can love, I feel perfectly certain that she requites him."

"Has she told him so?" demanded Adolphe, eagerly.

"I did not ask her," replied Lucy, with rather a quizzing
smile.   "First," she continued, "because I did not think it was
a discreet question to ask; and secondly, because I did not feel
it to be necessary."

"You mean that you discovered the fact, without putting her
to the embarrassment of confessing it," returned her husband.
"Then you were quite right to spare the question," he added;

"but would it not have been more honest, if you had given the second reason as number one?"

"And so put my discretion in the background?" she rejoined. "When I have told you more, Sir husband, I think it very probable that you may accuse me of displaying rather too much, than too little discretion. All the intelligence I have to give you is, that I think I left Gertrude more easy at heart than I found her. For the rest, I do most earnestly, most humbly advise the most cautious avoidance, on our parts, of everything in the least degree approaching interference."

Adolphe looked at her with such an expression of comic surprise, that she laughed.

"Thank Heaven!" he exclaimed. "It is, I assure you, Lucy, an immense comfort to see that your power of laughing has survived this mysterious visit. The profound gravity with which you uttered your humble advice rather frightened me. But now that the frigid solemnity of your aspect has begun to thaw a little, I hope we shall be able to understand each other. Alas! poor Gertrude!" he added, after the pause of a moment; "I suppose she has been imploring you not to repeat one single word of what she has said to you. God bless her, poor girl! She need not be afraid of me. I would help her if I could, though I do not know very well how to set about it; but, at any rate, she need not fear that I should betray her."

"Nor does she, Adolphe!" said Lucy, eagerly. "You have completely misunderstood me. The caution I enjoined was not dictated by her judgment, but by mine."

"And what indiscretion do you fear on my part, Lucy? Do you fancy, dearest, that I am likely to proclaim aloud to all who may be willing to listen, that I suspect the Baroness Gertrude von Schwanberg of being enamoured of her noble father's librarian?"

"Nonsense, Adolphe! You know I have no such fancy," replied his wife, endeavouring to look more light-hearted than she felt. "All I meant was, that I think the misery of Gertrude would become incalculably greater than it is, if we either of us were to utter a word which, by being repeated to her father, might awaken his suspicion. Your affection for Rupert might (perhaps) lead you to speak of him to the baron as a man who would not disgrace any alliance. And that might prove quite enough to awaken a suspicion."

"Fear nothing of the kind, Lucy," replied her husband. "I know the baron much too well to commit any such imprudence;

so be easy on that head, you dear, cautious, little soul! And
tell poor Gertrude to be easy about it, also. It would be barbarous to let any unnecessary doubts and fears be added to her
embarrassments. God knows there are few objects to which I
would so readily devote myself as the bringing these two dear
creatures together, as man and wife. Do make her understand
this, Lucy, will you?"

Lucy remained silent for a moment, and then she very demurely replied, "No, Adolphe. You must excuse me if I decline
saying anything whatever on the subject to Gertrude. Nothing
that I could say would add to the firm conviction which she has
already of our true affection for her; and I am quite determined
not to allude to the subject of her attachment in any way."

Adolphe looked at her stedfastly, and then performed one of
those elongated, and very impertinent whistles, which indicate
both disapproval and contempt.

"Then I presume, dearly beloved wife," he said, as soon as
he thought proper to bring his very long whistle to a conclusion;
"then I must presume that your confidential *tête-à-tête* together
was so managed as to lead, if not to an absolute quarrel, at least,
to a pretty decided estrangement."

"Then you will presume to make a great blunder, my dearly-
beloved husband," replied Lucy; "and if you were to out-whistle
all the railroads in Europe, and America to boot, you would not
persuade me to doubt for a moment the propriety of the resolution
I have taken. So far from there being any estrangement between
us, I do assure you, Adolphe, that we never parted more affectionately, nor with a more earnest wish to meet again, than we
did to-day. Nevertheless, I am quite resolved that for the future
I will most scrupulously avoid any allusion whatever to the
attachment which you and I have agreed in thinking existed
between her and your friend, Rupert Odenthal."

"And pray, Mrs. Mystery, have you any objection to telling
me whether it is your present opinion that we have been mistaken
on this point?" said Adolphe.

"No, husband. I cannot say that anything which has passed
between Gertrude and myself this morning has led to that conclusion," she replied. "But the subject is one," she added,
"that ought not to be discussed between us. I have too much
respect for her, and I might say too much reverence for her rectitude, and her judgment, to wish to influence her. She must
judge entirely for herself, Adolphe; and I have a very firm persuasion that she will finally decide upon doing what is wisest

and best both for herself and Rupert. I should be vastly delighted to congratulate them on their marriage . . . . but till the proper time for this arrives, she shall never hear the subject alluded to by me."

" Well, my dear, I daresay you are right, though I do not quite comprehend your tactics," replied Adolphe, with his usual good-humoured gaiety of tone. " But at any rate," he added more gravely, "nothing can have passed between you and Gertrude, which should prevent poor dear Rupert from having the comfort and consolation of opening his heart freely to me on the subject. That we are right in our conjectures respecting the important fact of Gertrude's attachment to him, you do not, with all your caution and mystery, deny. This, of itself, is quite sufficient to justify my talking with him freely on the subject."

Lucy was in general a ready, as well as a rapid speaker, and by no means in the habit of leaving anyone who addressed her, to wait long for a reply. But now she sat silent, with her eyes riveted upon her husband, and a considerable augmentation of colour on her fair cheeks.

Adolphe fixed his eyes upon her in return, for a minute or two, with a puzzled look ; but, as she said nothing, he rose from his chair with a great bound, exclaiming, " Well ! At least I shall have the satisfaction now, of talking to Rupert on the subject without any fear of deluding him into false hopes. I daresay he will call before the day is over. *Au revoir ! chère amie.*"

And having said these words, he quietly turned himself towards the door.

He did not reach it, however, before the hand of Lucy had seized upon his arm. " My dear, dear Adolphe ! " she exclaimed, looking very coaxingly in his face. " If you were not the best-tempered man in the world, as well as the most exemplary of husbands, I could not dare to make the petition I am about to do. . . . For I really feel that my interfering between you and your dearest friend, must appear to be an act of most detestable presumption. And yet, Adolphe, that is exactly what I am going to do. I am going to beg and entreat you, to say nothing whatever to Rupert on the subject of his attachment to Gertrude."

" You are coming out in a perfectly new character, Lucy," replied her husband, looking considerably more grave than was usual with him.

" Because I venture to give you advice, Adolphe ? " she replied, dropping the arm she had seized upon, and looking still more solemn than he did himself.

"No!" he returned quickly, and throwing his arm round her. "I do not mean *that*, Lucy, I should like to have your advice now, and always. But what puzzles me is your air of mystery. It is so unlike you."

"And in what does this mystery consist?" she replied. "I will tell you, Adolphe. It consists solely in my having nothing to tell you! Confess the truth!" she added, laughing; "you fancied that after a *tête-à-tête* with Gertrude, I must come home full of matter, and be able to tell you exactly on what terms these lovers stood together. *Lovers* I do certainly believe they are, but beyond that I know nothing; nor will I ever hint a wish to Gertrude, that she should confide to me anything that she may wish to conceal. So upon this point, dearest, you will always find me quite as mysterious as I am at present. For my own part, I am thankful that it is so! There is no way of keeping a secret so effectual, as carefully avoiding the knowledge of it."

"That is a truth, my dear, that I shall not venture to deny," he replied, in his usual cheerful tone. "But the thing that puzzles me, Lucy, is not that you should be silent (though there is certainly something out of the common way in it), but that you should insist upon my being so likewise. I really think that the kindest thing I could do for my friend Rupert, would be the leading him to open his heart to me."

Lucy shook her head. "It might, perhaps, seem to be the kindest," she replied, "but I am quite persuaded that it would not be the wisest. But as you have certainly the right to think yourself a better judge of this question than I can be, I will only ask you to indulge me in this whim, this notion of mine, for a very short time."

"And for how many days is this short time to last, Lucy?" he replied. "How long must I see this man, whom I love as if he were my brother, how long must I see him looking as miserable as he does now, and growing thinner and more hectic-looking every day, without giving him the consolation of knowing that I see no presumption in his love, and that I fully believe it is returned? For what length of time, Lucy, do you mean to insist upon my withholding this consolation from him?"

"Insist!" repeated Lucy, again shaking her head. "That is not a pretty word, Adolphe! However, you are, upon the whole, very condescending, if not perfectly gracious, and I will be moderate and reasonable in my demands. Moreover, the delay I will ask from you shall be only conditional. All I ask is, that, just for the present, Rupert should be received here with the same cheerful welcome as heretofore ; that no allusion should be made to his altered spirits, or his altered looks. Let this mode of treatment go on for a week or two, Adolphe ! That is not very long, you know ! If you will agree to this, on your part, I will agree on mine to withdraw all restriction on your confidential intercourse, provided that you do not perceive him to be improving in health and spirits. And in that case, perhaps, it may not be very long before he opens his heart to you."

" And in that case, Lucy, I shall be perfectly well contented, whether he opens his heart to me concerning this suspected love affair, or not. In the mean time, dear little wife, I readily subscribe to your conditions. Moreover, I will be honest enough to confess, that I think there is some wisdom in your counsel. If our surmises respecting their attachment be correct, we must confess, despite all our earnest wishes for its success, that it is a very thorny and difficult affair, and that, in good truth, our wishes and good-will cannot do much towards helping them."

Lucy put her loving arms round his neck, very unceremoniously pulled down his lofty head, and impressed a kiss upon his forehead.

" If Gertrude does marry Rupert," she said in a whisper, as if she were afraid the winds might hear it, " if she does, she will not have one quarter so charming a husband as I have."

CHAPTER L.

Either from accident, or design, on the part of Gertrude, or on that of Lucy, or both, no long *tête-à-tête* meetings took place between them for some time ; but, nevertheless, their intercourse was as frequent and as affectionate as ever.

They often dined together, sometimes at the home of the one, and sometimes at that of the other; but it so happened, that Madame Odenthal was always of the party.

As to the young men, their intimacy was in no degree less than heretofore ; but, nevertheless, there seemed to be something fitful and capricious in the manner of it.

It would, in truth, have been difficult for either of them, when within reach of the other, not to profit by the vicinity; for not only were they attached by the memory and the habits of many years of youthful friendship, but they had neither of them, as yet, ever met with any other man equally well qualified to satisfy both heart and intellect, as companion and friend.

Neither hard reading nor deep thinking is greatly in fashion among noble Austrians; and such a young man as Adolphe Steinfeld, would probably have felt himself more at a loss to find a companion to suit him in the brilliant and crowded salons of Vienna, than in the remote seclusion of his father's castle, for he found Rupert Odenthal within reach of him there. ·

Improvements of all sorts are going on so rapidly in this busy little globe of ours, that we may reasonably hope to see these elegant salons, at no very distant date, becoming a little more intellectual, without becoming less graceful. A sprinkling of Lansdownes, Carlisles, and Lord Johns, would speedily cure the species of inanity which, if report says true, still lingers in the perfumed drawing-rooms of this imperial metropolis; but, as yet, a man, like Adolphe Steinfeld, who has passed his happiest hours in reading, thinking, and discussing with a kindred spirit, themes capable of transporting him, not only beyond the silken walls of a drawing-room, but a little, too, beyond the boundaries of this fair globe, called earth, is apt to prefer the forest to the Prater. And such, in fact, was very decidedly the case with Count Adolphe von Steinfeld.

Perhaps it was because he had of late found his friend Rupert less prone than formerly to kindle with him into animation, at coming in contact with new trains of thought, that Adolphe just at this time conceived the project of writing a book; and it was thus he announced the project to his friend.

"Rupert!" said he, as that languid individual "dragged his long length" into the snug little parlour which Adolphe especially called his own—"Rupert! my dear fellow! I am very especially glad to see you at this moment, for I have just decided a question which has for some time been working in my brain . . . . 'To write, or not to write, that is the question.' And I have, within the last ten minutes, made up my mind in the affirmative. Rupert! I am going to write a book."

"I am very glad to hear it," replied Rupert, with a languid smile. "And what is the subject?"

"The title is to be 'East and West; or, Meditations on the Days that are Gone, and the Days that are to Come.'"

"A very pregnant theme," replied Rupert, gravely. "How do you mean to treat it?"

"The answer must be rather long, and very pedantic," rejoined Adolphe. "It must be treated traditionally, historically, critically, and prophetically."

Rupert looked at him earnestly, and something like a gleam of awakened interest seemed to flash across his countenance for a moment. "Comprehensive, beyond all question," he returned, with a smile, somewhat less languid. "What subject is there, relative either to Earth or Heaven, which may not fairly find its place under such a title?"

"True, Rupert! Perfectly true! And why should we not write it together? I should never have conceived such an idea, had not the Schwanberg library been within reach. The good old baron will trust me with his volumes more freely than I should trust him with the inferences I may chance to draw from them. The prophetic pages, Rupert, might make him wince a little."

"No!" replied the librarian, the transient gleam fading from his countenance, and a look of the deepest dejection taking its place. "If he believed in your prophecies at all, Adolphe, he would place their fulfilment at too distant a date for the chance of it to give him any annoyance."

The look and the words together made a nearer approach to the forbidden theme than anything which had passed between them before; and Adolphe thought that it would not be very difficult, by pushing this allusion to the baron's feelings a little further, to make poor Rupert lay before him the most sacred secret of his heart.

But Lucy had so earnestly begged him *not* to do this, and, in fact, he had so explicitly promised her not to do it, that he very honourably resisted the temptation, and suffered the conversation to settle itself on the books which he should first wish to borrow.

Count Adolphe was quite in earnest when he announced this intention of writing a book; and being in earnest, he was by no means likely to set about the undertaking negligently.

It might be very truly said, in the most important sense of the phrase, that Rupert had taught Adolphe to read; and the result of this teaching was every year becoming more and more apparent, more and more decided.

Count Adolphe was by nature a man of clear, vigorous, and healthy intellect; but had he passed the last ten winters of his young life in the salons and boudoirs of Vienna, he would not now have been contemplating a work stretching from east to west, and embracing such bold meditations on the days that are gone, on those days which are yet to come.

As it was, however, he was by no means unfitted for the task. It may occasionally happen, that meditations fairly deserving the epithet of deep thinking, may arise spontaneously in a healthful and active brain, even when unaided; but such meditations are marvellously nourished and strengthened by the constant companionship of thoughtful books and thinking men; and Adolphe was in a great degree what the Schwanberg library and his friend Rupert had made him.

And Rupert still proved himself the same ready helper now, and the same earnest and helpful friend; but he was no longer the same sympathising fellow-student; and though all the *matériel* for this great work was collected and arranged under his direction, and by his assistance, poor Adolphe very soon became aware, that though his learning, and even his reasoning powers, were present, yet that the spirit was absent.

This discovery put a very speedy stop to the literary labours of the young Count. The original idea of such an undertaking probably owed its birth to the notion that Rupert might be led to take such an interest in it as to conquer the languor which seemed to have taken possession of his mind, as well as of his body. But it took a very short time to convince the ambitious young author that if he laboured at all, he must labour alone; and, worse still, that if he submitted a deeply meditated page of the most original thinking to his friend, he would have forgotten the beginning, before he reached the conclusion of it.

Adolphe's literary enthusiasm was by no means ardent enough to resist such a check as this; and the enterprise was quietly abandoned without a word being spoken to explain, or even to announce this change of purpose. But the employment which had been furnished by preparing notes and references for this mighty undertaking, had sufficed, while it lasted, to keep Count Adolphe's mind so constantly occupied, as to render it a very easy matter for him to keep his promise to Lucy; for not only had it prevented his dwelling upon the much-changed aspect of his friend, but it so far occupied Rupert himself, as very naturally to suggest the idea that his condition was improving, and that whatever might be his malady, whether of mind or body, he was better.

But scarcely had the ambitious young author resigned himself to his disappointment, and recommenced his former habits of reading, instead of writing, than it really seemed as if this change had wrought a sudden and most complete cure in the health of his friend. If he had been better before, he was well now; and so sudden and so striking was the improvement, that he positively began to think that he must himself have been in some degree the cause of the heavy oppression of spirits under which his sensitive friend had been suffering.

"Lucy! I do believe I have found out the real source of Rupert's malady, and what is infinitely more important, I think he is cured!"

"I am very glad of it," replied Lucy, with a heightened colour, and a happy smile.

"Nay, my dear, I don't see why *you* need blush about it," returned Adolphe; "though perhaps, when I have told you all, you may be of opinion that *I* have cause to blush, though you have none. I have made no secret to you of the book-writing vision which has passed over me, but you do not know the whole history of it. To the best of my recollection, this nervous malady (for such it certainly was) began to show itself immediately after my father left home, and it was very soon after this, if you remember, that Rupert first began to droop, and show evident symptoms; first, of declining spirits, and then of declining health. You may remember this, but you cannot remember, because I took care that you should know nothing about it, that just at the very same time I was brooding by day, and dreaming by night, of my ridiculous project of writing a book. Did I ever talk to you about it in my sleep, Lucy?"

"Certainly not," she replied; "or if you did, my dear," she added, "it must have been in a very gentle voice, for it never waked me."

"I am thankful to hear it," resumed Adolphe, very solemnly; "for had it been otherwise, I might have brought a nervous fever upon you, as well as upon poor Rupert."

"But how is it possible, Adolphe, that your notion of writing a book could have given Rupert a nervous fever?" she replied. "It might have produced that effect upon yourself; but I really doubt if his sympathy could have gone to such an extent as to cause him a nervous fever."

"That is only because you don't know to what an excess I tormented him, poor fellow!" replied her husband. "The proof that I am right, Lucy, may be found in the fact, that when I ceased to expatiate on my grand theories, and set him to work on the matter-of-fact process of looking out books for me, and marking any particular passages which he thought might be useful, he almost immediately began to look better."

"Really!" said Lucy, gravely. "That is very remarkable."

"Decidedly, it is very remarkable," rejoined her husband; "and so remarkable, that it seems strange you should not have observed it. Did you not observe that the last time we dined at Schwanberg he was vastly more cheerful and conversable than we have lately seen him?"

"Yes, I did perceive it," returned Lucy; "and if I did not say anything about it, the reason, probably, was, that I thought his improved looks, and greater cheerfulness, might be only accidental. It might have been produced, you know, merely by the circumstance of our dining there."

"It was more likely to have been produced by the circumstance of my having ceased to plague him about my confounded book," said Adolphe. "But, my dear child, the improvement you remarked *then*, is not worth mentioning in comparison to what you may see now. And I can explain the reason of that, too; though the doing so, gives a painful pinch to my vanity. But the real truth is, Lucy, that I announced to him in good set terms, a few days ago, that I had abandoned my writing scheme altogether; and I give you my word of honour, that I have never seen a melancholy expression upon his features since."

"Well, Adolphe!" replied his wife, with every appearance of being perfectly satisfied, "I am sure you will easily forgive and forget the pinch to your vanity, and only remember the comfort of seeing poor, dear Rupert look like himself again."

CHAPTER LI.

The return of the widower Count von Steinfeld to his paternal mansion was still delayed; and as a beautiful autumn was beginning to fade into something very like gloomy winter, both Count Adolphe and his young wife began to think that the wide old house, with its multitude of useless rooms and long galleries, would be but a melancholy winter residence; and the more so, as Lucy was not in very strong health, and quite unable to enjoy the riding and walking, which constitute so large a proportion of country amusement. The old Count was at Vienna, and as he had more than once expressed a very earnest wish that they should join him there, Adolphe began to think that it would be both dutiful and agreeable to comply with his request.

Upon the arrival of a letter in which this proposal was very strongly urged, and backed with the assurance, that he had just seen excellent apartments, amply sufficient to accommodate them, at no great distance from his own ; the last shadow of reluctance at the idea of leaving the home he loved, seemed to vanish from the mind of Adolphe, and he said, "Lucy, I should like to go, and I should like to show you Vienna. Do you think you are well enough to undertake such a journey ?"

"Adolphe !" she replied, "if you really wish to go, how comes it that you have never told me so before ? I quite agree with you in thinking that this grand old mansion will be much less agreeable in the winter than the summer. And as to the journey, I think it will do me a great deal of good. All the country is new to me, and I don't want to travel through it full galop. Why did you not tell me before, Adolphe, that you wished to go ?"

"Because I knew that in that case you would have said yea, however much you might have preferred saying nay. It is only since the arrival of this last letter, that I began to think that you would really like it too."

"You are an accurate observer, my dear Adolphe. It is only since the arrival of this last letter, that I have *really* wished to go. You will not, I presume, be much surprised when I tell you that I have a very great affection for the Baroness Gertrude ; and my affection for her will prove a great deal more constant than yours did ; for I am quite sure that I shall never be cured of it, not even if the old baron, as in your case, were to quote the 'Almanack de Gotha' to me, in proof that I had no right to love her at all. In short, Adolphe, she is my only real sister, and if she were my twin, I do not think I could love her better. But you look as if you did not comprehend why this sisterly affection should influence my wishes respecting the going to Vienna, or remaining here."

"Then my looks are very honest looks, Lucy," he replied, "and they speak the exact truth. I do *not* see what this very natural and praiseworthy affection has to do with our complying with my father's request."

Lucy looked at him earnestly for a moment, to ascertain whether his total ignorance of her wishes were real, or feigned ;

but she speedily became convinced that there was no feigning in the matter, and that if she wished to be understood, she must explain herself distinctly.

"The truth is, Adolphe," she said at length, "that there is nothing in the world I should like so much as taking her with us."

"Take the Baroness Gertrude to Vienna, and leave the baron without her?" exclaimed Adolphe, in unfeigned astonishment. "My dearest Lucy! I should be delighted to let you have your wish gratified, if I believed it possible; but I feel about equally certain, that neither the father nor daughter would consent to the separation. I should have thought that you must have known as well as I do, that the baron was never separated from her for twenty-four hours together."

"Yes. I know," replied Lucy, colouring; "I know perfectly well that they are devoted to each other. But, perhaps, you will not think me so unreasonable, when I tell you that Gertrude is in great want of the services of a really skilful dentist; and Vienna, you know, is famous in this respect. Madame Odenthal says, that her only chance of saving one of her beautiful front teeth, which has a very threatening spot upon it, is by going to Vienna, and having it properly attended to."

"Well, dear wife, I leave the whole affair entirely to you," returned Adolphe; "I am sure I need not tell either you or Gertrude, that I should be delighted to have such an addition to our party. But when did you first form the wish of taking her with you, Lucy? Has this defect in her splendid teeth only been discovered now?"

"You mean to allude to my indifference about going to Vienna at all?" returned Lucy. "But I can easily explain that, Adolphe. From your father's first letter on the subject of our joining him, I thought he was inviting us to take up our abode in the same house with him, and I could not think of taking the liberty of proposing an additional guest. But this last letter says, you know, that he has seen apartments that will suit us; and as this, of course, indicates a distinct residence, I can have the great delight of my friend's society, without producing any inconvenience to him."

"That is quite true, Lucy. And as houses are often said to be elastic in accordance to the wishes and will of the mistress, I have no doubt that you will find means to accommodate our fair friend, although my father's letter only states that these apartments will suffice for us."

"Where there is a will, there is a way," replied Lucy, gaily. "I have no doubt that we shall make ourselves exceedingly comfortable."

"And pray, my dear, do you mean to undertake the task of proposing this startling scheme to the baron?" he added.

"Yes, Adolphe!" she very boldly answered. "I do not mean to insinuate that he is as much in love with me as he was with my sister Arabella," she continued; "but nevertheless, I think I have influence enough to obtain his consent to it."

"I should not be at all surprised if he were to propose to go too," rejoined her husband, with a very comic expression of dismay on his countenance.

"Set your heart at ease on that point," replied Lucy, laughing heartily; "if he were to hint at such a proposal, I would tell him candidly that you were of too jealous a disposition to make such a scheme desirable."

"And Rupert? what will reconcile poor Rupert to such a barbarous proposal?" said Adolphe, very gravely. "You are one of the kindest-hearted little angels in the world," he added; "but surely you are very thoughtless!"

"Remember our resolution, Adolphe," returned his wife. "Remember that we agreed not to interfere in any way between them in reference to their supposed attachment. If the invitation I wish to give Gertrude is, for any reason, such as it would be painful to her to accept, be very sure that she has *savoir faire* enough to decline it, without betraying to me any secrets which she may wish to conceal."

"Set off, then, and make the proposal," said Adolphe, seizing the bell-rope. "I am going to order the carriage for you at once, Lucy. You are such an impetuous, self-willed little creature, that it is lost labour to talk common sense to you. But I confess I shall feel considerable curiosity to learn the success of your enterprise. Shall we have a bet, Lucy? I will bet you five to one that the baroness declines your invitation. Will you take it?"

"Yes!" she replied, promptly, but immediately added, with a considerable augmentation of colour, "no, I will not make any bet upon the subject. If Gertrude refuses to go with us, the disappointment will be quite mortification enough for me, without my losing a bet."

No further time was lost in discussion. Horses, carriage, bonnet, and cloak were all promptly supplied, and the young Countess set off on her expedition.

The reader is already too well aware of the sincere affection which subsisted between the Baroness Gertrude and the Countess Adolphe, for it to be at all necessary that I should describe at any great length the scene which passed between them upon this occasion. It was very soon evident to the kind-hearted Lucy that her friend was very well disposed to accept her invitation; but they neither of them forgot that whatever readiness there might be on the part of Gertrude, she was not sufficiently a free agent to give a definitive answer before she had consulted her father.

"Go to him, then, immediately!" said the eager Lucy, "and let me know his reply before I return home."

Gertrude shook her head. She had been too long accustomed to the slow and ponderous movements of her father's mind, to wish that her friend should remain waiting for the result.

"But Adolphe will be so much disappointed if I return to him before the question is settled!" exclaimed Lucy. "Let me wait," she added, coaxingly. "Here are books enough, without going beyond your sofa, Gertrude, to amuse me much longer than it is possible your father can detain you, while he is weighing the comparative advantages of saying yes or no."

But the Baroness Gertrude probably knew considerably better than her friend, the length of time which it was not only possible, but probable, her father might take before delivering his answer, or, at any rate, before there was the least chance of his having said all that he might wish to say on the subject. After fondly and very gratefully embracing her, therefore, she saw her drive from the door, before she turned her anxious and not unembarrassed steps to the apartment where her father was sitting.

Father Alaric and the backgammon-board were both ready for use before him, but both were immediately dismissed as soon as Gertrude made her appearance, the baron condescendingly bending his head to his anointed friend, as he hinted to him that if he wished for an interval of holy meditation in the chapel of the castle, he could not find a better opportunity for it; adding, "I will let you know, my good father, by the entrance of one of my people into the chapel, as soon as I find myself again at leisure to receive you."

CHAPTER LII.

"I AM going to ask a very great favour of you, my dear father," said Gertrude, bending over him, "but I feel quite sure you would grant it, if you could understand how much I wish for it."

"Then I am sure I shall not refuse it, my dear," said the old gentleman, kissing her. "Sit down in your own place here, close to me, and tell me what it is."

"You are always so kind to me, my dearest father," resumed Gertrude, "that I do not much fear you will refuse me, but yet I think that it is possible you may feel surprised at my request, for it is one quite unlike any which I ever made you before. I want you, dear father, to consent to my going for a few weeks, or it may be for a month or two, to Vienna, with the Count and Countess Adolphe. She is very anxious that I should go with her, and I must confess that I do feel a very great wish to go."

"And it is very natural that you should wish to see such a metropolis as Vienna, my dear child," replied the baron, who, to say the truth, was so constantly in the habit of admiring and approving every word his daughter uttered, that he would have experienced great difficulty in finding any fitting phrase which could have expressed a different feeling.

"I told our friend, Lucy, that I knew you were too kind to refuse me," returned Gertrude, affectionately kissing his forehead.

"To be sure," said the old man, pondering, "it will seem rather strange to me at first, Gertrude. But as you will be staying with the Count and Countess von Steinfeld, you will not require such a suite as was necessary when we made our excursion to Paris. You will not think it necessary to be attended by my secretary?"

Poor Gertrude coloured violently; but it mattered not, for the eyes of the meditative baron were fixed upon the carpet while deciding in his own mind the equally important question as to the possibility of her also dispensing with the services of Madame Odenthal. But all his anxiety upon this really very important question was speedily removed by Gertrude's laughing gaily, as she replied, "No, no! dear papa! I must have no suite of my own, you know, if you trust me to the protection of our dear Countess."

"Then you do not wish to take Madame Odenthal with you, my dear?" said the baron, with very unwonted eagerness of manner.

"It would be quite impossible to think of it," replied his daughter, very gravely, and in a tone which plainly indicated that such a proposal would be a breach of etiquette. "If we decide, my dear father, that the Countess von Steinfeld is a proper chaperone for me, my taking any one else in the same capacity would not only be unnecessary, but uncivil."

"I daresay you are right, my dear. Ladies understand things of this nature very much better than gentlemen. Then you do not propose, my dear," he continued, "to take any of my people with you, excepting your own maid?"

"Nay, papa, I do not even propose to take *her*. I shall be waited upon entirely by that excellent person whom the Countess calls 'Nurse Norris.' I have taken a great affection for her. And besides, I do not think that there will be any room for Teresa."

"As to all that sort of thing, my dear child," returned the baron, "I shall by no means interfere, for I consider you to be a much better judge of such questions than it is possible for me to be. But there is another point, my beloved child, upon which I feel that it is my especial duty to speak. Though I am quite aware," he continued, with great dignity, "though I am perfectly aware that persons of my rank are, generally speaking, much longer lived than the great majority of ordinary individuals, yet I am, nevertheless, not insensible to the fact, that I myself, in common, however, with emperors and kings, am growing old.

" *Old* is, indeed, a word," he resumed, after allowing himself a short pause for reflection; " *old* is a word which ought properly to be only applied to persons of inferior station; at least, it does not recur to my memory, that I have ever heard such a phrase as 'great old man,' whereas 'poor old man' is perpetually repeated. But, nevertheless, though I am, I trust, in no way ungrateful to Providence for the many special blessings graciously bestowed on myself, and to the class whereunto I belong, it would partake of the nature of falsehood, were I to deny that I am conscious of increasing age. It is this consciousness, my beloved Gertrude, which causes me so cordially to approve the plan you now propose. I am perfectly aware that your position in life is such as to render the great retirement of my ancestral castle objectionable, if not varied by occasional absence, but I am fully aware also, my dear child, that I owe it to myself, and to my exalted station in life, not to expose my health to any unnecessary risk; and for that reason I am extremely well pleased that you should take advantage of the opportunity now offered you, of seeing Vienna, and all the splendour of the court and capital, without my risking my health to obtain it for you."

Long as this speech was, Gertrude listened to every syllable of it with pleasure, and a pleasure, too, that was quite unexpected. She knew her father's unbounded indulgence too well, to expect any very vehement opposition to her wishes; but his declaring himself so cordially pleased by the scheme, was certainly beyond her hopes.

Having again embraced, and thanked him cordially for his ready acquiescence in her plan, she was about to leave him; but he stopped her, by saying, "You must not go yet, my dearest Gertrude; I have more to say to you, and that too, on a subject most important. You will, doubtless, easily guess my dear child, that I allude to the probability of your being addressed, it may be by many persons, with proposals of marriage. We must, doubtless, both of us, be aware that this subject has been made painful to us by the disgraceful conduct of an individual whose name has never, I believe, passed our lips since we turned away from the city which he disgraced by his residence; and I only allude to him now, in order to account for the wish which I am about to express to you, and that is, that you would make me a solemn promise not to receive, or listen to proposals of marriage from anyone, however high his rank, or however large his revenue, without first referring him to me. Will you consent to give me this promise, my dearest Gertrude?"

It was not till after a momentary silence, that this appeal was answered. The eyes of Gertrude, which had before been affectionately fixed on the face of the baron, now sought the ground, and her colour was again very perceptibly heightened.

"Do you fear to give me this promise, my dear child?" said the old gentleman, looking at her with great surprise.

"No, father! no!" said she, as if suddenly recovering from a fit of absent musing. "I have no such fear! and I do promise you, and very solemnly too, that I will not listen to any proposal of marriage from anyone, however high in rank, or however rich in fortune."

"But do not mistake me, my dear child," returned the fond

father, drawing her tenderly towards him; "you must not suppose, Gertrude, that I am so unreasonable as to wish that you should always remain single; but whenever the important event of your marriage *does* take place, it must not only be with my consent, but with a very perfect assurance on my part that the individual is worthy, in all respects, of the honour and happiness to which he aspires."

"I have given the promise, dear father, and I consider it as a very solemn one, that I will listen to no proposal of marriage."

"Unless backed by my consent, my dear Gertrude, that is the condition upon which I ask for your promise; and depend upon it, my consent will be only given upon a full knowledge that the birth, fortune, and character of the individual are such as to justify his addressing my daughter."

A silent kiss was the only answer given to this important assurance; and then she said, "I must leave you now, my dear, kind father, because I have promised my friend Lucy not to keep her in supense, but to dispatch a messenger to her as soon as I had received your answer."

"Quite right, my dear, quite right; I do not wonder that she should be anxious for my decision. It will be no trifling addition to the consequence of the young Countess von Steinfeld, that she should be accompanied to court by the daughter and heiress of Baron von Schwanberg. But I wish that your note should convey to her the assurance, that I know no other chaperone to whom I would so willingly trust you."

This message was worth another kiss, and it was paid; but Gersrude had still to be detained a few minutes, while the baron inquired whether Madame Odenthal had been made acquainted with this intended excursion?

"Oh, no, papa!" replied Gertrude, with great sincerity; "I had no wish to name it to her, till I had your permission to consider myself as one of the party."

"You were quite right, my dear, as, in fact, you always are, Gertrude; a pre-eminence, under the blessing of heaven, we owe to your so decidedly inheriting these qualities of my character which are to be considered as the special mark of the race from which I have sprung. Few daughters, especially while still so young, have ever accorded so perfectly in opinion with a father, as you do with me. That this is the effect of the immediate intervention of Providence, it would be a sin to doubt; and it is one of those especial manifestations of the Virgin's favour, for which I have instructed Father Alaric to return especial thanks.

Now, then, leave me, my noble Gertrude, and let Madame Odenthal be made to understand that I wish for, and expect, her immediate presence here."

Had not Gertrude known her father as thoroughly as in truth she did, it is probable that she might have been tempted to relieve her over-full heart, by communicating to her ever-loved Madame Odenthal the expedition which she had in view; but this would have been defrauding the baron of his promised share in the business. The contrast between his vast conceptions of his own magnificence, and the miniature nature of the nutriment with which he fed it, was often very ludicrous.

The being the first to whom all news was communicated, and all gossip reported, ranked very high among the privileges which he enjoyed ; and the having to announce to Madame Odenthal the news of Gertrude's proposed excursion, made him feel much as a pompous Minister of State might do, if announcing to the cabinet news that was not only important, but of which he was the sole repository.

Gertrude's first care was, as she had truly said it would be, to dispatch a note to her friend Lucy, communicating the very satisfactory result of her petition to her father ; and having done this, and ascertained that Madame Odenthal was still with the baron, she turned her steps towards the library.

CHAPTER LIII.

It is probable that the Baroness Gertrude expected to find Rupert alone in the library, and if so, she was neither disappointed nor surprised. He was seated in his accustomed chair, and at his accustomed table, but in all other respects, he was as unlike the Rupert of former days, as the bright sun rising amidst the radiant splendour of a summer morning, is to the same orb when sinking into the clouds and darkness of a winter night.

As she opened the door, he started, and turned round, and for a moment remained without rising, probably in order to ascertain, beyond the reach of doubt, that no one accompanied, or was immediately about to follow her. But, before she had advanced

23—?

three steps into the room, the metamorphosed Rupert was at her feet.

"You have seen him, my Gertrude? You have told him of your wish?" he said, looking in her face with an aspect as nearly approaching adoration as "any mortal mixture of Earth's mould" could reasonably wish to inspire.

"Yes, dearest Rupert!" she replied. "Leave has been asked, and granted—most kindly granted; and, so far, all is well. But I almost begin to doubt my own courage, Rupert! How can I bear to leave you all? . . . My poor, dear father! He is getting both old and infirm; and how do I know—how do I ever dare to hope, with such sanguine security, that I shall ever see him again? How can I leave him? How can I leave you all?"

As she uttered this, her head drooped dejectedly on her breast, and she burst into tears.

"You should not attempt it, my beloved Gertrude," he replied, "were your friend Lucy less devoted to you, or even if she were less urgent in her entreaties that you should accompany her. Everybody, as she truly says, has been remarking that you do not look well, Gertrude; and change of air and scene, you know, is universally considered as beneficial to the health. Lucy will be a true sister to you, and my friend Adolphe, who does not yet know how much of his 'Almanack de Gotha' adventure he owes to you, will be all kindness! Think of all this, sweet love, and of fifty other reasons besides, if we had but time to rehearse them, and you will become better reconciled to the excursion."

"You are a man, Rupert, and a very wise one; and I (Heaven help me!) am only a woman, and not wise at all. Nevertheless, I will really and truly try to behave as well as I can."

Having said this, as cheerfully as her trembling voice could be made to utter it, she sat herself down on the sofa, and made Rupert place himself beside her.

"My dear father, and your dear mother, Rupert, are holding a conference, which, I daresay, will last a good while, so I think you must prepare to hear a little more of my moaning, because the opportunity is so favourable for it. Just think, dearest friend, of all that I must leave behind! What will become of me when I have no longer the power of seeing you, and hearing you repeat again and again that you have always loved me, even through the long years during which my morning and evening penance was ever and always the repetition of the killing words—'*he loves me not?*' Who knows that I may not fall back into the same mournful monody? Perhaps, Rupert, I may repeat it from the mere force of habit. . . . . And who knows, dearest, but I may die, listening to my own wailing?"

She looked pale, and her eyes were full of tears; and yet there was something almost playful in the manner in which she thus exaggerated the doleful anticipations of the future. But, neither in jest nor earnest, would he permit them; but painted with so much touching energy, and so much tender truth, the improvement of their mutual condition since the blessed accident of Miss Arabella's love-fit had opened the way to mutual confidence, that, before Madame Odenthal re-entered the library, he had brought her to confess that, notwithstanding her moanings, she was very much happier now than she had ever been before, during the whole course of her life.

Nor did her naturally firm spirit again fail her.

Madame Odenthal seemed, fortunately, very much to approve her taking this excursion. She had recognised so many excellent qualities in Lucy (which, with insular partiality, she was pleased to call "*perfectly English*"), that she declared she knew no one with whom she could see her set off on an excursion with more entire satisfaction.

"It is very right and fitting, my dear," said the good woman, "that you should see a metropolis so celebrated for its beauty and fashion as Vienna; and I really think it is about equally fitting that your good father should not again be tempted to leave the peculiar habits of life to which he has been so long accustomed, and every variation from which is, I know, a source of positive suffering to him. He married a lady so very much younger than himself, that he was for many years considered to be a man much younger than he really was; and, naturally enough, he seemed to fall into the same pleasant mistake himself. But now, my dear Gertrude, he certainly begins to be conscious that he is an old man, and very evidently prefers staying at home, to going abroad."

"And you, my dear maternal friend, will, I well know, contrive to make that home so happy to him, that he will not miss me so much as he would have done in former days, when our greatest mutual delight was riding together. I have heard him say repeatedly, within the last few months, that he did not think that he should ever mount again," replied Gertrude.

"And what do you mean to do about Teresa, my dear?" said Madame Odenthal, with a look and voice that manifested considerable interest in the question. "Is it your intention to take her with you?"

"I rather think not," replied Gertrude, carelessly. "I really do not think I shall want her. Madame de Steinfeld assures me that the old servant who has lived with her so long, is a most accomplished lady's-maid."

"Indeed, I think you have decided very wisely, my dear," was Madame Odenthal's reply. "Teresa," she added, "is in many respects a very good servant, but I cannot deny that she is a great gossip, which is just the very most disagreeable thing that any visitor can take into a family."

"Yes," replied Gertrude, after the silence of a moment; "I certainly think she has a strong propensity to idle talking."

At this point of the conversation, Gertrude took up a book which lay near, and soon appeared to be completely occupied by it. For a few minutes she was allowed to do so without interruption, but then Madame Odenthal called her attention, by saying, "Then I suppose, my dear, that you intend to dismiss Teresa before you leave home?"

Gertrude took a moment or two to think before she replied, and then she said, "No! I do not think I shall like to do that, Madame Odenthal, because I do not think she deserves it. She has been a very good servant to me, and I scarcely know how I can send her away without injustice."

"I am afraid that she may say something reproachful and vexing, when you tell her that you are going to Vienna, but that you do not intend to take her with you," replied Madame Odenthal. "I wish you would let me perform the task of telling her this."

"You are very kind, my dear friend, to volunteer thus to perform a task which, I am quite aware, must be disagreeable; and, I fear, it is very selfish in me to accept your offer. Nevertheless, I do accept it, and I confess it is a relief to me to be spared this task."

"It shall be done at once, my dear Gertrude," replied Madame Odenthal; "for the news of your intended departure will be sure to fly from Schloss Steinfeld to Schloss Schwanberg with wonderful rapidity; and it is far better that she should learn the whole arrangement from me, than that she should come to me to make inquiries concerning it."

And, having said this, Madame Odenthal impressed a fond kiss upon the forehead of Gertrude, and left her.

The place chosen by the kind ambassadress as the scene of this interview, was the bed-room of the young baroness, for she knew

that a bell rung from thence, would immediately bring Teresa.
And so it proved.

"Is my lady here?" was the question by which the conversation opened, and it was certainly asked in a tone which seemed to imply that if she were not, Madame Odenthal's right to ring the bell was a very doubtful one.

"No, Teresa. The baroness is not here," replied the *dame de compagnie*, seating herself on the sofa which stood at the bottom of the bed; "it is I who wish to speak to you."

"Well, ma'am," returned the waiting-maid, assuming an attitude that seemed prepared either for going or staying, as the case might be.

"I rang for you, Teresa, that I might let you know that you must get ready a moderate-sized travelling-trunk, and fill it with all that will be most wanted for the baroness on her first arriving at Vienna, where she is going with the Count and Countess Adolphe von Steinfeld."

"My lady going to Vienna, and not to tell me of it, herself!" exclaimed Teresa, with an aspect which very evidently threatened rebellion; "I don't believe a word of it!"

Madame Odenthal never forgot that she was the humble sister of the humble Father Alaric, and, moreover, the pensioned companion of the Baroness Gertrude; but she remembered also, that such authority had been delegated to her, as ought, if properly exercised, to keep the household in good order, without giving their young mistress the trouble of interfering in the matter; and it was, therefore, with the tone and manner of one who expected to be obeyed, that she replied to this uncivil speech, "Leave the room, Teresa."

The waiting-maid was not without her good qualities, but a gentle temper was not one of them; and she signified her intention of remaining where she was, by stoutly saying, "I shall do no such thing."

No person, holding the situation which Madame Odenthal filled in such an establishment as that of Schloss Schwanberg, could have retained her authority so long, and at the same time so smoothly, had she always been as ready to resent a hasty word, as she showed herself on the present occasion. "You will not only leave the room, but the house, Teresa, if you speak to me in that manner," said Madame Odenthal, with great sternness. "I am to be left in charge of the household," she added; "but I should scarcely accept the office, if the servants behaved as you are behaving now."

"At any rate, you need not trouble yourself by any fears about my behaviour," replied Teresa, with a saucy sneer; "for wherever my lady is, there, of course, I shall be too; and Vienna is far enough off for us both to snap our fingers at the other, without any danger to either of us."

"But you are quite mistaken, Teresa," replied Madame Odenthal, "if you suppose that your young lady intends to take you with her to Vienna. She has just told me that she shall do no such thing."

"Then they must find bars, and bolts, and chains, too, if they intend to keep me here till she comes back. I don't deserve to be treated so, and I won't bear it," returned the deeply-incensed waiting-maid, with a very alarming augmentation of colour; "and since you have chosen to make yourself the go-between, I advise you to tell my young lady. . . . But no! I will not send her any message at all. It is a great deal better that I should see her myself. She never used to treat me in this manner, and therefore I am quite sure that I have got some ill friend at court."

"Well, then, Teresa, go to her," said Madame Odenthal, very quietly. "I assure you I have no wish to prevent you; on the contrary, I shall much prefer it. Only I hope you will not forget yourself, and speak disrespectfully to her, for my lord the baron will certainly hear of it, if you do."

"Trust me, Madame Odenthal, for knowing how to manage my own affairs," replied Teresa. "You need not give yourself any trouble about me. If my lady does go to Vienna, you may depend upon it that I shall go too. . . . And if I do *not*, why then you may depend upon it, that I won't stay half-an-hour in this stupid old castle after she has turned her back upon it."

"Perhaps you are right, Teresa, though what you say would have a better effect if your manner were more civil. Nothing would be more easy, you know, than for you to come back after her return, if she wishes to have you; and, to tell you the truth, I would much rather you did not remain here during her absence."

Although there was nothing like positive anger in the tone and manner in which this was said, it had so much less of friendliness than was usual in the kind-hearted English-woman's accustomed mode of addressing the servants, that it really seemed as if she wished to have a little *fracas* with the vexed and disappointed Teresa.

For a minute or two, Madame Odenthal, who had risen from

her chair, stood beside the door, as if waiting for her; upon which, Teresa, rather fiercely knitting her brows, said, " I don't want your help, Madame Odenthal. . . . I suppose my lady and I may speak together, without being watched by you?"

" I am not quite sure that I think so," replied the old lady, gravely. " The Baroness Gertrude," she continued, " has never been exposed to any impertinence from her servants, and I do not wish that she should see such looks, or hear such language from you, as I have now done."

" And how will your being present prevent it?" returned the angry Teresa. " Do you think the sight of you will put me in good humour? But I will prove to you at once, Madame Oden-thal, that I am not afraid of you, so come along this very present time. The sooner the question is settled, the better."

Madame Odenthal said nothing in reply, but proceeded immediately to the room where she had left the baroness, and was followed by Teresa.

If it was the wish of Gertrude's maternal friend that this interview should terminate in the final dismissal of the offending waiting-maid (and the very unusual severity of her manner towards her seemed to indicate that such was indeed her wish), the scheme answered perfectly; for the temper of the unlucky *soubrette* was already so much irritated, that the quiet avowal of Gertrude that she certainly was going to Vienna, but certainly did not intend to be accompanied by her, was more than she could listen to with decorum, and the interview had not lasted long, before she was desired to leave the room.

The unfortunate young woman stood for a moment with her hand upon the half-open door, as if expecting a recal; but no recal came, and poor Teresa had to announce to the next assemblage of the household in the servants' hall, that her mistress was going to set off for Vienna without her; and what was, if possible, more extraordinary still, she had given her warning for good, and all for no other reason in the wide world, except that she had not treated old Mother Odenthal as much like an Arch-Duchess as she chose to be treated.

That she, probably, had herself been treated rather more harshly than she really deserved, may be inferred from the fact, that a very handsome gratuity was left for her in the hands of Madame Odenthal, which that kind-hearted person secretly doubled from her own purse, and then presented to her with many kind wishes before she left the house.

" Well, I won't deny that the old Englishwoman has a kind

heart at bottom," was the commentary of the ex-waiting maid, when discussing this termination of her service with the household, before taking leave of them; "but one might think she had been a spoiled child, she is so unaccountably whimsical. She does not seem to know her own mind for two days together."

CHAPTER LIV.

No journey could be freer from accidents, or *contretemps* of any kind, than was that of the Count and Countess Adolphe, and their friend the Baroness Gertrude; and they reached Vienna on the third day after setting off, with as little fatigue, and as much gratification from fine weather and fine country, as reasonable people could desire.

They found that the Count von Steinfeld had said no more in praise of the agreeable apartments he had secured for them than they well deserved; nor was the addition of Gertrude to the party productive of the least inconvenience; for the Count Steinfeld, like many others, was strongly persuaded, that *the English* were considerably more difficult to please in all matters of personal accommodation than all the other nations of the earth put together, and had therefore, in choosing apartments for his pretty daughter-in-law, Lucy, so far exceeded what was needful for her, as to provide what was amply sufficient for her, and for her friend likewise.

Who can enter Vienna for the first time, and not feel a sensation of delight at its aspect! To Adolphe, of course, it was not new, but it was the metropolis of his country, and he was as much delighted by the effect it produced on his fair companions, as if he had himself been looking at it for the first time.

He was delighted too at all the attentive preparations which had been made for their reception, and not a little pleased likewise, at perceiving that the depression of spirits under which his father had laboured when leaving home, had altogether vanished; for no widowed father of a married son ever looked more young, handsome, and *débonnaire*, than did the Count Steinfeld, when he came to welcome the travellers on their arrival.

It speedily became evident that he expected the young party

who had joined him to enter with zeal, at least equal to his own, into all the fascinating dissipations of that prettiest of capitals; but in this he was mistaken. The ladies drove about with great perseverance, saw everything, and admired everything; but when Lucy's gay and handsome young father-in-law began to talk of introductions, presentations, and visitings, which were immediately to take place, and which would be followed, he assured her, by his having the happiness of seeing herself, and her beautiful friend, become the most admired ornaments of the courtly circle to which he meant to have the honour of introducing them, he was startled and astonished by the assurance that they neither of them intended to enter into society at all.

So astonishing, indeed, did this determination appear to him, that it was some time before they could persuade him that they were really in earnest; and it was only when his son hinted to him, that he was again in hopes of his wife's presenting him, at no very distant day, with an heir to the family honours and estates, that the juvenile grandfather could be induced to withdraw his opposition to so melancholy a proposal.

But even after he had made up his mind, as all noble fathers-in-law do upon such occasions, that it was perfectly right and proper the Countess Adolphe should stay at home, and take care of herself, he still expressed his hope of being permitted to introduce some eligible chaperone to the Baroness Gertrude, who might have the honour and happiness of presenting her to the Empress, and to all other ladies of high distinction in Vienna.

But to this very kind and very proper proposal, the Baroness Gertrude would not listen, assuring Count Steinfeld, that her present visit to the capital was not intended to be one of gaiety, but of friendship; while at the same time, she begged him to believe, that, under other circumstances, she should be most happy to put herself entirely under his guidance.

" Well then, my fair baroness," replied the amiable widower, "I will look forward with hope to some future time, when I may meet you here under circumstances more favourable; but, meantime, I fear that you and dear Lucy will find me a very useless personage, for, at present, I cannot command my evening hours, having fallen into such a routine of engagements, as would make my withdrawing myself from society unpleasantly remarkable."

This candid avowal was, of course, replied to in a suitable manner; and before they had been many days at Vienna, the trio found themselves passing their days very nearly as they might have done, when reciprocally meeting in their respective castles.

Their mornings, however, had considerably more variety; for not only were there many interesting drives, but there were fine pictures, rich museums, and noble libraries, where they often enjoyed themselves for several hours together, without running the very slightest risk of being interrupted, for these precious repositories are not the most fashionable resorts in Vienna. In fact, the life now led by these much-attached country neighbours, was very much like what it might have been, had they remained at home, at least as far as society went; for the Countess Adolphe, though well inclined to make light of all evils, whether physical or moral, could not conceal, either from herself or her two watchful companions, "that she was not quite so strong as she used to be."

Had she never known the misery of losing a child, her usually gay spirits would not so easily have deserted her; but, as it was, the companionship of the much stronger-minded Gertrude, and the constant and assiduous attention of her truly devoted husband, were greatly needed, and of the most essential benefit to her.

Fortunately for them all, the accounts from Schloss Schwanberg were everything that the anxious Gertrude could wish them to be. The baron was in as perfectly good health as his three-score years and ten could possibly permit him to be; Father Alaric, it was evident, was always at his post, both in the chapel and out of it; and as for Madame Odenthal, her pleasant narrative letters were so charming, that their arrival was almost as satisfactory, Adolphe said, as a gallop from Schloss Steinfeld to Schloss Schwanberg could have been.

In respect to Rupert's part of the correspondence, it must be confessed, that his dispatches partook so much of the style and character of love letters, that it would be indiscreet, and in very bad taste, to examine them; but, nevertheless, it cannot be doubted that they very successfully fulfilled the purpose for which they were written, for as surely as the post conveyed one of them to the hands of Gertrude, so surely did she exhibit a very visible improvement both in health and spirits.

It must be confessed also, however, that our very domestic young trio had another source of interest, I will not say amusement, because under the circumstances, it would not be decorous so to describe it; but the facts of the case must be stated, because they eventually became of considerable importance.

It was Lucy, notwithstanding the languor and low spirits to which she occasionally gave way, who was the first to observe a considerable change in the general appearance and manner of Count Steinfeld. It has been already stated, that he was a very young father for a married son; but now this incongruity had become very greatly more remarkable. In truth, there would be little or no exaggeration in saying, that the effect produced by his general aspect was such as might have easily led to the belief that he was the younger man of the two.

Adolphe, though by no means slovenly, was very decidedly careless in his dress. Few hard-reading men are coxcombs in their attire, although they may occasionally be detected in bestowing rather an overweening attention to the attire of their books; but Adolphe was not a coxcomb, even here. He was a *genuine* hard reader, though scarcely conscious of the fact himself; for he still knew much too little of the general state of his fellow creatures in this particular, to be at all capable of forming a just estimate of himself.

The daily, or nearly daily, visits of his elaborately attired father, might have gone on for years, without its ever occurring to Adolphe to remark, that his father was one of the youngest, handsomest, and best-dressed men of his acquaintance, had Lucy not pointed out the fact to him.

On one occasion, when the Count made his paternal visit *en route* to a dinner-party, the contrast between the father and son struck her so forcibly, that, after he had bestowed his customary salute on her fair cheeks, and departed, she said, with one of her quizzical little smiles, "I almost wonder, Adolphe, that you should like to see your wife kissed by such a very handsome, elegant young man!"

"Handsome, elegant young man?" repeated Adolphe, looking infinitely puzzled. "Who do you mean, Lucy? Who is it that kisses you?"

"The person who kisses me, Adolphe—I don't mean yourself, remember—is by far the handsomest and best-dressed man of my acquaintance," she replied; "and, moreover, he does me this honour, every time I see him."

"You mean my father," said he, laughing; "and he certainly does look very young and handsome, considering that he is the father of such an uncouth old son as I am."

"Why, really, Adolphe, I do think it is very kind of him not to be ashamed of you," she replied; "ashamed of your looking so exceedingly old, I mean. I really think that he could not have quite given up flying kites and spinning tops, when he married. Depend upon it, my dear, he looks more fit to be a bridegroom now, than he did then. Don't you think so, Adolphe?"

"Nonsense, Lucy! A bridegroom? who could have put such stuff into your head? Not Gertrude, I am sure, for she never talks nonsense!" he replied, with a very awful frown.

"Don't look so very fiercely angry, husband, or you will make me cry," returned Lucy. "I won't say another word about bridegrooms," she added, in the very meekest accent possible, "if you will only make one innocent little wager with me. Will you bet me a solid, honest, English sovereign (I don't mean our well-beloved queen, but only one of her beautiful little golden portraits), will you bet me a sovereign, Adolphe, that your father is not a bridegroom before this day six months?"

Adolphe scolded a little, but he laughed a little too; and at last the bet was made, and moreover, the bet was won by the sharp-sighted Lucy, or rather, the bet was honourably paid, though not accurately won; for Count Steinfeld's marriage with a pretty young lady some half-dozen years younger than his son, did not take place till six months and seven days after the said bet had been registered in Lucy's pocket-book.

CHAPTER LV.

MEANWHILE the important hour approached, which was so anxiously looked forward to, and which, it was hoped, would repair the heavy loss which poor Lucy, with all her gaiety, had never ceased to deplore.

It unfortunately happened, that when this anxiously looked-for hour arrived, the Baroness Gertrude was too unwell to bestow on her beloved friend the personal attendance which her heart dictated. Happily, however, there was not much time for regret of any kind, for Lucy presented not only one baby to her delighted husband, but two, a boy and a girl, both strong, both healthy, and both greatly more likely to live than to die.

The contrast between the hours which precede such an event, and those which follow it, is too familiar to all the world to make any description of it necessary; even the gallant and handsome young grandfather, notwithstanding his approaching change of condition, seemed conscious of this, and looked as well pleased and happy as the rest of the party; although Lucy, with her accustomed sauciness, declared that though this handsomest of all her young men acquaintance behaved so admirably well upon the occasion, she could not help fearing that the having to announce *two* grand-children to his affianced young bride, must have been extremely disagreeable.

It was not very long after this happy event had taken place, that a letter from Madame Odenthal gently hinted to Gertrude that her father began to be anxious for her return; but the hint was so quietly given, that had not there been a postscript to the letter, it is possible that the receipt of it would not have greatly hastened their movements. The postscript said, "I should be very sorry, dearest Gertrude, that what I have written should hasten the homeward movements of your friends, but should a lengthened stay at Vienna be their purpose, I will make the journey myself, under the protection of the faithful Hans, and I think that between us we shall be able to conduct you home very safely."

This (feminine) postscript settled the business at once; neither of the party had, in fact, any great wish to remain longer in Vienna; and Gertrude's reply to Madame Odenthal assured her that they should meet in a very few days, without her enduring the trouble and fatigue of a long journey for the purpose.

Two babies and their two nurses formed, however, an addition to the party of a kind which prevented its being quite as rapid as it might have been without them; and Gertrude, on arriving, found that she had, for the last hour or two, been rather anxiously expected.

One carriage, containing Lucy and the children, drove to Schloss Steinfeld, the other, with Gertrude and Adolphe as her escort, took the road to Schloss Schwanberg. Their journey had been without *contretemps* or accident of any kind; but, nevertheless, the heart of poor Gertrude beat so vehemently as she approached her home, her father, and Rupert, that it was not without considerable effort, and considerable difficulty, that she sustained the appearance of composure.

On the steps which led up to the principal entrance to the castle, stood Rupert, precisely where he had stood three years before, waiting their arrival on their return from Paris. At the moment that Gertrude first caught a glimpse of him as he thus stood, pale with intensity of emotion, she was herself so nearly overcome by the same cause, that she shook from head to foot.

But the one quick backward glance which memory took to the moment when she had last seen him standing exactly in the same place and in the same attitude, did more towards reviving her exhausted spirits, than all the volatile essences which ever were applied to the most sensitive nostril.

The difference between the present and the past rushed upon her memory like a gleam of bright sunshine into a darkened room; and utterly forgetting the fears which had tormented her, lest she should find her aged father changed, or in any degree the worse for her long absence, she uttered the name of "RUPERT" in accents which proved plainly enough that, for the moment, at least, the feeling of very exquisite happiness was predominant.

Never was a genuine emotion of sympathy more clearly demonstrated than in the manner of Count Adolphe's taking leave of his late guest. He uttered no word of salutation to Rupert, no word of farewell to Gertrude; nay, he did not even shake hands with her, for he had a sort of instinctive conviction that she would have been quite unconscious of it, if he had. All he did in the way of leave-taking, was to spring out of the carriage the moment it stopped, take her in his arms just in time to prevent her throwing herself head foremost after him, then spring into it again, and drive off.

It is a most certain fact, that during many hours of this homeward journey, the thoughts of Gertrude had been very much occupied by the idea of her reunion with her father; but now that she had reached her long-distant home, he was, for a short interval, utterly and entirely forgotten. The same little parlour which had sheltered her during the first agitating moments after her return from Paris, sheltered her again now. But oh! the blessed change! She no longer shrunk from seeking Rupert's eye, from fear that she might find it averted; but, for a moment, the happiness of which overpaid (as she often declared in afterlife) all the misery she had endured, for one short dear moment, she rested her head upon his bosom, and whispered a word or two of seemingly very moving tenderness in his ear.

But this one dear moment passed, she lingered not for the enjoyment of a second, but exclaimed, "My father! and your dear mother, too, Rupert?"

"They are together," he replied; "but I cannot, I dare not, lead you to them."

"No, Rupert, no! It is far better that you should not. You are not by any means trustworthy at this moment. Fortunately,

I know my way, and therefore do not need your assistance. Stay where you are, and lock yourself in, if you please, for you are not at all fit to be seen. Alas! my Rupert! you are a very poor specimen of a philosopher! · But, if I mistake not, Shakspeare tells us somewhere, that there never yet was a philosopher that could endure the toothache patiently, so I suppose you must not lose caste for looking so very little stoical at this moment. Shut yourself up! shut yourself up, Rupert, and behave better when we next meet."

With her heart still beating joyously, and her cheeks flushed with emotion, Gertrude sought her father, and was not only most joyously welcomed, but highly complimented on her improved looks.

"Vienna seems to have agreed with you, my dear child, still better, if possible, than your own free native air. But I have no doubt, my beloved Gertrude, that with your peculiarly high-minded views respecting noble rank, and noble races, you must have felt in another sense, as if you were in *native air*. There is no capital in Europe where high birth so instantly finds its proper place, as in Vienna. No mistakes there, my dear; neither equipage, jewels, nor anything else that wealth can give, can stand in the place of high birth, at Vienna. I am sure you must have observed this with pleasure, my dear Gertrude."

"The Countess Adolphe was not very well, papa, and did not go much into society," replied Gertrude.

"I am sorry to hear it," replied the baron, very solemnly. "Not that I mean to blame her," he continued; "for her situation, probably, rendered it desirable that she should not fatigue herself. But it is probable, my dear Gertrude, that though she has allied herself to a family of very considerable distinction, she may not be herself aware of the real importance to the highest class of society in Vienna which your appearing among them would have been. You know what our alliances are, and have been, Gertrude, though this rather low-born young Englishwoman does not; and I cannot but think, my dear child, that you scarcely did justice to yourself, or to them, by remaining unknown among them."

"I did not think it would have been right, papa, for me to let her pass her evenings alone. I went to Vienna more for her sake than for that of the society I was likely to find there. Their being all personally strangers to me, would have made my going among them alone rather embarrassing to me."

"Perhaps you are right, Gertrude. Perhaps you are right.

I can perfectly well imagine, that your feelings on the subject would have been very different, if I had been with you," replied the baron. "You must have often felt that you wanted me, Gertrude."

"I can truly say, my dear father," returned Gertrude, with a heightened colour, "that no single day has passed during my absence, in which I have not thought of you."

During the whole of this conversation, the hand of Gertrude had been fast locked in that of Madame Odenthal; but it was perfectly well understood in the family, that when the baron was holding a conversation with his daughter, he did not approve of its being interrupted or broken-in upon by any "member of his household," which was a phrase that comprehended Madame Odenthal and her son, as well as the footmen, waiting-maids, and grooms. But Gertrude now begged permission to retire, for the purpose of changing her dress, which she averred, would be a very great refreshment after so dusty a journey; and as Madame Odenthal very respectfully attended her, as a matter of course, the two friends soon found themselves clasped in each other's arms.

Madame Odenthal looked wistfully in the face of Gertrude, as if she longed to ask her a hundred questions; but instead of asking her any, she only threw her arms around her again, and pressed her to her heart.

"And my father?" exclaimed Gertrude, after the pause of a moment; "tell me everything about him. Has he been constantly well? Has he, on the whole, been in tolerably good spirits since I left him?"

"Indeed, I think I may very honestly answer *yes*," replied Madame Odenthal. "His garden walks are certainly much shorter than they used to be, but with this one exception, I really think he is as well as I ever saw him. But come back with me this very moment, dearest Gertrude. or he will lose all the little patience he possesses."

The pleasure caused by the reunion between the father and daughter, seemed equal on both sides; and most assuredly, Gertrude had never before been so gay, so delightful a companion, as she was now; nor had her father ever before appeared to enjoy her society so much. But, nevertheless, it was a very obvious fact, that the Baron of Schwanberg was growing old, and it was fortunate both for him and his daughter also, that the daily intercourse between them and their Steinfeld neighbours seemed, by degrees, to become the only *visiting* they required, to make them perfectly happy. All the noble, but scanty, neighbourhood, of course, came to pay their compliments to the Baroness Gertrude on her return from the capital; nor was Lucy, notwithstanding her not very clearly understood English origin, welcomed home with less of cordial kindness; but when these visitings had been duly returned, and were then followed by dinner invitations from all the mansions within reach of them, it speedily became evident, that both the ladies had lost their taste for usual hospitalities. Nor is it, therefore, very extraordinary that they should both be accused of giving themselves airs of stateliness and superiority, in consequence of their three months' sojourn in the metropolis.

It was in vain that Gertrude pleaded her father's increasing infirmities, which rendered his leaving his own arm-chair a painful effort to him; for there was scarcely a single individual in the whole neighbourhood who was not ready to testify and declare that he had never been better, or more fit for society in his life.

Nor did Lucy and her stay-at-home husband fare at all better, when the former pleaded her daily increasing averseness to leaving her darling babies; and the latter ventured to confess that he had not courage to contest the point with her; so they were both accused of giving themselves intolerable airs, and of having been too much delighted with the dissipations of the capital, to retain any relish for the friendly hospitalities of the rural abode to which they had returned.

Even the friendly Doctor Nieper, though the last man in the world to increase the circulation of an opinion so unfavourable to his friends, had very decidedly strengthened this impression.

For one of the ladies of the neighbourhood wishing to ascertain, if possible, whether there was anything like truth and sincerity in the cause assigned by the Countess Adolphe von Steinfeld for staying at home, took an opportunity of asking the good doctor, whether these precious twin children were in any danger of following the one that she had lost; upon which he answered with the genuine satisfaction of a truly good-hearted man, that he was happy to say, that he had never, in his whole long life and practice, seen so magnificent a pair of twins. "Babies are always anxious joys," he added, "and particularly so, it must be confessed, in the case of twins; but I certainly see no reason whatever to fear for the life of either of these, at present."

So it was agreed by general consent among the provincial aristocracy, that the two friends should be permitted to shut themselves up alternately in each other's strongholds, as much as they liked.

Nor did any of the individuals concerned repine at the fate thus allotted them. Nothing pleased the old baron better than having Lucy and the nursery transferred to Schloss Schwanberg; and as Gertrude became every day more and more averse to leave her father, it was there, for the most part, that the two united families might be said to live. The library, too, had its share in strengthening this arrangement. Gertrude had not left off buying books; and remote as they might seem to be from the scenes where human intelligence is the most actively at work, they were more completely *au courant du jour* than many who bustle about in the midst of them.

CHAPTER LVI.

THERE was not a single individual of the party who formed this isolated group, the baron and Madame Odenthal included, who would not have been ready to declare, if questioned on the subject, that "let but *the same endure*, they asked not aught beside."

But this *same*, natural, simple, and unambitious as it was, nevertheless, was not destined to endure long. The first distant sound that disturbed it came from Vienna, and reached them in the shape of a report that the Count von Steinfeld was immediately about to unite himself in the bonds of holy wedlock with the young and fair Countess Wilhelmina Carolina Rodolphina von Kronenstern.

Then came a letter, written in the most affectionate style, from the Count himself, not only officially stating the same important fact, but adding thereunto the information that it was the intention of himself and his bride immediately to take up their abode at Schloss Steinfeld, which he earnestly requested might be made in every respect ready for their reception.

Though Lucy's prophecy had been at first considered as a joke, rumour had for some time been busy upon the same theme, so that the announcement of the fact did not take them by surprise;

but, nevertheless, the quiet establishment was put into considerable confusion by the efforts made, by every part of it, to be, as directed, in all respects ready for the announced arrival of the bride-folks; and it was immediately felt by them all, that one of the two happy homes which of late had, in a great degree, been in common to the two families, could continue to be so no longer.

But in order to make this inevitable change as little painful as possible, Madame Odenthal and Gertrude between them, contrived to prepare something so like a nursery for Lucy's twins, as might render Schloss Schwanberg as much like a home to Adolphe and his wife as Schloss Steinfeld had ever been.

And this precaution proved a very essential blessing to them all; for the gay Wilhelmina was much more disposed to remember that she was herself a young bride, than that her husband was a grandfather.

The return of the Count himself to his own domain, in the character of a bridegroom, was, of course, a signal for a repetition of all the hospitalities by which that of his son, when under the same circumstances, had been welcomed rather more than two years before; but what had appeared very amusing to Lucy when she enacted the part of bride herself, assumed a very different aspect now.

She and her beautiful sister had been welcomed almost like "foreign wonders;" and their bad French, and worse German, had been listened to, not only with indulgence, but, positively, with admiration. But now there was not a distinguished family in the neighbourhood that was not ready to avow its conviction, that a bride from Vienna was a much more valuable acquisition to the neighbourhood than it was possible a bride from London could be.

As to Gertrude, the excuse afforded by the fact that her father no longer went into company . . . never, in truth, leaving the house except for a short drive in a close carriage, was exceedingly welcome; and her declining all invitations in order to avoid leaving him, was a fact almost forgotten amidst the unwonted gaieties of Schloss Steinfeld.

And, assuredly, a more domestic partnership was never instituted than that which now united Gertrude and Lucy, under the hospitable roof of Schloss Schwanberg.

Though the nursery of the twins, in the mansion of the bride, was not wholly deserted, it was very nearly so; for it was impossible to deny the fact that Gertrude, Rupert, and the library, formed altogether an attraction that very decidedly overpowered that of all the festivities that were to be found elsewhere.

The increasing infirmities of the baron began, however, to disturb the serenity with which this was enjoyed; and at length his strength failed him so completely, that he could no longer leave his room.

But the master-passion failed not with his failing strength. While supported in his arm-chair, and then upon his sofa, and at last, when stretched upon his bed, his head, or heart, or whatever the seat of pride might be, still remained true to the feeling that had predominated throughout his life.

"Remember, my beloved Gertrude," he said, re-said, and said again, at least a score of times before his death—"remember that my obsequies must be in most respects, I think I might with propriety say IN ALL, totally distinct, and different, from those of inferior persons."

"Your instructions, my dearest father," she tearfully replied, "shall be exactly obeyed in every respect."

"I know it, my beloved child!" he replied again and again to the oft-repeated words, but never as if he thought that his injunctions could be given, or her obedience promised, too often. "I know it, my noble-minded daughter! You will never suffer your sorrow for our comparatively short separation to interfere with your performance of the duties which will devolve upon you at my death. Our opinions upon all points connected with our exalted station are, and ever have been, so exactly the same, my dear child, that, I confess to you, I consider your having remained thus long unmarried, as an especial dispensation of Providence. Had any reigning prince, or nobleman of the very highest rank, solicited your hand, Gertrude, it was more than probable that you might, by necessity, have been absent from me at this very important moment."

"I am, indeed, thankful, my dearest father," she replied, "that I have formed no connection which should oblige me to leave you! Let me but understand your wishes, and be certain that I will obey them."

"I have still much to say to you," he solemnly replied; "and I would wish our good Madame Odenthal to prepare me some restorative which I may take, from time to time, while I am giving you my final instructions. I would spare you the fatigue of listening to directions which must, of necessity, be long, and which you may feel, also, to be melancholy, my dear child; I would willingly spare you this, if I could, and make our good

Rupert the executor of my last wishes. But we know, my dear love, that the sort of intellect necessary for the full comprehension of such a subject, is not to be looked for in any class inferior to our own. People of high station, my Gertrude, ought to live for posterity; their manners, and habits of life, being the only safe standard by which those who come after them can be modelled. Nor is this all that we are bound to do for posterity; we ought not only to live, but to die also, in such a manner as may serve as an example for those who follow us."

The good old man had been so accustomed, through his whole life, to utter long harangues, that he had, like many extemporary preachers, acquired a habit of pausing, as if to give his hearers time to digest what he had said; and this skilful pause enabled him now to proceed, though in a voice considerably lower than usual.

"I have a high opinion of Rupert," he resumed; "indeed, I have a very high opinion of him. I think his abilities must be quite out of the common way, considering the rank in which he was born; but, nevertheless, my dear Gertrude, I do not believe him to be at all more capable of comprehending my wishes on this important subject than of managing an army, or of ruling a kingdom. My wish is . . . "—but here he became so evidently exhausted, that Gertrude, in her capacity of nurse, insisted upon his taking a little refreshment, and, if possible, of composing himself, and endeavouring to sleep for a few moments, before he proceeded with his instructions, which, as he himself very justly observed, were only the more fatiguing in their delivery, because he was so deeply conscious of their importance.

*   *   *   *   *

Meanwhile, a very different scene was going on at Schloss Steinfeld.

After having been exhibited in her bridal attire, at every mansion within visiting reach in the neighbourhood, the sprightly Wilhelmina made it clearly understood by her handsome bridegroom, that it was her inclination, wish, purpose, and intention, to give a series of fêtes at Schloss Steinfeld, which should prove most satisfactorily to all the world that she was not unworthy of the flattering reception which she had met in the neighbourhood.

Nor did the handsome bridegroom appear in the least degree averse to this gay project; and hospitable preparations of all kinds were accordingly commenced with great zeal from the garrets of the old mansion to its cellar, both inclusive.

But, unfortunately, the neighbourhood, though on the whole

very respectably aristocratic, was somewhat too widely scattered to be convenient for such an object, and in many cases, the personages with whom the ambitious young bride most eagerly sought intimacy, resided at too great a distance to permit their returning home after a ball; and therefore, whenever a ball, or even a sociable little waltzing party, was given by the dance-loving Wilhelmina, the garrets of Schloss Steinfeld were to be put in requisition as well as its cellars.

But let it not be supposed that the brilliant and quick-witted bride ever dreamed of lodging neighbours of sixteen descents in a garret. Assuredly no idea so preposterous ever entered her head. But if they were not to lodge there, somebody else must, or Steinfeld Castle could not be made to furnish pillows enough for its inhabitants.

Now, when Adolphe had brought home his young English bride (her forty thousand pounds sterling coming home with her), the handsomest apartments in the mansion had immediately been assigned to her and her husband, and these they had, of course, retained ever since. Moreover, the apartment which had been occupied by Arabella, and which had been selected not only as being second-best, but as being near her sister, had been appropriated to the babies ever since the return of the party from Vienna; nor had it been thought necessary to change the arrangement, because that portion of the mansion which had even been hitherto appropriated to the master and mistress of the family, was, of course, assigned to the Count and his bride on their arrival. But when the time approached for returning the festive hospitalities by which the Count and his young bride had been welcomed to the neighbourhood, it was discovered that it was absolutely necessary to invade the nursery apartments of the twins, in order to accommodate the guests.

The announcement of this necessity was not in any way agreeable to Lucy. The garrets might be very good garrets, as the gay Wilhelmina repeatedly assured her they were; but nevertheless Lucy did in no degree approve the proposition of lodging the precious babies therein.

But Lucy had too much good sense, as well as too much good temper, to make a family quarrel on the occasion. She knew, moreover, perfectly well, that "if he lived to be a man," her darling boy would some day be lord of the castle, despite all the beautiful brides that her youthful father-in-law could bring down upon them . . . . but the question was, what was to become of the dear babies now? Had it not been so perfectly obvious to everyone about him that the Baron von Schwanberg was positively dying (though he still found it very difficult to believe it), the natural remedy for this garret scheme would have been obvious enough, as nothing could have been more easy than the sending the two children to occupy the rooms at Schloss Schwanberg which had been long ago allotted to them.

But she knew that Gertrude would neither like to rouse him from his half lethargic state, in order to ask his permission for doing this, nor yet would she choose to take advantage of this same melancholy lethargy, in order to smuggle them into the castle without his knowledge.

Lucy had, however, the comfort of knowing, that her dearly-beloved Adolphe would not only tell her exactly what it was best to do, but that his constant good humour would enable him to take a more patient view of the case than she could do without him . . . . for in her heart she was very angry indeed, and therefore, like a good wife, and a wise woman, she dutifully determined to make over all her sorrows to her husband, leaving him at perfect liberty to do battle, or to yield, as he thought best.

The task she thus assigned him was not an easy one, and so conscious was he of this fact, that he looked an older man by half-a-dozen years while he was meditating upon it, than he had ever looked before. But notwithstanding both his bookish abstraction, and his constitutional good humour, Adolphe had sober judgment enough to perceive that Lucy's question, " What had we better do, Adolphe ? " was an important one, inasmuch as it did not concern the present moment only, but might have an influence on their domestic comfort for many a long year to come.

At the time of Adolphe's marriage it had been settled, without the slightest doubt or difficulty on either side, that Schloss Steinfeld should be the principal residence of the young couple ; and though Lucy's ample fortune had made it an easy matter to them to change the scene whenever inclined to do so, they had never, as yet, considered any other residence as their home.

But after very mature deliberation, Adolphe now began to think that this could be the case no longer ; and it was then, perhaps, for the first time, that he became fully aware that forty thousand pounds sterling might be a very important addition to the good gifts of a pretty wife, even if blessed with as sweet a temper as that of his Lucy.

To have asked his bridegroom father to have made him such

an allowance as might have enabled him to live elsewhere, in a style befitting his rank and station in society, would have been very painful to him, and probably in vain, also; for he had never as yet heard any allusion made to the personal fortune of his youthful step-mother, and it was therefore certainly with more satisfaction than he had ever felt before on the same subject, that he now recollected how perfectly it was in his power to let his dear little wife choose a home for herself.

Lucy was at first considerably more puzzled than pleased when Adolphe returned to her, after taking, as he said, a solitary walk to meditate, with a countenance much more indicative of enjoyment than of deliberation. Lucy could not look cross; Nature had denied her the power; but she certainly did look very grave, as he returned to her in her solitary boudoir, looking as blithe as a school-boy at the beginning of his holidays.

"Oh, Adolphe! Adolphe! you have not been thinking about the dear children, I am very sure!" she exclaimed, shaking her head. "At least you cannot have been meditating on the subject as seriously as I have done; for the difficulty only increases the more I think about it. Little Lucy has decidedly got a cold already, and I really would not have her taken out of her own warm room into that great wide garret for the world!"

"Lucy shall not be taken into that great wide garret, my dear," replied Adolphe, gaily; "nor little Adolphe, either. But I suppose you will not be terrified at the idea of my going there."

"Terrified," repeated Lucy, looking, if possible, graver than before. "Terrified is certainly a very strong word, and I don't suppose that I could truly say that I should be terrified, Adolphe, if you were to pass a night in the garret. But I will tell you fairly and sincerely that I shall not approve it at all."

"It will only be for one night, you know, Lucy, and if I do happen to sneeze, it will not much signify, will it?"

"I hardly know how to answer you, Adolphe," she replied, "because you are in jest, and I am in earnest. As to the mere inconvenience," she added, "I assure you that I could make quite as little fuss about it myself, as you can do, It is *not* the inconvenience. It is the . . . . the *principle*, if I may use so solemn sounding a word without your laughing at me."

"No, Lucy, for once in your life I will let you be solemn without laughing at you. On the contrary, I do not think you could choose a better word, and, like you, my dear, I do not approve the principle. But though I can forgive your solemnity, I doubt if I can forgive your folly. Lucy! Lucy! Lucy! will you agree to our both following the example of your beloved Dogberry? Will you write yourself down an ass, and obligingly permit me to do the same?"

"My dearest, dearest Adolphe!" she replied, with something very like a tear in her bright eye; "how I do wish you would be serious!"

"Serious!" he repeated, "which of us do you suppose to be the most serious at this moment?"

"Why, Adolphe! how can you talk to me so?" she exclaimed; "I really do not believe that you are exactly aware *what* we are talking about. It is about the health of the children, my dear Adolphe, that I am so anxious. I do not approve the Countess's proposal of removing them from their present warm nursery to the garret. Do you think there is anything really ridiculous in that?"

"Not exactly ridiculous, Lucy," he replied. "But the question is but trifling, my dear, that is, speaking comparatively. What should you say, for instance, of its comparative importance, if I were to name beside it the question of whether you, and I, and our children, present, and to come, were from henceforth, probably for the term of our natural lives, to remain the permitted guests of our blooming step-mother; or, that we were suddenly to turn ourselves to the right-about, and, dutifully asking papa's blessing, to march off, and find an independent home for ourselves, in whatever part of the world we might happen to like best!"

"My dearest, dearest Adolphe!" exclaimed Lucy, clasping her hands, and positively trembling with eagerness; "are you really in earnest in saying, that such a delicious idea has ever occurred to you?"

"Traitress!" he replied, holding up his fist in a very threatening attitude; "traitress! did such an idea ever occur to you, without your telling me of it?"

"Telling you of it?" replied Lucy, with an air of very superior wisdom. "Telling you of it, Adolphe! Just fancy the daughter of a plebeian English banker, telling the son and heir of an Austrian nobleman, that she thought the best thing they could do would be to run away from the ancestral castle, and its sixteen quarters, in order to amuse themselves by leading a sort of fancy life, heaven knows where!"

"You have put the case so well, Countess Adolphe," replied her husband, "that I should not find a single word to say in reply, were it not for one trifling little circumstance. If the daughter of the plebeian English banker had chanced to have no marriage portion more precious than that appertaining to the noble Countess Wilhelmina von Steinfeld, I am quite ready to confess that the best, and perhaps the only course they could pursue, would be to remain in the said ancestral castle, peaceably contenting themselves with whatever portion of it might be assigned to their use. But as the marriage portion of the Countess Adolphe von Steinfeld for the time being happens to consist in English pounds sterling, instead of German armorial bearings, the case is different. You know more about living in England, Lucy, than I do, and I have no doubt you will be able to tell me, with tolerable accuracy, whether the income arising from your fortune would enable us to exist there with tolerable comfort?"

"Exist there! Oh! my darling Adolphe! would you really consent to make the experiment? Exist? not a single comfort, not a single luxury that you enjoy here, shall be wanting there, Adolphe, save and except the pleasure of looking up at the great stone griffins over the gate, and telling your heart, with a complacent smile, that they were stuck up there by your ancestors in the year one! Adolphe! Adolphe! if you are in earnest, I shall be too, too happy! I shall indeed! I shall not know how to bear it." And so saying, the gay-hearted Lucy threw her arms upon the table, buried her face upon them, and began sobbing.

"My dear little wife!" said Adolphe, throwing his arms round her, "I shall have to quarrel with you at last! Why did you never tell me, never hint to me, in any way, that you should be happier in your own country than here? I give you my honour, Lucy, that I never suspected your having such a feeling."

"Nor had I any such feeling," she replied, with great sincerity, "as long as I believed that you preferred this home to every other. I daresay you will laugh at me, if I tell you that one reason for my never hinting at my occasional longings for a peep at Old England, arose from that sort of mysterious reverence which we feel for some of the mighty truths that we cannot understand. If any one had asked me, why I preferred England? I could have answered by the commonest of all English words: I should have said, 'Because it is more *comfortable ;*' but I never meditated, for a moment, upon your undoubted preference for remaining with your father, instead of having an establishment of your own (which I know very well you could afford to pay for); never, for a moment, did my vulgar English thoughts glance

that way, without my feeling that I was totally unable to form a
fair judgment on the subject; because I could not comprehend
the exact nature of the attraction which kept you here. For I
knew that nothing would be more easy than for you to pay your
good father a visit from time to time; and, besides the Count
himself, I could see nothing but the griffins outside the door, and
your gay, young step-mother within, which you might not have
found elsewhere."

This explanation, however, on the part of Lucy, was so far
satisfactory, that it produced a hearty laugh from her husband,
though the said laugh was occasionally interrupted, for the purpose of assuring her that she had behaved exceedingly ill.

The discussion ended, however, as most of their discussions did,
in a very perfect agreement of opinion on the subject before them.
Moreover, it was agreed between them, ere they parted, that the
precious babies should in no case be exposed to the doubtful
atmosphere of the threatened garret, a danger which was easily
avoided by Adolphe's quietly taking up his quarters on the sofa
in his wife's dressing-room, while the noble bed-room which had
been appointed for him and his lady on their arrival, was converted into a very satisfactory nursery; and of this nursery it
was decided, that she and the children should keep possession,
till their newly-projected scheme of taking refuge in England
from the enlarged hospitalities of Wilhelmina could be acted
upon.

<hr>

CHAPTER LVII.

THE last scene of the august Baron von Schwanberg's earthly
existence was, meanwhile, rapidly approaching. Fortunately,
however, for the harmony of the Steinfeld festivities, his death
did not take place till two days after the party assembled to partake of them had separated; and therefore the absence of Adolphe
and his wife, who immediately quitted the house of feasting for
the house of mourning, produced no discussion or objection of any
kind.

Gertrude had been to long prepared for this event for it to

overwhelm her; but, nevertheless, she felt it severely, and, like most other people,. probably, upon losing one whom they had dearly loved, and who had dearly loved them, she tormented herself not a little by dwelling upon all the circumstances in which she had recently opposed his wishes though not avowedly.

Her last consolation, under the weight of these painful thoughts, was the recollection of all the misery which she had inflicted upon herself in Paris, in order to obey and please him; and if, at length, her sensitive conscience permitted her judgment to acquit her, it was only by the help of her strong conviction, that had such misery been repeated, her reason, or her life, or both, would have been the sacrifice.

All that the most tender love, and the most genuine friendship, could offer, in the way of consolation, was not wanting to Gertrude now. She deserved to be loved, and to be esteemed, notwithstanding these untoward features in her destiny, which had made her past life such a curiously-mixed tissue of right and wrong. She had, in fact, been so placed, that no line of conduct which it was possible for her to pursue, could have left her wholly free from self-reproach; and gratefully did she listen to the reasonings of Rupert, which, without the aid of anything approaching sophistry, displayed to her very satisfactorily the undeniable truth, that by no other line of conduct could she have assured to her father the enjoyment and consolation of her presence, to the last hour of his life.

It scarcely need be stated, that the presence of her true friend, Lucy, and the active co-operation of Adolphe with Rupert, in all matters of business, were blessings gratefully received, and fully appreciated. But as one of the most urgent of the defunct baron's dying commands concerning his interment, specified the absolute necessity of his being embalmed, according to the most approved receipt at present known to mankind, it was necessary that Gertrude should remain in her dismal castle considerably longer than would otherwise have been necessary; for he had exacted from her also the promise, that she would herself see him deposited in his grave, with as much of dignity as it was in her power to obtain at so great a distance from the capital.

"All this to hear, did" the poor tearful Gertrude "seriously incline;" and she performed it too, by the active agency of Rupert, in a style which could not but have been highly gratifying and satisfactory to the spirit of the defunct nobleman, if, haply, it was within reach to witness it.

Neither Adolphe nor Lucy, anxiously bent as they were to withdraw themselves from the step-maternity of the brilliant Wilhelmina, could be induced to leave Gertrude till this stately pageant of her father's funeral was over; and even then, they felt that they would willingly have lingered with her still, had it not been for the persuasion that the most likely mode of obtaining a re-union with her, which they all hoped to render lasting, would be by setting off for England, while she was still engaged in arranging her affairs in the order in which she wished to leave them for the purpose of seeking a residence large enough to contain them all, till the heiress of Schwanberg had seen enough of this much-vaunted· English land, to decide whether it should be her permanent residence, or not.

Within a day or two after the funeral of the baron, therefore, the wandering pair, who did not as yet possess the shelter of a roof which they could call their own, set forth from Steinfeld Castle upon their long journey, the termination of which seemed as uncertain as that of our first parents, when they set forth with the world all before them; nevertheless, Lucy declared that she did not feel at all as if she were leaving Paradise.

Fortunately for Gertrude, Rupert's appointment of secretary to the baron had not been altogether a sinecure; but, on the· contrary, he had, ever since their return from Paris, been entrusted with all the business appertaining to the receiving rents, ordering repairs, and renewing leases, so that at the demise of their long-time landlord, the tenantry naturally applied to him for the arrangement of any changes which this event made necessary.

No property could have been left in better condition or in every respect in better order, to render the succession to it easy, and without embarrassment or trouble of any kind; yet, nevertheless, it did not take Gertrude any very long time to decide that, much as she loved the place, and much as she clung to the memory of both her parents, memories which every object in the neighbourhood suggested, it was not there that she wished to take up her rest.

But ample pecuniary resources furnish a wonderfully efficient assistance in all imaginable cases in which any alteration, or improvement, of any kind is contemplated.

The attachment which had long been growing, and strengthening, between the laughter-loving Lucy and the philosophical-minded Gertrude, had become too powerful, and too important to both of them, for either to contemplate any manner of life which was to keep them asunder, without more pain than any existing circumstances seemed to call upon them to endure; and if Gertrude did not immediately announce her intention of leaving the dreary splendours of her castle, for an abode less vast and more cheerful, it was only because she would not decide what her own movements should be, till she had been made acquainted with those proposed by her friends.

As little time as possible, however, was lost in deciding what these plans should be; and when a letter reached Gertrude from England, announcing the important and very agreeable fact, that Adolphe and his Lucy had settled themselves in an abode of ample room, and accommodation of all sorts, to enable them to receive Gertrude and her retinue, till such time as she should have selected a home of her own; a wonderful short delay was necessary before the heiress and her *retinue* were ready to set off on their long-contemplated journey to England.

The preparations for their departure were doubtless made with more facility because their numbers were few, for the whole of the retinue permitted to attend my high-born, wealthy heroine, consisted of Madame Odenthal and her son Rupert.

Madame Odenthal, indeed, did venture to suggest that Gertrude might find some inconvenience from not being attended by a more accomplished waiting-maid than she could herself hope to be; but Gertrude assured her, in reply, that by mutually practising this finest of the fine arts upon each other, they should both speedily become sufficiently accomplished in it to perform all its mysteries to their mutual satisfaction.

There certainly was a shade of sadness on the beautiful countenance of Gertrude, as she drove past the gothic window of the chapel in which both her parents lay interred; and for a few moments the travelling trio were very profoundly silent. But these few moments past, Gertrude's heart and head both told her that she belonged more to the living than to the dead; and the long journey upon which they had entered was performed with so much more of pleasure than of pain, that had they been less anxious to meet what they all hoped to find at the end of it, they might have been tempted to wish it longer still.

The careful and accurate instructions which they had received from Lucy, brought them at the end of ten days to a spot which, even had it not contained the living beings which their hearts most wished to meet, would have appeared to them all to look vastly likely a second Paradise.

On a level spot, containing within its smooth expanse about fifty acres, stood a modern mansion of very goodly size, but which, when compared to the mighty Schloss Schwanberg which they had left behind them, looked like a freestone toy.

The level space on which it stood, was about half-way up one of the steepest banks of the river Wye; but, being approached from behind, the first view of the sudden declivity produced the effect of a bold precipice, and the view commanded from its finely shorn lawn was one affording as fine a specimen of English river scenery, as it was possible for the eye to look upon.

Not to give an admiring and a lingering glance at this scene was impossible; but at the door of the mansion stood a group which caused even the strong-minded Gertrude to utter something very like a scream as she caught sight of it; and as the equipage swept round the lawn to the portico, she could not resist the impulse which caused her to attempt, somewhat vehemently, to open the carriage-door, though, had she succeeded in doing so, the result would probably have been her falling headlong on the ground.

Fortunately, this desperate attempt failed, and in another moment she was very safely in the arms of Lucy, while Adolphe, catching a baby from one of the nurses stationed at the door, placed it somehow or other on the bosom of the now weeping Gertrude.

And then the whole party, propelled by a little gentle violence from Rupert, was induced to enter first a handsome hall, and then a noble drawing-room at the further end of it, and there Gertrude, still pressing the favoured baby to her bosom, sunk down upon a sofa, and " tears began to flow."

And now it was the turn of Adolphe to exert himself, in order to render this scene more perfectly intelligible to some of the parties concerned in it.

The English nurse, however, who had been holding the babe when the travellers arrived, was not one of those whom it was his purpose to enlighten, and he, therefore, quietly told her to go to the nursery, where the baby should be brought to her presently.

On seeing this woman make her exit, closing the door after her, Gertrude cast an inquiring glance round the room, and perceiving that only Adolphe, Lucy, and the babe, which she still pressed to her own bosom, were present, in addition to the travelling trio, she rose, and approaching Madame Odenthal, placed the infant in her arms. "Take her, my second mother!" she exclaimed with deep emotion. "Love her, and cherish her! You

25

may may do so without a shadow of self-reproach!   I have kept
my secret from you, mother, that you might be innocent in all
ways!"

      *   *   *   *   *   *

Should any scrupulously correct persons honour this tale with
perusal, and feel, notwithstanding their long acquaintance with
Gertrude, any disagreeable uncertainty respecting some rather
mysterious passages in her history, they are respectfully referred
to the first chapter of this work, which, being rightly interpreted,
will solve all such painful doubts, although *this* "Almanack de
Gotha" may be the only one in which the authentic narrative
therein recorded is likely to appear at full length.

But there is a revolution, dearly beloved reader, which is
steadily at work among us, the progress of which is not the
less sure, because its onward movement is neither vehement nor
noisy.

We are all perfectly well aware that prosperous commerce, and
successful industry, will often cause so near an approach between
the toe of the commoner and the heel of the noble, as to run some
risk of galling a kibe; and this is a fact still more patent in our
days, than it was when the keenest of all observers first made the
remark.

But true as the remark was then, and more true as it is daily
becoming, by the eager onward movement of this successful industry, there is another cause at work also, which, I believe, is
likely to become infinitely more effective in *lessening* the distances
by which society is divided, than any which acquired wealth can
produce.

Nor is the lessening social distance its only effect.   Social distance may be lessened with very little chance of producing any
feeling of equality as its result.   But let the Barons von Schwanberg, who make the real "Almanack de Gotha" (not my almanack) their guide-book, let all such keep a sharp look-out upon
the species of *free trade in intellect*, which is so very obviously
threatening to set at naught the prohibitions of heraldic law-
givers.

The perils arising from a too close juxta-position between long-
descended rank and newly-accumulated wealth, are *as nothing*
when compared to the revolutionary influence of widely-diffused
education.

In proportion as that highest order of education which develops the *thinking powers* of human beings becomes general, the effort to separate society into distinct social classes becomes more difficult.

The system of enlarged education, which is so evidently gaining ground among us, will do more towards lessening the inequalities of rank, than all the heralds will be able to withstand.

Titles were abolished in France, yet no equality of condition ensued; but let the son of a tinker, born with a powerful and healthful intellect, have that intellect fully developed by education, and the effort to keep him within the tinkering sphere will be as vain as the attempting to make a thorough-bred race-horse pass for a fitting bearer of a pack-saddle.

SELECT LIBRARY OF FICTIO[N]

NEW VOLUMES JUST PUBLISHED.

Price 2s., boards.

CHARLIE THORNHILL; or, the Dunce of [the] Family. By CHARLES CLARKE.

ELSIE VENNER. A Romance of Destiny. [By] OLIVER W. HOLMES.

THE HOUSE OF ELMORE. By Autho[r of] "Grandmother's Money."

REUBEN MEDLICOTT, the Coming Man. [By] Author of "Bachelor of the Albany."

THE COUNTRY GENTLEMAN. By "S[PEC-]TATOR."

THE ORPHANS, and CALEB FIELD. [By] Mrs. OLIPHANT.

CARDINAL POLE. By W. H. AINSWORTH.

UNCLE WALTER. By Mrs. TROLLOPE.

THE MASTER OF THE HOUNDS. By "S[PEC-]TATOR."

CONSTABLE OF THE TOWER. By W. [H.] AINSWORTH.

THE LORD MAYOR OF LONDON. By W. H. AINSWORTH.

HUNCHBACK OF NOTRE DAME. By VICTOR HUGO.

YOUNG HEIRESS. By Mrs. TROLLOPE.

LONDON: CHAPMAN & HALL, 193, PICCADILLY.